DARE
DOCTOR...HUSBAND?

BY
ALISON ROBERTS

THE DOCTOR
SHE'D NEVER FORGET

BY
ANNIE CLAYDON

MILLS & BOON

Alison Roberts lives in Christchurch, New Zealand, and has written over sixty Mills & Boon Medical Romance™ books. As a qualified paramedic she has personal experience of the drama and emotion to be found in the world of medical professionals, and loves to weave stories with this rich background—especially when they can have a happy ending.

When Alison is not writing you'll find her indulging her passion for dancing or spending time with her friends (including Molly the dog) and her daughter Becky, who has grown up to become a brilliant artist. She also loves to travel, hates housework, and considers it a triumph when the flowers outnumber the weeds in her garden.

Cursed from an early age with a poor sense of direction and a propensity to read, **Annie Claydon** spent much of her childhood lost in books. After completing her degree in English Literature she indulged her love of romantic fiction and spent a long, hot summer writing a book of her own. It was duly rejected and life took over. A series of U-turns led in the unlikely direction of a career in computing and information technology, but the lure of the printed page proved too much to bear and she now has the perfect outlet for the stories which have always run through her head: writing Medical Romance™ for Mills & Boon®. Living in London—a city where getting lost can be a joy—she has no regrets for having taken her time in working her way back to the place that she started from.

DAREDEVIL, DOCTOR...HUSBAND?

BY
ALISON ROBERTS

MILLS & BOON

Published in Great Britain 2015
by Mills & Boon, an imprint of Harlequin (UK) Limited,
Eton House, 18-24 Paradise Road, Richmond, Surrey, TW9 1SR

© 2015 Alison Roberts

ISBN: 978-0-263-24730-5

Harlequin (UK) Limited's policy is to use papers that are natural,
renewable and recyclable products and made from wood grown in
sustainable forests. The logging and manufacturing processes conform
to the legal environmental regulations of the country of origin.

Printed and bound in Spain
by CPI, Barcelona

Dear Reader,

Sometimes my inspiration for a story comes from something tiny that I see or hear that strikes a chord and keeps resurfacing.

About two years ago I moved from my earthquake-damaged home of the last thirty years in Christchurch to come to New Zealand's biggest city: Auckland. I chose to live on the north side of the harbour bridge and found myself living within walking distance of a beach for the first time in my life. A very beautiful beach—Takapuna.

On a warm night last summer I was on the beach, looking out over a sea as calm as a huge swimming pool, enjoying the silhouette of the volcanic island of Rangitoto, when I saw something that was one of those tiny things: a paddle boarder, quite a long way offshore, who had a big dog along for the ride, lying on the end of his board. It tugged at my heartstrings to recognise the bond they clearly had, and it made me smile every time I remembered.

So that was my starting point. Now come and meet my heroine, Summer, who has a dog called Flint who rides on her board. You'll get to spend some time on Takapuna Beach, too, where my gorgeous hero Zac is lucky enough to live. The sea isn't always calm, of course. And what happens between Zac and Summer isn't either…

Happy reading!

Love

Alison xxx

CHAPTER ONE

HE WAS NOTHING like what she'd expected.

Well, the fact that he was tall, dark and ridiculously good-looking was no surprise for someone who'd been considered the most eligible doctor at Auckland General Hospital a couple of years ago but Summer Pearson had good reason to believe this man was a total bastard. A monster, even.

And monsters weren't supposed to have warm brown eyes and a smile that could light up an entire room. Maybe she'd made an incorrect assumption when she'd been given the name of her extra crew for the shift.

'Dr Mitchell?'

'That's me.'

'*Zac* Mitchell?'

'Yep. My gran still calls me Isaac, mind you. She doesn't hold with names being messed around with. She's an iceberg lettuce kind of girl, you know? You won't find any of those new-fangled fancy baby mesclun leaves in one of her salads because that's another thing that shouldn't get messed with.'

Good grief…he was telling her about his granny? And there was sheer mischief in those dark eyes. Salad greens and names were clearly only a couple of the many things Zac was more than happy to mess around with. Summer could feel her eyes narrowing as the confirmation of her suspicions became inevitable.

'And you used to work in Auckland? In A&E?'

'Sure did. I've spent the last couple of years in the UK, though. As the permanent doctor on shift for the busiest helicopter rescue service in the country.'

The base manager, Graham, came into the duty room, an orange flight suit draped over his arm.

'Found one in your size, Zac. And here's a tee shirt, too. I see you've met Summer?'

'Ah...we hadn't got as far as a proper introduction.'

Because she'd been grilling him like a prosecution lawyer in a courtroom—making sure of the identity of the accused before firing the real ammunition? Summer felt her cheeks getting pink.

'Sorry,' she muttered. 'I'm Summer Pearson. Intensive Care Paramedic. I've been with the rescue service for nearly three years now.'

'I've heard a lot about you.' An eyebrow lifted and his tone dropped a notch. 'And it was all good.'

No...was he trying to *flirt* with her?

I've heard a lot about you, too. And none of it was good...

Pretending she hadn't heard the compliment, Summer turned to Graham. 'I'll do the usual orientation while we're quiet, shall I?'

A groan came from the doorway as another man entered the room. 'Oh, no...did she just say the Q word?'

'She did.' Graham shook his head. 'What's your guess?'

'Eight minutes.'

'I'll give it six.' Graham grinned at Zac. 'Running bet on how long till a job comes in after someone says the

Q word. Worst performer of the week restocks the beer fridge. Meet Monty, Zac—one of our pilots.'

The men shook hands. Then they all looked at Summer and she tried to erase the expression that felt remarkably like a scowl from her face.

'Three minutes,' she offered reluctantly. Wishful thinking, maybe, but how good would it be if what was likely to be a complicated winch job came in and an untrained doctor had to be left on base in favour of experienced crewmen? 'So I guess we'd better get started on the orientation.'

'Just show him where everything is,' Graham said. 'Zac, here, is the most highly trained doctor we've ever had joining us. Fully winch trained. He's done HUET and he's even part way through his pilot's training.'

Summer could feel the scowl creeping back. She refused to be impressed but it was difficult. Helicopter Underwater Escape Training was not something for the faint-hearted.

Zac was shrugging off the praise. 'I'm passionate about emergency medicine, that's all. And the challenge of being on the front line is a lot more exciting than working inside a controlled environment like an emergency department. Maybe I haven't really grown up yet, and that keeps me chasing adventures.'

Immaturity was no excuse for anything. It certainly didn't mitigate ruining someone's life and then walking away. Summer tried to catch Graham's eye. Could she tell him she really wasn't comfortable working with this new team member?

She didn't get the chance. The strident signal from the on-base communication system told them a job had come in.

Monty checked his watch. 'Two minutes, ten seconds. You win, Summer.'

She picked up her helmet and jammed it on her head. She didn't feel as if she'd won anything at all.

She was nothing like what he'd expected.

Well, she *was* small. No more than about five foot four at a guess. Her head barely reached his shoulder and that was including the spikes of her short blonde hair. *Pocket rocket*, his ED colleagues had told him. *But don't be fooled. She's as tough as. And one of the best paramedics in the business.*

But they'd also told him she was Summer by name and sunny by nature. And that she was great fun to work with. *You're a lucky man*, they'd said.

He'd been expecting summer and he'd got winter instead. Funny, but he didn't feel that lucky.

Or maybe he did. Here he was in a chopper again and he hadn't realised how much he was missing the excitement of being airborne and heading for the unknown. Not only that, he was doing it over the sparkling blue waters of his home town instead of the grey British skies he'd become so familiar with. And they were heading for even more spectacular scenery on the far side of the Coromandel Peninsula—one of his most favourite places on earth.

'Car's over a bank,' he heard through the speakers built into his helmet. 'On the 309, between the Kauri grove and Waiau Falls. Ambulance and fire service are on scene.'

'The 309's still a gravel road, I presume?'

'You know it?' Monty sounded surprised.

'Spent most of my childhood holidays on the Coromandel. I'm into water sports.'

'Talk to Summer.' Monty chuckled. 'Queen of the paddleboard, she is.'

Zac would have been happy to do exactly that but it only took a glance to see that she had no desire to chat. Her face was turned away and she gave the impression of finding the view too fascinating to resist.

She still looked small, with the wide straps of her harness across her chest. The helmet looked too big for her head and while someone might be excused for getting the impression of a child playing dress-up, they'd only need to see her profile to sense a very adult level of focus and... what was it...judgement?

Yeah... He felt as if he'd been tried and judged and the verdict had not been favourable.

But he'd never even met the woman before today so what was he being judged on?

Was she some kind of control freak, perhaps, who didn't appreciate having someone on board who had a medical authority higher than hers? Or did she require confirmation that a newcomer's ability was what it appeared to be on paper?

Fair enough.

What wasn't acceptable was making said newcomer feel less than welcome. Undesirable, even.

As if she felt the force of his frown, Summer turned her head. Her gaze met his and held longer than could be considered polite.

Yeah...she was fierce, all right. Unafraid.

Who was going to look away first? Defusing tension was a skill that came automatically for Zac. He might have had to learn it for all the wrong reasons when he was too young to understand but shades of that ability still came in handy at times. All it usually took was turning on the charm. He summoned his best smile and, for a split second, he thought it was going to work because she almost smiled back. But then she jerked her head, breaking the eye contact.

A deliberate snub? Zac tamped down a response that could have been disappointment. Or possibly annoyance. Neither would be helpful in establishing a good working relationship with this unexpectedly prickly young woman.

'You should get a good view of the Pinnacles on your side in a few minutes,' Summer said.

'Might get a bit bumpy going over the mountains,' Monty added. 'I'll get an update on scene info as soon as we get over the top.'

When he'd first started this kind of work, Zac would be using this time to go over all the possible medical scenarios in his head and the procedures that might be needed to deal with them. A chest decompression for a pneumothorax, perhaps. Management of a spinal, crush or severe head injury. Partial or complete amputations. Uncontrollable haemorrhage. But the list was long and he'd learned that there was no point expending mental energy on imaginary scenarios.

He'd also learned that it was better to start a job without assumptions that could distract him from the unexpected. And that he could deal with whatever he found. This time was better used to relax and centre himself. The view of the spectacular bush-covered peaks below them was ideal—and definitely better than trying to make conversation with someone who clearly had no intention of making his life any more pleasant.

'ETA two minutes.'

'Roger.' Summer leaned forward in her seat to get a better view of the ground below. 'Vehicles at eleven o'clock. I can see a fire truck and ambulance.'

'Copy that,' Monty said. 'Comms? Rescue One. On location, on location.'

The chopper tilted as they turned. Monty was using the crew frequency now. 'Turning windward,' he advised. 'I think the road's going to be the only landing place.'

'Got a bit of a tilt to it. No wires, though.'

'No worries,' Monty said. 'Be a bit dusty, folks. Okay… right skid's going to touch first.'

They had the doors open before the dust cloud had cleared. Zac released the catch of his safety harness first and hoisted one of the backpacks onto his shoulder as they climbed out.

Summer picked up the other pack and a portable oxygen cylinder and followed. Weirdly, it felt like she was used to working with this guy already. Maybe that was because he seemed to know exactly what he was doing and he wasn't waiting to follow her lead. At least he stood back when they reached the knot of people standing by the side of the road near the fire truck so it was Summer that the fireman in charge of the scene spoke to first.

'We've got the vehicle secured but haven't got the driver out. It's a bit of a steep climb.'

'Single occupant?'

'Yes. An eighty-three-year-old woman. Frances.'

'Status?'

'I'd say two.' An ambulance officer joined them. 'GCS was lowered on arrival. She's confused and distressed. Airway seems to be clear but we haven't got close enough to assess her properly yet and, given the MOI and her age, there's every probability she has serious injuries.'

'Access?'

'Ladder. It's a few metres short of the target, though. You'll have to be careful but there's plenty of trees to hang on to.'

'Cool. We'll go down and see what's what.' Summer glanced at Zac. Tall and broad-shouldered, his size and weight would make the climb and access to the vehicle much harder than it was for her. It would probably be sensible for him to suggest waiting up here on the road while she did an initial assessment and made their patient stable enough to be extricated by the fire crew.

'Want me to go first?' he asked. 'And test the ladder?'

'If you like.' Summer passed her backpack to a fireman who was ready to secure it to a rope and lower it down. Not that it was needed, but she had to give him points for thinking about her safety.

Looking at the narrow ladder lying on the crushed and probably slippery ferns of the bush undergrowth on an almost vertical cliff face, she had to acknowledge those points.

'Yeah…you going first is a good idea, Zac. There'll be less damage done if I land on you rather than the other way round.'

'Impersonating a cushion is one of my splinter skills.' Zac handed his pack to the fireman and then turned without hesitation to climb onto the ladder. A rope attached to the top and anchored to the back of the fire truck was preventing it sliding downwards but it couldn't control any sideways movement. Another rope was attached to the back of the small car that could be seen protruding from the mangled scrub and ferns a good fifteen metres down the bank.

'She was lucky the scrub cushioned the impact,' the fireman said. 'Probably why she's still alive.'

Zac was halfway down the ladder now and climbing carefully enough not to make it swing. Summer caught the top rung and turned her body to find a foothold. She loved the kind of challenge this sort of job presented. The ladder was easy. Getting down the last stretch when you had to slide between trees was harder. There were fire crew down here but it was Zac who was moving just ahead of her and every time he caught himself, he was looking back to make sure she'd reached her last handhold safely.

It was Summer who needed to take the lead as they got close enough to touch the car. A small hatchback well buried in undergrowth left virtually no room for a large man to see much. The front passenger window had been smashed. Summer put her head in the gap.

'Hi there… Frances, is it?'

The elderly woman groaned. Her voice was high and quavery. 'Get me out. *Please*…'

'That's what we're here for. My name's Summer and I've got Zac with me. Are you having any trouble breathing, Frances?'

'I… I don't think so.'

'Does anything hurt?'

'I… I don't know… I'm *scared*…'

Summer was trying to assess their patient visually. Pale skin and a bump on the head that was bleeding. She could see the woman's chest rising and falling rapidly. The more distressed she was, the harder it would be to assess and try to move her.

The window on the driver's side was broken too and suddenly there was movement as the prickly branches of scrub got pushed aside. The face that appeared was wearing a helmet. How on earth had Zac managed to get down that side of the vehicle?

Not only that, he was reaching in to touch the woman. To put a calming hand on her forehead, probably to stop her turning her head to look at him in case she had injured her neck.

'It's okay, sweetheart,' he said. 'We're going to take good care of you.'

Sweetheart? Was that an appropriate way to address an eighty-three-year-old woman?

'Oh...' Frances didn't seem offended. 'Oh... Who are you?'

'I'm Zac. I'm a doctor.'

'Do I know you?'

'You do now.' He leaned in further, a lopsided smile appearing as he make a clicking sound like someone encouraging a pony to move. The sound was accompanied by a wink.

'Oh...' The outward breath sounded like a sigh of relief. There was even a shaky smile in response. 'Thank you, dear. I've been *so* scared...'

'I know.' His voice was understanding. Reassuring. Was he holding a hand or taking a pulse in there? 'Summer—are you able to open the door on your side? It's jammed over here.'

With the assistance of a fireman and a crowbar, the answer was affirmative.

With the new space, Summer was able to ease herself cautiously into the car. The creaking and slight forward movement of the vehicle made her catch her breath but it terrified Frances.

'*No...help...*'

This time it was Summer as well as their patient who took comfort from Zac's confident tone. 'The ropes just needed to take up the extra weight. You're safe. There's a great big fire engine up on the road that's not going anywhere and the car is very firmly attached to it. Relax, sweetheart...'

There it was again. That cheeky endearment. Summer wouldn't want to admit that skip of her heart when it seemed like the car was beginning to roll further down the cliff. She most definitely wouldn't want to admit that warm feeling the use of the endearment created. How powerful could a single word be? It could make you think that someone genuinely cared about you.

That you were, indeed, safe.

Suddenly, it was easy to focus completely on the job she needed to do. Summer unhooked the stethoscope from around her neck and fitted it into her ears.

'Take a deep breath for me, Frances.'

There was equal air entry in both lungs and a pulse that was a little too fast and uneven enough to suggest an underlying cardiac condition, although Frances denied having any. The worst bleeding from lacerations in papery skin needed pressure dressings for control because blood pressure was already low and Summer eased a cervical collar in place as Zac held the head steady.

'Sorry, Frances. I know this is uncomfortable but it's to protect your neck while we get you out. We can't examine you properly until we get you up to the ambulance.'

'That's all right, dear.' But it was Zac that Frances was looking at for reassurance. His hand she was holding through the window as Summer worked quickly beside her in the car.

'Are you sure nothing's hurting, Frances?'

'My chest is a bit sore. And my arm...'

'We can give you something for the pain.'

But Frances shook her head. 'I can bear it, dear. It's not that bad...'

Summer glanced up at Zac, who was still supporting the elderly woman's head and neck. 'We can reassess after we move her but I think we can probably wait till we get up to the top before worrying about IV access.'

'Absolutely.' Zac nodded. 'The tubing and trying to

carry a bag of fluids will only create a complication we don't need. Bit of oxygen might be a good idea, though, do you think?'

'Sure.'

They explained how they were going to get her out of the car, using a backboard to slide her towards the passenger side and then turning her to lie flat as they lifted her out onto a stretcher.

'You'll be quite safe,' Summer said. 'We've got lots of strong young firemen to carry you up the hill.'

'Oh... I've caused everybody so much trouble, haven't I?'

'It's what we do,' Zac told her. 'If people didn't have accidents or get sick, we'd be out of a job.' He was smiling again. 'And we *love* our job, don't we, Summer?'

This time, she really couldn't help smiling back so she tilted her head towards her patient. 'Indeed we do. Okay, Frances. You ready to get out of here?'

Getting her out of the car had to be done as gently as possible because there could be fractured bones or internal injuries that hadn't been recognised due to position and limited access but if there had been any increase in pain during the procedure, Frances wasn't complaining. Cocooned in a blanket and strapped securely into the Stokes basket stretcher, she looked almost relaxed as the rescue team began the slow process of inching the stretcher up to the road.

In the relative safety of the ambulance, it was Zac who led a more complete examination while an ambulance officer filled in some paperwork.

'Next of kin?'

'I haven't got any. Not now.'

'Is there anyone you'd like us to call?'

'Maybe my neighbour. She'll take care of the cats

if I don't get home tonight. Oh…that's why I was driving today. There's a special on in the supermarket at Whitianga. For cat food.'

Zac got an IV line through fragile skin with a skill that was unlikely to leave so much as a bruise and Summer hooked up the IV fluids, aware of how meticulous and gentle the rest of his survey was, despite being rapid enough to get them on their way as soon as possible. ECG electrodes, blood pressure and oxygen saturation monitors were in place and Zac was keeping an eye on all the readings. A raised eyebrow at Summer had her nodding. The heart rhythm wasn't dangerous but was definitely abnormal and would need treatment.

'You don't get dizzy spells, do you, Frances?' Zac asked. 'You weren't feeling sick before the accident?'

'I don't think so. I really can't remember…'

'What medications are you on?'

'I don't take anything, dear. Apart from my calcium tablets. I'm as healthy as a horse. Haven't needed to see a doctor for years.'

'Might be a good thing that you're going to get a proper check-up in hospital then. Bit of a warrant of fitness.'

'I don't like bothering a doctor when I don't need to.'

'I know. My gran Ivy is exactly the same.'

'How old is *she*?'

'Ninety-two.'

Summer found herself sliding a quizzical glance in his direction as she gathered dressings and bandages to dress some of the superficial wounds more thoroughly. It wouldn't occur to her to think about, let alone tell others, anything about her own family. What was it with him and his grandmother? Nobody could miss the pride in his voice and it just didn't fit with the whole cheeky, bad boy vibe. And it certainly didn't fit with his reputation.

'She still swims every day,' Zac added. 'Has done her whole life. Reckons she's half-mermaid. Does it hurt if I press here?'

'Ooh...yes...'

'Can you wiggle your fingers?'

'That hurts, too... Have I broken something?'

'It's possible. We'll put a splint on it and keep it nice and still till you get an X-ray. We might give you something for the pain, too. You don't have to be brave and put up with it, you know. Sometimes, it's nice to just let someone else take care of you.'

Frances got a bit weepy at that point but the transfer to the helicopter and their take-off a short time later was enough of a distraction.

It didn't quite distract Summer. Was Frances stoic and uncomplaining because there was no point in being anything else? Was there really nobody who needed to know she'd had a bad accident other than her neighbour?

The thought was sad.

Maybe more so because it resonated. As the chopper lifted and swung inland to head back to Auckland, Summer watched the people on the ground get smaller and a cluster of houses in the small township of Coromandel where Frances lived become visible. They vanished just as quickly and Summer turned, wondering if the elderly woman was aware and distressed by how far from her home they were taking her.

'Morphine's doing its job.' Zac's voice sounded loud in her helmet. 'She's having a wee nap.' His eyes were on the cardiac monitor. 'She's stable. Enjoy the view.'

But Summer still felt oddly flat. What if she'd been the one to have an accident in such an isolated location? Who would she call if she was about to be flown to an emergency department a long way from her home?

It was moments like this that she noticed the absence of a partner in her life with a sharpness that felt increasingly like failure since she'd entered her thirties and everyone her age seemed to be getting married and starting families. There was nobody to call her 'sweetheart' and really mean it. No one to make her feel cherished and safe. It wasn't that she hadn't tried to find someone—relationships just never seemed to work out.

If she was really honest, though, she hadn't tried that hard. She'd told herself that there was plenty of time and her career had to take priority but it went deeper than that, didn't it? Moments like this always made the loss of her mother seem like yesterday instead of more than fifteen years ago and what she'd been taught about not trusting men was as much a part of those memories as anything else.

Would she put her father down as next of kin? Not likely. She hadn't seen him since her mother's funeral and there was still anger there that he'd had the nerve to turn up for it.

She'd probably do what Frances had done and opt to put a call in to a neighbour to make sure her pet was cared for.

No. Her life wasn't that sad. She had a lot of good friends. The guys she worked with, for starters. And her oldest friend, Kate, would do anything to help. It was just a shame she lived in Hamilton—a good hour's drive away. Not that that was any excuse for the fact they hadn't seen each other for so long. Or even talked, come to that.

And, boy…they had something to talk about now, didn't they?

With Zac monitoring Frances during the flight and clearly happy that the condition of their patient was still stable, there was no reason why Summer shouldn't get her mobile phone from her pocket and flick off a text message.

Hey, Kate. How's things? U home tonite?

The response came back swiftly.

Late finish but home by 10. Call me. Be good 2 talk.

It would. Her friend might need some prior warning, though.

You'll never guess who's back in town!

CHAPTER TWO

'ZAC...WHEN DID you get back into town?' The nurse wheeling an IV trolley through the emergency department was overdoing the delighted astonishment just a tad when she caught sight of the helicopter crew coming out of Resus.

'Only last week. Didn't see you around, Mandy.'

'I was on holiday. Giving my new bikini a test run on a beach in Rarotonga.'

'Nice.'

'It was. Is. Pink—with little purple flowers. Might have to give it another outing at Takapuna on my next day off.'

It was no surprise that Mandy chose to assume he was referring to the bikini rather than the Pacific island. Confident and popular, she had flirting down to a fine art. There were rumours that it went further than flirting but Summer preferred to trust her own instincts and Mandy had always been willing to help when their paths crossed at work and good company at social events. The smile was as friendly as ever right now, but somehow it struck a discordant note. Maybe it had been the tone in Zac's voice. Or the warm glance that had flashed between them.

No surprise there, so why was it so annoying?

Because her instincts had been trying to convince her that Zac wasn't the monster she'd heard about? That someone who could treat a frightened elderly patient as if she was his own beloved granny couldn't possibly be that bad? They'd just finished handing Frances over to the team in Resus and Zac had promised to come and visit to see how she was as soon as he was back in the department again. There had been tears on her wrinkled cheeks as she'd told Rob, the ED consultant taking over, that this 'dear boy' had saved her life.

'That's our Zac.' Rob had grinned. 'We're lucky to have him back but we're letting him out to play on the helicopters every so often.'

It was a reminder that she was on Zac's turf now because his primary job was as another one of the department's consultants. After three years of working in Auckland, both on the road and in the rescue service, Summer felt as much at home in this environment as she did on station or at the base but something subtle had just shifted in unspoken ratings. Zac was the person Frances considered to be her lifesaver. He was also a doctor and clearly not only respected for his skills but well liked. Probably more popular than Mandy, even?

Did none of them know what she knew about him?

She'd been close to doubting the truth herself but seeing the way he and Mandy had looked at each other was a wake-up call. She'd been in danger of being sucked in by that charm. Like countless other women, including Mandy. And Kate's sister, Shelley. Had she really been prepared to dismiss how Shelley's life had been wrecked?

'Hey, Summer.' Mandy was still smiling. 'Have you guys stolen Zac away from us?'

'Wouldn't dream of it.' She kept her tone light enough for her words to pass as a joke. 'I'm sure he'll get sick of us soon enough and he'll be all yours again.'

Mandy's sigh was theatrical. 'Dreams are free,' she murmured.

A curtain twitched open nearby. 'We need that trolley, Mandy. When you're ready?'

'Oops.' Mandy rolled her eyes, blew a kiss in Zac's direction and disappeared with her trolley.

It was only then that Summer felt the stare she was receiving. A level stare. Cool enough to be a completely different season from a few seconds ago when Mandy had been present.

Had he guessed that she hadn't been joking? That she'd been wishful thinking out loud? Did she care?

No.

Then why was she suddenly feeling like a complete bitch? Helicopter crews were notoriously tight teams. They had to be. This was Zac's first day on the job and, under any other circumstances, he would be a welcome addition to the team. Perfect, in fact. She'd never gone out of her way to make a newcomer feel unwelcome. Ever.

She got a glimpse of how she must be coming across to Zac and she didn't like what she saw.

And that was even more annoying than feeling as if she had a running battle between her head and heart about what sort of person he really was. Or watching him confirm his 'bad boy' reputation by encouraging Mandy.

Summer was being someone she didn't even recognise.

'We'd better take this stretcher back upstairs. Monty'll be wondering where we've got to.' She couldn't meet his gaze any longer. Was this unfamiliar, unpleasant sensation what it felt like to be ashamed of yourself? She needed to find some way to rectify the situation. But how?

She manoeuvred the stretcher into the lift. They would be airborne again within minutes, either on their way back to base or onto another job. They had to work together so, at the very least, she had to be professional and to stop letting anything personal get in the way of that.

She broke the awkward silence in the lift just before the doors opened at roof level. 'Great job, by the way... with Frances.'

Talk about being damned by faint praise.

And she'd all but announced to Mandy that she'd be delighted if he decided he'd rather stay within the four walls of the hospital's emergency department from now on. How long would it take for that message to get dispersed amongst his colleagues?

He'd been looking forward to this. Coming into the department as a uniformed HEMS member to hand over his first patient. Showing everybody that this was where his passion lay and that he was good at it. This was supposed to be the start of the life he'd dreamed of. A job that used every ounce of skill he possessed and challenged him to keep learning more. A balance of the controlled safety of a state-of-the-art emergency department with the adrenaline rush of coping with the unexpected in sometimes impossible environments. The chance to do exactly the job he wanted in the place he'd always wanted to do it in—close to the only family he had, in a city big enough to offer everything, a great climate and, best of all, the sea within easy reach. Beaches and boats. The perfect playground to unwind in after giving your all at work.

But the blue sky of that promise of fulfilment had a big cloud in it. A dark cloud that threatened rain. Possibly even hail and thunder.

How ironic was it that her name was Summer?

'Yes?'

Oh, Lord...had he said something out loud? The microphone on his helmet was so close to his mouth, it could easily pick something up, even with the increasing roar of the rotors picking up speed to take off. Like the ironic tone of her name. He had to think fast.

'Cute name,' he offered. 'Can't say I've ever met a Summer before.'

'My parents were hippies. Apparently I got conceived on a beach. After a surfing competition.'

Monty's laugh reminded him that this conversation wasn't private. 'I never knew that. No wonder you've got sea water in your veins.'

It was the first piece of personal information Summer had offered. Monty's amusement added to a lighter atmosphere and Zac wanted more.

'A summer memory to keep, then?'

'Yeah…'

'Not many people know where they were conceived. I wouldn't have a clue.'

'Maybe you should ask your mother.'

'My mother died in a car accident when I was seven and I never knew my dad. I got brought up by my gran.'

'Oh…' She caught his gaze for a moment, horrified that she'd been so insensitive. 'Sorry…'

'No worries. It's ancient history.' Zac was happy to keep the conversation going. 'You got any siblings? Spring, maybe? Or Autumn?'

'Nope.'

The word was a snap. She could offer personal information but he wasn't welcome to ask for it.

Zac suppressed a sigh. Maybe he should have a word to the base manager about being assigned to a different shift on the rescue service.

The call coming in meant that wasn't going to happen any time soon.

'Missing child,' Comms relayed. 'Six-year-old boy. Red tee shirt, blue shorts, bare feet. They think he's been

swept off rocks at St Leonard's beach. Coastguard's sending a boat and the police chopper's on its way but you're
closest.'

A six-year-old boy.

How long would he last in the water? How frightened
would he be?

He was close to the same age Zac had been when he'd
lost his mother. Summer could only imagine how frightened *he* would have been. He would have had the same
soft dark curls by then. And big brown eyes.

Heart-wrenching.

She didn't want to feel sorry for Zac, any more than
she wanted his charm to get under her skin.

Maybe this kid could swim. She'd been able to at least
keep herself afloat by the time she was four but Monty
was right—she had sea water in her veins and life had
been all about the sun and sand and surf back then. Happy
days.

They were circling above the cliffs and rocks surround-
ing one of the many bays on Auckland's north shore now
and she could see the knot of people anxiously staring at
the sea. Others were climbing the rocks, staring down
into the pools where a small body could wash up with the
incoming tide. In the distance, as they circled again, she
could see a coastguard boat leaving a foamy wake behind
it as it sped out from the inner harbour.

Her heart was sinking. It was too hard to keep feeling
optimistic that this search would have a happy ending.

And one glance at how pale Zac was looking, with that
fierce frown of deep concern on his face, and it was too
hard to keep believing that he was some kind of monster.

Round and round they went. Monty focused on keeping them low and moving slowly over a small area, his

crew peering down, trying to spot the smallest sign of anything in the soft blue swells of water or the whiteness as they broke over rocks.

Emergency vehicles were gathering at a nearby park above the beach. A police car and then a fire engine. An ambulance...

'What was that?'

'Where?'

'I think I caught a flash of something red.'

'*Where?*' Summer narrowed her eyes, willing something to show up on the water below. The coastguard boat was there now. And a civilian dinghy. Even someone on a paddleboard.

'Not in the water. Up the cliff. Take us round again, Monty.'

Another slow circuit but Summer couldn't see anything.

'I swear I saw it. About halfway up, where that pohutukawa tree is coming out sideways.'

Monty stopped their circling and hovered. Took them in a bit closer. A bit lower.

'*There...*' Excitement made Zac's voice reverberate in her helmet. 'Two o'clock. There's a bit of an overhang behind the trunk. There's something there. Something *red...*'

They hovered where they were as the information was relayed to emergency crews on the ground. A fire truck got shifted and parked at the top of the cliff, facing backwards. Abseiling gear and a rope appeared and then someone was on their way down to check out the possible sighting. For an agonisingly long moment, the fire officer disappeared after climbing over the trunk and crawling beneath the overhang.

Summer held her breath.

He reappeared, backing out slowly so it took another couple of seconds to see that he held something in his arms. A small child, wearing a red T-shirt and shorts. And then he held up his hand and, despite the heavy gloves he was wearing, it was clear that he was giving a 'thumbs-up' signal that all was well.

The boy was not injured.

The relief was surprisingly overwhelming. It was instinctive to share that relief with someone, as if sharing would somehow confirm that what she was seeing was real. Maybe Zac felt the same way because their eyes met at precisely the same instant.

And, yes...her own relief was reflected there. Zac had probably dealt with the same kind of heart-breaking jobs she had in the past, where a child's life had been lost. The kind of jobs you would choose never to repeat if it was within your power—something they both knew was too much to hope for. But this time they'd won. The boy's family had won. Tragedy had been averted and it felt like a major triumph.

The momentary connection was impossible to dismiss. She and Zac felt exactly the same way and the depth of a bond that came from the kind of trauma that was part of what they did was not something everybody could share. Even amongst colleagues, the ability to distance yourself from feeling so strongly was very different. Summer still couldn't breathe past the huge lump in her throat and she suspected that Zac was just the same.

But he wasn't supposed to have an emotional connection to others like this, given what Summer knew about him. It was confusing. Not to be trusted.

The radio message telling the rescue crew to stand down broke the atmosphere. Monty's delighted whoop as he turned away and swept them back towards base added a third person to the mix and suddenly it became purely professional again and not at all confusing.

'How lucky was that?' They could hear the grin in Monty's voice. 'The kid decided to go climbing instead of getting washed out to sea.'

'Small boys can climb like spiders.'

'Only going up, though. It's when it's time to go down that they realise they're stuck.'

'He must have been scared stiff,' Summer put in. 'Good thing there was the overhang to climb under.'

'He probably knew he'd be in trouble. No wonder he decided it was safer to hide for a while.'

'He won't be in trouble.' Zac's voice was quiet. 'Or not for long, anyway. I'd love to have seen his mum's face when she gets to give him a hug.'

This time, Summer deliberately didn't look at Zac but kept her gaze on the forest of masts in the yacht marina below. She didn't want to see the recognition of what it was like to know you'd lost someone precious and what a miracle it would be to have them returned to you. Zac must have dreamed of such a miracle when he was the same age as that little boy in the red tee shirt. How long had it taken to understand that it was never going to happen?

She'd known instantly. Did that make it easier?

If she'd met his gaze, it might be a question that was impossible not to ask silently and maybe she didn't want to know the answer because that might extend that connection she'd felt.

A connection that felt wrong.

Almost like a betrayal of some kind?

Life didn't get much better than this.

A quiet, late summer evening on Takapuna beach, with

a sun-kissed Rangitoto island as a backdrop to a calm
blue sea. The long swim had been invigorating and it was
still warm enough to sit and be amongst so many people
enjoying themselves. There weren't many people swimming now but there were lots of small boats coming in
to the ramp at the end of the beach, paddleboarders beyond where the gentle waves were breaking and people
walking their dogs. A group of young men were having
a game of football and family groups were picnicking on
the nearby grassed area.

It was the kind of scene that was so much a part of
home for Zac he'd missed it with an ache during his years
in London. This beach had been his playground for as long
as he could remember. He loved it in all its moods—as
calm as an oversized swimming pool some days, wild and
stormy and leaving a mountain of seaweed on the beach
at other times. Little room to walk at high tide but end-
less sand and rocks to clamber over at low tide. Kite surf-
ers loved it on the windy days and paddleboards reigned
on days like this.

Funny that he'd never tried that particular water sport.
Maybe because it looked a bit tame. For heaven's sake—
it was so tame, there was somebody out there with a dog
sitting behind the person who was standing, paddling
the board.

A big dog. A small person. They were attracting attention from some of the walkers and Zac could see the pleasure they were getting from the sight by the way they were
pointing and smiling. More than one person was capturing
the image with a camera. He took another look himself.
The dog was shaggy and black. The paddler was a girl in
a bikini and even from this distance she was clearly at-
tractively curvy.

He'd finished rubbing himself down with his towel so

there was no reason not to head back to the house for a hot shower but there was still enough warmth in the setting sun to make it pleasant to stand here and that pleasure certainly wasn't dimmed by watching the girl on the paddleboard for a few more moments as she headed in to shore. How would the dog cope with the challenge of staying on board as they negotiated even small waves?

It didn't. As soon as the board began to ride the swell, it jumped clear and swam beside its owner, who stayed upright and rode in until the board beached itself on the sand. It was only then that Zac realised who he'd been watching.

What had Monty called her?

Oh, yeah…the queen of the paddleboard.

Who knew that that flight suit had been covering curves that were all the sweeter when there wasn't an ounce of extra flesh anywhere else on her body? The muscles in her arms and legs had the kind of definition that only peak fitness could maintain and she had a six-pack that put his to shame.

Zac found himself sucking in his stomach just a little as he moved towards where she was dragging the huge board out of the final wash of the waves. He couldn't pretend he hadn't seen her and maybe this was a great opportunity to get past that weird hostility he'd been so aware of today. There'd been a moment when he'd thought it was behind them—when they'd shared that moment of triumph that they no longer needed to try and spot a small body floating in the sea—but it hadn't lasted. Summer had been immersed in paperwork when he'd signed off for his first shift and she'd barely acknowledged his departure.

He summoned a friendly smile. 'Need a hand?'

'Zac…'

He was possibly the last person Summer might have

expected to meet here on the beach. The last person she would have *wanted* to meet? She was having to share yet another patch of her turf. First the base where she worked. Then the emergency department that was also part of her working life. Now this—not exactly her home but a huge part of when she spent her downtime and a place that was very special to her. And he was...he was almost *naked*.

Oh...my... The board shorts were perfectly respectable attire for the beach but the last time she'd seen him as he left the base that afternoon he'd been wearing real clothes. Clothes that covered up that rather overwhelming expanse of well tanned, smooth, astonishingly *male* skin. He'd obviously towelled himself off recently but droplets of water were still clinging in places. Caught in the sparse hair, for example, between the dark copper discs of his nipples.

'I've been swimming.'

Oh, help... He'd noticed her looking, hadn't he? Hastily, Summer dragged her gaze upwards again. His hair was wet and spiky and his expression suggested that he was as disconcerted as she was by their lack of clothing. Suddenly, it struck her as funny and she had to smile.

'No...really?'

'I'd offer you my towel but it's a bit damp.'

'I've been standing up. I'm not actually that wet.'

Just as she spoke, her dog emerged from his frolic in the waves, bounded towards them, stopped and then shook himself vigorously. It was like a short, sharp and rather cold shower.

'*Flint*... Oh, sorry about that. My bag's just over here. I've got a dry towel in there.'

'No worries.' Zac was laughing. He reached out his hand. 'Hey, Flint...'

The big dog sniffed the hand cautiously, wagged a

shaggy tail politely and then sat on the sand, close enough to lean on Summer's leg. He looked up and the question might as well have been a bubble in the air over his head.

Friend of yours? Acceptable company?

Summer touched the dog's head.

Yes. He's okay. I'm safe.

Maybe it was the genuine laughter that had made a joke of something many people would have found annoying. Or the way he'd reached out to make friends with Flint. She might not let people *too* close but she'd always trusted her instincts about their character and there was nothing here to be ringing alarm bells. Quite the opposite, in fact.

'So, do you need a hand dragging this thing somewhere? It looks heavy.'

'No. Jay'll come and get it soon. He's busy giving someone a lesson at the moment.' Turning the board sideways on the soft sand close to her brightly coloured beach bag, she sat down on one end. 'I'll just look after the board until he's done.'

'Jay?'

'He runs a paddleboard business. I hired one the first time I came to this beach and fell in love with it. I've been coming back ever since.'

'And Flint? He fell in love with it too?' Zac sat down, uninvited, on the other end of the board but somehow it felt perfectly natural. Welcome, even.

'He was in love with me.' The memory made Summer smile. 'Jay was going to look after him while I went for a ride, the first time I brought him here as a pup, but Flint wasn't having any of it. He just came after me. Luckily, Jay shouted loud enough for me to hear so I could fish him out of the water before he got so exhausted he sank. He fell asleep on the board coming back in and that's been his spot ever since.' She laughed. 'You're sitting on it right now. That's why he's standing there glaring at you.'

'Oh...my apologies.' Zac shuffled closer to Summer and Flint stepped onto the end of the board, turned around and then lay down in a neat ball with his nose on his paws.

Zac was so close to Summer now that she could feel the warmth of his skin. His *bare* skin. His legs were bent and she could see sand caught in the dusting of dark hair. The legs of his board shorts were loose enough to be exposing skin on his inner thigh that looked paler than the rest of him. Soft...

She cleared her throat as she looked away. Maybe that would clear inappropriate thoughts as well. 'So why Takapuna? Auckland's got a lot of beaches to choose from when you need an after-work dip.'

'It's been my backyard for ever. That's my gran's house up there.' He was pointing to the prestigious row of houses that had gardens blending into the edge of the beach. Multi-million-dollar houses. 'The old one, with the boat shed and the anchor set in the gate.'

It was impossible not to be seriously impressed. 'You *live* there?'

'I know...' Zac pushed his wet hair off his face. 'It's a bit weird. I'm thirty-six years old and I'm still living with my gran. But the house is on two levels. Gran's upstairs and I rent the bottom half and it's always just worked for both of us. She'd deny it but I think she's relieved to have me back. I'm relieved too, I have to admit. I worried about her while I was away. She's a bit old to be living entirely on her own.'

'A *bit* old? Didn't you say she was in her nineties?'

'Ninety-two. You wouldn't think so, though, if you met her. She reckons ninety is the new seventy.' Zac turned his head. 'She'd love to meet you. Would you like to come in for a drink or something?'

Summer turned her head as well and suddenly their faces were too close. She could see the genuine warmth of that invitation in his eyes. What was the 'something' on offer as well as a drink?

Whatever it was, she wanted it. The attraction was as strong as it was unexpected. She could feel the curl of it deep in her belly. A delicious cramp that eased into tendrils that floated right down to her toes.

She'd been fighting this from the moment she'd first seen this man this morning, hadn't she?

He was—quite simply—gorgeous...

It wasn't just his looks. It was his enthusiasm for his work. His charm. That smile. The way he loved his grandmother.

She couldn't look away. Couldn't find anything to say. All she could do was stare at those dark eyes. Feel the puff of his breath on her face. Notice the dark stubble on his jaw and how soft it made his lips look...

The board beneath her rocked a little as Flint jumped off. Maybe he'd knocked Zac slightly off balance and that was why he leaned even closer to her. It was no excuse, though, was it?

You really shouldn't kiss somebody you'd only just met. Somebody who you were probably going to be working with on an almost daily basis.

Summer couldn't deny that she'd been thinking about kissing him. Couldn't deny that sudden attraction. Had it been contagious?

Who actually moved first or was it just the result of that movement on top of already sitting so close?

Not that it mattered. Nothing seemed to matter for the brief blink of time that Zac's lips touched her own. The touch was so electric that she jerked back instinctively. She'd never felt *anything* like that...

Flint's deep bark couldn't be ignored. Jay was walking towards them. The random sound of a frog croaking from her beach bag was another alert. She had a text message on her phone.

Real life was demanding her attention but, for a crazy moment, Summer wanted it to just go away. She wanted to sit on the sand as the sun set.

She wanted to kiss Zac again.

Properly, this time...

'So...' Zac had noticed Flint's enthusiastic greeting and must have guessed that it was Jay coming to collect the board. 'How 'bout that drink?'

Summer was also getting to her feet. She'd scooped up her bag and was checking her phone. It could be an emergency call-out.

Except it wasn't. It was a text from Kate.

It's driving me nuts trying to guess. You don't mean Zac M, do you? OMG. If it is, stay AWAY.

Somehow Summer managed a friendly introduction between Jay and her new work colleague despite the chaos in the back of her mind as memories forced themselves to the surface.

Driving Kate up to Auckland late that night because Shelley had been hospitalised after an attempted suicide. Listening to the hysterical account of the man she'd been abandoned by. The father of her baby. The monster who'd tried to push her down a staircase when he'd learned that she was pregnant...

So many buttons could be pushed by memories that could never be erased.

And she'd actually wanted to *kiss* him again?

'I'll give you a hand closing up,' she heard herself saying to Jay as he picked up her board. She barely glanced over her shoulder. 'See you later, Zac.'

CHAPTER THREE

HE HAD NO one to blame other than himself.

How stupid had he been?

Even now, a good twenty hours after the incident, the realisation that he'd *kissed* Summer Pearson was enough to make him cringe inwardly. Or maybe it was an echo of the flinch his current patient had just made.

'Sorry, mate. It's just the local going in. It's a deep wound.'

'Tell me about it. As if it wasn't bad enough getting bitten by the damn dog, I had to rip half my leg open on the barbed wire fence getting away from it. Bled like a stuck pig, I did.'

'I'll bet.' Zac reached for the next syringe of local that Mandy had drawn up for him. 'Almost there. We can start stitching you up in a minute.'

'You won't feel a thing,' Mandy assured him. 'You've got the best doctor in the house.'

'At least he's a bloke. D'you know, there were two *girls* on the ambulance that came to get me?'

'Hadn't you heard, Mr Sanders?' Mandy's tone was amused. 'Girls can do anything these days. Can't we, Zac?'

'Absolutely. I'd say you were a lucky man, Mr Sanders. Can you pass me the saline flush, please, Mandy? I'd like to give this a good clean-out before we start putting things back together.'

He took his time flushing out the deep laceration. He'd do the deep muscle suturing here but he had every intention of handing over to Mandy to finish the task. It might do his patient good to realise that girls could be trusted to do all sorts of things these days.

Like fly around in helicopters and save people's lives. Not that he'd seen Summer do anything that required a high level of skill yesterday but he was quite confident that she had the capability to impress him. He was looking forward to a job that would challenge them both.

At least, he *had* been looking forward to it.

What had he been thinking on the beach yesterday evening? That because she seemed to be thawing towards him he'd make a move and ensure that she actually had a good reason to hate working with him?

Idiot…

Except it hadn't been like that, had it?

Zac reached for the curved needle with the length of absorbable suture material attached. He touched the base of the wound at one side.

'Can you feel that?'

'Nope.'

'Okay. Let me know if you do feel anything.'

'Sure will.'

Zac inserted the needle at the base of the wound and then brought it out halfway up the other side. Pulling it through, he inserted it in the opposite side at the same level and then pulled it through at the base again. This meant he could tie it at the bottom and bury the knots to reduce tissue traction, which would give a better cosmetic result.

His patient was happy to lie back on his pillow, his

hands behind his head, smiling at Mandy, who was happy to keep him distracted while Zac focused on his task.

'What sort of dog was it, Mr Sanders?'

'No idea. Horrible big black thing. Bit of Rottweiler in it, I reckon, judging by the size of those teeth.'

Zac tried to tune out from the chat. Tried not to think about big black dogs. But the suturing was a skill that was automatic and it left his mind free to circle back yet again to how things had gone so bottom-up on the beach.

He'd been enjoying himself. Taking pleasure in sitting beside an attractive young woman, sharing his favourite place with someone who loved it as much as he did. Feeling as if he was making real progress in forging a new professional relationship because of the way Summer had been telling him about part of her personal life. Loving the idea of such a faithful bond between owner and dog that a bit of ocean wasn't about to separate them.

And suddenly something had changed dramatically. He'd been shoved sideways by the dog and Summer had been looking at him and it felt as if he was seeing who she really was for the first time and he'd liked what he was seeing.

Really liked it.

But he didn't go around kissing women just because he found them attractive. No way. He would never force himself on a woman, either. *Ever.* Being made to feel as if he had done that stirred feelings that were a lot less than pleasant.

The needle slid in and out of flesh smoothly and the wound was closing nicely but Zac wasn't feeling the satisfaction of a job being done well. He was in the same emotional place he'd been left in last night, when Summer had virtually dismissed him and walked away without a backward glance.

If it wasn't beyond the realm of something remotely believable, he might have decided that it was Summer who'd initiated that kiss but the way she'd jerked back in horror had made it very clear that hadn't been the case.

He felt as if he'd been duped. Manipulated in some incomprehensible way. Pulled closer and then slapped down. Treated unfairly.

The final knot of the deep sutures was pulled very tight. The snip of the scissors a satisfying end note.

Okay…he was angry.

He needed to put it aside properly before it had any chance of affecting his work. At least he was in the emergency department today. He was due for another shift on the helicopter tomorrow but maybe he'd find time to ring the base manager later and ask if he could juggle shifts.

With a bit of luck, he could find another crew to work with, without having to tell anybody why he couldn't work with Summer again.

The call-out had been more than welcome.

'Big MVA up north.' Her crew partner today was Dan. 'You ready to rock and roll, Summer?'

'Bring it on.'

It was very unfortunate for the people in the vehicles that had collided head-on at high speed on an open road, but Summer had been suffering from cabin fever for several hours by now. She needed action. Enough action to silence the internal conflict that seemed to be increasingly loud.

The usual distractions that a quiet spell provided hadn't worked. She should have made the most of the time to catch up on journal articles or do some work on the research project she had going but, instead, she'd paced around. Checking kits and rearranging stock. Cleaning things, for heaven's sake.

A bit like the way she'd acted when she'd got home last night and couldn't settle to cook or eat any dinner because she kept going over and over what had happened on the beach.

Trying to persuade herself that that kiss had been all Zac's idea. That she hadn't felt what she had when his lips had touched hers.

She was still experiencing those mental circles today and, if anything, they were even more confusing, thanks to that conversation she'd had with Kate late in the evening.

Of course he's charming. Why do you think Shelley fell for him so hard?

But it was more than a surface charm designed to lure women into his bed on a temporary basis.

Zac cared. About elderly patients. About small boys who might have been washed off a rock and drowned.

Small boys. Children. Presumably babies. And if he cared about other people's children, it just didn't fit that he'd abandoned his own. The story was getting old now. Maybe she hadn't remembered the details so well. Kate had been happy to remind her.

Yes...of course he knew Shelley was pregnant. That was why he tried to push her down the stairs.

So why hadn't Shelley pressed charges or demanded paternal support?

She was too scared to have anything more to do with him. And she planned to terminate the pregnancy, remember? Only, in the end, she didn't...

And Zac had been on the other side of the world by then. And Shelley had had one health issue after another. Always at the doctor's or turning up at the Hamilton emergency department Kate still worked in. Things hadn't changed much, either—except now it was her son who always seemed to be sick or getting injured. The whole family had to focus on supporting Shelley and little Felix and sometimes it was a burden.

'Are you going to tell Shelley?' she finally had to ask.

God, I don't know... I might have a chat to her psychiatrist about it. The new meds seem to be working finally, at the moment. It might be bad news to throw a spanner in the works...

It had been Summer who'd thrown the spanner. Not only at Kate but, potentially, at Zac, too. What if Shelley was told? If she took legal action of some kind and demanded a paternity test and back payment of parental support? Or, worse—if she went public with accusations of physical abuse? It could ruin the career Zac was clearly so passionate about. She would not only be responsible for things hitting the fan but she would be stuck in the middle having to work with him.

Why hadn't she just kept her mouth shut? It wasn't as if she saw Kate much these days and she hadn't seen Shelley since that night at the hospital.

But—if it was true—didn't he deserve to face the consequences?

That was the problem in a nutshell, wasn't it?

If it was true. She had no reason to believe it wasn't.

Except what her gut was telling her.

Thank goodness she could stop thinking about it for a while now. She had a job to focus on. A huge job. She could see the traffic banked up in both directions below them now. A cluster of emergency vehicles. She'd heard the updates on the victims. One patient was dead on scene. Another two were still trapped and one of them had a potential spinal injury. The other was having increasing difficulty breathing.

'He was initially responsive to voice,' the paramedic on scene told Summer. 'But he's become unresponsive, with increasing respiratory distress. We've got a wide bore IV in and oxygen on.'

'The passenger?'

'She's not complaining of any pain but she can't move her legs and they're not trapped. She's got a cervical collar on and someone holding her head still while they've been cutting the roof off.'

'And the van driver's status zero?'

'Yes. He was dead by the time we arrived, which was...' the paramedic checked his watch '...twenty-two minutes ago.'

The next few minutes were spent on a rapid assessment of the driver, who was the most critically injured. Summer took note of the jagged metal and other hazards as she went to lean into the car's interior.

'Any undeployed airbags?' Summer had to raise her voice to be heard over the pneumatic cutting gear the fire service were still using to open the badly crushed car.

'No.'

'Is the car stable?'

'Yes. We can roll the dash as soon as you're ready and then you can get him out. Passenger should be clear for extrication now.'

'Dan, can you coordinate that? I might need you in a minute, though. I'm going to intubate and get another IV in before we move the driver.'

He was already in a bad way and she knew to expect a clinical deterioration as soon as they moved him, even when it was to an area where it would be easier to work. Due to his level of unconsciousness, she didn't need any drugs to help her insert the tube to keep his airway safe. By the time she'd ensured adequate ventilation and got both high flow oxygen and some intravenous fluids running, Dan and his team had extricated the passenger and had her safely immobilised and ready for a slow road trip to the nearest hospital by ambulance.

Summer coordinated the fire crew to help lift the driver from the wreckage and get him onto the helicopter stretcher but she wasn't ready to take off yet. She crouched down at the foot of the stretcher so that she could see his exposed chest at eye level.

'Flail chest,' she told Dan. 'Look at that asymmetrical movement.'

'Here's his driver's licence.' A police officer handed it to Dan. 'His name's Brian Tripp. He's forty-three.'

They already had that information from his wife. There was paperwork the paramedics on scene first had completed. Summer had more important things to deal with. She could hear more clearly with her stethoscope now and she wasn't happy with what she could hear.

'I'm going to do a bilateral chest decompression before we fly,' she decided. 'Can you get the ECG monitor on, Dan? And start fluid resus.'

The only procedure Summer had to deal with a build-up of air in the chest that was preventing the lungs from expanding properly was to insert a needle. It was a temporary measure and it didn't help a lung to re-expand. It also didn't help a build-up of blood instead of air.

And that was the moment—in the midst of dealing with something that was taking her entire focus—that she thought about Zac again.

If only he'd been on board today instead of yesterday. He could have performed a much more useful procedure by actually opening the chest cavity. Not to put a drainage tube in, because that would take too much time, but it was the same procedure and left an opening that would be of far more benefit than the tiny hole a needle could make.

One that could—and did—get blocked when they were in the air only minutes later, even though Monty was keeping them flying low to avoid any pressure changes that could exacerbate the problem.

It was touch and go to keep her patient alive until they reached Auckland General and Summer was virtually running to keep up with the stretcher as they headed for Resus in the ground floor emergency department.

Who knew that Zac Mitchell would be leading the team waiting for them? The wave of relief was odd, given that she had yet to see how this doctor performed under pressure, but there was no denying it was there. Instinct again?

Was it Zac's expression as he caught her gaze? Focused. Intelligent. Ready for whatever she was about to tell him. Not that there was any time for information about what they'd found on scene—like the amount of cabin intrusion that had advertised a potentially serious chest injury. Even the name and age of their patient would have to wait.

'Tension pneumothorax,' she told Zac succinctly. 'Came on en route. He went into respiratory arrest as we landed.'

Within seconds, Zac was performing the exact procedure she had wished he'd been there to perform on scene. And he was doing it with a calm efficiency that—along with the evidence that her patient was breathing for himself again—made Summer even more relieved.

Her instincts about his skill level had not been wrong.

She wanted to stay and watch the resuscitation and assessment that would, hopefully, result in a trip to Theatre to have the major injuries dealt with but another call took her and Dan away with barely enough time to restock their gear.

This was a winch job to collect a mountain biker with a dislocated shoulder who was on a track with difficult access. A road crew were there to take over the care and transport of the patient so there was no return trip to hospital that would have given Summer the chance to find out what had happened to Brian.

She would have been happy to wait until tomorrow. Zac was due to fly with them again and they could have discussed the case. But the base manager, Graham, caught her when she was getting changed at the end of her shift.

'What did you do to Zac yesterday?'

'What do you mean?'

'I had a call. He didn't come out and say it directly but he seems to think it might be better to be attached to a different shift. I told him there weren't any other slots and he said that was fine but...'

Monty was in the locker room at the same time. 'Summer doesn't like him.'

Graham gave her an odd look. 'What's not to like? He's got to be one of the best we've been lucky enough to have on board. What did you say to him?'

'I didn't say anything.'

'You didn't exactly roll out the welcome mat, Summer.' But Monty was smiling. 'And it's not like you to be shy.'

'It's got nothing to do with that.'

'What has it got to do with, then?' Both men were looking at her curiously.

What could she say?

That she knew things about Zac that they didn't know? She'd already caused disruption in other people's lives by telling Kate that he was back in town. How much more trouble would she cause by telling her colleagues? Word would get around in no time flat. She'd never been a troublemaker. Or a gossip, come to that. And it wasn't really any of her business, was it?

Or could she say that she'd met him on the beach last evening and ended up kissing him? That he was possibly so appalled at how unprofessional she'd been that he couldn't see himself being able to work with her again?

Things were getting seriously out of control, here.

'It's nothing,' she snapped. 'Leave it with me. I'll sort it.'

The excuse of getting an update on a major case was a good enough reason to pop into the emergency department on her way home.

Normally, it would be something to look forward to. A professional interaction and discussion that could well be of benefit in her management of similar cases in the future.

But what really needed discussing had nothing to do with her patient from the car accident. It was at the other end of the spectrum of professional versus personal. It felt like a minefield and it was one that had been created because she knew too much.

Or maybe not enough?

Summer felt ridiculously nervous as she scanned the department looking for Zac. He was at the triage desk, looking over Mandy's shoulder at something on a computer screen. When he glanced up and spotted Summer, he smiled politely.

She sucked in a breath. 'You got a minute?'

She looked different.

Maybe it was the clothes. He'd seen her in her flight suit and he'd seen her virtually in her underwear, given what that bikini had covered.

Even now, as he ushered her into his office, the memory gave him a twinge of appreciation that could easily turn into something inappropriate. Something to be avoided at all costs, given the way she had dismissed him so rudely on the beach last night.

It was easy enough to reconnect with the anger at being unfairly treated that was still simmering. Anger that had only received some new fuel by the demonstration of how Summer could blow hot and cold with no obvious encouragement.

He'd already been cool on greeting her. Hadn't said a thing, in fact. He'd just tilted his head with a raised eyebrow in response to her request and excused himself to Mandy before leading the way to his office. He'd seen the surprise in Mandy's expression that he was taking Summer somewhere private to talk. He was a bit surprised himself because there was no reason not to have a professional discussion in front of others and he suspected Summer had come in to follow up on that serious chest injury she'd brought in earlier today.

Except that she looked different. Nervous, almost?

Nah…that seemed unlikely.

Easier to focus on what she was wearing. Leather pants and a tight little jacket.

'You ride a bike?'

'Yeah… It's a requirement for employment on the choppers that you can get to base fast. Even a traffic snarl on the bridge is negotiable with a bike.'

'I know. I ride one myself. A Ducati.'

The quick smile was appreciative. 'Me, too. Can't beat a Ducati.'

'No.' His tone was cool again. Zac wasn't ready for another compass shift between hot and cold. It was too confusing.

Her smile faded instantly. She looked away. 'I won't take up too much of your time,' she said. 'I just came in to...to apologise, I guess...'

Whoa...this was unexpected. And welcome? Was she going to apologise for making him feel so unwelcome on shift yesterday?

She certainly looked uncomfortable. Zac perched on the corner of his desk but Summer ignored the available chair. She walked over to the bookshelf and looked as if she was trying to read the dates on the thin spines of the entire shelf of *Emergency Medicine Journal*s.

'What happened last night was extremely unprofessional.' Her voice was tight. 'I just wanted to reassure you that it would never happen again.'

She was talking about the kiss rather than her treatment of him as a team member but this was a good start.

Better than good. So why did he have that dull, heavy sensation in his gut that felt remarkably like disappointment?

'And?'

Her head turned swiftly. Her jaw dropped a little. 'And...and I hope you won't let it influence you working on HEMS. Everybody's saying that we're very lucky to have you.'

'Everybody except you.'

Good grief...why couldn't he just accept her apology gracefully? They could shake hands and agree to make a fresh start in their new working relationship, which could solve the issue in the long run.

Because it would be shoving the issue under the carpet, that was why. Yes, they could probably find a way of working together but he'd never know *why* he'd made such a bad first impression.

Summer had bright spots of colour on her cheeks and

her eyes were wide and uncertain. Almost…*fearful?* What the hell was going on here?

Zac stood up. He knew it was a bad idea the moment he did it because he was now towering over Summer. Intimidating her. To give her credit, however, he could see the way she straightened. Tilted her chin so that she could meet his gaze without flinching.

'What is it you don't like about me so much, Summer? You don't even *know* me.'

'I know *of* you.' There was a sharp note in her voice. A note that said she was less than impressed with what she knew. Disgusted, even?

Zac's breath came out in a huff of disbelief. 'You amaze me,' he said slowly. 'And I don't mean that as a compliment.'

Anger flashed across her features. 'I grew up in Hamilton,' she snapped. 'I had a road job there as an intensive care paramedic. One of my oldest friends worked as a nurse in the emergency department. Kate, her name is. Kate Jones.'

'How nice for you.' Zac shook his head. 'I have no idea where this is going. Or who Kate Jones is. Or what relevance Hamilton has.'

'Kate has a younger sister who's also a nurse. Shelley Jones. Shelley used to work right here, in Auckland General's emergency department.'

Zac knew he was glaring at her. His eyes were still narrowed as something clicked into place.

'I remember her.' He could feel his mouth twisting into the kind of shape that came when you tasted something very unpleasant. 'She was a bit of a nuisance, in fact.'

'I'll bet she was.' Ice dripped from Summer's clipped words. 'I hope you don't have that kind of *nuisance* in your life too often.'

'What *are* you talking about?'

Her tone was sarcastic now. 'I guess getting girls pregnant could be seen as a bit of a nuisance.'

'*What?*' Time seemed to stop. Alarms sounded. He'd heard of men having their lives destroyed by false accusations of something like sexual abuse. His word against hers and the guy was always guilty until proved innocent. Sometimes it didn't make that much difference when the truth finally came out. Mud always stuck.

But...*pregnancy*?

'I never even went out with Shelley.' The words came out slowly. Cloaked in utter disbelief. 'The nuisance was that she had a fairly obvious crush on me. Kept bringing in gifts, like cakes or flowers. Leaving notes on my locker. Turning up in my street, even.' His anger was surfacing. 'If a guy did that to a girl, he'd be had up for stalking. She was a head case but everybody thought it was a joke.' He pushed stiff fingers through his hair. 'She was pregnant? She *told* people that *I* was the father?'

Shock like this couldn't be feigned.

Summer's mouth had gone completely dry. No wonder she'd been having so much trouble fighting her instincts. Zac was telling the truth.

'Only me and Kate.' She tried to swallow. Tried—and failed—to meet his gaze. 'It was when we had to go and see her when she got admitted to psyche after a suicide attempt.'

And she hadn't thought to query how stable Shelley was at that point? To even wonder if her story was accurate?

'Oh, this just gets better and better,' Zac snapped. 'Don't tell me—I was somehow responsible for this as well?'

He might as well know the worst. Would she want to, if she was in his position?

It was hard to get the words out, though. She really, really didn't want to make this any worse for him. She was only the messenger but a part of her knew she deserved to be shot. She'd treated him unfairly. Appallingly unfairly.

'She…um…told us you'd tried to push her down a flight of stairs. After…um…she'd told you about the baby.'

'And where was I when this was going on?'

'I think you'd left for London the day before.'

'How convenient.' Zac was pacing. Two steps in one direction and then an about-face for two steps back as if he felt the desperate need to go somewhere. Anywhere but here. He shoved his fingers through his hair, making the dark waves stand up in a tousled mess.

Then he stopped still and turned slowly to stare at Summer.

'And you *believed* her?'

She'd never felt so small. Strangely, he didn't look angry at the moment, although that would undoubtedly resurface. She could see disbelief. Deep disappointment. Anguish, even…

'As you said… I didn't know you. I'd never met you. All I knew was your name.'

'You met me yesterday.' Yes. There was anger there as well and the words were accusing. 'And you still believed it.'

Summer bit her bottom lip. Would it help to tell him how she'd had doubts from the first instant she'd set eyes on him? How she'd had to fight the feeling of being drawn closer? Of a connection that would have been exciting in any other circumstances? Of a confusion that had ultimately ended in wanting that kiss?

No. She had no excuses. For any of it. She closed her eyes.

'I'm sorry.'

'So am I.'

There was silence for a long moment. A heavy—*where do we go from here?*—kind of silence that she had no idea how to breach.

And then Zac sighed. He perched himself on the corner of his desk again. Summer risked a glance but he was staring at the floor.

'I guess it's better that I know about it,' he said finally. 'At least I'll be prepared for when she turns up in the department again.'

'She gave up nursing. She's had a struggle with her... um...mental health issues.'

Zac snorted.

'I haven't seen her since she was admitted that time. I don't even see Kate much since I left Hamilton. Nobody else needs to know about this, Zac. I'm sorry I knew. Or thought I knew. I wish she'd never mentioned your name.'

'I'm sure you're not the only person she's "mentioned" it to. It's probably on some record somewhere. Like a birth certificate? Oh, my God...' It was clearly sinking home even deeper. 'She did *have* the baby?'

Summer nodded. Her cheeks were burning. 'She told us she was going to have a termination but she didn't. She went down south to stay with friends and apparently came back with the baby to land on her parents' doorstep, asking for help. It was a boy. Felix. He'd be about two and a half now.'

'So I'm probably on some social security list, somewhere. As a father who's failed to provide child support.'

Summer couldn't answer that.

'I hope I am,' Zac said surprisingly. 'A quick DNA test will sort that out.' His huff was incredulous. 'I never even kissed her.'

He caught her gaze with those words. She completely believed that he'd never kissed Shelley.

But he had kissed her. And, for a heartbeat, that was all Summer could think of. That jolt of sensation that had been like some kind of electrical shock.

'It wasn't an immaculate conception,' Zac said dryly. 'It was an entirely imaginary one. Why, in God's name, would anybody *do* something like that?'

'I don't know,' Summer whispered.

Except—maybe—deep down, she did know. Zac Mitchell was the embodiment of a fantasy boyfriend. The ultimate husband and father for your baby. Something to dream about that was never likely to happen for real.

If you were desperate enough and maybe *sick* enough then, yes...she could imagine how somebody would do something like that.

But to make it so completely believable? That was what she really couldn't understand. Her instincts hadn't warned her about anything remotely off, that night. She'd still believed it after talking to Kate last night. Until she'd heard and seen the irrefutable truth in Zac's voice and body language.

'I'll tell Kate,' she offered. 'She can confront Shelley and get the truth out of her. She owes you one hell of an apology. We *all* owe you that.'

But Zac shook his head. 'I'd rather not rake it up any further. Not unless I have to. I'd rather move on and do what I came back here to do. Focus on my career and combine my ED work with as much time as possible in HEMS.'

'But you'd rather work with another shift?' Summer was trying to find what it was on the floor that had caught Zac's attention earlier. 'I could talk to Graham.'

'He said there weren't any other slots available.'

'I'm sure something could be juggled. A team has to be tight. It just doesn't work if there's a...a personality clash or something.'

Another silence fell. Summer finally had to look up and meet Zac's gaze. An unreadable gaze but the intensity was unmistakable.

'But we don't, do we?'

'Don't what?'

'Have a personality clash.'

She couldn't look away. She was being sucked in again. Like the way she had been when she'd been sitting beside him on the paddleboard last night. In that moment before she'd kissed him.

'No...'

'So why don't we just try and make a fresh start and see how it goes?'

Hope was something wonderful. A close cousin of both relief and excitement.

'You'd be okay with that?'

'If you are.'

It felt like the first time she was smiling at Zac. The first time it was a truly genuine smile, anyway.

Nothing else needed to be said because Zac smiled back.

The moment seemed to hang in time. And then it became just a little bit awkward. As though more was being communicated than either of them were ready for.

Zac cleared his throat. 'Do you want to hear about the surgery on that tension pneumothorax guy you brought in?'

'Oh…' Summer's nod was probably a shade too enthusiastic. 'Yes, please…'

'Come with me. I'll show you the scans first. Man, that chest was a mess. I'm impressed that you got him here alive.'

Summer followed Zac out of his office. Their fresh start seemed to be happening now.

How good was that?

CHAPTER FOUR

ZAC'S BIKE WAS BIG, black and sleek.

It made Summer's smaller red model look feminine but the assumption would be deceptive. Only a certain kind of woman rode a machine like that.

Confident, feisty kind of women. And when they were wrapped up in a small package that could easily be seen as 'cute', it was a very intriguing mix. She must have arrived for work only seconds before he'd pulled into the rescue helicopter's base because she was standing beside her bike, pulling off her helmet. A glove came off next and the flattened spikes of her hair were fluffed up with a quick, spread finger comb-through—the feminine gesture at odds with the stance. With her feet apart and her helmet cradled under one arm making it look as if she had the hand on her hip, Summer Pearson looked ready to take on the world.

And she was watching him as he killed his engine and got off his own bike. Her gaze was…cautious?

Of course it was. This was the first time they were on base together after that extraordinary conversation in his office. And, yes, they'd agreed to make a fresh start and see how it went but how was that going to work, exactly? He'd had time to try and think it through but, if anything, he was finding it all increasingly disturbing.

Part of Zac—the angry part—wanted nothing more than to seek Shelley out and demand a retraction of accusations that were unbelievably malicious, but the voice of reason was warning him not to do anything without thinking it through very carefully. Yes, he could prove the child wasn't his but there were those appalling accusations of violence against a woman and that would be her word against his.

The people who knew him would never believe it but he didn't even want them to have to *think* about it. Imagine how upset his grandmother would be. It was something they never talked about these days—the way he'd seen his mother treated by the man who'd come into their lives when he'd been old enough to start remembering. Old enough to think that it was his fault and he needed to do something to defuse the tension that always ended with his mum bruised and crying.

Summer was taking his word for his innocence in regard to what she'd thought she knew about him. That was disturbing, too. Zac felt as though he still needed to prove himself in some way and he should never have had to feel like that.

There was a smudge of resentment in his mood and it was unfamiliar and unwelcome.

So maybe his gaze was just as cautious but they'd agreed to try a fresh start and Zac always kept his end of a bargain.

'Is that a Monster?'

'Yeah. A six five nine.' There was a definite note of relief in Summer's voice at the choice of an impersonal topic of conversation. A softening of her body language as she turned to look at *his* bike. 'About half the cc rating of yours, I expect.'

'Bet you'd still keep up. Maybe we should go for a ride

one day.' The invitation was deliberately casual. A little forced, even? They were both trying to create a new base for a working relationship but the ice was potentially a little thin and they were both treading carefully.

'Sure. I like stretching out on the open road when I get a chance.'

They walked side by side into the building and Zac could feel some of the tension ease. Maybe it was more important than he cared to admit that he could prove himself to Summer. That it wasn't just his word she needed to trust but that she would get to know him well enough to understand just how impossible it would be for him to act in the way she'd believed he had acted. If he could convince someone who had believed the worst, he wouldn't need to fear any repercussions if the story became public.

Thinking about a place they could head to on a bike ride—like a beautiful beach, maybe—was premature, however. It was quite possible that Summer was just being polite, the way she was making it about the ride rather than his company. She'd had time to think things through in the last couple of days, too. Time to talk to her friend Kate again, perhaps. She might have changed her mind about taking his word for his innocence but was giving him the benefit of some doubt in the meantime. It wasn't just that she needed to trust him—he needed to trust her, as well. And right now his trust in women was justifiably fragile.

It certainly wouldn't be helpful to mention a beach. To remind her of what had happened the last time they'd been sitting on a beach together. That had been even more premature. Unbelievably so, in fact. Zac still couldn't understand quite how that kiss had happened. Something else they needed to put behind them so they could move on with a more professional relationship? As far as building a base for their new working relationship, this was a minefield. Casual conversation was called for. The kind any new colleagues might have.

'You got four wheels as well as two?'

'No.' Summer gave him a quizzical glance. 'Why would I?'

'Doesn't it make things tricky when you want to take your dog somewhere with you?'

'We run.'

'*Everywhere?*'

Summer popped the studs on her jacket and started peeling it off. 'Everywhere we need to go, usually. If I have to take Flint to the vet or something, I'll get a friend to give us a ride. If I'm not at work or at home, we're generally at the beach. He gets a run there every day.'

'Guess I'll get to meet him again, then. I try and run on Takapuna beach every day.'

'Takapuna's our paddleboard beach. I have to use one of Jay's because it would be a bit tricky to carry one on a bike. If it's just a run or a swim we're after, we've got half a dozen beaches and bays to choose from. Or we can just jump overboard.'

'Sorry?' Zac was folding up his leather jacket. He couldn't see Summer because she was behind the open door of her locker now. He was sure he hadn't heard her correctly but then her face popped out and she was smiling. Really smiling. A real smile—like the one she'd given him in his office the other day, when they'd agreed to start again. A smile that could light up the darkest place.

'We live on a boat.'

'Oh…' Zac was lost for words. Just when he thought he was getting a handle on his new colleague, the rug got pulled out from beneath his feet. It wasn't just the unusual place to call home. That smile was doing something strange to his gut. It was more than relief that things seemed to be on a better footing. More, even, than the way it reminded him of what her lips had felt like for that brief instant. Maybe it was the impish quality—the hint of sheer *joie de vivre*—that made it impossible not to smile back.

'What sort of boat?'

'An old yacht. A thirty-foot Catalina. Her name's *Mermaid*. I'm not sure she'd be seaworthy to take out but I've been renting her to live in ever since I came up to Auckland. It's the only home Flint's ever known. He'd be a sad dog if he couldn't see the sea.'

'What does he do when you're at work?'

'Guards the boat. Or sleeps on the jetty. Everybody at the marina knows him. He's never wandered. Never needs a lead. He only wears a collar to hang his registration tag on and make him legal.'

Summer was pulling her flight suit on over her shorts and T-shirt. Her curves were disappearing beneath the shapeless garment and maybe that was just as well.

Zac was beginning to realise what an extraordinary woman Summer was. With the absence of the hostility with which they'd started working together, he was getting far more of a glimpse of what she was like. Fiercely independent, judging by her choice of lifestyle. Open-minded, maybe, given that she was prepared to take his word over that of a long-term friend. The relationship she had with her dog suggested a mutual loyalty and—a bit like her pet—maybe she was a free spirit who chose exactly where she wanted to be and who she wanted to be with. You couldn't lead Summer anywhere she didn't want to go.

But how privileged would you be if she chose to go with you?

Hang on a minute…she'd said 'we' live on a boat. He'd assumed she was talking about herself and her dog but what if there was another component to that 'we'?

That might go even further than both the misinformation on his past and prematurity in having made that kiss so shocking for her. No wonder this all felt so complicated.

Zac took a mental step backwards. Yep. He really did need to tread a little more carefully. There was still a lot more he needed to learn about Summer.

A trip to one of the inhabited islands right out in the Hauraki Gulf was always a bit of a treat. The longer flying time provided an opportunity to enjoy the spectacular views below. The harbour was busy, with ferries and yachts out enjoying the afternoon breeze. There was even a sleek cruise ship in the channel between Rangitoto Island and Takapuna beach.

'Tough day at the office.'

Summer laughed. 'You said it, Monty. And—even better—we're off to deliver a baby.'

'Might have arrived by the time we get there,' Zac warned. 'How far apart did she say her contractions were?'

'Five minutes. And Comms said she sounded a bit distressed.'

'I'm not surprised. It's an isolated place to give birth if something goes wrong.'

'She might be a bit earlier than full-term. It's usual practice for women to go to the mainland for delivery.' Summer was still enjoying the view. 'That's Tiritiri Matangi island. You ever been there?'

'No. Love lighthouses, though. It's a bird sanctuary, isn't it?'

'Yes. It's well worth a visit.' Summer took a breath, about to say something more, but then she closed her mouth.

Had she been about to suggest that they took a ride up to Gulf Harbour on their bikes the next time they had a day off at the same time? And then take the ferry and walk around the island, seeing things like the feeding stations that attracted hundreds of bellbirds and tuis?

Yep. Even now, the idea of spending a day like that with Zac was extremely appealing but he might have just been being polite, suggesting that they had a ride together. After all, it was a working relationship they'd agreed to make a fresh start on, not a personal one.

Wasn't it?

They were met at the landing site by a man called Kev, who was in charge of Civil Defence and the volunteer fire brigade for the small community. A retired fisherman with an impressive white beard, Kev had an ancient jeep to provide transport. The local nurse was unavailable to assist because she'd taken the ferry to the mainland to go shopping.

'Janine? Yep. I know where she lives. Haven't seen her for a while but she likes to keep to herself. She's sick?'

'In labour, apparently.'

'She's having a *baby*?'

Summer caught Zac's glance as he lifted the Thomas pack of gear into the back of the jeep. This was odd. In such a small community, surely a full-term pregnancy wouldn't go unnoticed?

Kev started the engine. It coughed and died so he tried again. This time it caught but he was shaking his head.

'A baby…well…how 'bout that?'

Summer climbed into the vehicle. 'You didn't know she was pregnant?'

Kev grinned. 'She's a big girl, is Janine. Can't say I noticed last time either, mind you.' He clicked his tongue. 'That was a sad business…'

'Oh? In what way?' Under normal circumstances, it might not be ethical to be discussing a patient with someone who wasn't a family member but the comment was ringing alarm bells. If the last birth had caused major problems, they needed to know about it.

'She did all the right things. Went to the big hospital in Whangerei to have the bub. Dunno what happened exactly, but it didn't come home. Janine was in bits. Broke her and Ev up in the end. He lives over on the mainland now but she goes off on the ferry to visit him sometimes so… Guess they must have decided to try again. She shouldn't be having it here, though, should she? Crumbs… what if something goes wrong again?'

'That's why we're here.' Zac's tone was calm. Reassuring. 'How far is it to her house?'

'It's not a house, exactly. More like a caravan with a bit built on. It's not too far. Up in the bush at the end of this beach coming up.'

'Does she have any family here?'

'Nah.'

'Friends?'

Kev scratched his beard as he brought the jeep to a halt. 'She gets on okay with everybody but, like I said, she keeps to herself pretty much. 'Specially since the trouble. Want me to come in with you?'

Summer caught Zac's gaze. There could be a reason why Janine had been keeping her pregnancy private.

'How 'bout you wait out here for us, Kev? We'll see what's happening and hopefully you can get us all back to the chopper pretty fast.'

Except that it didn't look as if they'd be moving their patient any time too soon.

Janine was inside the caravan, hanging onto the edge of the built-in table with one hand and clutching her belly with the other. She saw Summer and Zac ease themselves into the cramped space but clearly couldn't say anything in response to their introductions. Her face was contorted with pain.

'Contraction?'

Janine nodded, groaning at the same time.

'How long since the last one?'

Their patient shook her head. 'Dunno,' she gasped.

'Have your waters broken?'

A nod this time.

'We need to check what's happening,' Zac said. 'Would you prefer it if Summer examines you?'

Janine shook her head. 'You're the doctor. I'm... *scared*...'

'Let's get you on your bed.' Summer took Janine's arm to encourage her to move. 'We can help you. It might help us if you can tell us about what happened last time...'

But Janine burst into tears as she climbed onto the narrow bed. She covered her face with her hands. Summer could see the swell of the young woman's belly now that she was lying flat. She helped her bend her knees so that Zac could find out how advanced the labour was.

He was frowning when he looked up a short time later.

'No dilation whatsoever,' he said. 'No cervical softening, even.'

'Really?' Summer placed her hands on Janine's belly. 'Let's see if I can find out how Baby's lying.'

The swollen belly felt firm. And oddly smooth.

'Has Baby been moving?'

'Yes. Lots. Until this morning, anyway…'

Zac was unpacking the portable ultrasound unit. 'Have you been going over to the mainland for your antenatal checks, Janine?'

'No…' She turned her head away from them. 'I didn't trust the doctors at the hospital. Or the midwives. Not after last time…'

'What happened, love?' Zac paused, the tube of gel in his hands.

'It was all fine until I was in the hospital. They said it was a knot in the cord and it…it stopped the oxygen. I knew something was wrong but they were still telling me to push and I… I…'

'It's okay, Janine.' Summer caught her hand. 'You're having contractions now but you're nowhere near giving birth. We're going to get you to a safe place in plenty of time.'

Zac was pressing the ultrasound probe to Janine's belly, staring at the small screen of the unit. He was frowning again. He shifted the probe and tilted the screen so that Summer could see it. She stared too, totally bewildered.

'We just need some more gear,' Zac said calmly. 'We want to take your blood pressure and things, Janine. Be back in a tick.'

But… Summer stifled the word. They had all the gear they needed in the pack right beside them but she recognised the warning glance and followed Zac into the lean-to built onto the caravan that was a living area with armchairs and a potbelly stove.

She kept her voice low. 'There's no baby, is there?'

Zac shook his head.

'But she *looks* pregnant. She's having contractions. She's in *labour*.'

'She *thinks* she's in labour.' Zac spoke just as quietly. 'This is incredibly rare but I think it's a case of pseudo-cyesis.'

'Phantom pregnancy? Good grief...what do we do?'

'She needs help. When she finds out that she's not actually pregnant, it's going to be as devastating as losing her first baby. This isn't the time or place for that to happen.'

'So we go along with it? Transport her, believing that she's still about to give birth? Give her pain relief for the contractions?'

'What else can we do?'

There was no answer to that. Getting Janine to the specialist psychiatric help she needed was a no-brainer. Making the situation even harder to deal with would have been a stupid option. It took a lot of persuasion to get Janine to agree to transport at all.

'I want to have my baby here. Where it's safe.'

'But it's not safe, Janine. You're too far away from the kind of specialist people and facilities that make it safe. And it's not going to happen for a while. We can't stay but we can't leave you here by yourself either.'

Finally, she agreed. She told Summer where the bag was with all the things she would need for the baby. A glance inside the bag showed some gorgeous hand-knitted booties and hats. A soft pink teddy bear. She was blinking back tears as they helped Janine into the jeep.

'You should've told us, love.' Kev looked worried. 'We were worried about you.'

'I'll be fine, Kev. I'll be back soon. With the baby.'

It was the strangest case Summer had ever had. She was still thinking about it that evening when she was walking on the beach with Flint.

She'd known there was a good chance of meeting Zac

on Takapuna beach. It was easy enough to guess what time he was likely to be having a swim or a run. Maybe that was why she'd chosen this beach, despite not intending to go paddleboarding today. Maybe she wanted the chance to talk about such a puzzling case.

He'd been good to work with today. The fresh start was working well. Maybe there was even a pull to see him again that she wasn't about to admit to.

The excuse that this was where some of Flint's best dog friends came to play was a good cover. And Zac seemed happy enough to sit and chat.

'It was a good day, wasn't it? It's not often you get a "once in a lifetime" case like that.'

'I still can't believe that something imaginary could give rise to actual physical signs.'

'The power of the mind.' Zac nodded. 'It's extraordinary, isn't it?'

'The things she said when I was getting her history down en route. Like the date her periods stopped and the early nausea and breast changes. Feeling the baby starting to move at about sixteen weeks. Everything sounded so normal.'

'She'd been through it before. She knew what to expect.'

'But do you think she could actually feel what she thought was the baby moving?'

'I'm sure she could.'

'And the size and shape of her belly. I couldn't believe it when the ultrasound showed there was no baby.'

'I've read about it. They reckon it's due to changes in the endocrine system. When a woman wants to be pregnant so desperately, it can trick the body into believing it's pregnant, as well as the mind. That triggers the secretion of hormones like oestrogen and prolactin and that will stop periods and cause breast changes and nausea. And the weight gain and belly swelling. So, of course, there's no reason for her to stop believing she's pregnant—it just gets confirmed.'

'But for so many months? To actually go into an imaginary labour?'

'That's really rare. I think that psychiatrist that got called in looked quite excited about the case. He'll probably write it up for a journal article.'

'I just hope he takes good care of Janine. Poor thing.'

'Yeah... You have to feel sorry for her.'

They sat in silence for a while, then, watching Flint do the sniffing thing to greet a small black Spoodle. With an excited yap, the Spoodle ran in a circle and then dipped its head, inviting Flint to chase her. He complied and, a moment later, both dogs were splashing though the shallows at high speed against the backdrop of a pretty sunset over Rangitoto.

Summer felt her smile stretching. Life was good. Shifting her gaze, she found Zac smiling as well and, suddenly, there they were again. Looking at each other like they had been when they'd been sitting on her board the other night.

Only this time it felt different.

Relaxed.

The tension was gone and, just as suddenly, Summer thought she knew why.

'It's been bothering me,' she admitted. 'Why I believed Shelley. My instincts are usually so good about whether people are telling the truth. But it's like Janine, isn't it? What you said about the power of the mind.'

'Not sure I'm following you.'

'If we hadn't had that ultrasound with us, I would have believed Janine was pregnant.'

'She was certainly convincing.'

'So was Shelley.'

'But Shelley *was* pregnant.'

'I'm talking about the other stuff. About you being the father and…' No, she didn't even want to think about the accusations of violence. Zac had been so kind to poor Janine and the compassion in his voice had suggested he felt as sorry for her as others should. He'd made a terrifying situation bearable for Frances the other day. He adored his gran. It would be insulting to even voice something so unbelievable. 'But maybe she was believable because that's what she believed herself.'

Zac grunted. 'She's pretty sick, then.'

'Like Janine.'

'Janine's only hurting herself.'

'We don't know that for sure. There could be collateral damage for others—like her ex-husband? He might be involved enough to believe he's about to have another child.'

'I guess. You could be right. Maybe feeling sorry for Shelley is the best way to go.' Zac's sigh suggested that he didn't want to talk about it any more and that was fair enough.

Flint was shaking water from his coat as the Spoodle took off to rejoin its owner further down the beach. Any moment now and he'd probably come back, all damp and sandy, and she might have to excuse herself to go and finish their walk. Or maybe not. Zac might not want to talk about Shelley any more but he didn't seem annoyed when he spoke again.

'So you have good instincts, then?'

'I've always thought so.'

'Just out of interest—given what you thought you knew—what did those instincts tell you about me the other day?'

That was easy to answer. 'That you couldn't possibly

be the monster I'd assumed you were.' She smiled. 'No one but an exceptionally nice person could start talking about his gran the moment he opened his mouth.'

Zac grinned and Summer found herself saying more than she'd intended to say. 'I liked you,' she admitted. 'It felt wrong but I... I *really* liked you.'

Zac was silent for a moment. It looked as if he might be taking a rather slow breath. Then he cleared his throat. 'Just for the record, I really liked you too. I still do.'

Another silence as Summer absorbed his words. Oh, yeah... Life was good.

'And what did those instincts tell you when we were on the beach the other night? When I...kissed you.'

'But *I* kissed *you*.'

'I don't think so.' There was amusement in his tone. 'At least, that's not the way I remember it.' He caught her gaze. 'You wouldn't have been so shocked if it had been your idea,' he added. 'You jumped like you'd got burned.'

'That was because it felt...weird...'

'Weird?'

'Yeah...' Summer had to break the eye contact. 'Different. Yeah...weird.'

'Hmm.' Another pause and then the query was interested. 'Good weird or bad weird?'

Summer tried to remember that odd jolt. To feel it again. But all that she was aware of was a growing warmth in her belly, spreading into her limbs. A tingly, delicious kind of warmth.

'I think...good weird.'

'But you're not sure?'

'No...' *Oh, my...* That look in Zac's eyes right now. The sheer mischief. The *intent*...

'I'm thinking there's only one way to find out.'

Did he mean what she thought he meant? That he would have to kiss her again?

Had he really thought he'd been the one who'd initiated the kiss the other night?

There could only be one explanation for that. That they'd both been thinking exactly the same thing. At the same time.

And they were doing it again right now. Summer's heart skipped a beat and picked up its pace.

Or maybe not.

'Not here,' Zac said. 'It's way too public.'

The disappointment was fleeting because the prospect of being somewhere more private was infinitely more exciting. Zac was already on his feet, ready to take her to that private place. Summer's heart was still thumping and now her mouth felt a little dry.

Or maybe not.

'Come and meet my gran.'

CHAPTER FIVE

HE'D WANTED TO take her home.

So he could kiss her again. Properly. Last time it had been a kind of accident that didn't count but even the memory of that brief brush of their lips gave him a twist of very powerful desire. And Summer remembered it well enough to think it was different? Weird but good?

She had no idea how good it *could* be…

It would have sounded crass to say that out loud and it could well have scared her off completely so he'd had to come up with another reason to get them away from such a public place.

But introducing her to his grandmother?

Now they were stuck. Flint looked happy enough on the terrace outside and Summer looked happy enough inside. Zac had come back from taking a quick shower and changing his clothes to find her helping his gran put a salad together—to go with the massive salmon fillet that just happened to have been baking in the oven this evening.

Ivy Mitchell had been thrilled to meet Summer.

'So you're the girl who has the dog on the back of the board? I watch you every time, dear. With my telescope.'

'Really?' Summer looked disconcerted. 'I had no idea people were spying on me.'

'Oh, I spy on everybody, darling. I'm ninety-two. Nobody's going to tell me off.'

'I might,' Zac growled. 'You can't go around spying on people, Gravy.'

'I'm not gainfully employed. I sit on my terrace and the telescope's right there. What's a girl supposed to do?'

Summer was laughing. And shaking her head. '*Gravy?*'

Ivy smiled. 'I told Isaac's mum that I didn't want to be called Granny. I wasn't even sixty when he was born, for heaven's sake. Far too young! I said he could call me Ivy, like a real person, but she said I had to be Gran. So it was supposed to be Gran Ivy but it was too hard for him when he was learning to talk so it came out as Gravy. And it stuck.'

'I love it. The only grandmother I had was Nana, which seems terribly ordinary in comparison.'

'Had?'

'She died when I was quite young.'

'What a shame. The older generation is a blessing. Your family must miss that.'

'I don't have any family. My mum died when I was seventeen and my father was already well out of the picture.' Summer's tone was brisk and Zac recognised that it was not a topic open to further discussion. It reminded him of that first day in the chopper when he'd asked whether she had any siblings. The impression that she could offer personal information but he was not allowed to ask had been so strong he still hadn't tested those boundaries. He had boundaries of his own, didn't he? It might be unspoken but there was an agreement between them now that precluded any more discussion of Summer's friend Kate and her sister Shelley. Of the child he'd been accused of fathering.

Not that Ivy was likely to respect such boundaries.

Except that this time she did. She opened her mouth but then closed it again, simply handing Summer a jar with a screw lid. 'Throw this dressing on the salad, darling. I make it myself and it's got a lovely garlic punch. So good for you, you know—garlic.'

'It's your secret to a long life, isn't it, Gravy?'

'That—and champagne, of course. Speaking of which, let's refresh our glasses, shall we, Summer? Champagne and salmon—a marriage made in heaven.'

Zac took a pull at the icy glass of lager he held. The view from the upper level of this old house was extraordinary—like a huge painting of a beach scene with the background of the sea and the distinctive volcano shape of Rangitoto Island placed perfectly dead centre. Right now, there were vivid streaks of red in the sky as daylight ended with a spectacular flourish. He had always loved the changing panorama of this living painting. He loved this house. Right now, he loved that a contented dog lay with his nose on his paws guarding the house and its occupants. He could smell good food and he was with the person who meant the most to him in the world—his beloved Gravy.

Could life get any better?

Maybe it could.

He was also with an extraordinary newcomer to his life. The idea of getting to know Summer a great deal better was exciting. Maybe—just maybe—this was the woman who could capture him enough to be the person he had yet to find. The one who could come to mean as much—or possibly even more—than his only family member.

The possibility was as breathtaking as the view.

Zac watched the conspiratorial grin between the two women as they clinked champagne flutes and he had to smile. Kindred spirits? They were certainly getting on very well together. He just hoped that second glass of bubbles wouldn't loosen his grandmother's tongue any further. Bad enough that she'd already admitted spying on Takapuna residents as they enjoyed their beach. How much worse would it be if she started on another favourite theme—that it was high time her grandson found a nice girl and settled down to start making babies?

As if she felt both the gaze and his smile, Summer turned her head and her gaze locked with his. And there was that kick of desire in his gut again. How long would it take them to eat dinner and escape? To find somewhere they could be alone together?

Maybe Summer was telepathic. He could see the way her chest rose as if she was taking a deep breath. The way her eyes darkened, suggesting that her thoughts mirrored his. When the tip of her tongue appeared to wet her lips, he almost uttered a growl of frustration. However long dinner took, it was going to be too long.

If Summer was lucky enough to live until she was in her nineties, she wanted to be exactly like Ivy Mitchell.

A little taller than Summer, Ivy was very slim but it would be an insult to call her frail. She had long silver hair that was wound up into an elegant knot high on the back of her head and her clothing was just as chic, white Capri pants and a dark blue tee shirt with a white embroidered anchor on it. As someone with sea water in her veins, maybe that was why she'd instantly felt at ease with Zac's grandmother.

Unusually at ease. Was it the age gap? Way too much to be a friend or a colleague. Too much, even, to be an age group that invited comparison to her mother, which was a good thing because Ivy's relaxed confidence, that was so like her grandson's, would have made her mother's constant anxiety seem awkward.

Or maybe it was because she had the same warm brown eyes as her gorgeous grandson. Whatever the reason, Summer was enjoying herself and feeling increasingly relaxed, which was ironic because the energy level emanating from Ivy was leaving her feeling rather breathless.

Or maybe that had something to do with the way Zac was looking at her every time she met his gaze. As if he really liked what he was seeing. As if he couldn't wait to see more.

And eating dinner with these two...

Oh, my...

Watching food going into Zac's mouth and the way he licked the corners of his lips occasionally to catch a drip of salad dressing was doing very strange things to her equilibrium.

This was crazy. She'd only met him last week. Summer Pearson did not go around jumping into bed with men she'd only just met. Especially men she hadn't even been on a date with. But what if time together counted, even if it hadn't been prearranged? Sitting on a beach with someone was *almost* like a date, wasn't it?

If Ivy had any idea of where her thoughts kept drifting, she wasn't bothered.

'So you live on a boat? I love that. But isn't it a bit cramped?'

'We manage. You do have to be tidy. And not collect too much junk.'

'We?' Ivy's eyebrows shot up. 'You have a *man* in your life, Summer?'

'Ah...' Summer kept her gaze firmly on the flakes of salmon she was spearing with her fork. 'Only Flint. He has to be tidy, too.'

'Of course he does.' There was a satisfied note in Ivy's voice and Summer looked up to catch the significant look she was giving Zac. There might have been an eyebrow wiggle involved as well.

It was cringe-worthy but then Zac grinned at her and winked and suddenly it was fine.

More than fine.

Summer grinned back. She had just fallen a little bit in love with Zac Mitchell.

'You know, I think I've been a bit of a pelican,' Ivy declared. 'My eyes held more than my belly can. Do you think Flint might be able to finish this for me? Salmon's not bad for dogs, is it?'

'It would be a huge treat for him.'

'Let's bring him inside, then.'

'Oh, I don't think you want to do that. You have no idea how much sand gets trapped in those fluffy paws.'

'Pfft…' Ivy waved her hand. 'What's a bit of sand between friends? I track it in every day myself.'

Summer went to invite Flint inside. Ivy insisted on giving him the salmon off her own plate and Summer shook her head but she was smiling. She had just fallen a little bit in love with Zac's grandmother as well.

'Where does he sleep?' Ivy asked. 'On the boat?'

'Yes. He has his own bed under the cockpit. A double berth, even.'

'Oh… I hope you have a double berth, too…'

Zac's sigh was clearly audible but Ivy winked at Summer. 'Don't mind me,' she said in a stage whisper. 'When you get to my age, you find you can get away with saying almost anything. Sometimes I might get a wee bit carried away.'

Summer smiled. 'I have a very comfortable double bed, Ivy. It's even got an inner-sprung mattress. Speaking of which...' she only had to straighten and look towards the door and Flint was instantly by her side '... I'd better get going. I've got an early start tomorrow.'

Zac pushed his chair back and got to his feet.

The air seemed to have disappeared from the room. What was going to happen now? Would he show her out and kiss her goodnight? How likely was that when Ivy would probably be peeping from a window?

'I'll give you a lift,' he said. 'It's too late to be jogging around the streets.'

'Thanks, but I don't let Flint run after a bike. It's a bit dangerous.'

'Ah...' Zac was almost beside her now. 'Unlike you, I keep four wheels as well as two. I have an SUV with a nice big space for a dog in the back.'

'It'll get full of sand.' But Summer's heart was doing that speeding up thing again. Zac was coming home with her? Would he want to stay for a while?

He was close enough to touch now. She could feel the heat of his body. Or maybe that was heat she was creating herself. A warmth that kicked up several notches as he grinned lazily.

'What's a bit of sand between friends?'

He kissed his grandmother. 'Leave the dishes,' he ordered. 'I'll pop in and do them when I get back.'

Ivy waved them off. 'That's what dishwashers are for. I'll see you tomorrow, Isaac. Don't do anything I wouldn't do, now.'

Zac groaned softly as he closed the door behind them. 'Sorry about that,' he muttered. 'She's incorrigible.'

He'd never been in a yacht that was being used as a permanent home. He'd been sailing, of course. Anyone who grew up beside the sea in Auckland ended up with more than a passing acquaintance with sailing boats.

'She's thirty feet? Feels much bigger inside.'

'It's a great design. Small but perfectly formed.'

Just like Summer?

Zac had to drag his gaze away from her. He'd only just stepped aboard *Mermaid* and, while the invitation to see her home had been freely given, he didn't want to push things too fast, here.

He didn't want to wreck something. Not when so many possibilities were floating so close to touching distance. Mind you, if his gran hadn't scared her off, he was probably in a good space right now.

An astonishing space. There was colour from the warm glow of all the woodwork. A rich blue cushion and padding covered the built-in bench seating around a narrow table and the colour was repeated in a strip of Persian-style carpet down the centre of the floor. The front of the boat's interior was almost closed off by a folding fabric screen but he could see a glimpse of a raised bed with a soft-looking white duvet and fluffy pillows.

Once again, he had to avert his gaze before what he was thinking got printed all over his face.

'Cute sink.'

'It works well, even if it's a single rather than a double. Gives a bit more bench room for cooking. I've got an oven here and even a microwave in this locker, see?'

'Mmm.'

What he liked best about this space was that there wasn't that much room for two people to move around, especially when there was a fairly large dog to avoid, and it was inevitable that they ended up standing extremely close to each other. He had to bend his head a little to admire the microwave oven tucked neatly into its storage space and that put his face extremely close to Summer's as well. Without looking up, he lifted a hand to close the locker and, as he lowered his hand, it felt perfectly natural to brush the spikes of her hair. To let his hand come to rest at the nape of her neck.

To bend his head just a little further so that he could touch her lips with his own. Just a feather-light touch for a heartbeat and then he increased the pressure and touched her lips with his tongue. He felt Summer's gasp as a physical change in her body—the kind of tension that a diver probably had in the moment before she launched herself into space to perform some dramatic series of tumbles and then slice cleanly into the deepest pool. And, as Summer's lips parted beneath his, he knew she had taken that plunge and she was ready to fly.

He had no idea how long they stood there kissing. Zac was aware of nothing more than the delicious taste and the responsiveness of this gorgeous girl. And that the ground was moving slightly beneath his feet. Because they were on a boat? It felt more personal than that. His whole world was gently rocking.

Time had absolutely no relevance because it didn't matter how long it took to explore this wonderful new world. The map was coming into focus and there was no hurry at all to find the right path. The way Summer took the lead to follow that path was possibly the most exciting part about it. She wanted this—as much as he did.

It was her hands that moved first, to disentangle themselves from around his neck to start roaming his body, and that gave him permission to let his own hands move. To shape the delicate bones of her shoulders and trace the length of her spine. To cup the deliciously firm curves of her bottom and the perfection of those surprisingly generous breasts.

It was Summer who took his hand and stopped him undoing another button on the soft shirt she was wearing and, for a moment, Zac had the horrible thought that she was asking him to stop completely. He could, of course, but man, would he need a cold shower when he got home...

It was time to get rid of the audience. A quiet command sent Flint to his bed. Her voice might have wobbled a little but Summer was still holding Zac's hand tightly. She led him to the other end of the boat. Past the screen and up a step to where her bed filled the whole space.

No. It was Zac who was filling this space. The only light was coming from a lamp on the table and the shadows being created gave shedding their clothes a surreal edge—like a scene from an arty movie. And then Zac was kneeling on the bed in front of her and she could flatten her hands against the bare skin of his chest as she raised her face for another kiss and she stopped thinking about the way anything looked. She could only *feel*...

No wonder she'd been shocked by that first ever touch of Zac's lips. She'd never known that arousal could be this intense. That nerve endings could be so sensitised by the lightest touch that the pleasure was almost pain. It was still weird because she'd never felt anything like this before but it was most definitely *good* weird.

Oh, yes...the best weird ever, and she could get used to this.

She wanted to get very, very used to it.

CHAPTER SIX

'TARGET SIGHTED—TWO O'CLOCK.'

The helicopter dipped and shuddered as Monty turned to circle the area. The stiff breeze made the top of the pine forest below sway enough to make an accurate estimation of clearance difficult.

'Not sure I like this,' Monty said. 'Might need to winch you guys in.'

'There's more of a clearing at five o'clock. Where the logging trucks are.'

'It's a fair hike. The guy's having trouble breathing.'

'Winch me down,' Summer said. 'I'll scoop him into the Stokes basket and we can transfer him to the clearing to stabilise him.'

'You happy for Zac to winch you?' Monty's query sounded casual but this was the first time they'd been in a situation like this. In rough weather like this. Yes, Zac was winch trained but Summer would be putting her life in his hands.

She caught Zac's gaze, and even through the muting effect of the visor on his helmet she could see—or maybe sense—the anticipation of her response and, in that instant, a seemingly casual query became so much bigger than being simply about the job they were all doing.

Did she trust Zac?

She *wanted* to. She had never wanted to trust anybody this much. Not with her life because she did that every time she took on a tricky winching job and she was used to putting that kind of trust in her colleagues.

No. This was about trusting a man with her heart and she'd never really done that before. But she *wanted* to. With Zac...

Monty was hovering over the area where the felling accident had occurred. An ambulance was bouncing along the rough track and stopped with a cloud of dust billowing from beneath its wheels.

'Let's wait and see what the crew thinks. We've only had the first aider's story so far.'

The small reprieve in decision-making gave Summer the chance to let her mind go further down that secret pathway.

She was more than a little bit in love with Zac Mitchell. Maybe it had started that night he'd winked at her across his grandmother's table last week. Or maybe it had started even before that—when he'd called that frightened elderly woman 'sweetheart' on that first job they'd ever done together.

The point of ignition didn't really matter now, anyway. What did matter was what happened next. She might want to take that next—huge—step of trusting him completely but it was debatable whether she was capable of it. Summer had no experience of going that far in a relationship but a lot of experience in pushing people away when she sensed any kind of a threat. She'd learned how to do that a very long time ago, when she'd only been a teenager. When she'd pushed her previously beloved father completely out of her life. She'd pushed other men away too, when they started to get too close.

That excuse of her career being more important wasn't

really the truth at all, was it? She'd always had that whisper of warning that came in her mother's voice.

You can never trust a man. No matter how much you love them, it's never enough. They'll break your heart. Break you...

She was even pushing her best friend out of her life at the moment. There was a call she hadn't returned and a text message she'd brushed off with a breezy response that gave nothing away. Kate had no idea what was going on in Summer's life—that she was so far down the track of falling in love with the 'monster' who she believed had ruined her sister's life. Summer wasn't about to tell her, either. It was bad enough having the whisper of warning that was the haunting legacy her mother had left. Imagine adding the kind of poison that Kate couldn't help but administer, given her loyalty to Shelley? It would meld with that warning and she would have to start wondering if she was being as blind as her mother had been when she'd fallen in love so completely with her father.

That whole business with Shelley was a subject that she and Zac had put behind them by tacit consent and maybe she didn't want to hear what Kate had to say, anyway, because she wanted to trust Zac so much. She'd never met anyone remotely like him before and she instinctively knew that the odds of it happening again were non-existent.

This was her chance of finding out what it might be like. To be truly, utterly in love. And instinct was telling her more than how unique this situation was. Summer was also aware, on some level, that all it would require for her to take that final step of trust was to know that Zac felt the same way.

Telling Monty that she was prepared to put her life in Zac's hands on the end of the winch would have sent an unspoken response to that anticipation she'd sensed. It would have probably taken their newly forged bond to the next level—one that might have made it the right time to open their hearts a little further—but it wasn't going to happen today.

Another slow circuit in the blustery conditions and new information was available. The ground crew were going to scoop the patient and take him to the clearing. The patient was status two and was in respiratory distress but it wasn't a crush injury from the falling tree, as first reported.

It was far safer to land and preferable clinically, given that this was a chest injury and Zac could do more than any paramedic, but Summer was aware of a flash of disappointment. Had she wanted to publicly demonstrate the level of trust she had in Zac? Wanted the deeper kind of bond that would come from tackling—and winning—a tough challenge like this?

Never mind. It would no doubt come soon enough. And, in the meantime, they still had a challenge on their hands. A medical one.

'It's a penetrating wound,' the paramedic shouted over the noise of the slowing rotors as Zac and Summer ran, still crouching, towards the ambulance. 'The tree didn't land on him but it looks like he got stabbed with a branch or something. He's unresponsive. Now status one. Blood pressure's crashed and he's throwing off a lot of ectopics.'

This was an immediately life-threatening injury and it sounded as if a cardiac arrest was imminent. They worked fast and closely together as Summer intubated the young forestry worker and got IV fluids running as Zac performed the procedure she'd seen him do in Emergency on her car accident victim with the tension pneumothorax. But opening the chest cavity wasn't enough to allow the lungs to inflate, even when it had been done on both sides of the victim's chest.

'He's arrested.' Summer squeezed more oxygen in with the bag mask but this was looking hopeless. There was little point in starting external chest compressions when it was clear that there was some obstruction to the heart being able to fill and empty.

'The wound's within the nipple line on the left anterior chest.' Zac sounded calm but his tone was grim. 'It's not a pleural obstruction so it has to be pericardial. I'm going to open the chest with a clam shell thoracotomy.'

This was way beyond any procedure Summer could have performed. Beyond anything she'd seen in the emergency department, even. How confident would you have to be to actually open a chest in the field and expose a heart? But, if they didn't do something drastic, this young man was about to die.

Summer delegated the airway care to one of the ambulance paramedics so that she could work alongside Zac and pass him the necessary equipment. The sterilised strong scissors to extend the small opening that had been made in the hope of releasing trapped air or blood. The Gigli wire and forceps to cut through the breastbone. Rib spreaders to open the area and suction to clear it.

And then she watched, in amazement, as Zac used two clips to raise a tent of the covering around the heart and then cut a tiny hole before extending it. He used his gloved hands to remove massive blood clots. They could see the heart but it was still quivering ineffectually rather than beating.

Summer held her breath as Zac flicked the heart with his fingers. Once, then again, and she let her breath out in a sigh as she saw the heart contract. Fill and then contract again. She could feel the first effective beat as a pulse under her fingertips when she rested them on their patient's neck and a beep on the monitor behind them confirmed that a rhythm had recommenced. A movement of the whole chest was a first attempt by their patient to take a breath of his own.

Zac removed the rib spreaders and let the chest close.

'We'll put a sterile cover on this. We need to get him to Theatre stat.'

It still seemed like too big an ask to get their patient to hospital alive but, by some miracle, that was exactly what they managed to do. And, thanks to that achievement, the young forestry worker emerged from Theatre several hours later to go into intensive care. Still alive and looking as though he was going to stay that way.

It was all everyone could talk about, both in the emergency department of Auckland General and on the rescue helicopter base. It wasn't the first time such a major procedure had been attempted out of hospital but it was the first time it had had a successful outcome. Summer had never felt so proud of the job she did. Proud of the service she worked for. Proud of Zac...

'You're amazing, you know that?'

'So are you.'

They were still on base. Being professional colleagues. Nobody had guessed how close they'd become out of work hours yet and they were happy to keep it that way so all they could do right now was to hold eye contact long enough to communicate that the mutual appreciation went a lot deeper than anything professional. They would go over every tiny detail of this case, probably later this evening, and discuss the pros and cons of every choice and try to identify anything they could have done better. *Would* do better, if they were ever faced with a similar situation. She loved that they shared a passion for the same work.

Being able to debrief a case in detail with Zac was taking Summer's clinical knowledge to a whole new level and she knew it was giving her an edge in her job that others were beginning to notice.

Maybe that wasn't the only thing that they were beginning to notice.

'What about me?' Monty sniffed. 'It wasn't exactly a ride in the park, flying in that weather, you know.'

'We couldn't have done it without you, mate.' Zac gave the pilot's shoulder a friendly thump as he went past. 'You're a legend.'

'We're all legends,' Summer said. 'How 'bout a beer after work to celebrate?'

'I've got a date already,' Monty said. 'You two go off on your own.' He returned Zac's friendly thump and grinned at Summer. 'You know you want to.'

'Um...' Summer could feel her cheeks redden. 'We just work well together.'

'Yeah...right. So how come you suck all the oxygen out of the air for the rest of us when you stand around making sheep's eyes at each other?'

'Did he really say that we were making sheep's eyes at each other?'

'Mmm.' Summer tilted her head to smile up at Zac. 'I believe he did.'

Zac grinned back and tightened his hold on Summer's hand as he helped her over the boulders on the beach and back onto the track they were following. For a while, they were silent, enjoying the shade of the heavy canopy of native bush and the sounds of the birdlife they had come here to see.

The journey itself had been a joy. Being on the road with Summer, seeing her bike in his rear-view mirror, taking the corners like a faithful shadow. Riding a bike on the open road was always a pleasure but it could feel lonely. Being out with someone else changed the experience.

Being out with Summer Pearson changed everything. The sun seemed brighter. The smell of the sea as they stood outside on the ferry across to Tiritiri Matangi Island was fresher. Forgoing a guided tour so they could pretend they had the whole island to themselves had been a joint decision made with simply a heartbeat of eye contact. Walking hand in hand seemed like the most natural thing in the world. A pleasure shared being a pleasure doubled or something, maybe.

'What, exactly, *are* sheep's eyes?'

'Oh...you know...looking at each other for a bit too long, I guess. Like there's nobody else around.'

'I've always thought sheep were not particularly intelligent creatures.'

Summer laughed—a delicious ripple of sound that Zac immediately wanted to hear again.

'Are we being stupid, do you think?'

The glance he received was startled. 'How do you mean?'

'It's not against the rules, is it? To get involved with a fellow crew member? A colleague?'

Summer shook her head and her chuckle was rueful. 'If it was, you'd all be in trouble in the emergency department, wouldn't you?'

'It's a bit different on the choppers, though. Much tighter teams.'

'We're all adults. We get to make our own choices and deal with any consequences. The only trouble would be if you let something personal interfere with anything professional.' Summer dropped his hand as she climbed up a set of narrow steps that was part of a boardwalk. 'I'm surprised that anyone guessed about us so fast, though. I thought we were being really discreet.'

'Apparently we suck all the oxygen out of the room.' Zac's tone was light but he knew exactly what Monty had been referring to. Sometimes, it felt that way when he was looking at Summer. As if he'd forgotten how to breathe or something. A weird sensation that he'd never experienced before.

Good weird, though—he was pretty sure about that.

'Do you think Ivy knows?'

'Well...you know how you and Flint stayed around the other night, after we'd been out for that swim?'

'Mmm?' Something in her tone suggested that Summer was remembering how amazing the second time together had been. Any first time awkwardness had vanished and they had been ready to play. To get to know each other's bodies and revel in the pleasure they knew they could both give and receive.

'When I popped in to say good morning before I went to work the next day, she gave me a pile of new towels. Said that mine were old enough to feel like cardboard and they simply weren't suitable for delicate skin. I don't think she was referring to *my* skin.'

'But I snuck out well before dawn. It was still dark by the time Flint and I had jogged back to the boat.'

Zac threw a wry smile over his shoulder. 'There's not much that gets past Gravy. She's had ninety plus years to hone her skills, after all.'

'Oh... Do you think she disapproves?'

'If she did, I don't think she'd be supplying soft towels. She'd think that the cardboard variety would be a suitable penance. Oh...look at that.'

They had come to one of the feeding stations on the island. Cleverly designed platforms supported bottles of

sugar water. This station had attracted both bellbirds and
tuis and, for several minutes, they both stood entranced,
watching. The bellbirds were small and elegant, the tuis
much larger and more confident—the white ruff on their
necks being shown off as they reached to sip the water
from the metal tubes.

They saw stitchbirds and riflemen further along the
track and then the highlight they would be talking about
for days came when a group of takahe crossed their path.
The huge flightless birds with their blue and green plum-
age and big red beaks were fascinating.

'They thought they were extinct, you know. Like the
moas. There's only a few places you can see them now.
This is a first for me.'

'Me, too.' Summer's face was alight with pleasure.
'This was such a good idea, Zac. And I thought we were
just going for a bike ride.'

'I'm full of good ideas.' Zac caught her hand as they
started walking again. 'Stick around long enough and
you'll find out.'

'I might just do that.'

Her words stayed in the air as they walked on. Zac
could still hear them when they finally sat on the grass
near the lighthouse to eat the picnic they'd put together
from the shop near the ferry terminal. They were hungry
enough after all the walking to polish off the filled rolls
and muffins and fruit and then they lay back in the long
grass. They had some time to spare before walking back
down the hill to catch the ferry back.

It was inevitable that they started kissing. They were
lying so close together, well away from any other visitors
to the island. It was a gorgeous day and they had been
having the best time in each other's company. The kisses

were sweet. Perfect. Was that why Zac was aware of a warning bell sounding?

'It feels like we're breaking the rules,' he finally confessed.

'But we only work together sometimes. It's not like we're even employed by the same people.'

'I didn't mean that.' Zac propped himself up on one elbow but Summer had closed her eyes against the glare of the sun, a hand shading her face. 'I mean my own rules.'

Summer spread her fingers and peered up at him. 'You have rules?'

'Kind of.'

'What kind of rules?'

'Like not getting in too deep.'

'Oh...' She was really looking at him now but he couldn't read her expression. If he had to guess, he might say she looked wary. Almost afraid?

He had to kiss her again. To reassure her. Or maybe he was trying to reassure himself?

'This feels different. Weird.'

Her lips quirked with a tiny smile. 'Good weird or bad weird?'

'I think...good weird.'

'But you don't know?'

Zac sucked in a breath. Had he ever been this honest with a woman before? 'I do know. I'm just not sure I trust it. Because it's...too good?'

A single nod from Summer. She understood.

'I've never had a good role model for what can be trusted,' Zac said quietly. 'My grandad died before I could remember him and my stepfather...well, I prefer not to remember him.'

Summer nodded again. 'My parents weren't exactly a shining example to follow either.' She sat up, as if even thinking about her family had disturbed her. Zac wanted to ask about what had gone so wrong but he didn't want to spoil this moment because it felt important. A step forward.

'But we're adults,' he said. 'We get to make our own choices, don't we? And live with the consequences.'

'How do you know if you're making the right choices, though?'

'I guess you don't. I think that maybe you have to do what feels right and then hope that you *have* made the right ones.'

Did she understand what he was trying to say here, or was he being too clumsy? He didn't want to scare her off completely.

He didn't seem to have done that. If it had been a declaration of sorts, then Summer seemed to be in complete agreement. She stretched out her arms and linked them around his neck, pulling him towards her for another kiss.

'This feels right,' she murmured. 'Weird but good.'

Better than good. It felt as if they had agreed to make this choice. That there was a potential to trust on both sides. Almost an unspoken promise that they would both do their best for whatever was happening between them not to become an emotional disaster.

Inevitably, the real world had to intrude again. Zac checked his watch as he became aware that they really were alone here now. 'We've got two minutes and then we need to head back fast for the ferry. Gravy would be upset if we don't get back for the dinner she's cooking up for us.'

Her lips were moving against his. 'We'd better make the most of them then, hadn't we?'

'There you go, Gravy. A nice hot lemon drink to wash down that paracetamol. You'll feel better in no time.'

'I just hope I didn't give Summer this cold when she was here for dinner the other night after you'd been out to the bird island.'

'I think she's pretty tough. She'll survive.'

Ivy sniffed her drink. 'You know, I think a hot toddy might work faster. With a good slosh of whisky.'

'Hmm.' Zac took a mohair rug off the back of the couch and held it up but Ivy shook her head.

'Far too hot for that. Summer colds are the worst.' Ivy blew her nose and leaned back in her chair but she was smiling. 'Summer,' she murmured. 'Such a lovely name. Conjures up the feeling of blue skies and sunshine, doesn't it? The sparkle of the sea and long, delicious evenings to enjoy it.'

'Is there anything else I can do for you before I head downstairs?'

'Sit and talk to me for a minute. Unless you're meeting your Summer?'

'Not tonight.' Zac settled himself on the couch beside his grandmother. 'She's doing some crew training. And we don't spend every minute of our time off together, anyway.'

'You'll have to bring her to dinner with me again soon. I ordered some new champagne online yesterday and it looks lovely. I could do your favourite roast chicken.'

'You're not to do anything for a few days except rest and get better. If that cough gets any worse, I'll be having a chat to your GP. You might need some antibiotics.'

'I'll be fine. I can't have been eating enough garlic, that's what it is.'

'Maybe you should stop swimming when the weather isn't so good. I saw you out in the rain the other day.'

Ivy snorted. 'You know as well as I do that the weather doesn't cause a viral infection.'

'Getting cold lowers your resistance.'

Ivy flapped a hand in his direction. 'I'll stop swimming when I'm dead, thanks very much, and who knows how far away that is? I intend to make the most of every day I've got.'

'Don't say that.' Zac frowned. 'I expect you to be around for a long time yet.'

Ivy's smile was unusually gentle. 'Nobody lives for ever, darling.'

Zac smiled back and took hold of one of her hands. When had her skin started to feel so papery and fragile? An internal alarm was sounding faintly. This was what it was like when you had somebody who was this important to you. You had to live with the fear of losing them. His gran was all the more precious because of that knowledge he'd come by too early in life.

'You could try.' There was a tight feeling in his throat. 'You're my touchstone, Gravy. I don't even want to think about what life will be like when you're not around.'

'Maybe you've found a new touchstone.' Ivy turned her hand over and gave his a squeeze. 'Your little ray of summer sunshine.'

'You wouldn't have thought that the first time I met her. She's not only tough. She can be quite fierce.'

'Good.' Ivy sipped her hot drink. 'Being fierce is an attribute. Sometimes you have to fight in life to get through things. And it sounds like she's had to get through more than her fair share. Not that she said much, but it sounded like her mum was the only family she had and she lost her when she was far too young.'

'Mmm…' He'd had the opportunity to ask more about her background when they'd been on the island but he'd held back. Boundaries were still being respected. On both sides? Was that a good thing—or another warning?

'She's got a heart of gold, that girl,' Ivy said quietly. 'And she loves you to bits.'

'You think...?'

'It's obvious from where I'm standing. And I think you feel the same way.'

Zac pushed his fingers through his hair. That would certainly explain why this felt so different. 'Maybe...'

'But?'

'Who said there was a but?'

'You only mess up your hair like that when you can't decide something. You've been doing it since you were a little boy, Isaac. I always had to carry a comb whenever we went out anywhere.'

'Hmm. It's early days, I guess.'

Ivy snorted. 'Nonsense. When something's right, it's right. You should know by now.'

'I don't want to rush into anything.'

'You're already into it up to your eyebrows, from what I can see.'

Zac couldn't deny it. He'd never felt this way about any girl before but... Yes, there was a but...

'Maybe it's her independence that bothers me,' he admitted. 'How different she is. How many girls live by themselves on a boat? Ride a motorbike and kick ass in a job that would be too much for most people to cope with?'

'*Language*, Isaac. Please.'

'Sorry. But she's amazing at what she does. She's got this confidence that makes you think she'd cope with anything by herself. And yes, she probably did have to cope with too much when she was young. But would she want to fight to keep a relationship together if times got tough or would she just walk away and cope all by herself again?'

Ivy sniffed. 'Sounds like the pot calling the kettle

black, Isaac Mitchell. How many relationships have you walked out on so far when they didn't go the way you wanted them to? When they wanted more than you were ready to give? You've broken your share of hearts, you know.'

'It wasn't intentional.'

'I know that.' Ivy patted his hand. 'And you were always very kind about it.'

'I've just never found the person that makes me want to give everything I could to.' But he had now, hadn't he? The only thing stopping him was a fear of...what? Having his heart broken? Again?

Ivy was giving him a look that said she understood. That she remembered the small boy whose world had crumbled when he'd lost his mother. But it was also a look that told him it was time to be brave enough to break his own rules. The ones about working hard and playing hard and guarding your heart. That she knew exactly who the person was. A look that suggested he was being just a little bit obtuse.

Zac felt the need to defend himself. 'You only got married once,' he reminded her. 'I'm cut from the same cloth. If I give everything, it'll only happen once. I think if the trust it takes to do that gets broken, you never find it again. Never as much. So it has to be right.'

Ivy's gaze was misty. Was she remembering the love of her life, who'd sadly been taken before Zac was old enough to remember him?

'Nothing's ever perfect, darling. At some point you have to take a leap of faith and hope for the best. I hope you'll be as lucky as I was. But don't wait too long.' She closed her eyes as she leaned her head back against a cushion. 'I want to see you waiting for your bride at the end of the aisle. I want to throw confetti and drink a wee bit too much champagne and be disgracefully tipsy by the end of the reception.' She opened her eyes again and the expression in them gave Zac that tight feeling in his throat again. This time it felt like a rock with sharp edges.

'I want to know that you'll be living here in this house and there'll be babies playing in the garden and building sandcastles on the beach. Dogs tracking sand into the house and maybe a paddleboard or two propped up against that dusty old boatshed.'

Zac found his own eyes closing for a long blink. He could almost see it himself.

And it looked...perfect.

CHAPTER SEVEN

THE MORE TIME he spent with Summer, the more Zac could see that picture of a perfect future.

'D'you think you'll always want to live on a boat?' The query was casual. They were restocking gear during a quiet spell one afternoon.

'No way. I had no idea I'd be doing it for *this* long.' Summer turned to look at the pouch Zac was filling. 'Have you got plenty of size eight cuffed tracheal tubes in there?'

'Three. That's enough, isn't it?'

'Yes. Make sure we've got sizes three, four and five of the laryngeal mask airways, too. And we'll do the paediatric airway kit next.'

'Sure.' Zac checked the size printed on the sterile packages for the LMAs. 'So how long did you think you'd live on a boat, then?'

'As long as it took to save up a house deposit.' She snapped a laryngoscope handle into place to check the light and then folded it closed again. 'I was looking for a share flat when I moved up from Hamilton but then I heard about the boat and it was cheaper. I didn't expect house prices to go so crazy, though. It feels like I'm getting further and further away. And living on the boat's not helping.'

'Even if it's cheaper?'

'I'm getting spoiled. I can't imagine living far from a beach now and they're always the pricier suburbs.'

'I know. My grandparents had no idea what a good investment they were making when they bought a rundown old house on the beach nearly sixty years ago.'

'It's a perfect house.'

Zac opened the paediatric airway kit. He ran his gaze over the shiny laryngoscope blades and handles, the Magill forceps and the range of tracheal tubes and LMAs. There didn't seem to be anything missing from the slots. He checked the pocket that held the tiniest airways that could be needed in resuscitating a newborn baby and sent out a silent prayer that they wouldn't be needing to use any of them any time soon.

A quick glance at Summer took in the way she was sitting cross-legged on the storeroom floor. She had another kit open on her lap—the serious airway gear that made things like scalpels and tracheal dilators available when all else failed.

Her words still echoed in the back of his head.

The house that he would inherit one day was *perfect*. Like the life that Ivy had imagined him living in it one day.

He'd always loved the house but how much better was it on the nights that Summer and Flint stayed over? When they could all go out at first light and run on the beach or brave the cold water for an early morning wake-up swim?

It was like his job. Perfect but so much better when he got to share it with Summer. The bonus of seeing the crew in their orange flight suits arrive to hand over a patient when he was on a shift in Emergency always added something special to his day. Days like today, when he was actually working on the rescue base as her crew partner, were the best of all.

Ivy's warning of not waiting too long had been surfacing more and more in recent days.

He was coasting. Enjoying each day as it came. Trusting that it would continue for as long as they both wanted it to. Trusting that it was safe to give more and more because it could become stronger and potentially last for the rest of his life.

And there was the rub. He might be confident that Summer felt the same way he did but he couldn't be sure until he heard her say it out loud. And maybe she was waiting for him to say something first? Something else Ivy had said had struck home. He was the pot calling the kettle black. Maybe he and Summer were more alike than he'd realised. They both had the kind of skills that came from putting so much effort into their work. They chose leisure activities like ocean sports and riding powerful bikes that meant they could play as hard as they worked. Perhaps Summer's fierce independence came from self-protection and it would take something extraordinary to persuade her to remove the barriers that were protecting her heart?

But what they had found together was extraordinary, wasn't it? Surely he couldn't be the only one feeling like this?

The buzzing of their pagers broke the silence. Kits were rolled up and stuffed back into the pack with swift movements. They were both on their feet within seconds. Strapped into their seats in the helicopter within minutes. Heading west.

'Piha Beach,' Monty confirmed. 'ETA ten minutes.'

'I've been there for near-drownings,' Summer said.

'And falls from the rocks. I can't believe someone's been attacked by a shark.'

'We're being followed,' Monty told them. 'Reckon you'll both be starring on the national news tonight.'

Zac knew he would recognise the landmarks below with ease. Lion Rock was famous. Lying forty kilometres west of the city, Piha was the most famous surf beach in the country.

'I used to surf at Piha when I was a kid,' he told Summer. 'When I got my first wheels when I was seventeen, I chose an old Combi van and me and my mates were in heaven. We'd load up the boards and wetsuits before dawn and we'd get home, sunburned and completely exhausted, well after dark. There was always a big roast dinner on offer when we got back. It was no wonder I was so popular at school.'

The look he was getting from Summer suggested that there were other reasons he might have been popular. Her gaze held his with a tenderness that made something ache deep in his chest and her smile made it feel like whatever it was had just split open to release some kind of hitherto untried drug.

Love. That was what it was, all right.

Summer *did* feel the same way he did—he was sure of it. And he'd never loved anyone this much. Never would ever again. It was time he did something about making sure he never lost it. For both their sakes, he needed to be brave and be the first one to take those barriers away. To put his heart on the line.

The first chance he got—tonight—he was going to tell Summer how he felt. Maybe even ask her to move in with him.

Marry him...?

Whoa...where had *that* notion come from? And now

that it was here, it was the weirdest thought ever—maybe because it felt so right. The knowledge was fleeting, however. It couldn't claim even another second of headspace as the distinctive shape of Lion Rock—the formation that separated the two beaches at Piha—loomed larger.

Zac could see the knot of people on the beach below, including the red and yellow uniforms of the lifeguards, and many more were watching from a distance. Several bystanders were waving their arms, urging the rescue crew to land as quickly as possible. There was nobody in the water, surfing or swimming. It could be a while before this popular beach could be deemed safe, despite a shark attack in New Zealand being an extraordinarily rare occurrence.

One of the lifeguards met them as they raced from the helicopter over the firm sand they'd been able to land on.

'We've got the bleeding under control with a pressure bandage but he's lost a lot of blood. And his leg's a real mess, man… I hope he's not going to lose it.'

'Is he conscious?' The priority was keeping this patient alive, not discussing a potential prognosis. It sounded like preservation of blood volume was likely to be the key management, along with as swift a transfer to hospital as possible.

'He swam in himself with his board, yelling for help, but he was barely conscious by the time we got him onto the beach. We've got oxygen on and put some blankets over him to try and keep him warm and he's woken up a bit. He's in a lot of pain.'

The knot of people—including a skinny lad gripping a surfboard that had obvious tooth marks and a chunk bitten out of its end—parted to let Zac and Summer into the centre and place their packs on the sand. Summer immediately dropped to her knees to open the pack and start extracting gear they would need, like a blood pressure cuff and IV supplies. She reached for the man's wrist as Zac crouched by the patient's head.

'No radial pulse palpable,' she said.

The man looked to be in his early fifties and he was deathly pale but breathing well and Zac could feel a rapid pulse beneath his fingers from the carotid artery in his neck. It was a lot fainter than he would have liked and if it wasn't reaching his wrist it meant that his blood pressure was already dangerously low. Hypovolaemic shock was a life-threatening emergency and they might have to fight to keep this man alive. From the corner of his eye, Zac could see Summer unrolling the IV kit. She would be putting a tourniquet on and aiming to get a cannula in and IV fluids running as quickly as she could.

'Hey, buddy.' Zac shook the man's shoulder. 'Can you open your eyes for me?' Response to voice was a good indication of level of consciousness and he was relieved to see the man's eyelids flutter open and get a groan of verbal response.

Zac glanced up at the onlookers. 'Does anyone know his name?'

An affirmative chorus sounded from all sides.

'It's Jon,' one of the lifeguards told him. 'He's one of us—a Patrol Captain.'

'Jon Pearson,' someone else called. 'He's fifty-two. Lives locally.'

Pearson?

Startled, Zac's gaze swerved towards Summer and— just for a heartbeat—his focus was broken by regretting not taking that opportunity he'd had to find out more about her background. He really needed to know more than he did right now.

What little information he had flashed through his

brain with astonishing speed. Her parents had been hippies. She'd been conceived on a beach in the wake of a surfing competition. She had no siblings. Her mother had died when she was seventeen and her father was already 'well out of the picture'. Her parents had not been 'a shining example' of something to follow as far as relationships went. What had she meant by that? *Dear God*...had there been violence involved? Had she had to cope with the same sort of fear in her childhood as he had?

More importantly in this moment, however, if this man *was* Summer's father—and that seemed quite likely given that he was a surfer—how was she coping, seeing him for the first time in so many years, let alone in a life-threatening emergency? Having to treat him? It was a paramedic's worst nightmare, having to treat a loved one. How much harder could it be if the relationship was complicated and emotionally distressing anyway?

She seemed to be coping. She had a tourniquet around their patient's arm and was swabbing the skin on his arm.

'You'll feel a sharp scratch,' she warned. 'There. All done.' The cannula slid home into the vein and Summer released the tourniquet and reached for the connection so that she could hook up the bag of IV fluid she had ready.

And then she looked up and caught Zac's steady gaze as he did his best to communicate silently.

I understand, he tried to tell her. *I'm here for you. I'll do whatever it takes to help.*

She could do this. She could cope.

She *had* to.

It had almost done her in, though, that first instant she'd seen their patient's face. Of course she had recognised him—despite the differences that fifteen years had etched onto his face. For one horrible moment, she had frozen—assaulted by a flashback of the grief she'd had to deal with all those years ago when he'd chosen to walk out of her life.

The only way to deal with it had been to blank out those memories. The visceral knowledge that this was her only living relative. He had to become simply another patient. A man with hypovolaemic shock who was in urgent need of fluid replacement. All she had to think about was putting a large bore cannula into his arm and to get fluids running. Probably two IV lines—except that it was equally important to find out whether the loss of blood was actually as controlled as the first aiders had led them to believe.

'I don't like the staining on that pressure bandage,' she told Zac. 'It could be soaking up volume.'

Zac nodded. 'Have a look at what's going on.' He was still crouching beside her father's head. 'Jon? You still with us, mate? Open your eyes...'

'*Hurts*,' Jon groaned. 'My *leg*...'

'I'm going to give you something for the pain.'

Summer used shears to cut away the bandage. The ripped flesh on Jon's thigh was horrific. She could see the gleam of exposed bone in one patch and...yes...there was a small spurt of an arterial bleed still going on. She clamped her gloved fingers over the vessel and pressed hard.

Jon groaned and then swore vehemently. Summer had to close her eyes for a heartbeat as the cry of pain ripped its way through the emotional wall she had erected.

This was just another patient. *Jon*. Not Dad. Sometimes you had to cause pain to save a life. It didn't make it harder because he was her father. He wasn't her father any more. He hadn't been for fifteen years...

She opened her eyes as she sucked in a new breath, to

find Zac looking up from where he was filling a syringe from an ampoule. He was giving her that look again. The one that told her he had somehow made the connection the moment he'd heard their patient's name and that he knew exactly how hard this was. How much he wanted to make it easier for her.

He knew nothing about her history and yet he was prepared to take her side and protect her from someone who had the potential to be some kind of threat. Funny how she could still be so focused on what she had to do but be aware of how much she loved this man. How easy it would be to put her emotional safety in his hands for ever.

'The femoral artery's been nicked,' she said. 'I'm putting some pressure on it.'

'We might need to clamp it. I'll get some pain relief on board first.'

Yes. Knock him out, Summer thought. The pain of what she was doing had roused him. Any second now and he was going to look to see what was happening and...

'*Summer?*' The word was shocked. Disbelieving. Jon pulled at the oxygen mask on his face as if he wanted to make his speech more audible. 'Is that...*you*?'

'Keep your mask on, mate.' A lifeguard crouching at his head pushed the mask back into place.

The guard holding the bag of IV fluid aloft crouched to catch his arm. 'Keep your arm still, Jon. You don't want the line to come out.'

During the flurry of activity, Zac injected the pain relief and Jon relaxed, his arms dropping and his eyes closing. A flash of eye contact told her that Zac was relieved that things hadn't got any more difficult but it did nothing to interrupt his focus on what they had to do as soon as possible—to get this bleeding under control so that pouring fluids in to maintain blood pressure wasn't a futile exercise.

Forceps were a good enough temporary measure to close the artery. Sterile dressings covered the wound. It took only a few minutes to have their patient packaged onto the stretcher and stable enough to fly.

'Any family or close friends here?' Zac asked.

Summer deliberately avoided making eye contact with anybody. How many people had heard him say her name? The name that was embroidered on her overalls for anybody to check. A name that was unusual enough to be an accusation if someone knew that Jon had had a daughter in a previous life. It was normal to find out whether there was anyone who might want to travel with a patient who was seriously injured, anyway. These could be the last moments they had together.

'Me.' The skinny kid who'd been standing there, silently gripping the damaged surfboard, spoke up. 'I'm Dylan. He's my dad.'

She didn't manage to avoid Zac's glance this time. He was hiding it well but he was shocked. Did he think she'd known she had a half-brother? *Oh, man*...he couldn't be as shocked as she was. A half-*brother*?

She tried to shove the thought aside. This was her father's new family. It didn't have to have anything to do with her, other than as a professional. They couldn't just take a boy who didn't look any older than about ten or eleven with them. He would need to travel with an adult.

'Where's your mum?' The words came out more fiercely than she would have chosen.

'Haven't got one.'

'She died,' someone said quietly, close to Summer's shoulder. 'Couple of years back.'

'There's just me and my dad.'

The boy had blue eyes. And they were dark with distress—making him look a lot older than he probably was. A lot older than any kid should have to look. Summer had lost her mother. She knew what that was like but she couldn't afford to start feeling sorry for the kid. If she let him touch her heart, it might open the door to everything associated with her father and that was a world of hurt she thought she'd left well in the past.

But how could she not feel the connection? This kid even *looked* like her. Short and skinny, with bleached blond hair that was probably still full of sea water, which was why it was sticking up all over the place in the kind of spikes that Summer favoured for a hairstyle.

The unexpected mix of something so personal with what should have been a purely professional situation was impossible to deal with. Thank goodness Zac seemed to know exactly the right way to deal with it. He had his hand on a skinny shoulder.

'Want to come with us, then? We'll look after you, buddy.'

A single nod. The surfboard was handed over, with some reverence, to one of the lifeguards. The news crew, who'd been filming from a respectable distance, began to move closer. People would get interviewed. Close-up shots of that surfboard would probably be all over the Internet in no time. There could be more reporters waiting at the hospital and they'd be eager to get some sound bites from one of the crew.

Maybe Monty could deal with that. Or Graham, back at the base. All Summer wanted to do was get this job over with and find some way of getting her head around it all. But what was she going to do about the boy? She had a responsibility, whether she wanted it or not, and dealing with that was inevitably going to open a can of worms that Zac would want to talk about. That he had the right to know about, even?

A short time later, Dylan was strapped into the front seat of the helicopter beside Monty, and Zac and Summer were in the back with their patient. They were lifting off from the beach. They were in an environment totally familiar to Summer and heading back to the world she knew and loved.

But it didn't feel the same any more.

It was being shaken and it was impossible to know just how much damage might be happening.

Even Zac seemed different. Was it her imagination or was he treating Jon with even more care than usual? She didn't need reminding to keep a constant watch on his blood pressure and oxygen saturation. Surely he didn't need to keep asking about pain levels?

'It's down to three out of ten,' she finally snapped. 'And we're only a few minutes away from hospital. He doesn't need any more pain relief.'

Zac's expression was sympathetic but it felt like a reprimand. He was trying to do the best for everyone involved here but this was a decision their patient should be allowed to make. Was he providing an example of not letting anything personal interfere with something professional? 'How bad is it, Jon?'

'Better than before.' It was clearly an effort for him to open his eyes. 'Summer?'

It was easy to pretend to be absorbed in the measurements she was recording. To pretend she hadn't heard him call her name.

'Where's my boy?' Jon asked then. 'Who's looking after Dylan?'

'He's up front,' Zac told him. 'Coming to the hospital with us.'

'But who's going to look after him? He's just a kid…'

'Don't worry about it,' Zac said. 'I'll make sure he's taken good care of.'

What? Summer's frown was fierce. This felt wrong. This wasn't what he'd promised in that look. The one that had told her he was on her side and would protect her. He was treating Jon Pearson as if he was his girlfriend's father and not just a potential threat to her emotional well-being. As if this unknown and unwelcome half-sibling was part of her family.

And what did that say about Zac? That he'd think it was forgivable to cheat on your wife for pretty much an entire marriage? That it was okay to pack a bag and simply walk out when you decided that your daughter was old enough to be considered an adult?

'You're grown up now, chicken. It shouldn't matter that me and your mum aren't going to live together any longer. I won't be far away. I'll always be your dad.'

She'd only just turned sixteen, for heaven's sake. She'd been nowhere near old enough to handle her mother's emotional disintegration.

And it sure as hell *had* mattered.

'You're a cheat. A lying cheat. I can't believe you'd do this to Mum. To me. I hate you… I never want to see you again…'

She had seen him again, though, hadn't she? At her mother's funeral, less than a year later. Not that she'd gone anywhere near him. What could she have said?

This was your fault. It might not look like it to anyone else but, as far as I'm concerned, it was murder…

Murder by drowning in the dank blackness of the cloud that had been left behind in their lives.

The echo of her mother's voice was even more disturbing. Concentrating on recording a new set of figures wasn't enough to chase it away.

Blood pressure was ninety over sixty. Improving. At least it was recordable now.

You can never trust a man... No matter how much you love them—it's never enough...

Oxygen saturation was ninety-three per cent. Not enough but it had also improved from what it had been. There was enough blood—albeit pretty diluted now—to be keeping Jon alive.

'He's going to need blood.' Had Zac guessed her train of thought? 'Do you happen to know his group? Might speed things up.'

'He's O positive.'

'Really? Me, too.'

The coincidence was hardly impressive. 'So am I. It is the most common group, you know. Thirty-eight per cent of people are O positive.'

Her tone sounded off, even to her own ears. Cold, even. She turned to stare at the cardiac monitor.

He was in sinus rhythm so his heart was coping. The heart rate was too fast at a hundred and twenty but that was only to be expected with the low levels of circulating oxygen.

Looking up at the monitor made it inevitable that her glance would slide sideways at Zac but he'd looked away when she'd been making the comment about blood groups and seemed to be focused on checking the dressings over Jon's leg wound.

She couldn't shake that echo of her mother's voice. How could she when her father was lying there only inches away from her?

She loved Zac. More than she would have ever believed it was possible to love someone. And she trusted him completely.

Despite evidence to the contrary? How easily had she taken his word and shut those poisonous whispers from Kate out of her life?

The way her mother had always refused to believe rumours of her father's infidelity?

Her thoughts shouldn't be straying like this in the middle of a job. She was being unprofessional. She'd never felt like this. Well—maybe just a little—that first day she'd been on the job with Zac and she'd had to make an effort to separate the personal and professional, but that paled in comparison to the wash of mixed emotions she couldn't control right now. A mix of the present and past that was turning into a confused jumble.

Shaking things unbearably. Damaging things.

Nothing was going to be quite the same after this. Including how she felt about Zac?

Maybe that was the worst thing about it.

They were coming in to land on the roof of Auckland General. There would be a resus team waiting for them in Emergency. They could hand their patient over and if it had been any normal job that would be the end of it.

But Summer knew that, this time, it might only be the beginning of something else.

Something that had the potential to ruin her life all over again?

How on earth was she going to cope?

And then they were out of the helicopter and there was a flurry of activity as they got everybody out and ready to move. Summer gathered up the paperwork so she was a step behind as the stretcher started to roll. A nurse had taken charge of Dylan. For a moment, Summer stared at the entourage and it was hard to make her feet move to start following them.

But somehow Zac was right beside her. His side pressed against hers.

'It's okay,' he told her. 'We can deal with this. All of it.'

It was a good thing they had to move fast to catch up with their patient and take the lift down to the emergency department. A good thing that there were so many other people around because otherwise Summer might have burst into tears.

She had no idea exactly how they were going to deal with any of this but she desperately wanted to believe Zac.

There was the most enormous relief in the idea that, this time, she wasn't going to have to do this alone.

They could deal with this.

Together.

CHAPTER EIGHT

ZAC STOOD WITH Dylan in the corner of the resuscitation room, his arm around the boy's shoulders, as the team made their initial assessment of his father. Summer stood on the boy's other side. Not touching him but still close.

He could only imagine the mixed feelings she must be experiencing but she was standing her ground. Being protective of a scared ten-year-old kid who she happened to be related to. It made Zac feel enormously proud of her.

'Do a type and cross match,' Rob told one of the nurses. 'He's going to need a transfusion.'

'He's O positive,' Zac said.

'Thanks, mate, but we'll still have to check.' Rob's glance took in how close Zac and Summer were standing to Dylan but, if he was surprised, he gave no sign of it, with the same kind of professionalism that had stopped any of the team commenting that their patient's name was the same as Summer's. 'Bitten by a shark, huh? Your dad's going to have a great story to tell, isn't he?'

'Is he…is he going to be okay?'

'We're going to give him some more blood and make sure he's stable and then he'll be going up to the operating theatre so they can see what they can do. Try not to worry too much, okay?' Rob's smile was reassuring but he turned away swiftly. 'Has someone got hold of Orthopaedics yet? And where's the neurosurgical registrar? And Summer...?'

'Yes?' Summer responded to the tilt of the ED consultant's head. He wanted a private word. Was he going to warn her that Dylan might need to be prepared for the worst? That he might lose his father?

That she might lose her father again—permanently, this time?

It shouldn't make any difference but it did. There was new grief to be found. A grief mixed with regret and... and something that felt like...*shame*?

'We need to intubate,' Rob told her quietly. 'It's better if you take the lad somewhere else. Is he...is there some connection I should know about?'

Summer's heart was thumping. This was the moment when she had to decide how far she was going to go in opening a part of her life that had previously been out of bounds.

'Jon Pearson is my father,' she said aloud. 'And Dylan's my half-brother. I... I didn't know he existed before today, though.'

'Hmm...' Rob's look was searching. 'You okay?'

Summer's gaze shifted to where Zac was still standing with his arm around Dylan's shoulders. Skinny shoulders that were hunched in misery and fear.

'I think I will be,' she said quietly.

'I'll get Mandy to set up one of the relatives' rooms for you. She can take care of him if you need a break for any reason. If there's any way we can help, just say.'

Dylan wasn't happy about being taken somewhere else.

'I want to stay with my dad.' There was hostility in the glare being delivered as she and Zac ushered him out of the resus room. 'I don't want to go anywhere with you.

You're Summer. I know all about you. You were mean to Dad.'

Summer's jaw dropped. *She* had been mean?

'Um… I didn't know about you.'

'You would have if you'd talked to Dad. Like he'd always wanted you to.'

Summer tried to push away memories of things she wasn't proud of. Like the look on her father's face when she'd turned her back on him at the funeral and walked away. The letters she had ripped up. The parcels she'd had returned to their sender. Yes…there was definitely shame to be found in the kaleidoscope of emotions this day was creating.

'You don't care,' Dylan continued. 'You don't care if Dad dies. You don't care about *me*.'

'That's not true.' The sincerity in her words was a shock because it *was* genuinely sincere. She'd had no idea how much she *did* actually care, did she? But there was a huge part of her that still didn't *want* to care. There was a battle going on inside and it was hard to know which way to turn.

'He's not going to die, buddy.' Zac's voice was calm. 'What we don't know is whether they're going to be able to save his leg and we're not going to know that for a while yet. You can't stay while the doctors are doing their work and that's why we're taking you somewhere else. In here. Look, there's a TV and DVDs and that machine has lots of food.'

'Are you going to stay with me?'

'Sure.' Zac's smile was as reassuring as his calmness.

'So *she* doesn't need to stay then, does she?'

'She kind of does.' Zac let the door swing closed behind them.

'Why?'

'Well...she's kind of your big sister.'

Dylan's huff was dismissive and Summer could feel herself stiffen defensively. So what if this kid didn't want anything to do with her? Maybe she didn't want anything to do with him, either. She was just trying to do the right thing, here.

'And we're kind of together, you know?'

'You mean she's your girlfriend?'

'Yeah...' Zac's gaze found Summer's and held it. She felt some of the tension ebb away. Yes, there was a battle going on but she wasn't alone and if she had the choice of anyone to be on her side, she would choose this man.

Dylan's gaze went from Zac to Summer and back again. He shrugged and the look he gave Zac was an attempt at a man-to-man resignation that could have been funny if it wasn't heart-breaking at the same time.

'Guess that's okay, then.'

An hour of waiting brought the news that Jon had been taken into Theatre. Another hour passed and then another. The team of specialists had a huge job ahead of them to try and repair nerves and blood vessels and muscle if they were going to save his leg. Dylan had stopped talking as soon as the decision had been made regarding his company and all Zac and Summer could do was sit there with him and watch the cartoons he'd chosen as distraction.

Shared glances acknowledged how much they needed to talk about but none of it could be discussed in front of Dylan. Even the practicalities of where he would stay while his father was in hospital was something that needed to wait until they had confirmation that all had gone well in Theatre. The young boy seemed oblivious to the tension and frustration that slowly built around him. He shut himself away, seemingly absorbed by the meaningless entertainment, until, eventually, he fell deeply asleep on the couch. Mandy chose a moment a short time later to poke her head around the door.

'Looks like he's out for the count.'

'Yeah. Any word from upstairs?'

'Sounds like it got a bit dodgy for a while. He lost a huge amount of blood. Last I heard, he's stable again and the neurosurgeons are doing their bit.' Mandy took a blanket from the back of the couch and covered Dylan's bare legs. 'Why don't you two take a break? I'll stay in here with him. Even after his dad gets to Recovery it's going to be another hour or two before he'll be awake enough for a visitor.'

Zac stood up. 'Great idea. Let's go and get some coffee, Summer.' She looked exhausted enough to fall asleep herself but the lines of tension in her face suggested that was unlikely to be an option for a long while. She needed to talk more than she needed to sleep, but how much would she be prepared to tell him?

The sensation of being nervous was unexpected but this was a big ask, wasn't it? How close would Summer let him get?

How much did she really trust him?

He couldn't just ask, either. He knew that Summer guarded her privacy. He knew that he would probably get some answers by asking direct questions but he didn't want to do that. The information would still be guarded and the question of trust would not be answered. It mattered whether Summer was prepared to tell him what was important without being asked. Trust was like love, wasn't it? If it wasn't given freely—if you had to *ask* for it—it probably wasn't really worth having.

And it didn't seem as if it was about to be given. They sat in the cafeteria drinking bad coffee in the same kind of silence with which they'd been sitting in Dylan's company. Strained enough to make Zac's heart ache. He wanted to help but he couldn't just barge into a space he might not be welcome in.

It was still the early evening of what had been a beautiful day. Harsh sunlight had faded to a soft glow. How much better would it be if they could be sitting on the beach at Takapuna, watching the sunset over Rangitoto? They'd had their first moments of real connection on that beach and surely it would be easy to talk there. Apart from anything else, Summer needed a break from the emotionally traumatic situation she had unexpectedly found herself in. Some way to reassure herself that her life hadn't suddenly gone belly-up. They couldn't go to the beach right now, of course, but...

'Let's go back to the base,' he suggested.

Summer's immediate reaction was to shake her head. 'I can't leave. Not yet.'

But Zac could see the way her gaze went to the windows and beyond. That the notion of escaping was more than appealing.

'Dylan's being well looked after. He's probably going to sleep for hours, anyway. We don't have to be that long but we could get changed and bring our bikes back here and that way we'll be ready to go home later, when things are more sorted.'

Summer looked torn. 'It's a good idea,' she said. 'You should do that. I'd better stay, in case...in case...'

'I'm confident that your dad's not going to die,' Zac said gently. 'You'll be back by the time he wakes up and it can be you that takes Dylan in to see him...if you want,' he added hastily, seeing the way her eyes darkened with emotion. 'Only if that's what you want.'

'I don't. I told him I didn't ever want to see him again.

He… I…' Her voice cracked and she dropped her gaze, clearly struggling not to cry.

It broke Zac's heart. Here was this strong, capable and incredibly independent woman in front of him, but he could see a young girl as well. A girl who'd been unbearably hurt in some way.

*Oh… God…*had her father been violent to her? Snatches of memory flashed through his brain like a slide show that could be felt as much as seen. The fist that couldn't be avoided. The fear in his mother's eyes. Blood. *Pain…* The knot of overwhelming emotion in his gut was powerful enough to make him feel ill. There was grief there. And a white-hot anger. He had to move. Standing up, he held out his hand to Summer.

'You don't *have* to see him again,' he said, his voice raw. 'And you're not going anywhere alone.'

He loved the way Summer took his hand so readily. The way she kept moving as she got to her feet, coming into his arms as if it was the only place she wanted to go. He held her tightly, pressing his cheek to the top of her head. More than one group of people in the cafeteria were staring at them. The need to protect Summer kicked up several notches.

'Let's get out of here,' he said softly. 'Just for a bit.'

It was the right thing to do. It was Summer's idea to see if there was an ambulance crew who might be clear of a job in Emergency and have the time to drop them back at the helicopter base and that allowed her to step back into her own world. They changed out of their flight suits into civvies and that made it feel as if the job they'd been to at Piha Beach was really over. Best of all, they kicked their bikes into life and could roar through the city, weaving in and out of the traffic, feeling the freedom of their preferred mode of transport.

No. That wasn't the best of all. This was. Walking into the green space of the enormous park over the road from Auckland General Hospital. Walking hand in hand in soft light, mottled by the canopy of ancient trees, and feeling the caress of a gentle summer breeze.

It was as good as life could get in this particular moment, Zac decided. And then he changed his mind only moments later, when Summer's hand tightened around his and she started to talk, albeit tentatively at first.

'You never knew your dad, did you?'

'No. My mother never even told me his name. The only father figure I had came into my life when I was about four and...he was never a dad to me.' He could have said so much more but this wasn't about his story. Or was it? Would sharing something that was never spoken about be a way of showing Summer how much he was prepared to trust her? How much he wanted her to be able to trust him?

His hesitation made it irrelevant. Or maybe Summer was already lost in her own memories.

'My dad was the best,' she said softly. 'I adored him. Everybody did. He coached all the kids and was the chief lifeguard and a volunteer fireman and the go-to guy for the whole community.'

'Country town?' Zac was absorbing the undercurrent of her words. He could let go of the idea that her father might have been violent and the relief was sweet. But what else could have caused such a catastrophic breakdown in a relationship that should have remained strong for a lifetime?

'A beach community. Tiny. There was never much money but if the sun was shining and the surf was up, it didn't matter. We were all happy. Dad would be running his surf school or the shop and Mum made pots that she

painted and sold to the crowds that came in the summer
holidays. I had a long ride to school on the bus but that
was okay, too. We'd go with salt in our hair from a morning ride and we'd know there'd be time for the sea again
after school.' She was silent for a moment. 'I'll bet Dylan's
life is just like that. When I saw him on the beach today,
he looked like all my friends did at that age. Like I did. I
could have guessed who he was before he said anything
if I hadn't been trying so hard not to think about who it
was we were treating.'

'That must have been so hard for you. I can't believe
how well you coped with it.'

Her tone was suddenly shy. 'You helped more than I
can say. Thank you.'

Their steps had slowed and now they stopped. Zac
drew Summer into his arms. 'You would have managed
anyway but I'm glad I was there. I'm glad I'm here now.'

Summer pressed against him for a long moment but
then pulled away with obvious reluctance, shaking her
head. 'It's not over, though, is it? And I have no idea what
to do. It's all this confused jumble in my head. I've hated
Dad for so long. I want to hate Dylan too, but he's only a
kid. It feels like he's the cause of it all but he's not. It's not
his fault and…and he even looks a bit like me…'

Zac smiled. 'He does. He looks like a cool kid.' His
breath came out in a poignant sigh. 'I wish I'd been around
then.' He lifted an eyebrow. 'Maybe I was. Did you happen to notice a Combi van full of cool teenagers with their
surfboards at your beach?'

It made her smile. 'Lots. Did you happen to notice a
cool chick with a pink surfboard? My dad made it for my
thirteenth birthday.'

The smile vanished. Those big blue eyes glittered with

unshed tears and her voice was shaking. 'I miss him...
I've always missed him...'

In the silence that followed, they both sat down on
grass that was bathed with the last of the day's sunshine.
Zac let the silence continue but then decided that he could
ask a question now. He'd been invited into that private
part of her life. It felt as if she was ready to trust him but
he made his words as gentle as possible.

'What went wrong?'

Summer had picked a daisy from the grass and she
held it in one hand. With the fingers of her other hand,
she delicately separated a tiny petal from the others and
plucked it clear.

'We lived for surfing competitions,' she said. 'They
were the big, exciting days over summer and there were
always huge barbecues in the evenings. Everybody knew
each other and they were big social events.' Another petal
got plucked from the daisy. 'There was this woman—
Elsie—who turned up to a lot of the comps when I was a
kid. Mum said she was an old friend of Dad's but she was
weird about it. When I was thirteen—the year I got the
pink surfboard—I heard a rumour that there was something going on between Elsie and Dad.'

'Ohh...' Zac knew instantly where this story was likely
to go. He closed his eyes as if to hold back the distress of
a small family about to be broken apart.

'I asked Dad and he denied it. I asked Mum and she
said it wasn't true. She got really angry and told me never
to mention it again. Dad had married *her*. He loved *us*. He
was ours. For ever. She was always a bit over the top, you
know? When she was happy, she was super happy but little things upset her. A lot. I didn't dare mention it again.'

More petals were coming from the daisy. Half of its
yellow centre had a bare edge now.

'And then, one day—out of the blue—just after I turned sixteen, Dad told me that he had to leave. That he had to go and be with Elsie. That he'd been living a lie and life was too short to keep doing that. He thought I was old enough to understand, but all I could see was that he'd been cheating and lying for years—to the people who loved him the most in the world. I told him I never wanted to see him again.'

A whole bunch of petals got ripped clear. And then the daisy fell, unheeded, into the grass.

'Mum fell to bits. She wouldn't eat. She never stopped crying. I got her to see a doctor and he put her on medication but it was never enough. The pills got stronger and there were a lot of them. Enough for her to take so many that when I came home from school one day and found her unconscious on the floor, it was too late.'

'Oh, my God,' Zac breathed. He reached for Summer's hand and held it tightly.

'She never came out of the coma.' The tears were escaping now. 'They turned the life-support off a few days later.' Summer scrubbed at her face. 'Dad had the nerve to turn up at her funeral but, as far as I was concerned, he was guilty of murder. I refused to talk to him. Or even look at him. And I haven't, ever since...' Her indrawn breath was a ragged sob. 'But I had to, today. And I thought he was going to die and...and I realised I still love him. And when Dylan told me I'd been mean, I realised how horrible I have been. He tried to keep up the contact. He wrote to me. He rang me. He sent me presents. I ripped up the letters and blocked him from my phone. I sent the presents back. And then, when Mum died, I blamed him, even though I knew that wasn't fair. I'm... I'm not a very nice person, am I?'

Summer tilted her face up and her expression broke

Zac's heart. It was easy for it to crack because it had become so incredibly full as he'd listened to her story. No wonder she'd believed the accusations she'd heard about him with regard to Shelley after experiencing the pain that deception and denial could cause and yet she'd been prepared to take his word that the accusations were unjustified.

And how hard must it be for her to trust any man?

But she had trusted *him* with not only the story but her own fear about what kind of person she was.

He had to gather her into his arms.

'You're the nicest person I've ever met,' he said softly. 'And you don't have to do anything you're not ready to do. That includes talking to your dad or taking any responsibility for Dylan. I'll take care of everything.'

He pressed a kiss to the spiky hair that always felt so surprisingly soft. 'I'll take care of *you*,' he whispered. 'I love you, Summer.'

Those words blew everything else away.

It felt as if Summer had been adrift on a stormy sea for the last few hours, in a boat that was being dragged further and further into a storm where it would capsize and she would have no protection from the wild water in which she would inevitably drown.

But those words were an anchor. Something that could prevent the drifting and allow her to ride out the storm and then choose a safe path to find her way home.

They made the pain bearable. They made any doubts evaporate. Zac hadn't tried to defend her father in any way. He understood how hard it had been for her and he was ready to protect her completely. She didn't have to see her father or have anything more to do with her half-brother if that was what she wanted. He would take care of it all.

Those words made her feel safe.

It felt as if her own words had simply been waiting for the chance to escape. To be made real.

'I love you too, Zac.'

It was the moment for souls to touch through the windows that eyes provided. For trust to be offered. For lips to touch gently and linger to seal an emotional troth.

But the safety Zac's words promised gave Summer something else as well.

Strength.

'I think I do want to see Dad,' she said slowly. 'I've let this haunt me for too long. It's been like poison in my life. Probably in my relationships, too. I don't want that any more.'

Zac's smile was gentle. 'No poison permitted,' he said. 'Not for us.'

'I don't want it to hurt anyone else, either. Like Dylan.' The reminder that there was a scared kid curled up asleep on the couch in a relatives' room was a wake-up call. It was time to get back to reality.

'Let's go back.' Summer's limbs felt stiff as she got to her feet. How long had they been sitting there? 'We need to get stuff sorted. Like where Dylan's going to stay tonight.'

'He could come home with me. Gravy's really good at taking care of waifs and strays.'

'But he's not a waif. He's…he's part of my family.' Her breath came out in an incredulous huff. This was going to take some getting used to. 'I always wanted a sibling when I was a kid. Maybe this could be… I don't know… a gift, even?'

'Maybe it is.'

'So I guess I'll take him home with me. There's room on the boat. Flint will just have to sleep somewhere else.' She frowned. 'Except he might not want to. Dylan, that is. He thinks I'm mean. I suspect he hates me.'

Zac took her hand again as they crossed the road to the hospital entrance.

'He just needs the chance to get to know you. And I have a feeling that sleeping with Flint might be a pretty good place to start.'

'Maybe.' Summer smiled up at Zac as they headed for the lift. 'I think the only point in my favour right now, though, is that I'm your girlfriend. You're the hero who saved his dad. *My* dad,' she added in a whisper.

It still didn't feel real. Her world was still spinning.

It was undeniably weird. But part of that weirdness was very, very good.

Zac *loved* her.

She could deal with anything on the strength of that. Even this.

CHAPTER NINE

ZAC WAS THE HERO, all right.

It was Zac that Dylan chose to have by his side when he walked into the intensive care unit later that evening to see his father—leaving as much distance as possible between himself and Summer.

It was Zac who drew Summer closer to his other side as they reached the bed that was flanked by a bank of monitors, IV stands and the nurse who was monitoring her new patient carefully. Jon Pearson was awake, but only just. He was still weakened by the massive blood loss he had suffered and the medication for his pain made staying awake almost impossible.

But it was Summer that Jon focused on first when his eyes fluttered open and, for the first time in so many years, she met the eye contact—and held it. Neither of them smiled. The moment was too big for that.

But it was a start. A new beginning?

A smile appeared for his young son.

'Still got my leg.' Jon's voice was croaky. 'We'll be riding those waves again soon, kid.'

Dylan was clearly struggling not to cry. He inched closer to Zac and lifted his chin but his voice wobbled. 'Your board's munted, Dad. It got chewed to bits.'

'No worries. I'll make a new one.' Jon closed his eyes

and drew in a long breath before he pushed them open again. 'We'll put that one up on the wall. In the shop. People'll come from miles around to see it.'

His eyes drifted shut again. The brief conversation had exhausted him. The glance between the nurse and Zac gave the clear message that it was time for visitors to leave.

Zac put his hand on Dylan's shoulder. 'We'd better head off and let your dad get some rest, buddy. You can come and see him again tomorrow.'

'But I want to stay here.'

'Summer's going to take you home with her. On her motorbike. We found a helmet that will fit you back at the rescue base. She's got a cool bike—it's a Ducati. And it's red.'

The smile for Summer made her think of being out on the road with Zac's bike in front of her. Heading off so that they could spend time together somewhere special. The wave of longing was overwhelming. All she wanted to do right now was be somewhere with him again. Doing something that didn't involve such difficult emotional drama. They had only just declared their love for each other. How unfair was it that it was going to be impossible to spend this night in each other's arms?

Maybe Dylan noticed the look that passed between them. Or maybe he just wasn't impressed by the incentive that had been offered. He ignored Summer and fixed his gaze on Zac.

'Can't I go home with you?'

'Hey... I only live in a house. Summer lives on a boat and it's really cool. And she has a dog. His name is Flint.'

'I don't like dogs.' The words were sullen.

It was an obvious effort for Jon to open his eyes again. 'Go with Summer, lad. She's...she's your big sister...'

Another moment of eye contact and this time Summer found a smile, albeit a wobbly one.

'I'll look after him, Dad. You rest.'

It was a promise that wasn't going to be easy to keep, Summer realised a short time later when, thanks to the bike ride, Dylan was forced to make physical contact by putting his arms around this unwelcome newcomer in his life. It felt even harder after Zac's bike peeled away to leave her alone in Dylan's company. He had offered to come back to the boat with them but Summer knew she had to make the effort herself. Maybe it was a kind of penance. Or a need to prove that she wasn't the monster that Dylan believed she was—the unknown other child who'd always been so mean to his dad.

Looking after him in a physical sense wasn't the problem. She could give him a safe place to sleep and feed him. Finding him some acceptable clothes might be more of an ask, but she could sort that kind of issue tomorrow. It was the emotional side of things that was far trickier. Dylan had lapsed back into the miserable silence he'd displayed while they were waiting in the relatives' room. She didn't even have a television to distract him with on the boat.

At least there was Flint, who was overjoyed to have company after a longer day than usual, and feeding her dog gave Summer something to do after a tour of her home that took such a short period of time.

'I'll make us something next. Do you like bacon and eggs?'

Dylan shrugged.

'You'll just have to ignore Flint trying to persuade you that he's still starving. He'd do anything for a bit of bacon rind.'

Sure enough, it was Dylan's foot that Flint laid his chin

on when they were eating. Summer pretended not to see a piece of bacon rind being slipped under the table.

'Your bed is usually where Flint sleeps,' she told him, 'but I'll put some clean sheets on it and Flint can sleep somewhere else.'

Another shrug but it was clear that Flint intended to share his bed with the visitor when things were sorted for the night.

'Want me to put him somewhere else? Up on deck?'

'Nah.' Dylan climbed into the bed and edged to one side. 'I'm good. There's room.'

Summer took her hand off Flint's head and got a lump in her throat as she watched her dog step politely into the space provided and then curl up beside Dylan.

It was far too soon to offer the comfort of physical touch herself—for either of them—but Flint seemed to understand that that was exactly what was needed.

'Night, then. Just give me a yell if you need anything.'

A grunt indicated how unlikely that was but, as Summer turned away, she heard a small voice behind her.

'Did Zac mean what he said? About going for a swim in the morning?'

'Sure. Are you up for a bit of jogging, though? Flint will want to come and he can't go on the bike.'

Another grunt. 'Bet I can run faster than you can.'

He could. With his skinny legs and arms pumping, he stayed ahead of Summer with Flint close beside him and only slowed to wait for her when they got to an intersection and he didn't know what direction to take. By the time they got to the beach the first light of the day had strengthened enough to recognise the tall figure waiting alone and Dylan took off, even faster. Summer was a little out of breath by the time she caught up.

'You ready?' Zac asked Dylan. 'It'll be a bit cold.'

Dylan shrugged. 'Guess so. But there aren't any waves.'

He was right. Takapuna beach looked like a giant swimming pool this morning, calm enough to gleam under the rising sun. It would have been perfect for paddleboarding if they'd had more time.

'We get waves sometimes,' Zac told him. 'But this is just a wake-up dip. Last one in is a sissy...'

Maybe it was only Summer who noticed the tiny hesitation that gave Dylan the head start. The man and the boy ran into the sea, splashing through the shallow water and then diving as soon as it got deep enough. With a joyous bark, Flint took off to join them and Summer wasn't far behind.

The water was icy enough to make her gasp. By the time it felt bearable, it was time to get out. She and Zac both had to work today and there was a lot to get organised.

Zac seemed to have everything in hand, however, including towels waiting in a pile on the dry sand.

'Gravy's got breakfast ready. Do you like bacon and eggs, Dylan?'

Summer expected him to say that he'd had them already—for dinner last night—but she saw the way his gaze shifted to Flint, who was shaking seawater out of his coat.

'Yeah...bacon's cool.' And then he squinted up at Zac. '*Gravy?*'

It was such a perfect echo of the tone she had used herself the first time she'd heard the unusual name that Summer laughed. 'She's Zac's gran.'

Zac gave Dylan the same explanation as they headed for his apartment.

'Quick shower, then,' he ordered as they got inside.

'And I'll find some dry shorts for you. Might be a bit big, though.'

That shrug was becoming very familiar. 'Doesn't matter. My jacket's dry.'

The bright red and yellow jacket was the first thing Ivy commented on. 'Are you a lifeguard, Dylan?'

'Yep. My dad's in charge of the surf club. I help with Level One—the little nippers. We teach them about water safety and get them confident in the waves.'

Summer had never heard such a long speech from Dylan. There was something about Ivy Mitchell that broke through barriers of age or anything else, wasn't there?

'That's something to be proud of,' Ivy told him as she placed a laden plate in front of him. 'It's a wonderful organisation. I *always* swim between the flags.'

Zac snorted. 'You've never waited till the lifeguards are on duty to swim.'

Ivy looked affronted. 'But if I *did*, I'd swim between the flags.'

Zac and Summer laughed and, to her astonishment, a wide grin spread across Dylan's face a moment later. It was the first time she'd seen him smile. Even better, the smile didn't vanish as his gaze met hers. He even shook his head and then rolled his eyes as if to ask if this astonishing old lady was for real.

Ivy made it easy to organise the rest of their day.

'I can take Dylan into the hospital with me,' Zac said. 'And check on him during the day.'

'He can't stay in the hospital all day,' Ivy declared. 'And he needs some clothes. I'll take him shopping.' She winked at Dylan. 'I love shopping.'

'He needs to visit his dad,' Summer said. '... Dad,' she corrected herself.

The look that flashed between Zac and his grandmother told her that Ivy was already filled in on the fragile relationship but she gave no sign of any judgement.

'Of course he does. We'll go in on the bus after we've done our shopping. What do you need besides clothes, Dylan? A phone? Yes… You need to be able to text your dad. And your friends back home. And Summer, maybe, when she's at work.'

'I'll see what I can do about juggling shifts in the next couple of days,' Summer said. She was being excused from spending time with her father today and it felt like a reprieve. Or did it? 'But I'll drop in after my shift to visit and then I can take Dylan home.'

'Good.' Ivy wasn't going to allow for any more discussion. 'That's settled then. For today, anyway.'

'How long is my dad going to be in hospital?'

They all noticed the possessive pronoun that didn't include Summer.

'A fair while, I expect,' Zac told him gently. 'But we'll look after you, okay?'

'I've got a few days off coming up,' Summer said. 'First day's on Friday.'

'I've got Friday off, too,' Zac said. 'And you might be a bit over hanging around the hospital by then. We could do something fun, maybe.'

Dylan was staring at his plate. There was a pile of bacon rind carefully pushed to one side. Summer wondered how he might be planning to sneak it out to Flint, who was lying on the terrace with his nose on his paws, just inside the open French windows.

'Ever tried paddleboarding?' Zac continued.

Dylan snorted. 'Paddleboarding's for sissies.'

'Careful, mate… Summer's the queen of paddleboarding around here. And I'm learning and loving it.'

Ivy's lips twitched. Had she noticed how often Dylan's

gaze strayed towards the doors? 'It's Flint's favourite thing
to do,' she said. 'He rides on the end of Summer's board.'

Dylan's jaw dropped. 'No way...'

'Yes, way.' Summer nodded. 'And if you got good at
it, he might ride on the end of your board.'

The shrug seemed more like an automatic reflex than
something dismissive this time. 'Okay... I'll give it a go.
If Dad's okay.'

'Friday's a day or two away,' Ivy said. 'Let's take this
one day at a time, shall we? Now, scoot, you two. You've
got jobs to go to. Dylan and I need to do the dishes and
then go shopping. You'd better give that bacon rind to
Flint, Dylan, before Summer takes him home.'

Day by day, Jon Pearson continued to improve after being
moved from the ICU to a private room the day after his
long surgery. Visiting became less awkward for Summer
as she and Dylan got used to each other's company. While
he seemed to accept her presence in his life, though, he
wasn't in any hurry to share his father. She had yet to
spend any time in Jon's company without Dylan being
present and there were often others there as well. A steady
stream of friends came from the west coast to visit and,
in the first couple of days, there was the excitement of the
media interest in the survival story of man versus shark.
Dylan was clearly bursting with pride for his dad and that
meant he spent as much time as he could glued to the side
of his father's hospital bed.

And maybe the lack of any private time with her father
was a good thing as they also got used to breathing the
same air again. It meant that they only talked about safe
stuff. Like their jobs. They could swap stories about dramatic incidents or the kind of training it took to be able to
do what they did. Dylan was keen to share his own take

on dramas at the wild beach that was his playground. He became more and more interested in hearing about Summer's work, too. Especially if the stories included Zac. There was a bit of hero worship going on there and that was fine. Thanks to both Zac and Flint, Summer had something to offer in the way of being a potential part of his family.

Not spending time alone with her father made life easier for now. Not being able to spend time alone with Zac was less welcome. Oddly, though, the lack of physical contact was bringing them closer on a completely different level. One that was making Summer think more about the future. About what an amazing father Zac would make. He seemed to know instinctively how to relate to Dylan. When playfulness was needed. When a word to the wise was called for. Considering that he'd grown up without a father as a role model for himself, it was extraordinary. But, then, he'd been brought up by Ivy so maybe it wasn't so unbelievable.

The time they spent together on Friday felt like a family outing. Jay was happy to provide paddleboards for them all and, fortunately, it was another day with a sea calm enough to make it easy for learners.

Ivy was on her terrace in a deckchair, watching closely enough to wave whenever Summer or Zac looked up at the house. She was paddling slowly, Flint on her board, with Zac and Dylan not far away. Having been kneeling until he got used to the feel of the board, Dylan was standing up now. He had to be getting tired but he was giving it everything he had, trying to keep up with Zac.

'Hey… Flint…' he yelled. 'Come on *my* board…'

'Go on,' Summer urged. 'It's okay. I won't be offended.'

'Come on, Flint.' Zac joined in the chorus. 'Share the love…'

The big black dog obligingly jumped off Summer's board, making it rock. For a short time, all they could see was the black head above the water and then he was hauling himself up onto a different board. But not Dylan's. He had chosen Zac's. The dog was used to the effort it took but Zac wasn't prepared for how unstable it made his board and he lost his balance and fell off. Flint stood on the board, anxiously watching for him to resurface, and then barked in relief as Zac caught the board. Summer and Dylan were both laughing so hard they almost fell off their own boards.

It was a moment she would remember for ever.

Shared laughter that created a bond. A family kind of moment.

Even the mention of it later made them laugh, lying on their towels and soaking up the sun as they rested tired limbs.

'Wait till I tell Dad how you fell off,' Dylan said. 'You should have seen your arms. You looked like a windmill.'

Summer's smile was more poignant. 'He chose your board,' she said. 'I hope you realise how honoured you are.'

Dylan dug his feet into the sand. 'He was supposed to choose mine.'

'He wasn't being mean,' Summer said. 'Maybe Zac's board was just closer.' She held Zac's gaze, though. She wanted him to know that she didn't believe that. That her dog had chosen him because he was his person now, too. As important in his life as Summer was.

That they were a kind of family already?

It could be like this with their own children one day, couldn't it?

Was she ready to trust that much? To give herself so completely to Zac?

Maybe Dylan guessed where her thoughts were going and felt left out. That might explain the glare she could feel that made her turn her head.

'What's up?' she asked. 'You hungry again?'

Dylan said nothing and an echo of what she'd just said replayed itself, the words taking on a new significance. She sighed. Maybe they weren't becoming as close as she'd thought.

'You still think I'm mean, don't you?'

'Just because you go and visit Dad now doesn't make it all right,' Dylan muttered. 'It's just because he's sick.'

'Summer's not mean,' Zac said quietly. 'I don't like hearing you say that, buddy.'

'She was mean to Dad. I saw him crying one day, when I was little. After one of those parcels came back. I heard him tell Mum how much he missed her. How much he *loved* her.' The emphasis was a statement of how little she had deserved it.

Summer's heart ached. How much time had she missed having a father in her life?

'It's going to be different from now on,' she said. 'I'm sorry about the way I acted. I was…'

'Hurt,' Zac finished for her. 'Summer wasn't that much older than you are, Dylan. How would it make you feel if your dad decided he wanted to go away and make another family? With someone else?'

'She could have come too.' Dylan's feet were almost buried in the sand now.

Zac's hand moved discreetly between the towels. Summer felt his fingers close around hers. Offering support. An ally. Telling her that Dylan might not believe she had deserved her father's continued love but *he* did. Telling her that she had *his* love now as well. She had to swallow hard and scrunch her eyes shut so that the full feeling in her heart didn't escape as tears.

'She had to look after her mum,' Zac said carefully. 'Her mum got sick.'

'My mum was sick.' Dylan's voice wobbled. 'She... she died.'

'So did Summer's mum.'

There was something different this time in Dylan's gaze when he raised it to meet Summer's. Almost...respect?

Zac gave her fingers a squeeze and then let go, as discreetly as he'd made the contact. He must have been able to sense how big this moment was but, yet again, he knew how to lighten things and make it seem no more than a natural step forward.

'It's cool living on a boat, isn't it?'

'I guess. But it doesn't go anywhere.'

'It could.' Summer was happy to move away from anything intense. 'The sails aren't any good but it's got a motor. I turn it on every so often to make sure it still goes. I should do it tonight, in fact. I'll let you turn it on, if you like.'

Dylan didn't respond. He had rolled onto his side and was tickling Flint's tummy.

Zac smiled. 'You didn't really mean it when you said you didn't like dogs, did you?'

A skinny bare shoulder gave a single shrug.

Zac's tone was as light as it had been when he'd mentioned the boat. 'Sometimes, when things are tough, we say—or do—stuff we don't really mean. Sometimes it's good to just forget about them and start again.'

They all lay there in silence after that. Silence that made it easy to hear Ivy's call from the terrace above.

'Yoo-hoo! Are you lot coming inside for some lunch?'

They got to their feet and gathered damp towels to shake the sand out of them. Walking up to the house, Zac took Summer's hand. Flint was on her other side with Dylan close beside him.

The boy looked up at Summer. 'Do you reckon Flint'll sit on my board one day, too?'

It was another one of those moments to treasure. Zac's hand was warm around hers. She had her beloved dog by her side and she knew she was about to make her little brother smile.

'I reckon you can count on that. Maybe next time we go out, even.'

Going out on the boards wasn't going to happen again any day soon. A summer storm was brewing and the next day the wind came up and the sky darkened ominously.

'We'll go and visit Dad after lunch,' Summer said. 'We can go shopping this morning and find him some presents. Some nice things to eat, maybe, seeing as he's feeling so much better. Hospital food's not up to much.'

'Zac said I could go and see where he works and he'd show me some cool stuff. Like the saw they use to cut people's chests open.'

'Did he? Okay…we'll have to see how busy they are in Emergency, though. We can't get in the way if Zac's in the middle of saving someone's life.'

Dylan's nod was serious. 'I wanna do that one day. I think I'm going to be a doctor like him.'

'You could be a paramedic, maybe. We get to save lives too, you know. And being on the helicopter is pretty exciting.'

Dylan's grin was sympathetic. 'Zac gets to do everything. He's the best.'

Summer had to grin back. 'Yeah… I think so, too.'

The best boyfriend. The best lover. And he would be the best father for any children she had.

Oh, yeah…she was so nearly ready to trust that much. Maybe the only thing in the way was to deal with the ghosts still haunting her past.

It was time to talk to her father. Properly.

The opportunity came later that day when Zac appeared during their visit to Jon and told Dylan he could have the promised tour of the emergency department.

'You want to tag along, Summer?' he asked.

'No, I'm good. I'll stay.'

The sudden tension in the room advertised that the significance wasn't lost on anybody. Dylan hesitated, clearly feeling protective of his father. He eyed Summer.

'Is that cool, Dad?'

'It's fine, son. Come back and see me later.'

Summer gave Dylan a smile intended to reassure him that she wasn't about to start being mean. Zac got the message, even if Dylan didn't. His glance, as they left, told her that he was impressed she had chosen to stay and have her first time alone with her father. Proud of her, even?

It was impossible to know how to start. Summer fiddled with the supply of grocery items she and Dylan had chosen to bring in. Fruit and biscuits and ginger beer. She held up a packet of sweets.

'Do you *really* love sour worms?'

'No. But Dylan does.'

'Ah…that might explain the salt and vinegar crisps, too.'

'No. I *do* love them. Might need a beer to go with them, though.'

Small talk seemed to be exhausted at that point. Summer finally sank into the chair beside the bed as the awkward silence grew.

It was Jon who broke it.

'I can't tell you how sorry I am, love. About what happened to your mum. About not being there. I know you think it's my fault that she died...'

Summer shook her head. 'I did, I guess. But I'm a bit older and wiser now. I get that people make their own choices. And I know Mum wasn't the easiest person but... she really did love you...'

'I know that. I loved her, too.'

'Not as much as you loved *her*...'

'Elsie?' Jon's smile was sad. 'That was a very different kind of love. We'd grown up together. We started dating when we were fourteen. We were always going to be together.'

Summer's jaw dropped. 'So why did you marry Mum?'

Jon lay back against his pillows, his eyes closing. 'Elsie's family had moved to Australia and she was a couple of years younger than me. She was going to come back to New Zealand as soon as she turned eighteen. And then we were going to get married.' His breath escaped in a long sigh. 'I was nineteen. Elsie had been away for more than a year and I... I was lonely. Not that that's an excuse but there was this big surf comp and a party afterwards and your mum was there and she...she made it clear how keen she was on me and...'

'And she got pregnant?'

'Yes. I had to tell Elsie and...and she was devastated. Said she never wanted to see me again. It was the worst time. Your mum was in love with me and she said she couldn't live without me and she really meant that. I was scared she'd hurt herself if I left and, besides, there was a baby involved and I wanted to do the right thing by everyone. And then you came along and I found a new kind of love that I thought would always be enough. I didn't think I'd ever see Elsie again but she turned up for a comp when you were about eight or so. And it was still there. The way we felt about each other.'

Summer was silent. How would she feel, she wondered, if she and Zac were forced apart and then she met him again years later? Would she still feel the same way?

Yes, her heart whispered. It would never change.

'We tried,' Jon said quietly. 'And, when it became too hard to stay away from each other, we still tried not to let it hurt you or your mum.'

'Did she know?'

'I think so. But she chose not to believe it. I think she thought that if she simply refused to believe it, it wouldn't be true. Her mental health was always a bit fragile. She had a stay in hospital after you were born with postnatal depression. I had about three months of looking after you by myself and...it might sound horrible but I'd never been happier. You were my little girl and I loved you to bits. I never, ever wanted to make life hard for you.'

Summer had tears trickling down the side of her nose. 'I'm sorry, too. For shutting you out. And the longer I did it, the easier it seemed to just leave it all behind and not go back.'

'Ah...don't cry, love.'

'But Dylan was right. I was mean to you.'

'You were a kid. And you were protecting your mum. That's not something to be ashamed of.'

Jon stretched out an arm and Summer was drawn from her seat and into a hug that took her back in time. Back to before the tragedy of losing her mother. Back to a time when she and her father had shared so many magic moments. Like the moments she had had with Zac and Dylan so recently. The bonding family moments.

They didn't get wiped out, did they? Maybe they got

covered up but you could find them again and how good was that?

'I kind of like having a brother,' Summer admitted when they finally stopped hugging and both blew their noses and regained some composure. 'He's a nice kid.'

'He's very like you were at that age.'

Summer smiled. 'Yeah...he's got seawater in his veins, too.'

'Has it been okay—having him to stay?'

'I think he likes the boat. And he loves Flint. And Zac.'

'You and Zac—is it serious?'

Summer's nod was shy. It was as serious as it could be, wasn't it? She couldn't wait to tell Zac about this conversation. About the moment when she knew she had forgiven her father because she recognised that his love for Elsie had been the way she felt about Zac. That being with anyone else would be living a lie.

'It must be getting in the way a bit, having a kid brother on the scene.'

'It's fine. It won't be for ever.'

'It could be a while longer, though. They say I'm healing well but I won't be up on my feet for a week or so and I won't be going home any time too soon. I'm worried about Dylan missing too much school. I've got friends who've offered to have him stay. Parents of his friends.'

'He'd be worried about you.'

'It's not that far. Someone could drive him over almost every day for a visit. If I send him home, he won't be interfering in your life so much.'

It was unfortunate that Zac and Dylan arrived back in the room at precisely that moment. Just in time to hear those last words.

Zac's eyebrows shot up. Dylan visibly paled.

'Are you sending me away?' he demanded.

'I'm just thinking about all the school you're missing. Come and sit down and we'll talk about it.'

'I don't want to go away. I like being here. I like Flint and...and paddleboarding and stuff.' Dylan glared at Summer and her heart sank. She hadn't been included in why he wanted to stay. Of course he must think she'd been complaining about him interfering with her lifestyle but that wasn't true. She needed to talk to him as well. She cast a helpless glance at her father.

'I'll explain,' he said quietly. 'Don't worry.'

But Dylan's face had shut down. He shoved his hands in his pockets. And then he frowned.

'Oh, no...where's my phone?'

'You had it downstairs. You were taking a photo of the rib spreaders, remember?'

'I must have left it there.'

'I'll go and look. I have to get back to work, anyway.'

'I'll come with you,' Summer said. 'And then I can bring the phone back. You stay here with Dad, Dylan.'

It was a relief to be alone with Zac. 'He's got the wrong idea,' she told him. 'I'd said how good it was having him but Dad thinks he's getting in the way of *us* being together.'

Zac's glance as he pressed the button for the lift gave Summer a jolt of sensation deep in her belly.

'I guess there is a bit of truth in it,' she admitted, as the door closed behind them.

'You think?'

They were alone in the lift. Zac caught her chin with one hand and ducked his head to place a lingering kiss on her lips. By the time the lift doors opened on the ground floor, Summer's legs were distinctly wobbly.

Oh, yes...they needed some time alone together. Soon.

'I had the kit open in my office to show him,' Zac said. 'I reckon that's where the phone will be.'

They had to go through the emergency department to get to the office. To Summer's surprise, she heard someone calling her name.

'*Kate*...what on earth are you doing here?'

'I had to come in with Shelley. Felix broke his leg. It looks like... Oh, it's all such a mess, Summer. I'm so glad *you're* here...'

Kate's gaze shifted to the man by her side and there was no way Summer could avoid this.

'This is Zac,' she said quietly. 'Zac Mitchell.'

The door to the resus area behind Kate opened further and Mandy appeared. Summer could see into the room properly now. A young woman was sitting on the bed. She was crying and she had a small, limp boy in her arms. A boy who had dark curly hair and big dark eyes.

A boy who looked remarkably like Zac?

CHAPTER TEN

A PART OF Summer's brain had frozen.

She couldn't think straight and it was frightening. To be able to do her job, she *had* to be able to think straight no matter how many things were happening at once or how horrible those things might be.

But this was different. This involved a person she was intimately involved with and this time she couldn't step back and try to cloak herself with a clinical perspective, the way she'd been able to do when she had to deal with treating her father.

This was about Zac. And whether she'd been right in following her heart and giving him her trust. It had been given; there was no question about that. It had been given totally in that moment of connection with her father when she'd recognised that the strength of how she felt about this man would last a lifetime.

But even that truth seemed to be outside the anaesthetised part of her brain. Or maybe she couldn't catch it because too many other things were demanding her attention.

Kate had taken hold of her arm and her tone was urgent. 'I tried to call an ambulance but she said she had to take Felix to Auckland General and just put him in the car and took off. All I could do was follow. And now she won't let anyone touch him. Mum and Dad are on their way but...'

Rob was coming towards them, stripping off gloves. 'Right,' he said. 'I'm clear. We've got a two-year-old with a query fractured femur.'

'His GCS is down,' Mandy told the consultant. 'I'm worried about blood loss.'

Rob gave a curt nod. 'Children compensate too well to start with. Let's get a type and cross match stat, in case we need some blood products.'

'Do you need a hand?' Zac's voice was quiet. Calm. It made Summer think of the way she had been when faced with treating her father. At least Zac was managing to function professionally. His brain hadn't frozen.

Rob nodded. 'Hang around for a minute. Just in case.' He turned back to Mandy. 'Has the paediatric orthopaedic team been paged?'

'Yes...' Mandy lowered her voice. 'And we might want to page Psyche, too.'

'What?' Rob was instantly on the alert. 'Why?'

'It's a bit odd. She hasn't let anyone else touch him since she carried him in. She got hysterical when we tried so that's why we got her to carry him in here.'

Rob looked past Mandy. And then took a second look and stepped further into the room. 'Shelley, isn't it? Didn't you work here not so long ago?'

'Hi, Rob. You remember me?' Shelley's tears evaporated as she smiled. 'Not the best way to have a reunion, is it?'

'This is your son?'

'His name's Felix.'

'We need to look after Felix.' Rob moved closer but didn't try to touch his young patient. 'He's hurt his leg, yes?'

'I don't want anyone to hurt him.' Shelley's hold on the toddler tightened and the child whimpered.

The sound made Summer feel ill. It was the first sound she had heard Felix make and it wasn't the normal cry of a child in pain. She knew to worry a lot more about the quiet ones. Especially when they seemed so quiet and well behaved in a frightening situation. And this injury was serious. She could see how swollen the small thigh was and the odd angle of his lower leg. The colour of his foot wasn't good, either. Urgent treatment was needed.

Kate was still holding onto Summer's arm as she moved closer to Rob so she was forced to move as well.

'There's been a series of accidents recently,' she said. 'Some bad bruises. Shelley said it's because he keeps falling off the new bike he got for Christmas but...'

The look in her eyes said it all. Even Shelley's own family were suspicious that the injuries weren't accidental.

'Trampolines are dangerous.' Shelley's voice was calm. 'I *told* Mum and Dad he was too young to have one but they went ahead and bought it, didn't they?' She bent her head over Felix and rocked him in her arms. 'It's all right, baby. Everything's going to be all right...' She started humming a song.

Rob stepped back from the bed, his face grim. 'Yep. Page Psyche. And we'll go ahead with treatment without signed consent if we have to. Let's see if we can get an IV in and I want to get that leg splinted properly before we do anything else to try and prevent any more blood loss.'

He turned back to Shelley. 'We need you to sign a consent form, Shelley, so that we can treat Felix. You know the drill, don't you?'

Shelley stopped singing. She nodded without looking up. 'That's why I had to come here,' she said. 'I don't think I can bring myself to sign a form that means you're going to hurt my baby. His father can do that.'

'His father?' Rob looked sideways as if he expected to see someone else in the room but there was only Zac, standing near the door, Mandy, who was wheeling the IV trolley closer, Summer and Kate, who leaned in to whisper in her ear.

'I didn't mean to tell her that Zac was back in the country,' she said. 'It just slipped out…'

'Yes.' Shelley raised her head and she was smiling sweetly, her gaze fixed on Zac. 'That's his daddy. Zac. Dr Mitchell.'

It wasn't just Summer's brain that was frozen now. The whole world seemed to have stopped spinning.

'Oh, my God…' The packages containing the cannula and swabs dropped from Mandy's hands.

Rob's jaw dropped.

'Oh…no…' Kate buried her face in her hands.

Zac simply stared at Shelley, his face utterly blank and immobile.

Shelley smiled back at him, the Madonna-like expression completely out of place given that she was holding her badly injured child.

And then, as if given a director's cue, everybody turned to look at Felix. Still pale and limp, he looked back at all these strangers with those big dark eyes. From a perfect little face that was framed by soft dark curls.

The heads turned again, as if at some bizarre tennis match, to look at Zac.

There was no denying that it seemed quite possible he was Zac's child.

Zac's voice was as expressionless as his face. 'I am *not* his father.'

Mandy made an odd sound as she stooped to collect

the packaging. 'But... I remember now. Shelley was always bringing you stuff. Cakes. Even flowers...and...' She straightened and looked at Felix again, her words trailing into silence.

Doubt hung in the air. As palpable as thick smoke.

Summer stared at Zac. The numb part of her brain was coming back to life. Painfully. She had had those doubts herself but she had dismissed them on nothing more than Zac's word. On instinct. But her instincts weren't always to be trusted, were they?

She'd believed Shelley when she'd first proclaimed the paternity of the baby she was pregnant with and she'd been wrong about that. She'd believed her mother when she'd said that no man could be trusted and that love wasn't enough. That what had gone wrong in her life was her father's fault. She'd been wrong about that too and look at how much damage trusting her instincts had already done.

All she needed now was the reassurance that she was right to trust Zac.

To love him...

But she couldn't see anything. He could have been looking at Rob or Mandy or Kate. Possibly even Shelley. There was nothing there for her to read and, just for a dreadful moment, fear kicked in. A dreadful certainty that there was something he hadn't told her.

What if he *was* hiding the real truth?

And then something happened that forced an abrupt break to that desperate eye contact.

Felix screamed—a tortured sound that gave way to broken sobbing.

Rob spoke briefly to Zac and then gave Mandy a curt nod and took a tourniquet from her hand. It was past time they got some pain relief on board for this little boy.

Shelley burst into tears as well. 'I didn't mean it,' she sobbed. 'It just *happened*...'

Kate moved to touch her sister. 'It's okay,' she said. 'We're going to look after you. *And* Felix.'

More people arrived in the resus area. The paediatric orthopaedic consultant, who had two registrars with her. Another nurse, who was carrying a paediatric traction splint, and an older woman who didn't have a stethoscope around her neck. The psyche consultant, perhaps? Or someone from Social Services?

Zac was edged further back in the room and Summer couldn't catch his gaze again.

She didn't need that reassurance, did she? This was *Zac* and of course she believed him. Shelley was crazy. She wanted to say something but the noise level in the room was rising and the moment had long gone. X-ray technicians were getting ready to use the overhead equipment. Tubes of blood were being handed to a junior nurse. An IV line was in place and medication had been administered. Felix, thankfully, was now sedated and peacefully asleep.

Stuck in a corner behind Kate at the head of the bed, Summer couldn't even move without disrupting something that was far more important than her need to talk to Zac.

'Do you need blood on standby?' One of the ED registrars was by Rob's shoulder as he was getting the splint ready to go on the small twisted leg. Summer had been asked to provide support when they were ready to fasten the Velcro straps and put the traction on to straighten the leg.

'Yes, please. Just in case. Have we got the type and cross match back already?'

'Yes. And it's good that we checked. He's AB negative.'

Summer's brain raced. AB negative was the rarest

blood group there was. And she was pretty sure that the parents had to have the blood groups of A, B or AB.

'That means that someone who's an O couldn't be his father, doesn't it?'

Rob nodded. 'You ready?'

'Yes.' Summer lifted Felix's foot, keeping one hand under the calf. The splint was slipped into place and Rob began to fasten the straps. 'Zac's an O.'

The look Rob gave her was scathing. 'You didn't really think he was lying, did you?'

'No. Of course not. But this *proves* it...' But Summer could feel the colour flooding her cheeks.

She'd meant that it was proof for Shelley's family. For the psychiatrist. But she'd made it sound as if *she* had needed the proof. And she hadn't. But Rob didn't believe that. What if Zac didn't believe it, either? She would never be able to erase that last time their eyes had met. When she'd bought into that collective doubt for just a moment in time because she was so sure there was something he hadn't told her. A moment that could potentially have been long enough to destroy the trust they had built between them. Possibly irreparably. And she couldn't blame him entirely if it did.

She had to get out of here. She had to find Zac.

'I'm sorry, but I've got to go,' she told Kate. 'I'll be back later.'

Pushing her way out of the resus room, Summer scanned the emergency department. An ambulance crew she recognised were handing over a patient at triage. Orderlies were pushing patients in beds or wheelchairs. A nurse was wheeling a twelve lead ECG machine into a cubicle. A group of doctors were standing around a computer screen looking at the results of an MRI scan. There were people everywhere but no sign of Zac.

She went to his office. It was empty, but there, on the corner of his desk, was a mobile phone. Dylan's phone. The reason they'd come down here in the first place. The reason they'd had those brief moments in the lift when he'd kissed her with all the pent-up passion of not having been able to make love to her for days now.

And superimposed on those thoughts was the image of Zac's face and the way he'd looked at her that last time. As if he didn't even recognise who she was.

*Oh... God...*was it possible that that kiss in the lift was the last one she would ever receive from him?

Summer clutched Dylan's phone.

She could ring Zac. Or text him.

And say what? That the blood results were back and now everyone believed him? With the unspoken assumption that that 'everyone' included her?

No. This was too big for a message that could be misinterpreted in any way. Too big for communication that couldn't include body language or touch, even.

In the moment of indecisiveness, the phone in her hand began to ring. For a heartbeat, the wild hope that it might be Zac brought the sting of relieved tears to her eyes.

'Is that you, love?'

'Oh... Dad...'

'Dylan wanted to check that you'd found his phone.'

'Um...yes...'

'I need you to take him home. To collect his things. We've had a talk and I've got friends coming to collect him this evening.'

'Okay... I'm on my way. Just give me a minute or two, yes?'

She had to go back to the resus room first. Rob was amongst the team members who were standing back as a series of X-rays were being taken.

'Rob?' Summer tried to catch his attention discreetly. 'Do you know where Zac is?'

'I told him to go home early. To get himself away from this until it's sorted.' Rob's gaze was on Shelley, who was now flanked by two security guards and well away from her son. He shook his head. 'It's always so much worse when there are kids involved in this kind of crisis.'

Indeed it was. And now Summer had a child involved in what felt like a personal crisis of her own. She raced back to her father's ward. Dylan made no protest about being bundled into his jacket and helmet for the ride home and it took all of Summer's focus to cope with the traffic and blustery conditions as she rode over the exposed harbour bridge. Rain wasn't far off now and it could well be accompanied by a thunderstorm by the look of the turbulent sky.

Dylan ignored Flint when they arrived at the boat, which should have been a warning sign, but Summer had too much else on her mind.

'I've got to go and see Zac—just for a minute,' she told Dylan. 'I'm sure he'll want to see you before you go tonight.'

His look was as scathing as the one Rob had given her not so long ago but she couldn't explain why she had to see Zac face to face instead of ringing him. Or to try and reassure him that Zac didn't want him out of the way and not interfering with his life any more than she did. She wouldn't know where to begin, trying to explain any of it to a young boy, and there simply wasn't the time.

'It'll take fifteen minutes. Twenty, tops. You pack up

your stuff and, as soon as I get back, I'll take you back to the hospital so your friends can collect you.'

'Fine.' Dylan turned away from her, the word a dismissal.

It was only a few minutes' ride away but the lower level of Ivy's house had an empty feel to it. Summer kept knocking on the door but the sinking feeling got stronger. Nobody was there to answer it.

A voice came from the balcony above, though.

'Is that you, Summer?'

'Yes.' She stepped back until she could see Ivy peering over the railing. 'I'm looking for Zac.'

'He's not home yet. Come inside and wait for him. This weather's getting dreadful.'

'I can't. I've got to get back to Dylan. If you see him… can you tell him I'm looking for him?'

'Of course.' Ivy pushed wind-whipped strands of hair back from her face. 'Is everything all right, darling?'

Again, Summer had no idea where to begin. She could only nod, emphatically enough to try and reassure herself. If nothing else, the action had the bonus of holding back tears.

If Zac wasn't home by the time she'd taken Dylan back to the hospital and returned, then she would tell Ivy everything. Surely this amazing woman was old and wise enough to be able to tell her how to fix something that seemed to be more and more broken with every passing minute.

It had probably been a little more than twenty minutes when Summer eased her bike into the stand at the marina. She hurried down the jetty to the mooring. Past all the yachts she knew almost as well as *Mermaid*, all of them bobbing on an increasingly disturbed bed of water.

Most were empty, waiting for their owners to have some spare time at the weekend. A few, like hers, had people living in them.

Clive was the closest marina neighbour and he was the friend who could look after Flint if she was ever caught out on a job.

He was out on his deck right now, tying things down in preparation for the coming storm. He stopped what he was doing and stared at her, a rope dangling from his hands.

'*Summer!* What on earth are you doing here?'

The odd query stopped her in her tracks. Why wouldn't she be here, on her way to her home?

'I saw you going out. Fifteen or so minutes ago. Thought you must be getting the boat out of the water or something.'

'*What?*'

Summer started running, her boots thumping on the wooden boards of the jetty. She got to the point where Flint was usually sitting to await her return. Beside the bollards that her ropes were always curled around to anchor the boat.

There was nothing there. Just an empty space—the water dark and rippled.

Summer looked out at the harbour. It was already darker than it should be for this time of day. There were plenty of small yachts anchored away from the marina and they were all moving in the wind and the roll of the sea so it took a minute to make sure that none of the movement was as purposeful as it would be if there was anybody on board.

If there was a motor running.

She couldn't see *Mermaid* anywhere.

Dylan had taken her. With Flint on board.

He'd run away.

Thank goodness her brain didn't freeze this time. Summer knew exactly what she had to do. She pulled her phone out and made two calls.

The first was to the coastguard to raise the alarm.

The second was to Zac.

'Summer?' His tone was wary. Had he been reluctant to even answer her call?

'Zac…where are you?'

'I'm at the rescue base. I came in to have a chat to Graham.'

About giving up being a HEMS member, perhaps, so that he didn't have to work with her any more? The thought intruded even if it was completely irrelevant right now—fear for others was overwhelming any fear for herself.

'Dylan's gone. He's taken *Mermaid.*'

'No way… *How?*'

'I showed him how to start the motor last night. And I…' Summer squeezed her eyes shut. This was all her fault. She'd taught Dylan how to make the boat move and then she'd left him alone long enough to give him a head start. She'd known he was upset and *that* was her fault, too. He'd overheard the tail end of the conversation she'd had with their father and he had only been beginning to be ready to share the most important person in his life with the girl who'd been so mean to him for so long.

'There's not much petrol,' she added desperately. 'He could be drifting by now. He doesn't know how to use the radio and he's got Flint on board as well and…' Her voice caught in a strangled sob.

Zac's voice was calm in her ear. Any wariness had vanished. 'Have you called the coastguard?'

'Yes. Of course.'

'There'll probably be a call coming in here soon, then. Monty's on base. I'll ask him whether it's possible to go out in this weather. How soon can you get here?'

Summer was already running back towards her bike. 'I'm on my way.'

CHAPTER ELEVEN

As a doctor, Zac Mitchell knew that a heart couldn't actually break.

As a man, he knew that that was exactly what happened to his heart the moment he saw Summer arrive at the rescue base.

One look into her eyes and he could feel it happening with a pain like no other he had ever experienced.

Of course she was afraid. Her young brother and her beloved dog were out there on an unforgiving sea in a small boat in a breaking storm but—as he held the eye contact for a heartbeat longer—he could see another layer to that fear.

Summer could feel the distance between them.

And she knew why it was there.

She had doubted him. He might love her more than he thought it was possible to love anyone, but how could he commit to spending his lifetime with someone who had doubted him—about *that*—even if it had only been for an instant?

But right now that didn't matter.

What mattered was that Summer needed him and he could be here for her a hundred per cent, even if it would be for the very last time.

He closed the physical distance between them with a

couple of long strides and then he gathered her into his arms and held her close enough to feel his heart beating against her small body.

'We'll get through this,' he promised. 'Together.'

The hug was a brief one. They weren't alone, even though most of the day's crew had gone home.

Graham's face was grim. 'The coastguard's boat has been tied up with an incident out on Waiheke Island. They're on their way but conditions are worsening and the light's fading fast.'

'We've got to find them.' Summer's face was white. 'What if they drift into a shipping lane? With no lights?'

The thought of what would happen to a small boat, unseen by a container or cruise ship, was horrific.

Monty looked away from the weather maps and rain radar he had on the computer screen in front of him. 'We'll take the chopper up. Turn on the sun.'

Graham shook his head. 'It's getting marginal for flying.'

Monty's chair scraped on the floor. 'We'd better get on with it, then.'

Summer raced to her locker to grab her gear. Zac was right behind her.

'You don't have to do this,' she told him. 'I would never ask you to put yourself in danger for my sake.'

Zac could only meet her gaze for a moment. 'You would never *have* to ask,' he said. 'And I'm coming. End of story.'

Every minute that passed was a minute too long.

It took time to scramble into the gear they needed for an offshore rescue mission like this. A titanium under-vest and Poly-Lycra under-suit and then the specially designed wetsuit. The lifejacket came equipped with a range of accessories like a strobe light and mini flare, a whistle and a knife and even survival rations.

They strapped themselves into winching harnesses even though they knew how unlikely it was that it would be safe to be winched onto a moving target like a boat in this kind of weather. It took more time for Monty to complete pre-flight checks and get them airborne. And then minute after minute flicked past as they circled the inner harbour, working out from the marina where the *Mermaid* had been moored.

There was no sign of any small craft, including the coastguard vessel. Even the larger ferries were on the point of suspending services and the only people going near their yachts were those who were trying to make them more secure as the storm bore down on the city. The flash of lightning on the horizon heralded the first squall of rain that obscured visibility enough to make Monty curse.

'We'll have to abort if this keeps up.' But there was no indication that the pilot had any intention of calling it quits yet and Summer knew that this was the kind of challenge that Monty thrived on. He'd keep them as safe as possible but would also take them right to the edge if that was what was needed to save a life.

The squall passed and the helicopter rode the rough air to move further towards the open sea. They were over the shipping lane between Rangitoto and Takapuna beach now—the track that the big container and cruise ships took to gain entry to the city's harbour. Fortunately, there was no sign of any large vessels. Unfortunately, there was no sign of any smaller ones either.

'The swell's getting big enough to make it hard to see,' Zac said. 'Turn on the sun, Monty.'

The night sun was a light attached under the nose of the

helicopter that had the strength of thirty million candles. Below them, the white foam of breaking waves on the big swells covered the inky blackness of the deep water below.

Summer's stomach sank and then rose with every air pocket that Monty negotiated. Her heart just kept on sinking. They weren't going to find the *Mermaid*. It would get thrown onto rocks and there would be no way to rescue Dylan. Or Flint.

'There...' Zac's shout was triumphant. 'Nine o'clock.'

'Where?' Summer's heart was in her mouth now. 'I can't see them.'

'Wait...'

The water rolled and, yes...there she was, riding the swell. Still afloat but clearly without power. Being washed towards the rocky coastline.

Monty was on the radio instantly, relaying the coordinates to both the coastguard and the team ready to mobilise on shore.

'Can you get me down?' Summer's hand was already on her harness, her gaze on the winch cable that would need to be attached.

'Bit dodgy...' Monty's tone was a warning. 'You sure about this, Summer?'

'No.' It was Zac who spoke—the word an appalled exclamation. 'I'll go down.'

'The coastguard's not far away,' Monty said. 'They'll be able to get someone on board.'

'My brother's down there,' Summer responded. She surprised herself with how calm she sounded. 'He's just a kid. He must be terrified.' She caught Zac's gaze and held it. Flashing through her head was the memory of the last time they had faced the possibility of a tricky winch job—when they'd been called to that young forestry worker with the chest injury. When the question of how much she really trusted Zac had been raised. When she'd known how much she *wanted* to trust him and she'd wanted the chance to demonstrate that trust. Wanted the kind of bond that could only be forged by meeting—and winning—a life-threatening challenge.

She should have been careful what she'd wished for...

But here it was.

'Please, Zac...' Her voice was almost a whisper but seemed magnified by both the internal microphone system and the desperate plea in her tone. 'I need you to winch me down.'

He didn't want to do it. She could feel the strength of how much he didn't want the responsibility of her life dangling on the end of a wire. Trying to time the descent so that she didn't meet the deck of the boat as it came up on a rising swell. She could break her legs. Get tangled on the mast. Smash her head against the side of the boat...

He could refuse and that would be an end to it.

But he knew how much she needed to do this.

And he had to know she would only ask because she trusted him completely.

'Okay...' The word was almost a groan. 'I'll do it.'

It was possible to lock into his training and keep things completely professional up until the moment when Summer stepped off the skid to dangle in the air below the helicopter. Monty had just as much responsibility for keeping her safe but it felt as if he had her life in his hands.

And he couldn't let anything happen to threaten that.

Right now, the pain of knowing she had doubted his word was utterly irrelevant. She was trusting him with her life.

And he *loved* her...

How could he have even believed for a moment that he would prefer to live without her in his life?

Nothing mattered other than keeping her safe. Keeping Dylan safe. Even keeping Flint safe because Summer loved him.

And he loved her...

The tense minutes of the descent had sweat trickling down his spine beneath the layers of safety gear.

'Minus six metres.' Summer sounded remarkably calm. 'Five...four...no, five...'

It was so hard to judge with depth perception changed by the artificial light, let alone the heaving sea changing the actual distance. They had to time the swells and wait for the moment when they could—hopefully—get the meeting of Summer's body and the solid deck of the boat exactly right.

And, somehow, they did.

There was an awful moment as Summer fell on landing and slipped across the sloping deck. It looked as if she would go overboard or potentially get caught and he would have to fire the charge that would cut the cable and prevent the helicopter being pulled from the sky. How had she managed to find a handhold and release her connection to the cable at the same time? But there she was, clinging to a handrail and holding the cable clear as she gave the signal to wind it back in.

'Take it up, Zac...' Her words were a breathless but relieved statement. 'I'm good.' He must have imagined the grin because he couldn't possibly see from this distance, but he could still hear the words despite how quiet they were. 'Thanks, mate...'

And then she disappeared into the interior of the yacht and, only seconds later, the lights of the coastguard boat could be seen approaching. There was nothing more that the helicopter crew could do except provide light as another difficult mission was launched to take the disabled *Mermaid* under tow and get her back to safety.

It was over.

Every bone in Summer's body ached.

Her heart ached now, too. For a while, she had forgotten the finality of the way Zac had looked at her when they'd been in the emergency department with Shelley and Felix.

Fear had taken over. And then the adrenaline rush of the rescue mission. By the time the *Mermaid* had been safely towed into port, the helicopter had long since landed, which was just as well as the storm had well and truly broken. Dramatic forks of lightning and crashing thunder were a background for getting Dylan safely back to the hospital and his father.

He stayed glued to Summer's side as they walked towards the ward.

'Dad's going to be so mad at me, isn't he?'

'No. He's going to be too relieved that you're okay. Like I am.'

The look that passed between them acknowledged the bond that had been forged under circumstances neither of them could ever forget. In the moment she had climbed into *Mermaid*'s cabin to find a terrified boy crouched in a corner with his arms tightly around a big black dog and she had put her own arms around both of them for a long wordless hug.

There were more hugs in that hospital room. And words of reassurance from both Jon and Summer that Dylan wasn't being banished. That they were a family now and nothing was going to be allowed to break that.

Yes. A poignant joy had taken over from the fear.

The dramatic start of the storm had settled into steady,

drenching rain by the time Summer and Flint were given a ride home by Monty, who had come to pick them up from the coastguard's base.

And it was then that Summer realised she had no home to go to. The *Mermaid* couldn't be towed back to her marina until the weather improved.

'Come home with me,' Monty said. 'We can collect your gear from the boat tomorrow.'

But Summer shook her head. Because the fear had returned. The overwhelming relief that her brother and her dog were safe was wearing off. The joy of knowing she had a real family again was also being pushed into the background. What if she had lost Zac from her life? She hadn't seen him for hours now. Hadn't heard from him either, but then her phone had got wet during that rough ride back on the coastguard vessel and it was completely dead.

As dead as that dreadful message in the look that Zac had given her when she'd been seeking reassurance? As dead as the future she had started to dream of? One that had included children that they would take to the beach and build sandcastles with. Teach them to paddleboard so that they could stand up one day and wave at their great-grandmother, who would be watching from her deck.

Ivy...

The yearning for the kind of wisdom and warmth and humour that only Ivy Mitchell could dispense was suddenly overwhelming.

'I need to go to Takapuna,' she told Monty quietly. 'Down by the beach. I'll show you which house.'

The rain was so heavy that both she and Flint had runnels of water cascading off them by the time the knock on Ivy's door was answered.

Not by Ivy.

It was Zac who wrenched the door open but that was

all he did. He simply stood there, staring at her. She could see the breaking tension in his face. Relief. *Love...?*

'For heaven's sake, Isaac...what are you *thinking*? Get them inside...' Ivy tugged her grandson away from the door. 'Come in, darling. Oh, my goodness. You're completely *soaked...*'

Flint stayed where he was as Summer moved.

'You too,' Ivy ordered and Flint stepped cautiously onto the polished floorboards, puddles gathering under every paw. 'I'll get towels. Isaac, take Summer downstairs to your place. She needs a shower.' She waited until they were both at the head of the internal staircase, Summer's hand tightly encased in Zac's. 'And a proper hug,' she called after them. 'Don't forget your manners. I'll see you both in the morning.'

It was an instruction they should both have been able to laugh about as soon as they closed the door to the rest of the world behind them but neither of them was even smiling.

Zac pulled Summer into his arms and held her so tightly she couldn't breathe.

'Don't ever scare me like that again,' he growled. 'I thought.... Oh, my God... I thought I was going to lose you.'

It didn't seem to matter that he was getting wet. Or that she couldn't breathe. The hope that this meant Zac still loved her as much as she loved him was enough to survive on. Summer never wanted to move. She wanted to feel his heart beating against her cheek like this and feel his arms around her like the strongest, safest protection ever.

It was Zac who released the hold enough to move and see her face.

'Are you okay? You didn't get hurt?'

'I'm fine.'

'And Dylan?'

'He got the fright of his life but he's okay, too. He's with Dad—waiting to get taken back to the west coast tonight.'

The breath that Zac released was a long sigh. 'And Flint's good. He'll get dried off and we'll be lucky if there's any bacon for us at breakfast. That's all that matters.' His mouth quirked into a crooked smile. 'I'm not sure what Gravy meant by a "proper" hug but a hug is not quite what I'm thinking about right now.'

Summer's gaze dropped from those gorgeous dark eyes to the mouth that she loved almost as much. Her eyes drifted shut as her lips parted to murmur agreement but the only sound that emerged was a whimper of need as Zac's lips found hers.

And, for a very long time after that, the need for a shower or anything else was completely forgotten.

It was a time for a reunion—both physical and emotional. A time to celebrate a bond that could survive testing times and only become deeper.

Stronger.

A time for the kind of honesty that provided the glue for that kind of bond.

'I'm sorry I doubted you,' Summer whispered in the quiet hours of the night, as she lay in the warmth of Zac's embrace. 'It was only for a moment.'

'You weren't the only one.'

'Everybody knows the truth now. And I don't think it was about Felix that made me feel that way. I just couldn't help feeling that there was *something* you hadn't told me.'

'There was.' Zac was silent for a long moment. 'Because it's something I've never told anyone. Nobody knows, except for Gravy. I don't even like thinking about it.'

Summer waited out the new silence. Only her fingers

moved where they lay splayed on his chest—an almost imperceptible caress of encouragement. She was being invited into possibly the most private part of Zac's life, here.

'It wasn't the accusation that I was the father of Shelley's baby that shocked me the most,' Zac told her. 'It was the idea that I could have pushed her down any stairs. My stepfather...he was abusive. Violent. I could never hurt a woman. *Ever...*'

'I know that,' Summer said softly. She pressed her lips against the soft skin close to her face. 'I couldn't trust you any more than I do now. I love you so much.'

'Not as much as I love *you*.' Another soft sigh escaped Zac. 'So much I can't begin to find the words.' He moved, bending his head so that he could place another tender kiss onto Summer's lips. A kiss that was enough to move them onto a new space. One that accepted the past and made it part of a foundation instead of a barrier.

'Gravy's got a dream,' he told her then. 'She wants to live long enough to throw confetti at our wedding and drink too much champagne at the reception. She wants dogs tracking sand into the house and babies playing in the garden and on the beach. She even mentioned a paddleboard or two propped up by the shed.'

'Ohh...' Summer was smiling but she could feel tears gathering in her eyes.

Tears of joy.

'You like that idea too?'

The question was almost shy.

'It sounds like the best idea *I've* ever heard.' It seemed an effort to draw in a new breath and it seemed as if the whole world was holding it with her. 'Do you?'

She didn't really need to ask. She could feel the answer in the way Zac was holding her. The way he pressed his lips against her hair.

But it was still good to hear the words. So, *so* good…
'I don't think I could come up with a better one.' But
then his voice took on a wicked edge as his lips found hers
yet again. 'Or maybe I can,' he murmured. 'Just for now…'

* * * * *

THE DOCTOR
SHE'D NEVER FORGET

BY
ANNIE CLAYDON

Published in Great Britain 2015
by Mills & Boon, an imprint of Harlequin (UK) Limited,
Eton House, 18-24 Paradise Road, Richmond, Surrey, TW9 1SR

© 2015 Annie Claydon

ISBN: 978-0-263-24730-5

Harlequin (UK) Limited's policy is to use papers that are natural,
renewable and recyclable products and made from wood grown in
sustainable forests. The logging and manufacturing processes conform
to the legal environmental regulations of the country of origin.

Printed and bound in Spain
by CPI, Barcelona

Dear Reader,

There are times when being a writer gives me the opportunity to have a great deal of fun. Sophie Warner's part in a film set in the 1940s meant I needed to know something about the costumes she might wear. And how better to find out than to ask two ladies whose memories stretch way back? I owe a big thank-you to Joan and Betty, who told me everything I needed to know—along with some funny stories that I don't dare repeat! Thanks also to Lynne, for bringing both laughter and cake.

It makes me smile just to think of that morning. As I wrote this book I came to understand how much I define myself by the things I remember. Sophie's traumatic brain injury has deprived her of the ability to retain all her memories. Some aren't important, but what happens when you can't remember the name of the man you might be falling in love with? And how can she defend herself when she doesn't remember those compromising pictures on the internet ever being taken?

It's not easy for Drew Taylor either. A love affair is all about memories—the first time you kissed, that first touch. He's not sure how he would cope if Sophie were to wake in the morning with no idea of what had happened the night before.

Thank you for reading Drew and Sophie's story. I always enjoy hearing from readers, and you can contact me via my website at annieclaydon.com.

Annie x

To my dear friend Betty

Books by Annie Claydon

Mills & Boon® Medical Romance™

Snowbound with the Surgeon
A Doctor to Heal Her Heart
200 Harley Street: The Enigmatic Surgeon
Once Upon a Christmas Night...
Re-awakening His Shy Nurse
The Rebel and Miss Jones
The Doctor Meets Her Match
Doctor on Her Doorstep
All She Wants For Christmas
Daring to Date Her Ex

**Please visit the author profile page at
millsandboon.co.uk for more titles**

**Praise for
Annie Claydon**

'A compelling, emotional and highly poignant read
that I couldn't bear to put down. Rich in pathos,
humour and dramatic intensity, it's a spellbinding
tale about healing old wounds, having the courage
to listen to your heart and the power of love that
kept me enthralled from beginning to end.'

—GoodReads on
Once Upon a Christmas Night...

'Well-written, brilliant characters—I have never been
disappointed by a book written by Annie Claydon.'

—GoodReads on
The Rebel and Miss Jones

CHAPTER ONE

FIVE MILES FELT a lot further than it had used to. The final hundred yards of Drew Taylor's morning run left him feeling dizzy and sick from exertion.

'Morning.'

If he hadn't been so keen to gulp down a pint of water and collapse into a chair, Drew would have noticed the canary-yellow sports car parked across the street from his house and reckoned that Charlie would be around somewhere. As it was, the voice behind him came as a surprise.

'Morning...' Now that he'd reached his destination, Drew's body gave up and bent double, his lungs craving air.

'You're out of shape, old man.'

'Very probably. Is that what you came to tell me?' Drew gripped his knees, staring hard at the paving stones at his feet, gasping for air.

'Nah.' Charlie shrugged and waited until Drew had recovered sufficiently to let them into the house. 'I have a proposition for you.'

Charlie's propositions were liable to get him into trouble. Their friendship had lasted since their university days on the basis that Drew was choosy about which of them he took seriously. 'What?'

'Hydrate first. You look as if you need it.'

'That sounds ominous.'

'Nah. This one's a stroke of genius.'

'Yeah. They always are.' Drew poured himself a glass of water, while Charlie flipped open the kitchen cupboard, looking for coffee.

'You've only got one coffee pod left.'

Drew shrugged. 'Take it. I'm not drinking coffee at the moment.'

Charlie twisted the edges of his mouth down, and put the pod into the machine. 'Not sleeping?'

'I'm not used to doing nothing…' Drew took a mouthful of water. That was only half the story and they both knew it.

It was his own stupid fault that he was stuck at home with nothing to do. When the hospital he'd worked in—actually lived for—had first been threatened with closure, Drew had spearheaded the campaign to keep it open. It had been a two-year struggle, culminating in failure and defeat.

When he'd finally faced the inevitable, and begun to look for another job, he'd landed one with relative ease. Head of a new memory clinic in London, which was due to open in three months' time. In any other circumstances it would have been the job that Drew's dreams were made of but now it was tainted by loss, and he was having difficulty working up much enthusiasm for it.

'You'll be thanking me in a minute, then.' Charlie smiled beatifically.

Drew gave up. When Charlie got hold of an idea, he didn't let go. They weren't always good ideas, but enough of them had been great to make his friend a millionaire before his thirtieth birthday.

'Okay. What am I going to be thanking you for?'

'Someone I know has asked me for a favour, and I think it could work out perfectly for you. It's a job...'

'I have a job, remember?'

'This is temporary. It's a fantastic opportunity to get away from it all, take a bit of a break. Two weeks, a month tops...' Charlie stopped, pressing his lips together. 'This is absolutely top secret. Totally confidential and between ourselves.'

Generally Charlie's idea of confidential was that it didn't get as far as the newspapers quite yet, but it appeared this really was a secret. Drew chuckled. 'Understood.'

'Okay. Well, you've heard of Sophie Warner?'

Drew thought for a moment. The name rang a bell, but he couldn't place it. 'I don't think so.'

Charlie rolled his eyes. 'She's a big star. Gorgeous. Didn't you see *MacAdam* on TV?'

'I doubt it. Look, I'll take it as read. Sophie Warner, brightest star in the firmament. What's that got to do with me?'

'Well, a friend of mine from America has contacted me. Carly's an assistant director and she's known Sophie Warner for years, since before she was famous. The two of them are working on a film together down in Devon at the moment.'

Friends of friends of friends. In Charlie's world it was all about who you knew, not what you knew. Drew bit back the comment, reckoning that Charlie would get to the point quicker if he didn't interrupt.

'So they did the first lot of filming over here last winter. Just caught that heavy fall of snow we had, which was a bonus, and everything went like clockwork. Now they're back again to do the summer scenes, and they've run into trouble.'

'What kind of trouble?' Drew couldn't think of anything that his particular skills might help with on a film set. Apart from an outbreak of food poisoning, and a local doctor could deal with that.

'There's something the matter with Sophie. She's acting like a diva—tantrums on set, turning up late, not learning her lines. She's had a load of bad press in the last couple of months...' Charlie shook his head. 'We won't go into that.'

It must be very bad if Charlie's sense of discretion had kicked in. The woman sounded like a nightmare. 'And what's that got to do with me? I'm a neurologist, not a minder for spoilt children.'

'That's just the thing. Carly knows Sophie and she swears that this is not just the usual film star bad behaviour. She's sticking her neck out here, and putting her own job on the line to protect Sophie, because she thinks there's something wrong with her.'

'What sort of something?'

Charlie rolled his eyes. 'If we knew that, we wouldn't ask you, would we? Apparently Sophie was in a car accident a few months back and she just hasn't been right since. She's been shutting herself away for days, running off no one knows where. You get the picture...'

The picture was becoming horribly clear. 'And your friend wants me to go down there and examine an errant film star, to see if I can come up with some medical excuse for her bad behaviour?'

'No.' Drew heaved a sigh of relief. 'Carly's already tried to get Sophie to go to a doctor and she won't have any of it. Sophie's playing a doctor in this film and so Carly wants to take you on as a set medical advisor. So you can watch Sophie and see if there really is anything wrong with her.'

'What? You *have* to be joking...' Drew drained his glass, setting it down on the kitchen counter with a crack. 'I can't do that, Charlie. It's an ethical minefield.'

'No, it's not. I've seen you step into situations before without being asked. What about that time you bundled my gran into the car and took her up to the hospital?'

'She was having a series of mini-strokes, Charlie. That's completely different.'

'No, it's not. You saw something that no one else could see, and you acted on it.'

'Yeah, and Doris isn't some wild child looking for excuses.'

Charlie shot Drew an outraged look. 'So it's okay if it's my gran, because nice little old ladies deserve your attention, is that it? You're far too eminent in your field to bother with people who might be a bit awkward.'

'No, of course not. You know me better than that, Charlie.'

'It'd be a challenge...'

Charlie knew exactly what buttons to press. He always had with Drew.

'Look, even if you could just talk to Carly, as a friend. Convince her to think about her own career for a moment and not let this Sophie character drag her down with her. I'd count it as a personal favour. At the very least it'll be a couple of days out of town to clear your head. And the bike could do with a bit of a run.'

The thought of garaging the car, and just getting on his motorbike and riding somewhere, anywhere, seemed suddenly like a plan to Drew. Alone, on the open road, he might just be able to leave the bitterness over a past that couldn't be changed behind him.

'All right. I'll talk to Carly.' He sighed. 'You'd better tell me whereabouts in Devon I'm supposed to be going.'

* * *

To give Charlie his due, everything had gone like clock-work. When he arrived at the comfortable country hotel, the receptionist was expecting him and directed him straight up to a sunny room, overlooking a nearby golf course.

He dropped his overnight bag on the bed. The drive down here had given him time to think. He'd seen this world, or one very like it, before. People who didn't say what they meant. People who pretended to be one thing when, in fact, they were another. Beautiful people, like Gina, who had taken a young doctor's heart and squeezed it hard until it had felt empty of anything but pain.

He was older now, and a great deal wiser. He'd talk to Charlie's friend, make her see sense and go back to London in the morning. No real need to even unpack. Drew was halfway to the bathroom when a knock sounded on the door.

'Carly DeAngelo.' A young woman with dark curls, an American accent, and a no-nonsense air held her hand out for a brief handshake. 'I really appreciate your coming all this way.'

'My pleasure.' It seemed that Charlie had already alerted Carly that he was coming and there was no need to seek her out.

'Is it okay if we get together in half an hour? I've got another meeting later on this evening.'

That would be more than enough time to take a shower and change out of his grime-stained clothes. 'That's fine. I'll meet you downstairs.'

Carly nodded. 'Ask for the Blue Room. I'll get them to bring us something to eat.'

The Blue Room turned out to be a small, private

dining room, overlooking the sea. The highly polished table was set with heavy silver cutlery and Drew moved the centrepiece of dried flowers before he sat down. He had a feeling that eye-to-eye contact was going to be necessary to persuade Carly that this arrangement really was a bad idea.

'I'm afraid I'm going to have to ask you to sign this.' Carly extracted some stapled sheets of paper from a bulging portfolio she'd brought with her, and pushed them across the table towards him. 'It's a confidentiality agreement.'

That was fine. Drew didn't intend to even think about this after tonight, let alone talk about it. He picked up the pen that Carly had placed ready, and she shook her head. 'Read it first.'

Drew read the pages carefully and signed. 'Now we can talk.'

The appearance of a waiter put the moment off. Carly ignored the menu and ordered a salad, and Drew decided that he was too hungry to bother with food that could be picked at during the course of a conversation and ordered steak and chips. He wasn't considering saying much anyway. *No* just about covered it.

'Charlie's told you a bit about this.' She waited for the waiter to close the door behind himself before she spoke.

'He's told me that you're worried about your friend. That her behaviour's been erratic recently and she won't see a doctor.'

'Yeah. I'm a third assistant director here...' Drew raised a querying eyebrow, and Carly smiled. 'That sounds a bit more important than it is. I'm pretty low on the pecking order. Sophie helped me get the job and when we were over here last winter, doing the first lot of shooting, everything went really well.'

'And now you're back, things have changed?'

'Yeah. Joel, the director, knows that Sophie and I are close, and he's assigned me to her in the hope that I can get her under control a bit. But it's just impossible. The film world's a very small one, and no one's going to touch her when she's finished here if she's not careful.'

First things first. He wasn't a career consultant. 'If you think your friend is ill, then my first advice to you, or to her for that matter, is that she sees a doctor.'

'You're a doctor. If you stay here for a couple of weeks, then you'll see Sophie all the time.'

'I can't make any kind of diagnosis by just looking at someone. It doesn't work that way.'

'But you could tell me what you think. What the best way to proceed is. Charlie says you're a neurologist, you must be able to recognise the symptoms…'

'The symptoms of what?'

Carly flushed, looking down at her hands. 'Sophie was in a car accident about four months ago, when we went back to the States after we were here last winter. She hit her head, the side of her face was all bruised up…' Her hand wandered to her own temple and along the side of her jaw.

'And she saw a doctor after the accident?'

'Yes, she was taken to the hospital. They looked her over, X-rayed her, gave her some painkillers and released her. Told her to come back again if there were any problems.'

'And did she?'

'No. She called me and said she was going away for a holiday, and she disappeared completely for a couple of weeks. When she got back she was…different. She's vague, and defensive, and… She's just not Sophie any more.'

It was obvious what Carly was thinking. Drew knew that this wouldn't be the first case of traumatic brain injury that had been overlooked in a general examination after an accident, and imagined it wouldn't be the last. If TBI *was* what they were dealing with here.

'I have to ask you this. Are you aware of her being involved with drink or drugs at all?'

Carly's mouth twisted. 'You've been reading the scandal sheets, haven't you.'

'No. I'd ask that question of anyone.' Maybe not quite anyone. Drew rejected the thought that it had been a little higher on the list than usual.

'She drinks a glass of wine with dinner sometimes, that's all. And it's not drugs.' Carly flashed him a defiant look. 'I'd know.'

'Would you?'

'I've been around this business long enough. I'm not stupid. For a start…'

Carly bent her little finger back, as if she was about to give a list of all the signs of drug abuse, and then swallowed her words as the waiter entered with their food.

'Something to drink?'

Drew was about to say no. It was early enough to eat and then get back on his bike and go—he'd be home by midnight. Then he caught sight of the tears brimming in Carly's eyes.

'A glass of house red would be great. Thanks.'

Carly nodded, and ordered the house white for herself. 'She's not using drugs. I'd swear to it. She doesn't even take painkillers when she has a headache, just shuts herself away in her trailer.'

'She has headaches?'

'Yeah. Fewer than she says, sometimes she just

doesn't want to talk to anyone, but there are times when she's telling the truth.'

How was Carly so sure? Drew's experience of show business was limited to a couple of photographic shoots he'd been to with Gina, but his impression then had been that everyone treated the truth as if it was an optional extra. Gina had confirmed those suspicions herself, by lying to him with startling aptitude.

The waiter returned with their drinks, and Drew took a sip from his glass. At the back of his mind it registered that it was a very good red, and he took another swallow. 'Look, Carly...'

'Don't. Please don't tell me you can't help because I know that you can. Please...' Carly picked up her glass with a shaking hand and then put it down again and blew her nose on her napkin.

Perhaps Charlie had tipped her the wink that tears would help her case. Drew rejected the unworthy thought and apologised silently to his friend. Lying and manipulation were Gina's style, not Charlie's.

'Okay. What do you want me to do?' He could at least listen.

'I've got the okay to employ a medical consultant on set. I said that it might help Sophie and right now the director would try just about anything to get her to pull herself together.'

'I understand that she plays a doctor in the film.'

'Yes. It's set in 1944...' Carly pulled a large, spiral-bound document from her portfolio before Drew had a chance to object that he knew nothing about historical medical techniques.

'We've got this manual, written by an eminent medical historian. That'll help you. And injuries are injuries, so you won't have any trouble talking to the special effects guys about making them look authentic.'

'But you've managed this far…?' Drew picked his knife and fork up, in a signal that none of this held any water, and he was going to eat. The knife sliced through the tender, succulent steak as if it were butter.

'We had a set consultant when we were here last winter, but we didn't reckon we needed anyone this time around because there's less medical emphasis. But when I told the director it might help Sophie, he agreed like a shot. No one cares about the cost of it, we're talking a multi-million-dollar project here.'

Drew wondered what those many millions might have done, applied a little more usefully. Kept his old hospital open maybe. 'Even assuming I take the job, I can't do what you ask, Carly. The thing that will really help Miss Warner is to see a doctor, in a professional setting.'

Carly's stricken look would have made Drew relent if he hadn't been so sure that he was right. 'Okay, then. What *does* work for you?'

'What works for me is that I go back to London in the morning. If you want set advice, you get in touch with someone who's interested in that kind of thing. And if you want advice on Miss Warner's condition, you persuade her to go and see a doctor.'

Carly thought for a moment. 'That makes sense. Now, given that Sophie's adamant that she won't see a doctor, and that I'm out of options and pretty desperate, is there anything else you can suggest?'

It was a straight question, with an easy enough answer. 'I could stay on for a day. I'd be happy to meet with Miss Warner and try to persuade her.'

'And she'll say no, and then you'll walk away. Job's

done as far as you're concerned and nothing changes.'
Carly's lip curled in contempt.

'That's not...' Drew swallowed his words. It was exactly how it was. He was the one engaging in half-truths and excuses, not Carly. If he didn't want this job, he should just say so.

But he couldn't. However unlikely his role here and despite the fact that it wasn't going to push the boundaries of medical science, it was somehow intriguing. Did he even have the right to call himself a doctor if he chose to turn his back now?

'If I decided to do it, and I haven't yet, there'd be conditions.'

'Fair enough. I want you to tell me how to do this, not the other way around.' Carly nodded him on, obviously aware that she'd found a chink in his armour.

'I'm not Miss Warner's doctor. I'm not going to guess at a diagnosis and I'm not going to report back to you on anything. If I have any concerns, I'll speak only to her about them and advise she gets proper medical help.'

'Just advising isn't going to get you anywhere. Do you plan on being a bit more assertive than that...?'

Carly's gaze met his and Drew held it for a moment. 'What do you think? Do I seem assertive enough to you?'

'Yeah. You do.' She stretched her hand out towards Drew. 'We have a deal, then?'

CHAPTER TWO

THE NEGOTIATIONS HADN'T quite finished there. Drew had insisted that a week was quite enough for them both to see whether or not the arrangement would work. For her part, Carly had vetoed his intention of returning to London the following day to pack for the week and suggested he let Charlie throw some things into a bag for him, for the set runners to collect. When he'd acquiesced, Carly had produced a contract, written in the dates by hand, and given it to Drew.

Armed with four hours' sleep, and the knowledge that he might well have signed away his sanity for the next week, Drew was on the bus with a sleepy film crew at six the following morning. Carly had told him to consider today as an orientation exercise, and Drew was more than content to maintain a watching brief.

'Five dollars on ten o'clock.' An American accent sounded from the seat behind him.

'I'm not taking dollars. I'll give you three quid that it's closer to eleven.' A woman's voice this time, speaking in a laughing, London drawl.

'You're on.' Silence for a moment and then a chuckle. 'C'mon, Madame Sophie. If you get outta that bed now, Dawn'll have to buy me coffee.'

'In your dreams. She'll have to disentangle herself

from last night's waiter and wait for the uppers to kick in.' Dawn yawned loudly. 'It's not fair...'

'You had your eye on a night of passion with one of the waiters, did you?'

'No.' Dawn scoffed at the idea. 'If *we* turned up four hours late we'd get the sack. *She* does it, and Joel's all over her, grateful that she's made it at all.'

'She's the star. We can be replaced, she can't.'

'True enough. Though we've still careers when this job is finished. I'd like to be a fly on the wall when she tries for her next part.'

Drew stared straight in front of him. If this was true, then Sophie Warner was more of a nightmare than he'd reckoned. If not... The remote chance that Carly was right suddenly seemed worth taking. If Sophie *was* sick, and she continued to keep quiet about it, then things were only going to get worse.

The bus drew into a cluster of vehicles parked at the end of what looked like the main street of a small village.

'Looks as if you owe me that coffee, Dawn...' Drew couldn't help but look out of the window, in response to the voice behind him. 'She's here already.'

'Yeah, she's not going to be ready for a while. Look, she's on her way to her trailer. What's the betting she'll stay in there for another four hours?'

Drew saw Carly walking towards a group of trailers with another woman. Small and blonde, almost swamped in the large mackintosh she was wearing against the morning's chill air. They disappeared in between two of the vehicles and he craned his neck to see where they'd gone but he couldn't.

The set began to come alive for the day, and Drew maintained his watching brief. Before long, a concentrated buzz of movement centred around the main street of the village, which was a meticulous re-creation of wartime England. Further out, people in period costume mingled with the crew, almost as if the scene was dissolving, melting back into the present day.

From his vantage point, sitting in a fold-up chair at the edge of the activity, Drew suddenly saw a blonde head at the centre of it all, around which the whole shebang seemed suddenly to revolve. He looked at his watch. Eight-thirty. It looked as if Dawn was going to be paying for coffee today.

At lunchtime, the privileged few made for the group of trailers, and everyone else made a rush for the catering truck. Drew decided to wait until the scrum had died down a bit and flipped open the pages of his book.

'Hello.' Someone interrupted his reading, and Drew turned into the gaze of the greenest pair of eyes he'd ever seen. Shiny blonde hair, pinned in a wavy arrangement that was reminiscent of his grandmother's, but to quite a different effect. A dark skirt and a white blouse, under a lacy hand-knitted sweater.

'Sophie Warner.' She was looking at him as if he was a mere diversion, in the absence of anyone more interesting to talk to. 'You're the new medical consultant.'

Now that she wasn't half-obscured by distance and the milling entourage of people, he recognised her face from somewhere. Probably the TV, when he'd thought he'd only been half watching it. But he couldn't have been watching at all because it hadn't registered that she was gorgeous.

Drew smiled at her. Despite her obvious indifference to him, it was surprisingly easy to do. 'That's right. Drew Taylor.'

She nodded, as if there wasn't much more to say.

Drew stood, and pulled an empty chair across the grass for her and she looked at it uncertainly and then sat down.

'Nice to meet you…um…'

'Drew.'

She gave a little nod. 'I'm not very good with names.'

Clearly that was an excuse. But whether it covered a lapse in memory or profound disinterest in him, it was impossible to tell.

'Have you been watching this morning?'

'Yes.' Drew gestured to the copy of the script that Carly had supplied him with. 'You're not filming this in the same order that it's on the page, are you?'

'No, we're not. We go to one location, shoot all the scenes we need to do there, and then move on to the next.' She gave a little shrug.

'That sounds pretty confusing.'

Her mouth hardened suddenly. 'I'm a professional. It's part of the job.'

'Yes. Of course.' Drew had known that it would be difficult to get through to Sophie Warner. What he hadn't expected was that he'd want to, so very much.

'So have you worked out what the story's about yet?' The canvas chair creaked slightly as she settled back into her seat. Her face took on a look of composed interest, which gave Drew the distinct impression that she was doing exactly the same as he was, and prolonging the conversation in order to fish for information.

'Your character is Dr Jean Wilson, and you work at a hospital in a seaside town. Major Alan Richards is an engineer, working on a top-secret project, building and testing a new submarine. Dr Wilson meets Major Richards when she gets involved with treating some of the men who are injured during testing.'

'That's right. Only it's called a submersible. A submarine's usually bigger and can work on its own, but a submersible needs to have an outside supply of power and air.'

'Right. I'll remember that.'

'I suppose you must specialise in accident and emergency medicine.' She hardly even acknowledged his querying look. 'Since that's the kind of thing we're portraying in the film.'

A yes would have been enough. But if Drew wanted her to trust him, then it wasn't the way forward. 'I'm actually a neurologist, but I was a member of the hospital's trauma team. I have plenty of experience of all kinds of injuries, so I'm well qualified to advise here.'

'Neurology.' It was interesting that she picked on that one word. For a moment her composure faltered and then she shot him a smile, soft enough to break the strongest man, and clearly calculated to make Drew forget what she'd just let slip. 'It sounds important.'

'Yeah. I'm taking a break from important at the moment.'

Her face hardened suddenly and Drew regretted the words. He hadn't been thinking, and he'd let his prejudices show. That wasn't going to encourage any confidence on Sophie's part.

'Why?' She almost snapped the word at him.

'The hospital where I worked closed last month. I'm taking some time to look at my options for the future.'

'I'm sorry to hear that. It must have been a painful time for you.' Suddenly the ice cracked and the look of concern on her face seemed meltingly genuine. Drew reminded himself that Sophie was an actress. However beautiful she was, however much she made him long to make her smile, it was all an illusion.

He searched for something else to say. He didn't want to talk about the hospital or the closure, or how much it had hurt. They were real things, and they had no place here. 'Your English accent is very good.'

'I should hope so. I *am* English.' She waved away his apology. 'It's okay. A lot of people who saw me in *Mac-Adam* assume that I'm American.'

'The TV cop show? I saw the trailers.'

She gave him an amused look. 'Have you seen anything I've been in?'

'I...' Drew gave up the unequal struggle, remembering that his first task was to gain her trust, not impress her. 'I haven't had much time for TV recently, I've been pretty busy. Are you going to be making another series?'

'What?' Her sudden glassy-eyed look turned quickly into a frown.

'Another series.' Drew deliberately didn't proffer any more information. If she'd lost the thread of the conversation, he wanted to see if she could pick it up again, without prompting.

'How would *I* know?' She made it sound as if this was a detail that didn't warrant her attention.

'I just thought you might.'

'Well, you thought wrong.' She'd scanned his face, as if looking for clues, and then the frown gave way to a don't-mess-with-me glare. Sophie got abruptly to her feet and stalked away from him.

Drew watched her go. As soon as she'd put thirty yards between them her pace slowed a little, almost as if she'd calculated that she was now at a safe distance. Her angry movements gave way to a more graceful rhythm and Drew forced himself to forget the way her waist moved, and consider dispassionately whether she showed any signs of impaired co-ordination.

Nothing. She carried her beauty in a different way from Gina. Gina had known she was beautiful and had used it to wind Drew around her little finger, rock his world, and then smash it. But Sophie dealt her bewitching smiles carefully, playing her cards close to her chest. It occurred to Drew that it was a far more effective form of enchantment, and a great deal more dangerous.

She shouldn't have done that. Snapping at him and walking away only drew attention to the fact that her mind had suddenly blanked, right in the middle of a conversation. She should have thought of something clever to say to change the subject.

Clever was a bit beyond her at the moment. But she knew enough to know that no medical scenes this morning meant they didn't need a medical consultant, and Sophie had wanted to find out what he was really here for. And somewhere, hidden deep in those cool grey eyes, she'd found it. A spark of knowingness, as if he already knew the secret that no one else did.

'Forget it.' She muttered the words to herself, smiling grimly at the thought that forgetting came far too easily to her these days. People could, and would, suspect anything they pleased. If she didn't confirm those suspicions, they were nothing but idle speculation.

Carly was sitting on the steps leading up to the door of her trailer, basking in the midday sun. 'Where have you been, Soph?'

'I met the doctor.'

'Yeah? What's he like?'

'Good looking.' Sophie had always liked dark hair and light eyes in a man. 'Very good looking, actually. I don't think he approves of us much, though.'

'Why, because he's a doctor? Just because your

father disapproves, it doesn't necessarily follow that *all* doctors disapprove.'

What followed or didn't follow was more than Sophie could think about at the moment. And she didn't want to think about her father either.

'He might just be shy. He's new here…' Carly warmed to her point.

'No. He's not shy.' Those grey eyes, the assessing gaze had been anything but that.

'Perhaps you are, then. You said he was good look-ing.' Carly shrugged, betraying a slight unease with the gesture.

'I don't know what he's doing here today. There's nothing medical in the script.'

'Forget it. Just sit back and enjoy the scenery.'

'You'll enjoy it with me?' If Carly was around, per-haps the effect of the doctor's all-too-knowing gaze would be diluted a little.

Carly grinned. 'Sorry. Can't help you with that. I've only got one piece of male scenery on my mind, and he's back in the States.'

'So sweet. I'll tell Mark you said that.' Sophie smiled. Mark and Carly were solid, best friends, lovers… Just the sort of thing that she had dared to hope for with Josh. Everyone had told her that he was a risk, that he was a little more in love with her fame than he was with her, and Sophie had refused to believe it of him. But just when she'd been at her most vulnerable, Josh had dealt his most crushing blow.

Carly chuckled, opening the door of the trailer. In-side, the table was set for two, and lunch was waiting for them, the paper cups and plates of the catering truck banished in favour of china and glass. Sophie almost en-vied the altogether simpler life of rushing for a place in the queue, chatting with the film crew about the morning's work.

'Carly...'

'Yes?'

Wordlessly, Sophie hugged her friend. How could it be that one secret could erode almost everything between them? She missed being able to talk to Carly about everything, but even her closest friends were an unknown quantity these days. And Sophie knew that if she said anything, Carly would only tell her what she didn't want to hear, and insist she go for a check-up with a doctor.

'What's this for?' Carly was clinging to her tightly.

'Nothing. Does it have to be for something?' Sophie gave a final squeeze of her arms around Carly's shoulders and then let go. 'Come on. Let's eat.'

After the noise and chatter of the bus back to the hotel, Drew savoured the quiet of his hotel room for ten minutes, then opened his laptop and typed Sophie's name into the search engine. Maybe if he could watch a couple of episodes of *MacAdam* online, he'd get more of a feel for how Sophie had been before the accident. He wasn't convinced about that—after all she was an actress, playing a part—but he'd be damned if he'd admit to himself that he just wanted to see more of her.

It seemed that the internet knew all about Sophie. Her own website had pictures, a biography and a list of her acting roles, and Drew studied them carefully. Drama school and then some theatre work. She'd done Shakespeare, had small parts in a couple of blindingly awful films, and received critical acclaim for her last three films and for *MacAdam*. If it was even half-true, Sophie Warner wasn't all tantrums and bad behaviour.

The bad behaviour was there as well, though. When Drew clicked again, there were reports of reckless driving, an exposé by an ex-boyfriend, and a video clip of her slurring her words on a talk show. Drew watched it carefully, seeing the same look of glassy-eyed confusion on Sophie's face that he'd noticed this morning.

Drew shook his head. It could be anything. The papers interpreted it as drink or drugs, and Carly thought it was a brain injury. Either of them could be correct, and deciding which was true on the evidence he had so far was impossible.

His finger hovered over a link that mentioned scandalous photographs, then he decided that gossip and rumour weren't going to get him any further forward. He set about streaming the first episode of *MacAdam,* and within ten minutes of the opening credits he was well and truly hooked.

CHAPTER THREE

DREW HAD SPENT the whole of the previous evening with Sophie. He'd sat down to watch one episode of *Mac-Adam* and ended up watching four, back to back. He'd told himself it was an interesting show, with a great plot, but, in fact, it was Sophie he'd been unable to take his eyes off, and Sophie who'd inhabited his dreams, until it had been time to peel himself out of bed for another early start. This morning, it was in the large conference room at the hotel, which had been temporarily set aside as a rehearsal area.

Sophie looked different again. Different from the tough cop, with personal problems and a heart of gold that he'd watched last night. Different from the neatly dressed doctor he'd met yesterday.

Today she was the actress, dressed in an oversized sweatshirt, which fell by design from one shoulder, exposing the curve of her neck and the narrow strap of her top underneath. Her blonde hair was tied up in a messy bundle at the back of her head, a few wisps framing her face.

And she was alone. Sitting in one of the chairs that had been cleared against the wall to make some space in the centre of the room, yawning as she leafed through the pages of a small, leather-bound notebook.

The swing doors slapped closed behind Drew and she looked up. Even Sophie's frown was like a ray of sunshine, waking him instantly from the drowsy hangover of too little sleep.

'Hi.' She didn't say his name, and Drew wondered briefly whether she'd forgotten it again. After last night, when he'd thought he'd got to know her so well, it was a humbling experience.

'Morning. Are you ready to start?'

She shrugged, as if being in attendance was about all he could reasonably expect of her. 'I already know CPR.' She slipped the notebook into a large designer handbag, which lay on the seat next to her. He'd give a lot to know what that notebook contained.

He called her bluff, walking towards the dummy, which someone had arranged in a seated position, legs crossed, on one of the nearby chairs. 'The script says that you're resuscitating someone who's been knocked down in the street by a truck.'

Drew arranged the dummy on the floor, in a pose that vaguely resembled the kind of position a road-accident victim might end up in. Sophie looked at it with the bored air of a film star who had better things to do at seven o'clock in the morning.

'You're standing on the pavement, right?'

She nodded and he pointed to a spot a couple of feet away from the dummy. 'So that would be about here.'

'Yes, that's right.' When she stood, she seemed even smaller than she had yesterday, more fragile. Drew thought he saw a flash of uncertain fear in her eyes.

He needed to show her that he presented no threat. 'Okay. I'll give the signal and you just do what comes naturally. We'll work from there.' He gave her his most reassuring smile.

'All right.' She nodded quietly, and Drew took a couple of steps back, giving her some room. Then he clapped his hands to indicate the sickening thud of metal meeting flesh.

She jumped, whirling round in the direction of the dummy, for all the world as if she'd just heard the screeching of brakes and the rending of tyres. Then she moved. Confident, assured, with the professional focus that he'd seen so many times on the faces of the people he'd worked with.

Kneeling by the dummy, she was examining it, counterfeiting perfectly the checks and precautions that a real doctor would take in this situation. Bending over the dummy's head, she tapped its face with two fingers.

'Unresponsive... Not breathing...' She muttered the words to herself, almost as if he'd walked out of the room and she was alone.

'Great. That's good.' As Drew knelt down beside her, her scent brushed against his senses. Sophie smelled like every desire he'd ever experienced.

She tipped her face up towards him and suddenly he was falling, unable to catch his breath. One of her eyes was the same gorgeous green he'd seen yesterday. The other was light brown, shot through with gold. The effect was stunning, the one irregularity in an otherwise perfect face. He was bewitched.

The doctor was staring at her, and this wasn't his suspicious, searching stare. If she had to put a name on it, she would call it...

No. She was mistaken, it was far too early in the morning for him to make a pass at her. And, in any case, he clearly disapproved of her, and she didn't like him all that much. Whatever had put that possibility into her head?

'Have I got breakfast all over my face?' She brushed one of her cheeks, wondering whether she'd had time for breakfast today.

'No. I...' He seemed to force his gaze downwards, towards the dummy that lay between them. The sudden, almost apologetic gesture sent tingles to the tips of her fingers.

'What is it?' She brushed the other cheek and then realised what he'd seen. 'This?' Sophie made the well-worn joke that she used whenever anyone noticed her eyes. Opening and closing each one in turn, she described a circle in the air with her finger, intoning a spooky melody.

He had such a nice smile. One that could get her into trouble if she wasn't very careful. 'You have heterochromia.'

'Yes. I wear a contact lens in my brown eye for filming, so it doesn't look weird.'

'It doesn't look weird. It's...' He shrugged, seemingly at a loss for words.

'I was born with it. It's just a pigmentation thing, nothing else.' Sophie was aware that heterochromia could sometimes be the result of an injury, and she didn't want him getting the wrong idea.

'It's beautiful.' Clearly his mind was on the aesthetics, rather than any medical implications.

Suddenly, even though neither of them was moving, the space between them seemed to close. As if all the air were being sucked out of the room, and they were being forced together by some trick of physics.

Then the vortex seemed to throw itself into reverse, and he drew back. 'The patient's probably dead by now.'

He gave a regretful twist of his mouth, and Sophie's heart lurched.

'No one ever dies in a film unless the script says so. We'll perform a medical miracle.'

'Be my guest.' He sat back onto his heels, waiting for her to make the next move.

Suddenly she felt strong. She knew exactly what to do next. 'Thirty compressions and two breaths?'

'That's right.'

'But I have a second qualified person available.' She took the risk of testing her recall a little further.

'In which case?'

'One delivers compressions and the other rescue breaths. We switch every two minutes or so to avoid getting tired.'

He grinned. 'So we'll take it from the top, then?'

Sophie took a breath. Yes. It all came to her, like a well-understood routine. She checked for a response again, coming to the same conclusion as she had before. He helped her position the dummy, and she tilted its head back, ready to deliver rescue breaths.

'You start with the compressions.'

He nodded, doing as she'd told him, counting aloud when he got to twenty-five. She gave the rescue breaths right on cue, and he nodded his approval, starting the compressions again straight away.

'Do you want to try a switch?' He was concentrating on what he was doing and didn't look up at her.

'Sure. On your signal.'

The switch was perfect. Almost without thinking, Sophie fell into the lifesaving rhythm, picking up the compressions where he'd left off, using her body weight to help give her the amount of pressure that the doctor had applied. They carried on for five repeats and then switched back again.

'Perfect.' He finally sat back on his heels.

'Not so bad for an airhead, you mean?' She gave a half-smile to indicate that he could take that as a joke, if he chose.

'You said it…'

And Sophie knew beyond a doubt that he'd thought it. He hadn't been able to disguise the surprise in his eyes when she'd shown she really did know how to perform CPR.

'My father's a doctor. He taught us all what to do in emergency situations. I've never had to do it for real…' She couldn't keep the trace of bitterness from her tone. Her father had always assumed she'd become a doctor, and instead she'd taken up a profession that had no value in his eyes. His only response to the news that she was making this film had been a back-handed compliment, saying he was glad she was at least pretending to do something useful.

'Well remembered, then.'

He smiled, and pleasure trickled across the dull pain of rejection. Sophie wondered whether he'd adjust his opinion if he knew that she was still searching her mind for his first name. Dr Taylor seemed a little formal, since they'd just saved the life of a props dummy together.

'As you already have a good idea of how to resuscitate someone, you understand the theory behind it all.'

'Yes.' Sophie nodded. When he put it that way, she supposed that she did.

'Which will stand you in really good stead for this.' He got to his feet, producing a copy of the medical techniques document. She'd studied her copy for hours, hoping that she might retain at least some of it. 'I guess you haven't had much of a chance to look at it.'

'No. Not really.' He was giving her a way out, and Sophie took it gratefully.

He grinned. 'I guess that's my job. It gives a detailed description of how resuscitation was carried out in the nineteen-forties—which is a little different from the way we do it now.'

'They did chest compressions but no rescue breaths.' A fragment of fact suddenly popped into her mind.

He nodded. 'Yes, I've managed to find a couple of old training films on the internet. But it may be easier to just try it ourselves.' He knelt down next to her. 'Do you want to start with the compressions?'

'Okay.' Sophie could do that. She already knew how to do compressions. This morning was going a lot better than she'd expected it to. No tantrums needed to cover her lapses in memory, and the doctor seemed to be going out of his way not to spring anything unexpected on her.

'Right, then.' He flashed her a grin. 'Here we go...'

The morning's work had been a success. Starting with what Sophie knew and then using gesture and move-ment to reinforce the new information seemed to have worked. The atmosphere on set lightened considerably as she sailed through her scene that afternoon, even manag-ing to bestow a few smiles on her co-star and the crew.

Joel, the director, spared a nod of satisfaction for Drew, clearly pleased with his tutelage. Carly gave him a beaming smile when she thought no one else was look-ing, and Sophie ignored him completely.

Even though she clearly didn't want to think about him unless she absolutely had to, Sophie dominated Drew's thoughts. He watched her carefully, and as dispassionately as he could. And the more he watched her, the more he realised that he knew what was wrong, and that she was trying desperately to cover it up.

CHAPTER FOUR

THE FOLLOWING DAY didn't start well. The script had said
rain, but real rain seemed to be a problem, and an un-
scheduled downpour had stopped filming for a while.
Rumour had it that Carly was confined to her room at
the hotel with a stomach bug, and Sophie's face was set
in a hard, concentrated frown. She avoided him as if he
had something catching.

Joel had called cut, and the clapperboard signalled
the tenth rerun of a scene that should have been easy.
Each time she'd fluffed her lines Sophie's air of prickly
uninterest had increased markedly.

'It's all a matter of...' She stopped suddenly, frowning. 'This isn't right, Joel.'

'Oh, for goodness' sake...' Todd Hunter, her co-star,
turned away suddenly, frustration and anger showing on
his face. Joel moved in to smooth things over.

'What's the matter, Sophie?'

'It's not right... Give me the script...' Sophie looked
as if she was about to burst into tears.

A copy of the script appeared out of nowhere, and
Sophie leafed through it, seemingly too dissatisfied to
find the right page, and then threw it to one side. Drew
got to his feet, navigating through the circle of cameras
and sound technicians around her.

'It's nearly lunchtime. We'll take a break.' Joel seemed resigned to handling Sophie's moods and perhaps he thought that the catering truck could do what he couldn't and get today on a better footing. 'Sophie...'

Joel's mouth quirked in an expression of helplessness as he found himself speaking to thin air. Sophie was already on her way to her trailer, cutting a swathe into the crowd around her as they moved to get out of her way.

Jennie, a bright, usually happy young woman, who had introduced herself yesterday to Drew as Sophie's assistant, ran after her. He saw Sophie turn, aiming a couple of angry words in Jennie's direction and gesturing to her to go away. Jennie fell back, her face reddening, and Drew frowned. That kind of behaviour really wasn't necessary.

Drew pushed through the groups of people who were putting some distance between themselves and Sophie. She could act up with Joel, and he'd try to smooth things over to get her co-operation. Everyone else would cave in to her tantrums, in fear for their jobs. But this was one job he didn't need to keep.

Dammit! One curse vied with another in her head, filling her thoughts with the kind of obscenities that she never spoke out loud. She was turning into a monster. Slowly and irrevocably, and there was nothing she could do to stop it.

'Sophie...'

The one voice she didn't want to hear. The doctor. Damn him, too.

'Sophie...?'

He didn't give up, did he? She was twenty feet from

her trailer and then she could slam the door in his face, lock him out.

She didn't make it. With just a couple of paces to go before she reached safety, she felt his hand on her arm.

'Let go of me.' She whipped her arm away as if he'd grabbed it, not just touched it lightly.

'Wait, Sophie.'

His tone was so sure, so commanding, and in a sea of misunderstandings and unknowns it was the only thing that seemed to make any sense. Despite herself, she stopped.

'You haven't figured out how things work around here yet, have you?' She glared at him. 'I'm at the top of the pecking order and you're at the bottom. You don't tell me what to do.'

That bloody smile again. Relaxed and assured, the smile of a man who already knew his place in the world and didn't need anyone to tell him what it was. And dangerous in the extreme. 'I thought that was exactly my role. I'm an advisor and so I advise.'

'Don't be smart with me.' Sophie rolled her eyes and turned away from him, as if what he'd just said didn't deserve a proper answer. That always seemed to work when she couldn't come up with the words she wanted.

He slipped past her, opening the door of her trailer and walking inside. *Her private trailer.* The only place where she could take some refuge from the noise and bustle of the set. Panic started to rise in her chest.

'Get. Out.'

'There seems to be something wrong. I'd like to help.'

'I don't need help.' Anger wasn't working, and she tried another tack. Right on cue she summoned tears and a look of melting supplication. 'Please, go…'

He smiled, sitting down in one of the comfortable arm-chairs in the seating area. 'Nice one. You're very good.'

'What's that supposed to mean?' Sophie scowled at him.

'It means that you're a tremendous actress. And that you'll do anything to stop anyone finding out the difficulties you're having right now. Only I see through it.'

If he'd had any doubts about his conclusions before, the mock tears and that look of seductive pleading banished them altogether. She knew exactly what was wrong with her. If he could get through to her, just talk to her and make her see sense, then he'd be out of here in a week and back to a world where sanity was more of a guiding principle.

She sat down opposite him. That was something. Sitting was better than running.

'Who sent you to spy on me? Who are you reporting to?'

'No one. It's not like that at all, Sophie. When Carly spoke to me she mentioned…'

Wrong move. All the colour drained from Sophie's face and her hand flew to her mouth. Tears formed in her eyes and this time they looked like the real thing.

'Carly…? No…'

'Carly happened to mention that you were under a bit of stress.' That was stretching the truth to breaking point, but he'd already landed Carly in enough hot water.

Sophie stared at him blankly. Drew had seen that look before, when everything became too much and someone started to shut down.

'Sophie, listen to me. It's okay…'

'You think that any of this is okay?' she flashed back at him.

Time for the truth. 'All right. I don't know anything for sure, but here's what I think I know. You're having difficulties with your short-term memory. The things you've known for a while are no problem, it's new information that you can't process properly. It's possible that you sustained a mild traumatic brain injury in your recent car accident.'

'Carly just happened to mention that as well?' She'd composed herself now, and was staring straight at him.

'She's a good friend to you, Sophie, and she's trying to help you.' If he could do nothing else, at least he could try to repair the damage he'd done. So far he'd only managed to isolate Sophie even further from the one person who seemed to care about her.

'Whatever. That's not really your business, is it?'

'No, it's just an observation.'

'Yes, it's all just observations, isn't it? I think it's all in your imagination.'

'What's my name, Sophie?'

She shot him a defiant look. 'Dr...'

'My name.'

'What do I care?' She looked as if she was about to launch into another diatribe about how *she* was the important person around here, and his status was that of a cockroach, when a knock sounded on the door.

'Catering...'

'Come in.' Sophie pulled herself together and gave the young woman who entered a composed smile, watching as she set a covered plate on the table and got water from the fridge in the tiny kitchenette at the far end of the living space.

'Would you bring another plate, please?'

'For Dr Taylor? Sure.' The woman turned to Drew. 'What would you like?'

'Anything's fine.' Sophie's sudden turnaround was a surprise, but if accepting lunch meant that she was going to let him stay a while longer then he would eat whatever anyone put in front of him.

'Chicken in a cream sauce, sautéed potatoes, green beans…?'

'Sounds great. Thank you.'

The woman nodded. 'Back in a tick.'

He picked up the bottle of water from the table and filled her glass, aware that she was watching every move he made. 'Thank you.'

'Don't get any ideas. It's only lunch. We're not best friends yet.'

'I know.' She'd obviously come to the conclusion that she couldn't get rid of him so she was calling a truce. Drew nodded at her plate. 'Don't wait for me, yours will get cold.'

He knew. It was one thing for people to speculate, but he was a doctor and his word held some weight. And he wasn't just speculating, he knew. The only way out of this mess was to stop denying the obvious and try to get him to keep quiet about it.

Lunch gave her an opportunity to think. The doctor never mentioned anything to do with her memory until they were sipping their coffee, but Sophie knew this was temporary. He was biding his time, in just the same way she was.

'There's something I have to know.'

'Okay.' He handed her the mint chocolate that had come with his coffee. He must have noticed that she'd eaten hers straight away. He seemed to notice far too much.

'I need you to be discreet.' She unwrapped the chocolate, nibbling at the edge of it.

He nodded. 'Carly's already taken care of that.' He reached into his pocket, taking out a couple of sheets of paper, stapled together. Sophie wondered if he'd been carrying them around with him in anticipation of just this moment.

She scanned them carefully. A standard confidentiality agreement, with his signature and Carly's on the bottom. 'You plan to honour this?'

'Yes. Even without it, anything you say is confidential. I'm a doctor.'

'I don't recall asking for your professional services.' The jibe came out of nowhere, from the place where everything was a threat and no one could be trusted.

'No, you didn't. I'm offering them anyway.'

She shrugged. 'Do you understand how dangerous rumours like this can be? No one wants to employ an actress who can't remember what comes next. In big-budget projects like this, it's too much of a financial risk.'

'I understand. And it doesn't matter what your reasons are. Confidentiality is confidentiality.'

Sophie supposed that she would have to take him at his word. 'I want to make it clear that I've never taken drugs and I don't have an alcohol problem. My accident was nothing to do with either of those things.'

'Okay.'

'You believe me?'

'Yes.'

'Right. Thanks.' He could have believed her in a few more words but a yes would do. It was unequivocal enough, particularly when said the way he'd said it.

'I know it's tough, Sophie. When you remember some things and not others in what seems to be a completely random way. And the toughest thing is knowing that your memory's not working properly, and never being sure if there's something you've missed.'

'If you say so.' Actually, that was a pretty good description of how she felt. Never being sure of anything.

'Is it all right if I ask you some questions?'

'If I say no, you'll only ask them anyway. So you'd better get on with it.'

'Okay.' He grinned at her, and suddenly it seemed so much easier to just go along with him. He did have a very nice smile. 'This all started around the time of your accident?'

'Yes. It was much worse at first, and it's been improving over time.' There had been no recurrence of the lost days that she'd experienced right after the accident. And she didn't want to tell him about them. She didn't even want to think about the photographs that had appeared on the internet afterwards. Sophie couldn't bear to see the judgement in his beautiful grey eyes.

'Any clumsiness, loss of co-ordination?'

'I used to drop things quite a lot. And I'd forget how to do little things, like how to turn the shower on. I knew about traumatic brain injury from my father talking about it, and I knew that I could practise and relearn things.'

'That must have been very hard to do on your own.'

'I'm an actress, I've been taught how to be aware of movement and gesture.'

'Even so, it's a huge achievement. You should be proud of yourself.'

'Thanks.' This was the first time that someone had understood. The first time that anyone had praised her for the little things that had been so hard for her. She felt lighter than she had done for a very long time.

'That's good to see too…'

'What?'

'Your smile.' His gaze dropped from her face, as if that was the one thing he was embarrassed to have noticed. 'You've never seen a doctor about any of this?'

'No. I have to keep it quiet.'

'I understand that but you need to have a proper diagnosis. I can arrange for you to see someone discreetly. No one will know.'

'I'll think about it.'

'Don't put this off, Sophie.'

'I'll think about it. Don't push me. I can still have you thrown off the set.'

His gaze held hers for a moment, and then let go. They both knew she wouldn't do that now.

'All right. So shall we concentrate on getting through today, then? Leave the other things until later.'

That would be good. 'What do you suggest?'

'Why don't you lie down for half an hour then I'll go through your lines with you. See if we can crack this scene together.'

The way he'd helped her with the CPR scene. She did need some help, and he seemed to know how to fix memories into her head.

'Okay. Thank you.'

Drew found Joel eating a sandwich and talking to one of the cameramen. With the practised instincts of a man who missed nothing of what was going on around the set, Joel propped his plate on top of his script and rose to meet him.

'How's Sophie?'

'Fine. She's calmed down and I suggested she take a rest for a while. She'll be ready to start work in an hour.'

'You're sure about that? If she's going to be spending

the whole afternoon in her trailer, I'd rather know now.' Joel eyed him suspiciously.

'I'm sure. She'll be back here in an hour.'

'Okay, thanks. Keep me informed, will you?'

'Of course.' Drew turned before Joel could ask any other awkward questions. The next task, was make sure that Sophie was word perfect and ready to face the world in exactly one hour.

CHAPTER FIVE

THE HAMMERING ON the door of his hotel room was in-
sistent. Drew looked at the travelling clock at his bedside. Half past eleven. Probably someone who'd just been
ejected from the hotel bar.

'Please... It's Sophie...' When he hadn't answered
immediately, the knocking got louder, and Sophie's voice
sounded through the door, propelling him out of bed
and onto his feet.

'What...?' He stepped back as she almost fell into
the room. If she'd decided that seducing him would get
him to let up on her, a white cotton nightie with a long
cardigan over the top of it wasn't the obvious choice of
outfit, but on Sophie it looked entrancing. Something
at the back of his mind screamed that being alone in
a hotel room, half-naked, with a scantily dressed film
star who had a patchy memory showed spectacularly
bad judgement.

'It's Carly. She's sick. Please, come.' She frowned at
him. 'Put some clothes on.'

He was beginning to like it when Sophie put him
firmly in his place. Drew reached for his jeans, dragging
them on over his boxer shorts, and caught up a T-shirt.
'What's the matter?'

'I don't know. She seemed better this evening. Her

room's next to my suite and I left the adjoining door open and went to bed. When I woke up just now I heard her crying. She's in such pain...'

'Okay, which way?' Drew hoped she could remember, because he had no idea where Carly's room was.

She led the way through a maze of corridors, taking a few wrong turns before she reached one of the rooms at the front of the hotel. Carly was curled up on the bed, her knees almost touching her chin, tears streaking her cheeks. Untypically for someone who was obviously feeling very ill, she didn't look particularly pleased to see a doctor.

'I'm all right. It's just a...' Whatever Carly thought she might be suffering from was lost as she caught her breath in pain.

'Okay, then. Let's just have a look.'

Carly resisted him, and Sophie's voice sounded, firm and calm. 'Stop messing about and just do what the doctor tells you.'

'You're a fine one to talk.' Carly cursed under her breath but she let Drew roll her over on the bed and pull her hand from her side.

'Is this where it hurts?'

'Yeah...'

He pressed gently and Carly winced. When he removed the pressure she cried out in pain. Drew didn't need a thermometer to tell him that she was running a fever, burning up.

'Sophie, do you have your phone?'

'I think so.' She looked in the pocket of her cardigan and found it, handing it over to Drew. He dialled quickly, telling the ambulance controller that he was a doctor and that he had a patient with all the signs of acute appendicitis.

'Get off…my case…' Carly paused to catch her breath. 'It's a stomach bug. I'll be fine in the morning. I'm not going anywhere.'

'Carly, you're sick. Please.' Sophie was standing behind him, close to tears now. 'You have to go.'

'Soph…' Carly was clearly in a lot of pain, but all she could think about was her friend.

'Look, Carly. I know you brought him here to help me, and I've told him everything.'

'You told…*him*?'

'Wasn't that your plan all along?' Drew wondered whether he should leave the room to allow the two of them to argue about him in private.

'None of that matters now, Carly. Since the accident, I can't remember stuff, but I've admitted it now, and everything's going to be okay. You have to go. Please, I promise I'll let the doctor help me.' The words tumbled from Sophie's mouth in a rush of anxiety for her friend.

'Is that true?' Carly looked at Drew.

'It's true. You need to go with the ambulance. I'll look after Sophie.'

'You only signed for a week…'

'Forget the contract. I'm staying here until you're well.'

Carly gave a small nod and let him roll her over onto her side, drawing her knees up in a position that would make the pain easier for her to bear. Sophie pushed past him, getting onto the bed and holding her friend as best she could.

'Hang onto me, honey. It's going to be all right.'

Tears began to roll down Carly's cheeks, and she started to sob. 'I want Mark…'

'I know you do. We'll call him as soon as we have you safe in the hospital.' She turned her head towards

Drew. 'Mark DeAngelo, Carly's husband. His number's in my phone. Will you remember that I have to call him?'

'I'll remember.'

It had taken this for Sophie and Carly to finally talk to each other. Drew watched the two of them, curled up together on the bed, holding each other tightly, and hoped that Sophie would remember at least something about her promise to take some help.

The ambulance crew arrived and Sophie slipped away, letting Drew talk to the woman paramedic. He could hear her banging around in the suite next door and he resolved that he'd go and see what she was up to as soon as he could.

'Okay.' The paramedic bent over Carly. 'Carly... Carly, we're going to take you to hospital. The stretcher's coming up now and we'll get you comfortable and carry you down to the ambulance.'

Carly nodded wordlessly. She was lying quietly now, which wasn't necessarily a good sign. Sudden relief of pain usually occurred when the appendix burst, and Drew wouldn't put it past her to give a busy A and E department the slip and simply walk out of there.

A noise behind him made him glance around. Sophie was standing in the doorway, fully dressed, her designer handbag slung across her body, looking as if she was planning on going somewhere. That was all he needed. Drew had no intention of letting Carly go to the hospital alone, but Sophie was only going to get in the way.

'Sophie...' He walked towards her, leaving the paramedic to tend to Carly. 'I want you to stay here.'

'Forget it.'

'The ambulance won't take two passengers.'

'Then I'll get a taxi and follow you.'

Like hell she would. Having Sophie wandering around a strange hospital in the middle of the night wasn't his idea of looking after her.

'I can't watch out for both of you at the same time. Work with me, Sophie. I want to go with Carly to make sure she's all right, but I can't do that if I'm not confident that you're going to stay here.'

Her defiant, odd-eyed gaze met his. 'Okay, then.' She pushed past him, waiting for the paramedic to finish with Carly.

'Would you mind if I came in the ambulance too. Please? She's my friend. And he's a doctor, so he doesn't really count as a passenger.'

The paramedic flipped her gaze towards Drew, who nodded grudgingly, and then grinned at Sophie. 'Okay. I can make an exception this once.'

The A and E doctor's reaction was just as Drew had expected. He examined Carly and then got straight onto the phone. Sophie had hung onto Carly's hand, comforting her, and even though Carly had protested that they should go, she was clearly relieved that neither of them would.

He'd noticed that Sophie had kept her head down and walked close to him as they'd hurried through the busy public area of the hospital, and also that the nurse who attended Carly obviously recognised her. Nothing had been said, though, and he was grateful that Sophie had been allowed the space to be just another worried friend.

That anonymity was ripped away from her as soon as Carly was taken away for an emergency appendectomy, and Sophie walked back through into the waiting room. A girl, who looked too young for the short skirt and sequinned top that she was wearing, came straight up to her, grabbing her arm.

'You're Sophie Warner…' Her face was flushed and her eyes shone.

If Sophie was surprised, she didn't show it. Somehow she managed to extricate herself from the girl's grip without making a big thing of it and smiled as if she'd just met a long-lost friend.

'My friends said I shouldn't speak to you.' The girl gestured towards a group of half a dozen teenagers sitting in the corner of the waiting room, all dressed up to the nines and all staring at Sophie. 'But I still love you…'

In spite of what the papers said. In spite of what her friends said. Sophie's resigned half-shrug indicated that she had a pretty good idea of how the conversation between the girls must have gone.

'I'm so glad you did come over to say hello. What's your name?'

'Gillian.'

'Gillian.' Sophie shot Drew a glance as she repeated the name, and he made a mental note, in case he needed to prompt her with it later. 'Thank you for believing in me.'

The blush spread from Gillian's cheeks to the roots of her hair. 'I said it wasn't true.'

'All my real friends know that it isn't.'

Sophie had barely got the words out before Gillian flung her arms around her, enveloping her in a hug. Drew stepped forward to intervene and then saw Sophie's face. Eyes squeezed shut, to hide her tears.

Gillian let go of her and produced a phone from her pocket. 'Can I have a photo?'

The girls in the corner were talking excitedly now, and one of them was already weaving unsteadily on her high heels past the rows of seats. The situation was about to turn into a commotion.

'Let's go over there.' Sophie indicated an empty alcove, which contained a drinks machine and some chairs. 'We don't want to cause a disturbance.'

She seemed to have won the girls over completely. Sophie walked quickly over to the alcove, sitting down in the corner, and they followed her like a swarm of heat-seeking missiles. Drew kept as close as he could to Sophie, but he was elbowed out of the way, and she was surrounded.

It was impossible to say which one of them needed the services of the A and E department. They were chattering excitedly and Sophie quieted them, making a good-humoured game out of not drawing attention to themselves.

She smiled, hugging Gillian, while the girl took selfies. Then went to sit down next to one of other girls. Drew saw that her tights were ripped and she had blood caked on her leg.

'You fell over?' Sophie had disregarded the large graze on her knee and was looking at an inch-long cut on her cheekbone. 'Have you seen a doctor yet?'

'Yes.' The girl wriggled with pleasure at her concern. 'I've got to wait to have it stitched. It takes so long, though. I want to go home.'

'No, you must stay here,' Sophie reproved her gently.

'Do you think so?' Sophie's opinion was obviously more important to the girl than anything the doctors could possibly say to her.

'Yes, I do. Would you like a photo?'

The girl proffered her phone uncertainly, her hand wandering to the cut on her face, and Sophie handed the phone to Drew. 'Would you do it?'

He bent down to take the shot. Sophie put her arm around the girl, and they put their heads together, cheek to cheek. Then she waved Drew to the right a little, and he realised that at this angle the cut wouldn't show at all.

He took three shots, just in case, and handed the phone back. Sophie took it, expressed delight with two of the images and disappointment with the third, gently suggesting that it might be deleted.

'Those two are great. Thank you…' The girl flung her arms around Sophie and kissed her cheek, and phones were raised to capture the moment.

'Are you someone?' Drew found that he was suddenly the object of everyone's attention.

'He's a doctor.' Sophie leaned in, as if she was imparting an important secret.

'Is he your boyfriend?'

Drew felt the back of his neck start to itch with embarrassment. A simple enough question, with a simple enough answer. Why did it make him feel so uncomfortable?

'No, he's here with my friend. She was taken ill tonight.'

'Is she all right?'

Finally. Someone had thought that Sophie might have more important things to think about than taking selfies and signing autographs.

'Yes, she's going to be fine. But I have to go and check on what's happening with her now.'

The girls were unwilling to let her go, and it was time for Drew to step in. Allowing each of them one final hug, and the girl who had cut her face a few words of comfort and reassurance from Sophie, he put his arm around her shoulder and guided her away.

She looked suddenly tired. He felt her body trembling with fatigue against his, and he wrapped his jacket around her shoulders, hoping that they could get out of there before anyone else recognised her.

'Are we waiting?' She pulled his jacket around her.

'No, Carly's in surgery. And she'll be sleeping for some time after that. We can come back in the morning.' He adopted a firm tone. There was no more they could do here and Sophie had already had enough for tonight.

'Yes. I feel... I'm sorry. I feel so tired.'

'We're going back to the hotel, right now.' Drew guided her through the doors and towards a taxi rank, where one solitary taxi waited, its driver lounging against the side of the car. He hurried her across, thankfully managing to get the driver's attention before anyone else got there, and put her into the back of the cab.

Sophie opened her eyes and then closed them again. Hotel room. Yeah, she knew where she was. Slowly she oriented herself, not searching for the memories, just letting them come in their own sweet time.

'Carly!' She sat up in bed, pulling the bedspread off herself, and realised that she was still fully clothed, apart from her shoes, which lay neatly on the floor beside the bed.

She covered her face with her hands. She remembered now. She'd fallen asleep in the taxi, and woken to find him carrying her upstairs. She'd snuggled into his arms, letting him lay her on the bed and take off her shoes.

'Hey...' Sophie froze. That was his voice. He was still there. 'It's okay, everything's fine. We took Carly to hospital last night with appendicitis and she had an emergency operation.'

Yes, she remembered that. She still wasn't sure what had happened after he'd taken her shoes off, though. The thought of another night that she couldn't remember made her feel sick.

'You're...' Still here? Dressed? He was clearly both, but Sophie was lost for a way to enquire tactfully as to whether the latter had changed at some point during the night.

She still had her jeans on. And she could feel her bra strap under her T-shirt. No one had sex and then put their clothes back on to go to sleep...

'You went to sleep in the taxi. I brought you up here and stayed around to fill you in on the details when you woke up.' He was sitting in the large armchair tucked in the corner of the room, and Sophie noticed that one of the pillows from the bed was propped under his shoulders.

'That's it?' Perhaps she was panicking over nothing. There was nothing to indicate that she'd forgotten anything, only the uncomfortable knowledge that she was quite capable of doing so.

'Yes. That's it. You opened your eyes when I took your shoes off, and then you went right back to sleep.'

So there really was nothing to remember. Relief was tainted by guilt. 'I should have stayed awake. At least until Carly was out of surgery.'

'You were exhausted.'

'I haven't been sleeping all that well recently.' Sophie pressed her lips together, aware that she'd probably just admitted to another of the symptoms of traumatic brain injury. She should be a bit more careful.

'I need to phone the hospital and see how Carly is.' She looked around for her bag and spotted it beside the bed.

'I've done that already. She's fine. She came through the operation with flying colours and she's sleeping now.

And the last thing you did before you went to sleep in the taxi was to give me your phone and ask me to call Carly's husband.'

'Mark's okay?'

'Yes. He's worried, of course, but I texted him this morning to let him know how she was and give him the number for the hospital.'

'Thanks. I'll call him later. When can I go and see Carly? She'll want to speak to him.'

'You can go and see her whenever you want. We've got the day off today.'

That she'd forgotten. Her eyes wandered to the clock on the nightstand. As it was nine o'clock and no one had come to hammer on her door yet, she supposed he must be right. She twisted the corners of her mouth downwards.

'I forgot. Sorry…'

He shrugged, as if it didn't matter. 'I can't think you're the only one who woke up this morning thinking there was somewhere else they ought to be.'

She doubted she was. But for most people the information came to them. She had absolutely no idea what day it was, and, however hard she tried, she couldn't work it out.

'It's Saturday.' He walked towards the bed and sat down on it, holding her phone out towards her. Sophie took it quickly, trying not to either visibly shrink from him or get too close.

'Thanks. Saturday.'

'What do you say we meet downstairs for breakfast in half an hour? Then I'll take you to see Carly.'

'Breakfast would be nice. But I can get a taxi to the hospital.'

'I'll take you.' He smiled, and suddenly she felt very

alone with him. 'I'm not having Carly discharging herself over some mistaken idea that she's needed here.'

'I can manage.'

'We've been through this one already. I told Carly I'd look after you.'

'I appreciate that, but it was only to get her to go. I'm not going to hold you to it.'

'You promised you'd let me look after you. I'm going to hold you to that.' His gaze slid towards her handbag. 'You want to write that down?'

He'd noticed the notebook, then. Of course he had.

'No, I'll remember.' Sophie scrambled off the bed and he took the hint, following her into the sitting-room.

'Half an hour. Breakfast. If you don't turn up, I'll come and get you.' He grinned at her, and disappeared through the door of her suite.

CHAPTER SIX

HOWEVER MUCH HE tried to keep it simple, things seemed to be getting more complicated by the minute. Initially, Drew had made up his mind he disliked Sophie and that she was a beautiful, spoilt star, who needed a good shake. Then grudging respect had begun to creep in. Sophie might be volatile and difficult, but she was facing impossible obstacles, and it had taken a lot of guts for her to get this far.

Now he found himself wishing that Carly could be persuaded to go away and recuperate for a couple of weeks, so he could get to know Sophie a bit better. It was the start of a very steep and slippery slope, and what made it even more hazardous was that he had no intention of changing his course now.

He took the day slow and easy. A late breakfast and then a taxi ride to the hospital to see Carly. Sophie went to her room to rest in the afternoon, and met him downstairs for dinner.

Drew selected their table carefully, in a quiet corner of the hotel patio. They could talk there, without being overheard, and, more importantly, the area was a little removed from the noise and bustle of the main restaurant. Sophie would be able to gather her thoughts better there.

Joel joined them for dessert, chatting about nothing but watching Sophie carefully. When he rose, after fifteen minutes, to move on to another table, he gave Drew an almost imperceptible nod, which Drew studiedly ignored.

'He's doing the rounds.' Sophie leaned towards Drew slightly, speaking quietly. 'Have you noticed that he generally sits down with everyone at least once a day? Doesn't say much of any importance but he listens a lot.'

'Yes, I'd noticed.' Drew grinned at her. 'MBWA.'

'What's that?'

'Management By Walking Around. If you do it right, you get to know a lot about what's going on.'

She was watching Joel thoughtfully as he meandered across the dining room, her expression taking on an almost haunted quality. 'I have to be so careful.'

'About what?'

'That I don't give any clues...' She was twisting her fingers together in her lap. 'If Joel works it out...'

'You haven't worked it out properly yet. You're assuming that you have a brain injury.' Drew didn't really want to go into the other things that might cause a loss of short-term memory. It was unlikely, particularly in the context that Sophie's condition was improving. But they had to be ruled out.

'That's what makes sense. My father—'

'I know. Your father told you all about brain injuries. Have you considered that he might also tell you that self-diagnosing is never a good idea?'

'He doesn't think anything that I do is a good idea. I'm used to that.' Sophie's face took on a pinched look. 'I still think I should read up a bit so I know what I'm pretending not to have.'

Reading up on the many and varied symptoms of

traumatic brain injury, and concentrating on not showing any of them, really wasn't the way to go. It would just put Sophie under even more stress. 'I think that's a bit paranoid, isn't it?'

The last vestiges of the easy atmosphere that had kept them going throughout the day dissolved into the night air. 'You think I'm paranoid?'

'No, I didn't mean that...'

'You said it.' Her face was blank of emotion. Drew had come to see that as a warning sign. 'Perhaps paranoia is just another symptom, eh? Or maybe it's just a hazard of my job.'

Before Drew could find a way to disagree convincingly, she stood up. Avoiding his gaze, Sophie marched away through the dining room and out into the hotel lobby.

Drew had spent the last hour shut away in his room, deep in thought. Each time he considered it anew, the conundrum seemed to unravel a little, then twist itself into an even more torturous set of questions.

He wasn't maintaining a proper professional distance. He was reacting like someone who was emotionally involved.

He *was* emotionally involved. He couldn't help it. She'd walked away from him, and he was angry with her like some spurned suitor, instead of understanding the issues the way a doctor should.

He jumped as a knock sounded through the door. 'Room Service. Room 339.'

The voice calling was heavily accented and Drew shook his head. Wrong room. Someone else was waiting for whatever the woman outside had brought him.

He went to the door and opened it. Sophie was there,

wearing a pair of stunningly high black court shoes, which brought the top of her head up to the level of his cheekbone. Neat black slacks and a white shirt with a scarf tied at the neck, in the manner of the waitresses in the hotel. A napkin over one arm, and a large tray in her hands.

'You missed out on coffee after dinner.' Something in her eyes begged him not to slam the door in her face, however much he was tempted to. And Drew couldn't resist Sophie's eyes.

'Yes, I did.' He stood back from the doorway, and she walked past him into the room, setting the tray down on the small table by the window, next to the chair he'd been sitting in.

She poured the coffee and turned to him. 'Milk and sugar, sir?'

If she was going to play the waitress, she may as well get it right. Most of the staff here knew his name, and used it. It was only Sophie who didn't seem to be able to get her head around it, and that felt like a personal slight.

'No one else around here calls me sir...' The words slipped out before he could stop them.

A flicker at the side of her eye betrayed that she knew he was angry. 'No. Of course... Milk and sugar... Taylor?'

It was as if she'd jabbed a pin into his over-inflated pride. He'd belittled her, asking for something that everyone else found so simple and she found horribly difficult. And instead of running away, she'd done the best she could. It was an odd mixture of defiance and a heart-wrenching attempt to please.

'I'll take it black thanks, Warner. Will you join me?'

She nodded, splashing coffee into the other cup on the tray and perching herself on the edge of the second chair by the table. Her coffee cup rattled a little in the saucer as she picked it up and Drew realised that she was shaking.

'I'm sorry, Sophie.'

'No… You're right…'

'Drew.' He helped her this time, smiling as he did so.

'Yes. Drew.' A single crease of concentration appeared on her brow. 'I knew it was something like that. I don't know why I keep forgetting it.'

'It doesn't matter, Sophie. You can call me any damn thing you like, I know that it's not your fault.'

She nodded. 'I want to get it right, though. Drew.'

'Short for Andrew. Only my parents only ever called me Drew, and it stuck.'

'I prefer Drew.'

'So do I.' Now that the layers of defiance and fear had been peeled away, she seemed very sad. Very hurt. Drew's heart ached for hers.

'It's all a matter of finding hooks to hang the memories onto. They can be jokes, or visual images, or gestures. Whatever works for you.'

She thought for a moment. 'It's that easy?'

'No, it's not easy. But you can do it.'

She took another sip of her coffee, her brow creased in thought. He wanted to kiss away the stress, replace it with quite a different kind of tension, but those thoughts were unacceptable. Instead, he picked up his coffee cup.

She hadn't messed everything up after all. Sophie had stormed to her room, found her notebook and scribbled crossly in it so she wouldn't forget how angry she was with him. Then she'd scored the words out. He was probably right.

Anyone in her position *would* be paranoid. Photographs of her naked, on the internet, that she couldn't remember being taken, the press hounding her, everyone believing the lies. But when she was with him, it was as if all that didn't exist.

She drank her coffee, allowing the good feelings to seep in, displacing the bad. She hadn't said what she'd come to say to him yet.

'I'm sorry... Drew.'

He grinned. However much he said he didn't care what she called him, he clearly did.

'I know I shouldn't just walk away when things get difficult. It's rude and dismissive.' She took a deep breath. 'I know I don't have any second chances left, but if I asked you for just one more...'

'You've got it. And you didn't have to ask.'

'Thank you. I appreciate that.'

He reached towards her, tipping her chin up gently. His gaze was right there, with all the warmth she hadn't dared hope to see.

'I'll be there for you, Sophie.'

'You'll help me? If I promise to try and do better, you'll hold me to that?'

He chuckled. 'I'll hold you to it.'

'Thank you.' Relief couldn't stop the mist of fatigue that was descending on her, and the coffee wasn't helping either. 'I feel really tired. I...think I probably ought to go now.'

He put his cup down, grinning. 'I'll walk you to your suite. Do you need a wake-up call in the morning?'

'Carly usually...' Carly wasn't here. 'I can get the hotel to send someone up.' Hopefully whoever it was wouldn't leave until she was on her feet and talking coherently. Just having her eyes open was no guarantee that she wouldn't doze off again for another couple of hours, however hard she tried not to.

'No need. Wake-up calls are my speciality.' Something about the sudden glint in his eye told Sophie that they probably were.

Sophie was grateful that he didn't keep her talking at the door of her suite. When she tried to stifle a yawn he smiled and pocketed the key she'd given him, his parting goodnight aimed over his shoulder. When she bade him goodnight in return he raised one hand in a signal that he'd heard, without looking back.

Turn, turn, turn...

Drew wasn't going to. The swing doors at the end of the corridor would have been an ideal place to look back, but he missed the cue. Took those comfortably wide shoulders and his slim hips through the doors and out of sight. Sophie sighed. Her co-star, Todd Hunter, would have milked the moment and turned to flash his trademark smile, but suddenly that seemed like overkill. Drew was a better hero any day of the week.

She might have to revise that assessment. Sophie had slept for three hours then spent another three tossing and turning in her bed. It seemed that she'd only just closed her eyes, when she felt a hand on her shoulder, gently shaking her.

'No...'

'Coffee.' His voice was firm. She could smell the coffee. Sophie squeezed her eyes shut.

'I can't. Leave me alone.'

'Yes, you can. If you wake up at the proper time, it'll help you to sleep at the proper time.'

'Go away. It's too early for advice.'

She felt his arm around her shoulders. He smelled of soap. Gorgeous. Before Sophie could wriggle free of him, she was sitting up in bed. He was a lot more gentle about this than Carly generally was.

'Come on. Open your eyes.'

She opened one, and saw his smile. Maybe that was worth opening the other for. He proffered the cup, and she took a sip of coffee.

Then he was gone. The sound of the shower running in the bathroom reached her ears. No way…

By the time he got back she had disentangled one foot from the duvet, and it was hanging over the edge of the bed. She felt his fingers brush her instep and heard him chuckle. Then he lifted her out of the bed, setting her onto her feet.

'Okay? Can I let go of you?'

Actually, she'd prefer it if he didn't, his arms were so warm. But she was steady enough on her feet. 'Yeah. I'm fine.'

'Okay. Coffee.' He handed her the cup and she took another sip. 'Now walk a bit.'

She was wide awake now. 'All right. I've got it. I can take it from here.'

'I'll see you downstairs for breakfast.' He turned on his heel, and was gone, closing the door quietly behind him.

He must have been studying the script. Drew was not only word perfect with her part, but with everyone else's. At lunchtime, they sat together in her trailer, his smile rewarding her when she got things right and carrying her over the bits where she stumbled.

'Almost…' He didn't even seem to notice that this was the third time she'd fluffed that particular line. 'Imagine Todd in a tank of water. With piranhas nibbling at his toes. *I can't help you with that…'*

Sophie snorted with laughter. 'Okay… *I can't help you with that. You have to find your own way…'*

'And do it…?'

'And do it quickly.' She grinned at Drew. 'The piranhas will be up to your knees if you don't.'

'Okay, what's next?' He covered her copy of the script with his hand.

'Long spiel from Todd… He's torn between…'

'The piranhas and the shark that's circling, over there.' He jerked his thumb behind him.

'Oh. Big tank of water, then?'

'Yep, big as you like. Now what?'

'I can't save you, Todd.' The image of her own character in a lifejacket floated into her head and she hung onto that.

'Great. Perfect. Shall we try it again, from the top?'

She'd thought this scene was going to be a killer. But with the help of the images that Drew put into her head, the movements that he associated with the lines, the whole thing seemed, quite literally, to take shape. He was liberal with his praise and patient when she stumbled. When it was time to do the scene for real, in front of the cameras, she sailed through it.

'You did brilliantly.' He was sitting in a fold-up chair on the edge of the set and Sophie sat down next to him.

'Thanks. The piranhas helped.'

That grin of his, which seemed to frame the day, keep her on course. 'I'm sure they were more than glad to be of service. Looks as if we'll be finishing on time today.'

Probably due to the fact that Sophie hadn't held the filming up once. She was grateful to Drew for not mentioning that. 'I'll be able to go and see Carly before dinner.'

He thought for a moment. 'Why don't I take you to the hospital and then on to dinner? We could have a quiet meal somewhere, away from the hotel.'

That might not be as easy as it sounded. In Drew's world, you just walked into a restaurant, and if there was a spare table that was it. In hers, there was always a spare table, but with it went the complications of being recognised.

'I'd love it. Do you think we can find somewhere we won't be interrupted, though?' An image floated into her head. Lying on a beach, shaded by palm trees. Drew gently working the knots out of her spine, taking them one at a time. Not a bad analogy for the hundred small concerns that he seemed to have the solution for. Actually, not a bad daydream to have, just for the sake of it. Since it was a beach, and all in her mind anyway, it was entirely up to her what he was or, more to the point, wasn't wearing.

'If I can find somewhere out of the way…' He had obviously been applying himself to the problem in hand while she'd been daydreaming. 'How do you feel about motorbikes?'

Odd question. Sophie decided to go with the flow and work out what he was getting at later. 'My eldest brother had one. I used to love it.'

'So you've ridden pillion before?'

'Yes, all the time.'

'In that case, we could take my bike if you like. It's a lot easier to find somewhere quiet than having to cruise around in a taxi.' His eyes became serious. 'You'll be quite safe.'

'You have a motorbike?'

'Yeah, in the hotel car park.'

She'd seen it. A black and chrome machine that generally attracted a second glance from any of the men who happened to be passing. It had attracted a few second glances from her as well.

'Sounds great.' She put the beach image away for another time. She now had a new one to remind her that she was going out with Drew tonight.

CHAPTER SEVEN

DREW KNOCKED ON her hotel room door at exactly five o'clock. Sophie had been sitting on the bed, waiting.

He was all she'd hoped for, in a thick black leather jacket that somehow made his hair seem darker and his eyes a softer grey by contrast. Sophie swallowed hard.

His assessing gaze looked her up and down. She'd reckoned that jeans and a pair of ankle boots would be most appropriate, and had thrown in the pink lacy top just for fun.

'You'll need a jacket...' His gaze travelled over her bare arms, and Sophie shivered.

'Will this do?' She held out the thick waterproof jacket that she usually kept in her trailer for night shoots.

His fingers brushed the material of the sleeve. 'That'll be fine.'

Drew turned abruptly, leading the way down to the hotel car park, and Sophie wondered whether he was having second thoughts. Maybe the pink top had been too frivolous. He obviously took his bike pretty seriously.

'We could still get a taxi.'

He nodded. 'Whatever you prefer. If you don't fancy the bike...'

It would have been easier to have shrugged and left

the decision to him, as if she didn't care one way or the other. Sophie took a breath. Mentally walking away was just as bad as physically walking away. 'Are you thinking that I'm worried about being safe?'

A glint of relief showed in his eyes. 'Yeah. It's not that long since you were injured in an accident.'

'I'd rather be in your hands than those of a crazy minicab driver.' Sophie felt herself blush. Maybe she could have phrased that a little better. 'Anyway, most real bike riders I know are pretty hot on safety. And this does look like a real bike.'

She grinned at him, running her hand appreciatively across the leather saddle, and he smiled. 'Yeah. All right. Careful of my ego, it'll explode in a minute.'

He rather unnecessarily checked that her jacket was firmly zipped up and the helmet strapped firmly under her chin. Sophie let him do it. The brush of his fingers on her neck might be businesslike, but it still made her shiver with pleasure. He swung his leg over the bike, settling himself in the saddle, and she took hold of his shoulder to steady herself as she climbed on behind him.

'Put your feet on there…that's right.' He was acting as if she'd never ridden a motorbike before. 'And watch out for the exhaust, it gets hot.'

'Got it. Piranhas again.' Little biking piranhas this time, with motorcycle helmets and big teeth.

He chuckled. 'Yeah.'

Drew put his helmet on and reached back, taking hold of her gloved hands and pulling them around his waist. She held onto him, relaxing against him, feeling the pliable strength of his body. She'd known all along that this was going to be the very best part of the trip.

A few turns around the car park seemed to satisfy him that she was confident enough for the open road.

On the back of a large, heavy bike like this one a pillion rider had to go with the flow, following the movements of the driver. This seemed like a marvellous adventure, riding with him, trusting him to keep her safe. Sophie hadn't reckoned on trusting any man to do that in the foreseeable future.

When they arrived at the hospital, Carly put the lid on her exhilaration. She subjected Drew to ten minutes of rigorous questioning and a couple of stern exhortations as to the need for absolute discretion, which prompted urgent gestures to *cut* from Sophie, from behind his back. Then she relaxed against her pillows and professed herself glad to see them both.

'She seems to be doing well.' They were strolling through the hospital car park to where they'd left his bike.

'Yeah. If she can manage to divert some of that determination of hers to getting better, and not worrying about everyone else, she'll be out tomorrow.' Drew had good-humouredly said as much to Carly. 'Then we inherit the problem of finding a way of getting her to rest. She really shouldn't just get up and start work again straight away. She needs to take things very easy for a couple of weeks.'

'I think I've got the solution to that.' Sophie grinned smugly. It was nice to have a solution rather than be the problem for a change.

'What are you intending doing? Sedating her and tying her to the bed? I might be able to help with the sedation...'

'That's my second option. The first one's better. I emailed her husband, Mark, and he can fly over to fetch her in a couple of days. He'll take her home to recuperate.'

He chuckled. 'Passing the problem over to him, huh? Sounds like a tremendous idea.'

'Glad you like it. Mark will drive down here, spend the night and then take Carly back with him the next day, in time for their flight in the afternoon.'

'It's a lot of travelling. Would it be better if I hired a car and drove Carly up to London? They could spend the night in a hotel and then fly back the following day, it would be easier on them both.'

'Would you?' Sophie had thought of that, but not known how to ask. Drew had already done so much. 'I don't dare take another day off filming. I've been trying Joel's patience enough already.'

'Leave it with me. If you let me have Mark's email address I'll contact him and sort the details out.'

'I...' Sophie pressed her lips together.

'You what?' He grinned.

'I told Mark to leave the flights and the hotel to me. I want her to be comfortable, so I was thinking first-class tickets.'

'That's nice of you. So you'll arrange the flights and the hotel, and I'll do the driving, then.'

'You trust me?' After all the slips, all the lapses in memory, he had every reason not to. Sophie had only just got to grips with Drew's full name.

'You're just as capable of making a couple of phone calls as I am. Write a list and tick everything off. That's what most people do.' There was a hint of humour in his eyes.

'Okay. Deal.' Sophie pulled her notebook from her bag, and Drew waited while she wrote a note to herself. 'Are we going for something to eat now? I'm hungry.'

She didn't ask where they were going. Sophie submitted to the ritual of having him check that her helmet was on correctly, and climbed onto the seat behind him. Melting with him into the anonymity of two riders, who stopped at an organic burger stall then headed out of town.

They were free. Away from everyone and everything. There were too many layers of clothing between them to feel his body, but his solidity, his strength were there. Sophie thrilled at the way he pushed her a little, opening up the throttle slowly until she clung to him much tighter than she really needed to.

He turned into empty country lanes and then again onto a dirt track. The bike climbed the steep pathway, winding through a copse of trees, and then suddenly the horizon opened up in a wide panorama. They were on a clifftop, the sea thirty feet below them, the sky above them. Nothing else but a few gulls, wheeling above them.

'Wow!' She took her helmet off, shaking her hair out into the breeze, her legs still trembling from the exhilaration of riding with him. Drew manoeuvred the bike off the track and swung out of the saddle, taking the foil-wrapped packages from the pannier.

'These smell good.' He investigated the contents of one. 'And they're still hot.'

Sophie sat down on the grass beside the bike. 'How did you find that place?'

'I asked at the hospital. Nurses always know where to get the best takeaways in town.' He grinned, sitting down next to her. 'Is this okay?'

That could mean one of many things. Are *you* okay? Is *this* okay? He probably meant all of them, and Sophie decided to answer all of them.

'Yes. It's great.'

* * *

It had been sheer self-indulgence on his part. Having her ride with him on the back of the bike, bringing her out here where they could be alone, was the stuff that dreams were made of. His dreams, at any rate.

And she was enjoying herself. She seemed to visibly relax, to give up the constant struggle to remember, the constant search for things she may have forgotten. Drew told himself that this had been the real plan all along.

'Do you want to walk a bit? There's a path down to the beach a couple of miles along here.' Every one of his senses was putting in urgent requests for this evening to last as long as possible.

'Sounds great. I could do with a walk, blow the cob-webs away.'

She clung to him as he manoeuvred the bike back onto the track, her arms clasped tightly around his waist. This felt too good to question, too good to do anything other than enjoy it while he could, because it wasn't going to last for ever. Following the curve of the coastline, he drove towards the steps, which led down to sea level, and a sheltered beach.

There was no particular need to help her down the steps, but he did so anyway. Sophie didn't seem to mind, and it was just one more thing that added to the magic. They walked slowly in the gathering dusk, and Drew searched the sky, looking for the first glimmer of an evening star.

'Can I ask you something?'

'Of course. What do you want to know?'

'The things I've forgotten. Do you think they'll ever come back again?'

Perhaps this was the real nature of the bargain. Someone as beautiful as Sophie, who had everything going

for her apart from this one thing, probably wouldn't
have given him the time of day if she hadn't needed
him so badly. He forced his mind away from evening
stars and all the things that they seemed to represent at
the moment.

'I think you have to prepare for the fact that there are
some things you'll never remember.'

'But...' She slipped her hand into the crook of his
arm, hanging onto him tightly. 'I'd try anything. Drugs,
meditation. What about hypnotism?'

'Like in the films? Someone goes to a hypnotist and
remembers every detail of something they didn't know
about before?' He took the risk of chiding her gently and
she shrugged, giving a little laugh.

'It's so important to me, Drew.'

He was blinded for a moment, lost in the sheer delight
that this was the first time she'd called him by his first
name without having to think about it. Drew reminded
himself that he ought to be concentrating on the rest of
what she was saying.

'I'm sorry, but it doesn't work that way, Sophie. In
a lot of cases like yours, it's not the ability to retrieve
memories that's impaired but the process by which
events are written into the memory in the first place. If
something isn't there, it can't be retrieved.'

'So there's no hope?' She gave a little gesture of frustration with her free hand.

'I think that pinning your hopes on the future would
be more productive. How you can improve things now.'

A huff of disappointment escaped her lips. They
walked in silence, Sophie seemingly lost in her own
thoughts.

'Does it matter so very much to you, Sophie?' It

seemed that the past was more important than either the present or the future to her at the moment.

'Yes. It does.'

'Is it the accident? It's very common for people who've been injured in accidents not to be able to remember.'

'Partly. I was driving and the car ran off the road and into a tree.' She gave a little shrug. 'Since it wasn't the tree's fault, I guess it must have been mine.'

Something about the way she was clinging to him told Drew that there was more to it than that. 'And there are other things?'

'Yeah. I don't remember very much about the fortnight afterwards either. What I did...' She sighed. 'Have you ever begged someone to tell you the truth?'

'Yeah.' Sophie looked as surprised as Drew felt at his admission. 'A woman. I begged her to tell me the truth, and she said that I was crazy. That everything my common sense was telling me was a lie.'

'Does it still hurt?'

'No. It was a long time ago.' What Gina had done didn't hurt any more. It had just made Drew more wary, convinced him that most things that glittered weren't gold. And that included the world that Sophie inhabited.

She tipped her face up towards him, and suddenly it felt as if her gaze really was golden. 'I begged, too. And Josh told me I was crazy. Only I can't remember...'

'Tell me about it.'

She seemed about to say something and then turned her head away, looking out to sea. The evening breeze swirled around them, seeming to snatch the moment away.

Drew hung onto it doggedly. 'Tell me, Sophie. I won't tell you that you're crazy.'

'There's not that much to tell. I met Josh on set when I was making my last film. He had a smallish part.' She shrugged. 'Very small, actually. Everyone said that he cared about my fame a bit more than he cared about me, but I didn't listen. There was something about him and I thought he loved me.'

'But?' Sophie raised an eyebrow, and Drew shrugged. 'There's always a *but*.'

'I'd like to think not. But… When I got this film he demanded that I only take it on condition that he got the male lead. He wasn't right for it, and even if he had been, that's not something that I have the power to do. So he dumped me.'

'Because you couldn't further his career.'

'Yeah. More or less. But then, while I was here last winter, he got in touch again. Said he wanted me to take him back, and when I went back to the States… I did. He walked the red carpets with me, got the column inches. But that was all it was to him. I could see that by then.'

'So you left him.'

The sadness in Sophie's sigh made his heart lurch. 'I was going to tell him. But he asked me to go away with him for a couple of weeks, see if we could work things out, and I went. That was when I crashed the car. He wasn't injured, and we went on to the hotel after the hospital discharged us.'

'And you don't remember any of that?'

'Not much. I remember going back to Los Angeles on my own. Then three weeks later the stories started to hit the newsstands. He'd sold his story. I think he got quite a lot for it, but there was spite in there as well. How he was the guy who went out with a bad girl who broke his heart. That's when all the rumours started about my drinking.'

'He made it up?'

'He said I'd been drinking when I crashed the car, and somehow managed to get out of being breathalysed. I don't know whether that's true or not.'

It was then that it hit Drew. As if a massive, freak wave had rolled in from the sea, engulfing him and leaving him struggling for breath. Some events defined you in life. Sophie couldn't remember those all-important moments, so she couldn't remember who she really was.

'Sophie...' He wanted to give her some comfort, throw her something to hang onto, but he had nothing. For all his arsenal of coping strategies and carefully thought-through responses, there was nothing that could deal with this.

'It doesn't matter. If I can't remember, that's an end to it.' She was moving onto the defensive now.

'So what, then? You're just going to give up?'

She pulled her hand from the crook of his arm, roughly. 'You think I'm giving up? Look again.' Sophie began to walk down to the water's edge, as if plunging into the sea was the only way that she could get away from all of this.

'Don't walk away from me, Sophie.'

When she turned, she was trembling. 'You just told me it was no use. If I can't remember then so be it, there's nothing more to say.'

'There's plenty more. Like going to see a specialist, being properly diagnosed. Getting some help with the here and now. Coping strategies...'

She held up her hand to stop him. 'All right. You've said it once, and I heard and wrote it down. I'm thinking about it.'

'And what are you doing in the meantime? Wearing a tin-foil hat to bed?'

'Fine doctor you are. You think bullying your patients is the way to go?'

She was right. One hundred per cent. This was no way to treat a patient, taking them out into the middle of nowhere and arguing with them. 'You're not my patient.'

'Maybe you should wear a sign. *The doctor is in. The doctor is out.* I'm beginning to lose track…'

She was suddenly silent as he took her by the shoulders. Looking up at him, her lips parted slightly, almost as if she expected him to shake some sense into her, somehow wanted him to.

'The doctor's out right now Sophie. And I'm telling you now that if you don't agree to go and see someone and get your condition properly diagnosed, I'm going to throw you over my shoulder and carry you there.'

'Really?' There was a strange light in her eyes. Almost as if she'd been waiting for him to finally break and say something like this. 'That's not very sympathetic.'

'It's not meant to be. Sympathy can't change what's happened. You deserve to have a different future.'

'I want a different future.' She seemed to be mulling the idea over. 'You'll suggest someone?'

'Yeah. I can do that.'

'Okay. You tell me where to go, and I'll go.'

All he could think about was her face, tipped up towards him in the gathering gloom. And all he wanted to do was kiss her, but that was a bad idea. Drew contented himself with taking her arm in his again. The first stars were appearing in a violet sky, and for the moment it was more than enough to be able to walk with her under their meagre light.

CHAPTER EIGHT

A CAR ACCIDENT. An ex-partner who had clearly done something but she couldn't remember exactly what. It was little enough to go on. The irony of the situation didn't escape him. He had to do just what Sophie did every day, piecing the truth together from disparate half-remembered clues.

He stowed one of the motorcycle helmets away in the back of the wardrobe, leaving the other one on the bed. Despite his own best resolutions to leave it alone, he couldn't help wondering, nagging away at the problem. Maybe he'd go out again, ride for as long as it took to clear his head.

That wasn't going to work. Drew had the feeling that he could drive halfway across Europe and back, and it still wouldn't be far enough for him to come to any conclusion at all. He fell asleep in the armchair in the corner of his room, waking to the sound of his phone.

'Charlie? What's up?' He tucked the phone against his shoulder, trying to massage some feeling back into his cramped arm.

'Are you alone?'

'Yeah, of course. It's six in the morning.'

'Just asking. Have you seen the papers yet?'

'No.' Something about Charlie's tone indicated that this wasn't just an idle question. 'Should I have done?'

'Apparently Sophie Warner's got a new mystery man.'

'What?' This had to be another lie. Sophie had spent almost all of her time in the last few days with him. When had she even had time for a mystery man?

'There's a picture in this morning's paper of her perched on your bike. Holding a motorcycle helmet and looking pretty stunning, actually.'

'Me?'

'Yeah, you. I'd recognise your bike anywhere. Wake up, will you?'

Drew was wide awake now. Sophie had waited with the bike when he'd gone to get the burgers yesterday evening. She'd taken her helmet off... 'Are there any of me?' A sudden, irrational sense of dread engulfed him.

'There's another one of the two of you riding off. But you can't see who it is she's with. You've both got your helmets on. So what's the story?'

'I gave her a lift, that's all. Carly's in hospital—'

'Really? Is she all right?'

'Yeah, she's fine. Appendicitis. They operated the night before last and she's already sitting up in bed and arguing with everyone.' For once, Drew's mind wasn't on the medical details. He was wondering whether there was any way that his prospective employers would see the photographs and identify him from them.

'Where is she? I'll send her some flowers.'

'She's probably going to be coming back here today.' Drew couldn't work up much enthusiasm for Carly's flowers either. 'Can you actually...see my face?'

'In the photos? Nah. Like I said, I recognised the bike.'

That was something, at least. No publicity was bad

publicity in Sophie's world, and she could ride around with as many mystery men as she liked. But it was unlikely that being associated with a film star who had a reputation for bad behaviour could do Drew's medical career all that much good.

Suddenly he was ashamed of the thought. The lies and half-truths in the press gave Sophie enough pain already, without him adding to it all by being ashamed to be seen with her. 'Charlie, would you do me a favour?'

'Fire away.'

'If you happen to run across anyone who has any media influence, perhaps you could mention that...' Drew thought better of the idea. The media was a complex and dangerous animal, and he was beginning to realise how little he understood it.

Charlie came to his rescue.

'I guess that since you're still there, and you've taken the lady for a ride on your precious bike, she's not as bad as she's painted.'

'No, she isn't. Not at all.'

'But you can't talk about it?'

'No. I can't. Confidentiality agreement.'

Charlie chortled. 'Okay. I get it. Look, the best thing that you can do is to get her to talk to her media people, give them something concrete to back up her side of the story.'

'Okay.' Sophie was never going to agree to that. 'Thanks.'

'No problem. Call me if you need me. I got you into this...'

'Nah. I got myself into this one.' Drew squinted at the clock and decided that he had some more time. 'So what have you been up to?'

'Bit of this, bit of that...'

Drew grinned. That generally meant that Charlie's ever restless attention had been caught by something that interested him. 'Bit of what?' He stood up to stretch, and then flopped down onto the bed, lying on his back, looking at the ceiling. He had another half-hour before he needed to get into the shower and then go and wake Sophie.

She'd woken him. Drew had finished his call with Charlie and then fallen asleep on the bed. The next he knew was that Sophie was hammering on the door and when he opened it she was wearing a smile that said that she rather liked switching roles with him once in a while.

After a slightly shaky start, the day gradually turned into a success. No one seemed much interested in the papers, and when Sophie found Drew studying the pictures, she twisted the edges of her mouth down and then shrugged helplessly. The whole set was beginning to relax now, and Joel seemed anxious to keep it that way, making sure that he bumped into Drew at least three times in the course of the day, asking him each time if everything was okay with Sophie.

They returned to the hotel to find that Carly was out of hospital. Sophie went straight upstairs to see her, and Drew gave them half an hour alone together before he popped his head around the open door of Sophie's suite, knocking as he did so.

Carly was lying propped up on the sofa, obviously in fighting form. 'No, Soph, it sounds like a pretty bad idea to me.'

'No, it's not.' Both faces swung round towards Drew as they heard him by the door.

'I'll…come back later.' If they were in the middle of an argument, Drew didn't want to intrude.

'No, that's okay. Come in.' Sophie shot him a *please stay* look, while Carly's face hardened into a *just go* stare. Drew pretended not to notice either of them and gave Carly his most innocent smile.

'You're looking better, Carly.'

'See.' Apparently he'd just provided Carly with a piece of ammunition to hurl at Sophie.

'I…hope you're resting up.'

Apparently that redressed the balance. Sophie shot Carly an *I told you so* look.

The two of them seemed at an impasse. What was it Charlie always said? Never get between the girl you fancy and her best friend. Drew wondered whether his status as a doctor would protect him a little from the consequences of breaking that apparently sensible rule, and realised that he couldn't hide behind that whenever it suited him.

'Your shoulder hurts?' Drew noticed that Carly was absently rubbing her right shoulder.

'Yeah, a bit. I must have been lying on it.'

'Not necessarily. They pump gas into your abdomen to do the laparoscopy. It can cause you pain for a little while afterwards.'

Carly frowned. 'I've got gas? In my shoulder?'

'No. It's probably referred pain from your diaphragm. I don't suppose you told your doctor about this at the hospital?'

'I didn't think it was relevant.'

Sophie rolled her eyes. 'You're supposed to tell the doctor what your symptoms are and let him decide what's relevant.'

He shot her a grin, wondering if she remembered who she'd got those words from. Sophie's slight shrug told him that she was owning up to nothing.

'I imagine the doctor said you should walk around a bit, as soon as you feel able.' He fixed Carly with what he hoped was a no-nonsense look.

'Yeah. And I will be walking around. I'll be getting back to work soon.'

'Walking about a bit is not the same as being on your feet for sixteen hours a day. Did you think to mention that your job isn't exactly a nine to five?' Drew had seen how hard everyone on the set worked. Early mornings, evening shoots, night shoots. It was relentless.

Carly didn't reply to his question, so Sophie provided the answer. 'Obviously not. You need a bit of time to recuperate, and I've been on the phone to Mark. He'll be here in a couple of days to take you home.'

A tear glistened in the corner of Carly's eye. 'But, Soph… What about you?'

'I'm fine. Drew's been helping me, and I'm going to see a doctor that he knows. I feel much better, just knowing that I'm doing something, and that there's a lot more that I can do. You're best off at home with Mark and I'm best off here.'

Drew couldn't help grinning. The Sophie who spoke wasn't the one he'd first met, vague and temperamental. Her voice was firm and assertive, and she knew exactly what she wanted.

Carly frowned in Drew's direction and he shrugged. 'Don't drag me into this. I just do whatever I'm told.'

'I bet you do.' Carly folded her arms across her chest. 'All right. Have it your way. I never thought you'd turn into such a diva, Soph.'

Sophie laughed and hugged her friend. As Drew turned to leave them alone, he saw grateful tears glistening in Carly's eyes.

Sophie was proud of herself. She'd made a list, carefully ticking off each task as it was accomplished and making notes under each entry. It would have been easy— no, expected—that she would just have asked Jennie to do it but doing it herself had brought with it a feeling of power. A feeling that she could do these things if she tried.

The airline tickets were booked and Carly's husband was arriving in London in two days' time. He and Carly were booked into a hotel for the night, and the car was hired so that Drew could take Carly to London to meet him.

'Is that everything?' She pushed the piece of paper with her carefully transcribed notes across the breakfast table towards Drew.

He scanned it carefully. 'Looks like it. I have something for you.' He passed a business card to her.

'Dr Henry Chancellor.' She whispered the name quietly. It seemed almost like a magic spell.

'Yeah. I've spoken to his secretary. I didn't give your name, but he's going to make himself available for an appointment at short notice.'

'I don't know when   '

'You can come to London with Carly and me.'

It all seemed so sudden. So soon. 'But... I don't think I can make it, Drew. The filming schedule. Like I said, I don't want to mess Joel around any more than I already have.'

'I spoke to Joel. He's happy to reschedule to give you a couple of days off to come to London with us.'

'You did...what?' Sophie got to her feet and then sank back down into her chair. She didn't do that any more, she didn't run. She stayed and fought. 'You promised me, Drew.'

'I didn't tell him anything. He mentioned to me that you might want to go down to London to see Carly off, and I said I thought it would be a good idea.'

'Joel never *just* mentions anything.'

'Well, maybe I just happened to mention to him that we were going...' Drew had a look of studied innocence on his face, and the conversation clearly hadn't been as casual as he was making out.

'Come on, Drew. I'm paying you the respect of not walking away, so perhaps you can return the favour and give it to me straight.'

'Okay. You've got a point. Joel knows that something's going on, and he realises that it's being sorted. He hasn't pushed me for any details, and if he's willing to give you a bit of space without asking why, then I think you should take it.'

'And what *did* you say to him?'

'Just that I'd have you back on Saturday evening, ready for work on Sunday.'

'And that's what you intend to do?'

Drew grinned at her. 'That's exactly what I intend to do.'

It sounded like a plan. Now that she had the card in her hand, it sounded like a very good plan. 'So you'll call your friend?'

He chuckled. 'What, too much of a diva to make a phone call for yourself?'

'Don't make fun of me.'

His face was suddenly tender. 'I'm sorry. It's up to you, though, to make a time you feel comfortable with and to ask any questions that you want to ask when you make the appointment.' He took the card from her hand, writing on the back of it.

'Speak to Molly, Henry's secretary. He may well want to have an MRI scan done on the Friday, and see you to discuss the results on the Saturday. Is that okay?'

'Yes. It's good.' Sophie reached into her handbag for her notebook, and slipped the card between the pages. 'Shall I make a booking at the hotel?'

'For yourself, if you want. My place is in London, so I'll go back there and pick up my post. And if it's not too humble for a diva to stay overnight…?' He ducked back, as Sophie swatted the notebook in his direction.

'Mark and Carly aren't going to need me hanging around. And I think I can rough it for one night.'

CHAPTER NINE

'I'M SCARED, DREW.'

Everything had gone without a hitch so far. They had driven from Devon to London early that morning, and Mark had been waiting for Carly at the hotel. Hugs and kisses were exchanged, and then Drew drove Sophie to a private hospital in Harley Street, using the car park under the building and hustling her straight into the lift.

She was booked in for a MRI scan as Sophie DeAngelo and had reminded Drew to give her a nudge if she failed to respond to the name. Now came what felt like the scariest bit of the whole weekend.

'I'm *really scared*.' She picked up a magazine from the table in the private waiting room, flipping through it without reading anything. 'What if I panic in the machine? People do, you know.'

'Yeah, sometimes. But it's not the end of the world if you do. And you've already been through a lot worse, and held your nerve.' He laid his hand on hers, and she realised that she had been shredding the pages of the magazine between her fingers. 'Stop that. You're tearing me in half.'

Sophie focussed on the glossy paper. Drew's smile sparkled up at her, despite her having ripped one of his ears off. She smoothed the page, reading the heading of the article.

Dr Drew Taylor talks about the diagnosis and treatment of brain injuries.

'I might have to retract a couple of things I said in the article. In the light of recent experience.' He was grinning.

'Why?'

'Because I said that early diagnosis and therapy is vital. That was before I met an actress who decided she didn't need either of those things, and still managed to keep working.'

'I haven't exactly been at my best.'

'Well, maybe I'll just leave that bit in, then.'

'Why didn't you say something about this?' Sophie flipped to the cover of the magazine. It was a serious, well-regarded publication, aimed at educating lay people about medical matters.

'I didn't think you much liked guys who wrote magazine articles…' His lips twitched in wry humour and when Sophie started to laugh he grinned.

'Idiot. This couldn't be more different. Do you think they'd mind if I took this home to read?'

'I imagine they'll insist on it, now that you've torn it to pieces. They've probably got a few of them, they're good to put in the waiting room.'

Sophie slipped the magazine into her bag. 'I'll give the receptionist the money for it.'

'If you must. Now, what were we saying? About you panicking?'

'I can't remember.' Suddenly she felt safe. She was with Drew, and nothing bad was going to happen.

They waited another five minutes, then a nurse showed her to a small cubicle, and Sophie undressed, folding her clothes carefully. Drew was waiting for her outside and walked with her into the stark, white-painted room that housed the scanner.

'Sit up here.' He laid his hand on the long padded bench in front of the machine. It looked as if it was about to eat her.

'It's big, isn't it?'

'Yeah. It'll be a bit noisy when it gets going as well, but that's nothing to worry about. I'll be through there, and I'll be watching you all the time.' He took her hand in his, smiling down at her. 'It'll be over before you know it.'

A pinprick in her arm, which she hardly felt, because she was looking at Drew. A technician positioned her head, and a doctor took Drew to one side for a few words. Then he had to go.

He brushed his fingers against hers, told her that everything was going to be okay and walked away. Then the technician's voice over the intercom, quiet and reassuring, telling her when to breathe in, when to hold her breath...

Then it was over. The nurse helped her up from the bench and she changed back into her clothes, her hands shaking with relief.

'Did you see the results?' She found Drew pacing restlessly outside and caught at the fabric of his sleeve. Someone had said something about results, she was sure of it.

'The results need to be analysed by computer first. Henry Chancellor will have them tomorrow, and when you go and see him he'll explain everything to you.'

'Okay. Thanks. Can we go now, then?'

'All right.' Winding his arm around her shoulder, he guided her towards the lift.

Downstairs, he put the keys into the ignition of the hire car and left them there untouched, turning to face her. 'I was thinking we might go somewhere tonight.' He shot her a mouthwatering smile.

He was keeping her busy, trying to stop her from fretting about tomorrow. It was an obvious ruse, and it seemed to be working. 'Did you have anywhere in mind?'

'Not really. I thought we could go to my place, book somewhere quiet and go out for a meal. Catch the cinema if we felt like it.'

A tingle ran down Sophie's spine. She knew an opportunity when she ran across it, and this felt like one. She'd been passing her opportunities by for too many months now, just drifting in a world where nothing made sense to her.

'I've got a better idea. Let's go out somewhere bright, and noisy and full of people having fun.'

He grinned. 'Yeah?'

'Don't you like the idea?'

'What's not to like? A gorgeous movie star on my arm for the night.'

'A minor movie star…'

'If you say so.' He didn't seem to bother much about the intricate hierarchies of fame. 'We can get my old banger out of the garage, give her a run. She gets a bit choked up when I don't drive her for a while.'

'An old banger?' Sophie couldn't imagine Drew driving an old banger of a car. He liked anything mechanical far too much for that.

'Well…' His grey eyes glinted. 'She's sleek, beautiful.

Smells nice. But she is a little temperamental at times. It's nothing I can't handle.'

'Your ideal woman, then.'

'Well, she doesn't have much of a sense of humour.' He chuckled as if that was a private joke between a man and his car. 'What do you think?'

That sounded like a challenge. And Sophie wasn't going to be upstaged by a car. 'We'd have to do it properly.'

'Yeah? What do you suggest?'

She took the opportunity to look him up and down, imagining him darkly handsome in a dinner suit. 'I need a dress. A really nice one…'

Something ignited in his eyes. He liked the idea. A lot. And Sophie knew that this was something she could do for him. Probably better than Drew could imagine.

It was almost surreal. Sophie had made a phone call and given his address. By the time they got home, a courier was waiting on the doorstep with half a dozen large boxes. He helped her carry them up to the spare room and stacked them next to the wardrobe, and then she'd shooed him away, without giving any hint of what they contained.

The silence in the house for the next thirty minutes indicated that Sophie had done as he'd suggested, and lain down for a nap. When Drew heard the noise of the shower from upstairs, he changed into his best suit and waited.

An hour later, he was sitting in the lounge, trying to pin his attention on the pages of a book, but actually wondering whether a black hole had opened up in his house and she'd fallen into it. A noise at the doorway grabbed his attention.

Wow. Just... *wow.*

By some unknown process that defied medical princi-
ples, blood rushed simultaneously to his head and down
to another part of his body that he'd been trying to ignore for the last two weeks. Sophie had pulled out all
of the stops this time, and the transformation made him
want to fall to his knees.

She glittered...no, she shimmered...in a dark blue sequinned dress that clung to her curves, high-heeled silver
sandals, which made her legs look impossibly long, and
a small silver and blue clutch bag. Her hair was done in
a gravity-defying arrangement of curls, which framed
her face perfectly.

'You look...' Words failed him.

She smiled and a bright shiver ran down his spine. 'Is
that good speechless, or bad speechless?' She knew exactly what effect she was having on him, and it seemed
that was exactly what she'd wanted.

'Good. Definitely good speechless.' Confounded as
he was by her magic, Drew still couldn't quite square
the mathematics of six boxes and only one dress. 'So
what did your fairy godmother put in the other boxes?'

'I had a choice of dresses.' She giggled at his obvious confusion. 'Designers lend things out all the time.
It's good publicity for them if a celebrity wears their
latest creation.'

A sudden desire to see her in all six was quenched by
the thought that she looked just perfect, and he wouldn't
change a thing. He rose, pulling his jacket on, and she
smiled, looking him up and down unashamedly.

'You scrub up pretty well too, Drew Taylor.'

It still gave him a thrill whenever he heard his
name on her lips. He wondered if she'd used it because
she knew...

'I'm still getting used to seeing the many faces of Sophie Warner.' At first it had unnerved Drew that she seemed to be able to slip from one character to another so easily. But this was completely different. She wasn't trying to beguile him, or pull the wool over his eyes. She'd done this for him. To give him pleasure.

'Do you mind my many faces?'

'I find them endlessly entrancing. And having you on my arm tonight is the best gift you could give me.'

She nodded, as if she'd got the answer she wanted, walking over to him and slipping her hand into the crook of his elbow. This he was going to enjoy.

Drew's sitting-room was warm and welcoming, filled with books and photographs, a feeling of space and light. A pair of vintage red leather chairs matched the throw, slung across the back of a modern sofa. It put the carefully designed interiors of the faceless homes that Sophie had rented of late to shame. This was all about comfort, individuality and effortless style.

The garage lay on the ground floor of the three storey house and she followed him downstairs with a little thrill of anticipation, blinking as he switched on the lights. It was white painted, orderly, with a space for his bike. And a small, neat sports car.

'She's beautiful, Drew. Fabulous...'

'You like her?' he asked with a smile. 'I hope she doesn't get the sulks.'

'Why would she do that?' Drew had obviously lavished a great deal of care on the car. The opalescent grey paintwork gleamed. Through the window, she could see a fifties-style dashboard and cream leather seats.

'She's used to being the most beautiful thing in this garage. You've just changed all that.'

Yes! She'd gone out to wow him, and she'd obviously succeeded. Sophie shivered with pleasure.

'Thank you. How old…? What year is she?' It probably wasn't a good idea to ask the lady's age.

'Nineteen fifty-seven. When I got her she was just a rusted chassis. Took me six years to rebuild.'

'And you painted her to match your eyes?' She couldn't resist teasing him a little.

He opened the passenger door, grinning. 'That wasn't my thought at the time.'

It was tricky getting into the low seat with such high heels, but Drew's arm was there to steady her. When he slid into the driver's seat, the look on his face made her heart turn over. Pure enjoyment. And she was a part of it. He'd wanted to share his most treasured possession with her, and he'd said that she was *more* beautiful. Sophie sent a mental apology to the little car, and hoped it understood that this was a special night for her.

'Ready to go?' He grinned at her, darkly handsome.

'Yes.' She was ready for anything tonight.

He'd chosen a West End theatreland restaurant for cocktails and then dinner. The maître d' recognised Sophie and tried to usher her to a better table than the one that Drew had been able to procure, but she waved him away.

'Don't you want to sit over there?' Drew nodded towards the table she'd been offered, close to the piano.

'Not particularly. They always want you to sit somewhere that people can see you. I'm not here for that tonight.'

'What about the dress? Doesn't your designer want some photos in the morning paper?' It would be good to know when to expect a camera lens, so he could melt quietly into the background.

'I told him tonight was a private engagement. I've worn plenty of his stuff on the red carpet and he's happy to do me a few favours in return once in a while.'

The small, circular table in the corner of the restaurant suddenly became Drew's whole world. This was for him. Not the cameras, or the publicity people. All for him.

'Would you like a cocktail?'

She turned the shimmer of her smile onto him, and he almost blinked in its brilliance. 'Yes, I'd love one.' She picked the cocktail menu up from the table and held it up in front of her face, peering over the top of it at the bustle and noise around her. Only Drew could see the curve of her red lips. 'This is fun, isn't it?'

The service was a great deal better than he was used to and the meal was excellent. When an elaborately arranged confection was placed in front of her for sweet, she leaned towards him confidingly.

'I think the people at the next table have just recognised you…'

Drew chuckled. 'You mean they've recognised you.' He was pretty sure that he didn't warrant this kind of attention.

'Maybe. Although you're much more useful to have around.'

'What makes you say that?' Drew couldn't imagine that he could be more important than Sophie in the eyes of the people around them. He was just a dark suit, which served only to emphasise her gleam.

'If someone were to be ill…' she said, looking around, as if checking that everyone within view seemed healthy '…you'd go and do your thing.'

'I suppose so.' Drew hoped fervently that no one at a nearby table was going to use this moment to collapse. 'It would depend...'

'Depend on what?' Her gaze was on him now, making him shiver.

'Well, if someone cut their finger, I might just leave them to it.'

'And if someone had a heart attack?'

'If someone had a heart attack, I'd wish they'd chosen another time, but...' Drew shrugged '... I'd have to go.'

'Yes. My father was a doctor. Did I mention that?'

That little quirk of her lips again. Drew probed gently. 'I guess he wasn't always around, then.'

'He was never around. Not like you.'

Drew ignored the obvious unfairness of the statement. He'd been accused of being never around enough times to know that he was no angel in that department. And he knew that he couldn't change. 'Have you told your family about the difficulties you've been having?'

'No.'

'Don't you think they might want to know?'

She shrugged, the shimmer of her dress sparkling suddenly. 'My mum and dad are abroad. Dad works for a medical aid agency. I know what he'd say...'

'What's that?'

'He'd say that he can't get away at the moment.' She looked up at him, wrinkling her nose slightly. 'I'm the black sheep of the family.'

'Really? Surely they're proud of your success.'

'To my dad it's all Hollywood nonsense. My two older brothers both followed in the family footsteps and became doctors. He reckons that they're the ones who are doing something useful with their lives.'

At one time Drew might have unthinkingly agreed with that. That had been before he'd really got to know Sophie.

'I suppose your father thinks that medicine is all about what *he* does.'

'I don't understand.'

'Doctors can only do so much. We can diagnose, and often we can treat. We rely on people like you to give our patients the will to keep going.'

She narrowed her eyes. 'That's a generous thing to say. I'm not sure that anything I've done gives anyone the will to keep going.'

'Not on your own maybe. But never underestimate the power of a smile to make someone feel better. And that's your territory, not mine.'

'You want to try telling my father that?' She grinned at him, obviously pleased with the idea.

'No. I think you might, though.'

She shook her head. 'I need all my wits about me for that kind of discussion.'

'Then that's one hell of a good reason for you to work on getting better.'

'Okay. Remind me to write that down when we get back to your place. My notebook wouldn't fit in this evening bag.' Suddenly her gaze was on his face. 'I'd like to know something.'

Drew could tell that the something mattered to her. 'What do you want to know?'

'It's your job to look after me, I know that. Everyone wants me to come up with the goods, to get this film finished…'

Drew had been telling himself the same thing. But he couldn't pretend any more. Sophie herself was far more interesting to him than any medical condition she could possibly contrive to manifest.

'Soph... I look at you, and I see...' He shrugged. 'What I don't see is a traumatic brain injury, or a case of heterochromia. I see a strong, beautiful woman, with eyes that fascinate me. I don't want to be your doctor, or your minder, and getting the film made isn't that high on my list of priorities.'

Her smile radiated through the space between them, seeming to light up the room. 'What is high on your list of priorities?'

'Right now? Asking you to dance with me comes in as the clear favourite.' He nodded towards the piano at the far end of the restaurant, where people were dancing to a slow, lilting melody.

She smiled, holding out her hand, and he rose, hardly able to believe his good fortune. Drew led her through the maze of tables, aware that all eyes were on them, and not caring. For tonight, at least, he felt like the luckiest man in London.

They'd danced, gone back to their table for coffee, and then danced again. It was heaven. Feeling his body against hers, strong and graceful. His smile, his scent.

He was every birthday, every Christmas that her father hadn't been there rolled up into one. All the bad decisions she'd made in her life, and all the good ones, everything she'd remembered and forgotten, they all seemed to have led up to this night. She was playing the fairy-tale princess, and he filled the part of her Prince Charming so very well.

Drew paid the bill, brushing away the manager's protests that their meal was on the house. The car was on a meter a little way along the road, but instead they walked, finding themselves on the Embankment, the Thames glittering darkly on one side of them and the bright lights of the city on the other.

'What are you going to do next?' Sophie had been too busy trying to push Drew away to bother with that up till now.

'I've got a job that starts in two and a half months. Director of a memory clinic, here in London.'

'Sounds like a great opportunity. A chance to make your mark on something, right from the very beginning.' Deep in the pit of Sophie's stomach, she was almost disappointed. If Drew had said that he was entirely at a loose end, then the chances of their paths crossing on a rather more permanent basis were greater.

'It is.' His chest heaved in a motion of regret. 'I'd rather it hadn't come my way in quite the way that it did.'

'Your hospital closing, you mean?'

'Yeah. I put everything into that place and when the local authority said it was to close, I fought as hard as I could. We had an action group, we lobbied everyone we could think of, got a local petition going.'

'It sounds as if you were very determined.'

'I was.' His fingers had been resting on the hand that she had looped through his arm, and suddenly he took them away. 'I didn't always have time for the people around me. My family and friends.'

Sophie caught her breath. He was warning her off. Telling her that he wasn't so different from her father. In one way that was a choking disappointment, but in another way... If he felt nothing for her, why would he even bother to say it?

'You have time tonight, though.'

They'd been walking more and more slowly, and suddenly he came to a halt. When Sophie faced him, standing right in his path, he took off his jacket and wrapped it around her shoulders in a gesture that screamed of gentle protectiveness.

'Tonight is... It's just tonight.'

'That's okay.' She wanted to shrug off his jacket and demand a more intimate warmth. The warmth of having his arms around her, right here, right now.

She knew he was tempted. But he shook his head. 'We shouldn't get carried away.'

'Do you mean *I* shouldn't get carried away. I've been doing some reading on the internet. Isn't there something about traumatic brain injury affecting your impulse control?'

'It can do. That's just one possible symptom.'

'Do you think that's the case here?'

His eyes searched her face. 'No. I don't.'

'Then maybe you're afraid that if you kiss me, I might forget all about it.'

One hand cupped the side of her jaw and she tilted her face up towards his. So close. Then she felt his other arm around her waist, almost lifting her off her feet, pulling her against him. He kissed her, brushing his lips against hers as if he was feeling his way forward, gauging her reaction.

A little sigh escaped her lips. Couldn't he feel that she wanted more than that?

He kissed her again, properly this time. Deep and full of longing, offering himself up to her and taking what he wanted, all at the same time.

'You won't forget.' He almost growled the words, challenging her on the most primitive of levels.

'Do it again, then. Make sure...' She'd heard voices as people strolled past them in the darkness. Right now, she didn't care who recognised her or what they might say or do. All she cared about was Drew.

'Kiss me now, Taylor.'

His lips quirked into a smile. He knew that she was teasing him. 'That will be my pleasure…'

CHAPTER TEN

SINCE THE CRASH, waking up had been a slow process. Sophie had lost the ability to hit the ground running, knowing everything she had to do that day, remembering everything she'd done the day before. She took a breath, giving the memories time to come back and organise themselves in her head.

Opening one eye, she consulted the message written on her forearm in magic marker. Carly was with Mark at the hotel. She was at Drew's house, in his spare room. The door was open and the landing light was on. She must have asked him to do that last night so that she wouldn't wake in darkness and wonder where she was.

And he'd kissed her. She didn't need a note to herself to remind her about that. Even if a few of the delicious details had slipped her mind, her body remembered them. The way he'd kissed her until she'd been breathless. The way his lips had whispered everything that his body had said.

Big Ben had tolled midnight, the deep chimes echoing along the river. He'd tenderly let her go, and Sophie had reluctantly allowed him to. She hadn't run from him, leaving her glass slipper behind, but 'just for tonight' had meant what it said, all the same.

She rolled over, picking her phone up from the nightstand. She didn't remember putting it there, it should be in her bag. Sophie shrugged. Last night she'd done a lot of things to break her familiar routine.

The phone responded to her touch. Ten past nine. There was plenty of time before her appointment in Harley Street. She put the phone back onto the nightstand and lay back against the pillows.

Wait. That wasn't her phone... She stared at the corner of the instrument. It must be Drew's. He had the same model as her. But what was it doing in here? For the life of her, she couldn't remember him with it.

Doubt gnawed its way towards her heart. She didn't remember the photos that were on the internet being taken either. They'd been taken with a phone, too...

Drew wouldn't do that. He wouldn't. But trust and logic only went so far, and fear was a much more potent emotion. She sat up, reaching for the phone. She hated herself for finding the photo icon, in just the same place as it was on her own phone. It was wrong to tap it, and then scroll through the pictures.

A couple of photos of a woman, who resembled Drew, hugging a toddler. She remembered him saying he had a sister, who was married with a young child... She scrolled past them, and found a couple of pictures of his motorbike, and four of various bits and pieces that looked as if they came from an engine. Then nothing.

She was on a roll now. Somehow, relief didn't stop her from tapping to see whether he'd sent any texts or emails. Nothing. The last call listed was the one he'd made to book the restaurant yesterday. There was an incoming text...

Sophie couldn't help it. She opened the text. She vaguely remembered Carly and Drew talking about someone called Charlie, and supposed that was how Carly had got into contact with Drew in the first place.

You're in the papers again, mate.

Then she remembered. She and Drew had walked back to his car, and as he'd been helping her in she'd heard the sound of a shutter and been blinded for a moment by a bright flash. Drew had smiled, motioning the man with the camera away and shrugging the incident off.

Charlie obviously didn't think he'd be so indifferent to it. Maybe Drew was keeping score, the way that Josh probably had. How many times he could get himself in the papers, by dint of having Sophie on his arm.

A noise in the doorway made her jump. The phone slithered out of her hand and onto the floor.

'You're awake.' A faded pair of jeans, slung low on his hips, and a black T-shirt. Could he really have looked any more like the guy she should have had sex with last night?

He wasn't much of an actor, though. However much he wanted to pretend that he hadn't seen what she'd been doing, his body language said it all.

There was no point in trying to pretend that she hadn't been caught. He'd been caught as well. 'I seem to have ended up with your phone. You've got a text.' She got out of bed, recovering the phone from the floor, and held it out towards him.

'Yours is in the usual place, in your bag. I gave you mine last night so you could set an alarm for this morning.' He gave her the cup of coffee and inspected his phone. Shrugged and slipped it into his pocket.

That cleared up one unknown, but the other was still tearing at her. 'You saw the photographer last night...'

'Of course I saw him. I don't know how he caught up with us.'

'You didn't call him, then. Or this friend of yours... Charlie. It would have been a better shot if he'd got us...' She couldn't say *kissing*. She already felt as if the delicious audacity of that had been wrenched from her. '...on the Embankment.'

His face darkened. 'You think I *wanted* to be in the papers this morning?'

'Didn't you?'

'I'm a doctor, Sophie. I have a reputation to consider. I'm not some fly-by-night hanger-on, who thinks it's a good idea to wake up in the morning and read what he did last night.'

'Oh, so you think that I'm a fly-by-night do you?' He might have pretended to value what she did, but when it came down to it, his attitude was just the same as her father's.

'I didn't say that. If you want it in words of one syllable, then here it is. I'm not Josh.' He turned, pausing in the doorway. 'Get dressed. You have an appointment this morning.'

She'd never seen him so angry. He banged the door as he left, and Sophie heard his footsteps, marching along the hall and down the stairs.

Knives, forks. The butter dish, absolutely straight and in line with the marmalade. Drew arranged the breakfast table with ruthless accuracy, in an attempt to stop thinking about everything else.

The moment he'd seen her, sitting up in bed, looking at his phone, Drew had realised that she didn't trust him. And when she'd seen him, the look of guilty panic on her face had confirmed it.

Rationalise. He had to remember that Sophie had just woken up, and probably hadn't had a clue what his phone was doing beside her bed. She'd looked at it, and the text from Charlie had made it seem that he was just like Josh had been. How could she know that it was just the opposite, that he dreaded seeing his picture in the papers?

But she should have trusted him. She'd kissed him...

And that had been last night. They'd agreed that. Just one kiss, just one night.

Drew couldn't even bring himself to think about it. Of course it hadn't been *just* a kiss. He knew what just a kiss felt like, and it didn't leave his body aching for more, far into the night. Just a kiss would have felt uncomplicatedly good. Just a kiss didn't care if she didn't trust him.

A chair scraped as it was pulled back from the kitchen table, and Drew turned. She was wearing a pair of smart trousers with low pumps and a lacy sweater. Her hair pulled back in a ponytail, a couple of last night's curls escaping around her face. No one had any right to look this beautiful first thing in the morning.

'I want to apologise.' She looked at him determinedly, and all of Drew's anger melted. 'It was wrong of me to look at your phone, and your private texts, and it was wrong of me to suggest you had anything to do with the press finding us last night. I was being paranoid.'

'I was...' He shook his head. There was no excuse for his behaviour, other than the hurt of having those moments they'd had together twisted and warped by suspicion. 'You've every right to be concerned, after what you've been through. I should have understood that.'

He walked over to the table, pulling his phone from

his pocket and putting it down in front of her. 'You can look at my phone any time you like. You can look through my laptop, through every drawer in this house. I promise you that you'll find nothing that compromises you.'

Her hand trembled as it hovered over the phone. Then she picked it up and handed it back to him. 'I don't need to, Drew. I know there's nothing.'

The impulse to kiss her was almost overwhelming. 'Are we good, then?'

She nodded, looking up at him with the smile that made him want her in the very worst of ways. 'Yeah. We're good.'

Drew had taken the hire car up to Harley Street this morning, loading their bags into the boot so that they could drive straight down to Devon after Sophie's appointment. As arranged, he drove into the narrow, paved mews which ran behind the impressive Georgian façade of Henry Chancellor's consulting rooms.

'Molly...?' His phone lay in the hands-free cradle on the dashboard.

'You're early.'

Drew grinned. Early was always a point in any patient's favour in Molly's book as it allowed her to run Dr Chancellor's diary with the minimum of fuss and the maximum of efficiency.

'It's the green door. I'm opening up now.'

A brightly painted garage door, one of the row that lined one side of the mews, began to move, sliding upwards to reveal a garage. Two cars inside and one free space. Drew turned into it and switched off the ignition, and the door closed behind them.

A switch, probably flipped from Molly's desk, and the light came on. Sophie turned to him, smiling.

'Very neat.'

He'd promised to get her inside the building without anyone seeing her, and had been gratified when she'd just nodded and taken him at his word, not demanding to know how he was going to manage it. Molly had come up trumps, allowing him to use the garage usually reserved for the doctors who worked in the building, and negating the need for Drew to roll Sophie up in a carpet and carry her up the front steps on his shoulder.

He got out of the car, squeezing through the gap he'd left between the driver's door and the wall, and opening Sophie's door as wide as the cramped space would allow.

'This way...' He led her up the steps to the door into the main building, and found Molly waiting there for them.

'Drew. How nice to see you.' Molly smiled at him, and then turned her attention quickly to Sophie. 'Welcome...'

It was the first time he'd ever heard Molly not address a patient by their name. Perhaps that was taking things a little too far, but after this morning the gesture was appreciated.

'Thank you.' Sophie was beginning to shake now, and Molly took her arm, leading her towards the back stairs.

'Dr Chancellor's the best in his field. Although he'd tell you that Drew is. A case of the pupil outstripping the teacher...'

'Drew's a bit of an upstart, then.' Sophie looked over her shoulder at Drew, giving him a tremulous smile.

'Definitely.' Molly laughed quietly. 'There are a few stories I could tell you...'

'Look after him.' Drew only just caught Sophie's whispered words and Molly's nod in response as they reached the top of the stairs. His heart almost burst. The one time when she should be worried for herself and she'd remembered him.

He walked through to the reception area at the front of the building and started to fiddle with the coffee machine next to Molly's desk. Sophie would be a while with Henry Chancellor, and suddenly each minute seemed to drag out in front of him like a potential eternity.

'No coffee…' Molly walked around her desk, bending to flip the switch of a socket on the wall, and the lights on the coffee machine went out.

'What?'

'I'll make you some herbal tea, Drew. I'm not having you sitting here drinking coffee and twitching like a cat on hot bricks.'

Drew sat down. This was Molly's waiting room, and he knew from experience that she ruled it with a rod of iron. Molly disappeared for a minute and returned with a cup and saucer, placing it firmly on the side table next to him.

'Drink that. Then you're going for a walk.' She pulled at the cuff of her smart blue jacket and glanced at a silver bracelet watch. 'Half an hour at least. You can pop down to Oxford Circus and do some shopping.'

'You want me to get something for you?'

'No, I want you out of here. Your friend will be fine, but Dr Chancellor needs to examine her and go through the results of the MRI scan. Then he'll be wanting to have a talk with her.'

Drew knew better than to argue with Molly. She was probably right anyway, she usually was. He shrugged, picked up his cup and sipped the tea.

* * *

When he arrived back at the consulting rooms, Molly
was chatting to a young couple, taking their toddler onto
her knee so she could play with the picture calendar on
her desk. There was an agonising five-minute wait, and
then Molly answered the phone, nodded into the receiver,
and gave the child back to her mother. A glance in his
direction indicated that Drew should follow her.

She led the way through to the back stairs, arriving just as Sophie appeared at the top of them. A warm
smile in Sophie's direction, and then the two of them
were bundled through the door that led to the garage,
as Sophie stuttered out her thanks.

He shouldn't ask yet. He should let Sophie gather her
thoughts and tell him in her own time. Drew opened the
passenger door for her, squeezing around to the other
side of the car and getting in. The garage doors opened,
presumably under Molly's direction, and light filtered
through into the gloom.

Drive. Just drive. Sophie was staring straight ahead
of her, her face impassive. He knew that look, and she
didn't need to have him question her at the moment. She
was busy processing everything that had happened in
the last hour. He put the car into reverse, cursing softly
and jamming his foot on the brake as the sound of the
front bumper touching the wall reached his ears.

That was all he needed. Rolling the car forward, he
was about to try again when Sophie's voice sounded
beside him.

'Steady… Everything's okay, Drew.'

His heart jumped. Okay how? Really okay? Drew
was shaking now, and he took a deep breath before he
turned towards her. He hadn't been prepared for this.
The sudden realisation that Henry's assessment of the

MRI scan results meant everything to him. That he needed to know, just as desperately as she did.

Then he heard her crying, softly. 'Soph...' Drew switched the engine off, turning to her. She was gulping for air now, her cheeks streaked with tears. 'Soph, it's all right. Whatever it is, we can face it.'

We can face it. It was no longer a matter of encouraging her, telling her that she was strong enough to deal with this. Drew realised that however hard he'd tried to stand back, however much he'd felt that was the best thing he could do for himself and for Sophie, that they were now in this together.

'It's...' She flung her arms around him, crying into his shoulder, her words coming between fits of tears. 'He said it was okay... The scan...'

It was as if his skin was suddenly porous, soaking up happiness. Drew felt it permeate through his body and he twisted in his seat, holding her tightly. 'It's okay. Just let it out, sweetheart...'

She clung to him for a long time. Finally she seemed to catch her breath and pulled away from him, her face shining. 'I want to get this right.' She pulled her notebook out of her bag.

'Take your time.' Drew grinned at her as she tore one of the pages, in her haste to get to the right place.

'Dr Chancellor said that the MRI scan showed up some microscopic lesions on the site of the impact...' She looked up at him, shrugging. 'Basically, I hit my head and that caused a mild traumatic brain injury. There's every reason to be optimistic about my symptoms improving and, of course, there are plenty of things I can do to manage the condition. There are no signs of any other bleeding or of any tumours.' She snapped her notebook closed triumphantly.

'Is that what you were worried about, Sophie?' Drew had never voiced his own concerns to her, knowing that they were not the most likely scenario, and that they would only feed her own fears.

She shrugged. 'I knew it wasn't likely. But anything's possible.'

'And now you know for sure.'

'Yes. Thank you, Drew. I wouldn't have had the scan or seen Dr Chancellor if you hadn't made me.'

'Did I make you? I thought it was just a little gentle encouragement.'

She snorted with laughter, reaching into her handbag for a tissue and blowing her nose. 'Were you going to let me get away with not going?'

'Now you mention it…' He grinned at her. 'I would have carried you here if you hadn't agreed to come. But that's not the point. You made that step yourself, and that means something.'

She nodded, her brow furrowing in thought. 'I'm ready now. I'm going to stop messing around and really work on coming to terms with this. Dr Chancellor's given me a whole list of things to do…' She reached into her bag and pulled out some sheets of paper, stapled together. 'He's given me a copy of the results and his recommendations, so I've no excuse for forgetting.'

Drew's fingers itched for the paper. He trusted Henry's judgement better than his own. Henry had been his guide and mentor since medical school. All the same, he wanted to see the results for himself, read them three times and check each word.

'I imagine he intended me to show them to you. I don't understand the medical bits.' She smiled at him. 'His recommendations were much the same as what you've been saying to me.'

The temptation to snatch the sheets from her fingers almost overwhelmed him. 'What do you say we find somewhere to have lunch and look at this? We'll go to Regent's Park, there must be a café there…'

'Okay.' She put the precious papers back into her bag, reaching for her seat belt and then changing her mind and letting it snap back into the housing. 'Thank you, Taylor.'

She planted a soft kiss on his cheek. Drew felt his skin tingle with pleasure where her lips had touched it. Then she grabbed the front of his shirt, pulling him as close as the restricted space would allow.

Her lips were so close her scent overwhelmed him. Drew meant only to brush his lips against hers, but that didn't work out. He found himself kissing her, his hand on the back of her neck, his thoughts racing in a dance of sheer delight. She responded to him so readily. So completely.

His phone beeped and he ignored it. Then, out of the corner of his eye, he caught sight of a tiny red light, flashing somewhere up by the roof of the garage.

'Soph… Sophie.' He let her go, feeling the loss immediately.

'What?' Her eyes sprang open, widening in confusion. 'I'm sorry…'

'Are you?' He grinned, running a finger along her jaw. 'I'm not. But perhaps this isn't the place…' He pointed to the CCTV camera mounted on the wall. He'd forgotten all about the screen on Molly's desk, where the feeds from the security system were displayed.

'Oops. We've been caught…' She put her hand to her mouth. Drew was tempted to get out of the car, tear the camera from its mounting and kiss her again. Instead, he reached for his phone.

A text from Molly.

Let me know when you've gone so I can close the garage doors.

Sophie looked over his shoulder and giggled.

'She's very tactful.'

'Yeah. Molly's the soul of discretion.'

She wound down the car window, waving to the CCTV camera with a smile and blowing a kiss. Drew's phone beeped again, and he showed Sophie the smiley face that Molly had sent. It was time for them to go. He started the car, backing carefully out of the cramped parking space in the garage.

CHAPTER ELEVEN

SOPHIE SEEMED TO be blooming. She had studied Henry Chancellor's recommendations carefully, and with Drew's help she was sticking to them. Her confidence seemed to grow by the day, and she became more relaxed and a delight to be with on set.

And then, unexpectedly, they both had a day off. This time it was Todd's scenes, not Sophie's, that needed to be reshot, and neither Drew nor Sophie were needed. He expected that she'd take the opportunity to have a lie-in and a lazy day.

Instead, she appeared at breakfast looking like a million dollars. A little make-up, skilfully applied to make it look as if she was bare-faced. A pretty top, swirls of green and blue, with a matching necklace.

'What are you up to today?' She plumped herself down opposite him.

'I've nothing planned.' Sophie clearly had, and whatever that was he suddenly craved the opportunity to be a part of it.

She grinned. 'In that case, can I persuade you to give me a lift? I need to go into town and then I'm going to visit the hospital.'

'What for?'

'I'm going to visit the children's ward. I made up my

mind that I would when we were visiting Carly. I got lost on the way to the drinks machine and ended up in there.'

He chuckled. 'I thought you were just taking your time, so that I could persuade Carly to behave.'

'Nothing that premeditated. I phoned the administrator yesterday and he said it would be fine for me to go. I want to stop off in town to get something for them first. I can't go empty-handed.'

She didn't need to take anything, just being there would be more than enough. But he supposed a little memento of the afternoon for the kids would be nice.

'Sure. You want me to borrow a car? You might arrive a bit windblown if we take the bike.'

'Oh, windblown is fine.' She obviously had everything planned and was on a roll. 'I like the bike.'

He liked the bike, too. Particularly with Sophie riding behind him, her arms firmly around his waist. He took the longest route he could into town, hoping that it wasn't too obvious that he was just riding around with her for kicks.

'Phew!' She climbed off the back of the bike, removing her helmet and unzipping her jacket. 'I love those country lanes. There seem to be such a lot of them.'

She shot him a knowing grin, looked around and then made a beeline for the door of the large electrical store that he'd parked outside. The automatic doors swooshed open, and Drew followed in the wake of her bright enthusiasm.

Suddenly she stopped short, a frown puckering her brow. 'I didn't come in here for a vacuum cleaner, did I?' She was looking at the display straight in front of her.

'I wouldn't have thought so. You didn't say what it was you wanted.' Drew looked around for a clue.

She'd consulted her notebook and a grin spread across

her face. 'Yeah, I think that would be good. What do you reckon?' She flipped the notebook around so that he could see what she'd written.

'A tablet computer. Yeah, that would be great to have on the ward. The kids can watch films, play games…'

'Good.' She looked around and then set off towards the far side of the shop. 'Come along.'

She listened to the salesman's spiel, tried out a few for herself, and then ignored his recommendation completely, choosing a model that Drew thought would be perfect. 'I'll take one. No, actually, I'll take two.'

'Yes, miss.'

Sophie leaned towards Drew, whispering in his ear. 'Do you think that's okay? I'm not having a problem with impulse control here, am I?'

'Maybe. You can afford it?'

She rolled her eyes. 'Of course I can.'

'And the kids will love these. When an impulse is as good as this one, who cares?'

She brightened. 'Yes… Of course. Who cares? What do you think about headphones? They might like headphones…' Her gaze searched the display behind the counter.

'It's a nice idea, but the hospital will want to have a different set for each patient. They probably already provide single use ones.'

'Good point. What about… If I get one of those gift cards, they can download some games and films.'

Drew nodded his approval. She was bright with enthusiasm, and totally irresistible along with it. 'It's a very generous gift. I imagine they'll be well used, a lot of hospitals are collecting money to buy these at the moment.'

'Hmm. Wonder if it was my idea or the admin

guy's…' She shrugged. 'Doesn't really matter. As long as they like them.'

'No, it doesn't matter.' Drew suspected that she would have fretted over the point a few weeks ago, trying to remember something that wasn't there, and it was good to see her dismiss it with such carelessness.

'I thought about what you said. The other day. About believing in me.'

'Yeah?'

'I reckoned if someone like you could believe in me, then I'd give it a try.'

Drew caught his breath, humbled by her faith in him. 'And how's that going?'

'Not sure yet. Working on it.' She slipped her hand into the crook of his arm, watching while the salesman wrapped her purchases.

She made a point of taking the ward sister and the administrator to one side and handing them the bag containing the tablets privately. And Drew made a point of watching her do it. He enjoyed her delighted smile when the ward sister saw what was in the bag and thanked her.

He hung back, letting her work her magic. No fuss, no big entrances, she just chatted briefly to a couple of the nurses, then let the ward sister lead her to one of the beds, where a small girl was dwarfed by the medical equipment around her. Sophie was introduced to the woman by the bedside, who smiled, pulling up a chair for her, and she took the little girl's hand.

It was almost too much to bear. Drew thought that he'd seen just about everything that could happen in a hospital, both good things and bad. But this was an aspect of healing he hadn't seen before. She made sure that she went to each of the beds, taking a little joy with

her as she did so. Talking to the staff and the families.
Seeming to see only the kids, and not the paraphernalia
that surrounded them. Playing with them, making faces,
anything to make them smile.

And smile they did. Drew didn't blame them one bit.
She was more beautiful than he could ever have imagined a woman could be, and if there had been a spare
bed in the place, he'd have been tempted to get into it,
just for that smile and the touch of her fingers on his.

Finally she found her way back to him. 'Sorry. I've
been so long…'

He shook his head in astonishment. 'Don't. I love
this.'

'Drew, there's this little boy. In the third bed along…'

'Yeah? What about him?'

'He loves motorbikes. He has a toy one, and I told
him that I'd come on a motorbike…' Her expression was
somewhere between imploring and embarrassed. 'I don't
suppose you could…' She waved her hand vaguely at
the window.

'Leave it with me. I'll be back.'

She brightened immediately. 'Thank you.'

Drew turned on his heel, grinning to himself.

He'd spoken to the ward sister and to Tommy's mother.
It had been decided that, as the day was fine and warm,
the young boy could be taken out into the grassy area
outside the ward for a while. Drew went to fetch his bike
from the car park, and rolled it as close as he could to the
ward entrance, making sure that the stand held it firm
and steady on the uneven ground.

Sophie had come outside with a little girl and one
of the nurses, and the three of them were busy with the
inevitable photographs. Drew sat down on a bench to

wait, nodding at the burly man who was already sitting
at the other end, drinking from a can.

'That's Sophie Warner.' The man nodded towards
her knowingly.

'Yeah.' Drew wondered if the man saw what he saw,
and came to the conclusion that he must do. It was impossible not to notice her smile.

'It's all very well, coming here, taking photographs.
You'd think they wouldn't have the nerve.'

'It's nice for the kids. And the parents.' Drew wondered what planet the guy came from. Couldn't he see
the pleasure that Sophie's visit was giving everyone?

'Then she'll go home and take a few more pictures.
Put them up on the internet and then pretend she doesn't
know how they got there.'

'And you're her best friend. Which is how you know
all this.'

The man missed his sarcasm entirely. 'They all do
it. Media whores, the lot of them. And from the sounds
of it, she's the worst. I read what that bloke said in the
paper, he seemed like a genuine type. Whore's the right
word for her.'

The keys of his bike fell to the ground at his feet as
Drew's hand balled involuntarily into a fist. 'Apologise.'
He choked out the word. One last chance for the man
before he punched him.

'Who to? Not you. And not *her* either.' The man got
to his feet, throwing his half-empty can at a waste bin
and missing it entirely. Drew stood, towering over the
man, who realised he was outmatched and almost ran
in the opposite direction from where Sophie was standing at the entrance to the ward.

The temptation to drag him back on his knees to
apologise to Sophie almost overwhelmed Drew. Then

he heard her laughter. Sophie was enjoying her day. He couldn't spoil it all for her, by letting her know that someone had called her a whore.

Every tendon ached for action of some sort. Punching something, kicking something—the inoffensive brick wall of the building seemed like a reasonable candidate at the moment. Instead, Drew bent, picked up his keys and slipped inside, making for the gents.

He filled a bowl with cold water, splashing his face and the back of his neck. Stared himself down in the mirror until he was able to breathe again. He had to calm down. If Sophie could deal with this, and still smile and face the world, then so must he.

Finally, he was calm enough to consider venturing out. He dried his face and hands and walked outside, making his way back to the ward. At the door, he ran headlong into Sophie's smile.

'There you are. Are you ready?'

'Yes, the bike's outside.'

'We're all set, too.' She grinned over to where Tommy had been seated in a wheelchair, beaming with happiness.

'Great. Let's do it.'

Tommy was wheeled out of the ward by a male nurse, his mother walking by his side. He was full of questions about the bike, and Drew bent down by the side of the wheelchair, giving the boy all the specifications, details of petrol consumption and how it ran on a long journey.

Then Drew helped Sophie into the saddle, and Tommy was wheeled in close beside her for the inevitable photographs. 'Can I sit on it?' Tommy's imploring voice was directed at his mother.

The question was passed along the line to the ward sister, who nodded a yes and supervised as Tommy was helped from his wheelchair and lifted onto the saddle in front of Sophie. She curled one arm protectively around his waist, and the male nurse stood behind them, supporting Tommy but looking for all the world as if he just wanted to be in on the photographs.

Drew approached Tommy's mother, who was waving at her son's delighted smile, tears streaming down her face. 'Why don't you go and stand with them? I'll take a picture.' He gestured at the phone in her hand.

'He doesn't want me...' The woman smiled up at him 'When a guy's sitting on a bike with a film star, he generally doesn't want his mum around.'

'I can understand that.' It wasn't just Tommy who felt that way. 'But he'll have plenty of pictures with Sophie. Perhaps you'd like one to remember today by, too.'

She pressed her lips together. 'I look a mess.'

Drew smiled. 'You look fine.'

He held his hand out and she dropped her phone into his palm. Her hand flew to the elastic tie that held her hair back in a ponytail, and she produced a comb from her handbag, scraping it across her head.

The little group around the motorbike was about to break up but Drew signalled to Sophie, who spoke quickly to the nurse who was holding Tommy, and they waited. A dash of lipstick, and Tommy's mother stepped forward. Sophie put her arm around her, pulling her a little closer so that she was in the centre of the frame with her son. When Tommy turned, beaming at his mother, Drew got the shot. Three more, for good measure, and then tears blurred his vision.

CHAPTER TWELVE

HUGGING HIM TIGHTLY all the way back to the hotel was the perfect ending to a perfect afternoon. Drew had seemed to take as much joy from it as she had and he'd talked about how much good it did the kids and their parents. Despite her father's clear disdain for the callow and useless profession his daughter had chosen, in Drew's eyes she was doing something important. Something that had brought him to tears at one point. He'd wiped them away quickly, but she'd seen them.

'Everyone looks busy.' He'd waited for her to get off the back of the bike and was surveying the scene of activity in front of the hotel.

'Looks as if Joel's happy with the scenes they shot today. We might be on the move.' Sophie had tried not to think about the impending move. A new set of hotel corridors to get lost in. Pages of notes that needed to be made, just so she could present some semblance of normality to the world around her.

He pulled one of his gloves off and his hand wandered to her arm, as if he was steadying her. As if he knew that she was standing on the edge of a dark precipice and that all she could do was jump, along with the others, and hope that everything was going to be okay.

'I thought we weren't moving to Hertfordshire until

the weekend.' He swung off the seat of the motorbike, unzipping his jacket.

'We've been making good time. If everything went well today, then there's only another day's filming before we're ready to go.'

'In that case...' he started to stroll towards the entrance of the hotel and Sophie followed him '...there's something I've been meaning to discuss with you.'

'What's that?'

'This might be a good time to think about restructuring things so they work a bit better for you.'

'You mean, facing the facts instead of hiding from them?'

'I wouldn't put it in those words exactly.'

She grinned up at him. 'Stop being nice to me, Drew. It unnerves me. And you know I get confused when you don't say exactly what you mean.'

He chuckled, taking her key along with his own from the receptionist. 'Okay, then. Now you've finally decided that being a diva isn't going to solve your problems, it's about time you looked squarely at your other options.'

'That's better.' She grinned up at him. 'So what *are* my other options?'

'Staying somewhere away from the crew, where you can get some peace and quiet...' He counted on his fingers. 'Having a therapist with you for all or part of the day. Telling Joel...'

She took the key to her suite from his hand and opened the door. 'Telling Joel. Are you sure about that one?'

'No. It's just a suggestion. You know your own business better than I do, and you can assess the possible implications, but I think that Joel knowing could help you with the day-to-day things.'

Sophie sat down with a bump.

Everything he'd said was perfectly reasonable. It would all help her cope on her own. That wasn't what was tearing at her.

'What about you, Drew?'

His gaze became solemn. 'What about me?'

'Are you...thinking about leaving?' Sophie felt a lump rise in her throat.

'It's a possibility. I'm going to have to at some point. I've got a job to go to, and you're going back to the States when filming's finished here.'

And that was set in stone. No way out for either of them, unless... No. It was too big a step to take. She couldn't see everything she'd worked for crumble, just for the sake of a man, not even Drew. She just didn't have the ability to trust that much any more.

'You're saying that I don't need you around any more?'

'That's up to you to decide.' Something in his eyes told her that her decision was important to him.

'Okay. You're right. I don't actually need you. Henry Chancellor could suggest a good memory therapist, couldn't he?'

'Yes. He'd do that.'

She looked into his face. Saw the tightening of his jaw and the slight beat of a pulse at his temple, which answered the biggest question of all.

'I don't *need* you, Drew. But if you feel able to, I really *want* you to stay.'

His smile was all the answer she needed. 'Yeah. I want to stay.'

'Life on set's not so bad, then?' He didn't seem to bristle with disapproval now, the way he had when he'd first arrived.

'I'm getting to like it.' He grinned. 'It's not what I thought it would be.'

'Is that settled, then?'

'Yeah. It's settled. There's another thing I was thinking of asking you.'

'Go on. We may as well get it all over with in one go.' Sophie was almost breathless with relief. There was nothing which could hurt her now.

'We're going to be in London and my place is forty-five minutes' drive from the set. If you wanted, you could come and stay with me. You'd have a chance to settle a bit. Not so difficult to find your way around...' He shrugged, as if that probably wasn't an option at all.

'Are you sure? You might find the paparazzi on your doorstep. That wouldn't do your career much good.'

A slight flicker, at the side of his eye, attested to the fact that it had occurred to him, but it seemed that Drew was dealing with it. 'I want you to stay, Sophie.'

'In that case, I guess I don't have much choice.'

It was all settled. After some thought and a great deal of discussion, Drew called Joel, who appeared at the door of her suite inside two minutes.

'Sophie. You want to talk?'

'I do...' Drew took the initiative, seating everyone comfortably, keeping the atmosphere friendly and relaxed. He explained Sophie's condition clearly, the way he'd already discussed with her, emphasising the ways forward now that she'd been diagnosed and could get proper treatment.

'This is... There's no cure for this?' Joel rubbed his forehead thoughtfully.

'Time is the cure.' Drew smiled. 'Sophie's already made enormous improvements, working on her own.

With a proper support framework, she can do every-thing she used to.'

Joel nodded. 'I was looking at some of the footage last night. The scene in the tea shop.'

'Yes?' Sophie gulped out the word. Joel was going to tell her that he wanted to reshoot. That was going to mean expense and inconvenience for everyone.

'It's fantastic, Sophie. There's a real depth to your performance, you've caught all the underlying sadness of the situation perfectly.'

'Thank you.' She didn't quite believe it, but Joel didn't lie about this kind of thing. That was what made him so good at his job.

'I wish you'd come to me with this sooner.'

So did she. It was the one thing she had no answer for, but Drew was there with one.

'You have to understand how difficult it's been for Sophie. Brain trauma isn't like a cut or a bruise. There's a long sequence of coming to terms with it, trying to understand what's happened.'

Yes. That was it. Sophie waited for Joel's response, her mouth dry.

'I'm glad you've talked to me now, then. Whatever you need, I want to hear about it.'

'Yes.' Sophie nodded. 'Thank you.'

'There is one thing,' Drew cut in smoothly. 'We've already agreed that this conversation remains between the three of us. I just want to reiterate it.'

'I hear you. But releasing this to the press, carefully and in the proper way, might get them off your back a bit, Sophie. It might give you a bit of leverage with re-gard to those photographs that got leaked onto the in-ternet. If you weren't well when they were taken, that has to be grounds to suppress them.'

Drew's gaze flipped to her face. She could almost see him putting two and two together. Sophie had never quite been able to fathom whether Drew knew about the pictures or not, but now it was pretty clear. He hadn't known and now he did.

She wanted the earth to open up and swallow her. Or maybe it would be better if it swallowed Joel, before she decided to strangle him.

'Anything to do with the press is Sophie's decision. Not yours or mine.' Drew had regained his composure quickly, and was talking now to Joel. 'It's very important that Sophie's the one in control here. It's her memory that is impaired, not her understanding or her decision-making process.'

Right. In control. Whatever had made her think that was even possible.

'Okay. Understood.' Joel made a zipping motion across his mouth. His own, familiar way of confirming that his lips were sealed. That was all a bit late now.

'Is there anything else?'

'No...' Drew leaned back in his chair in an unconvincing parody of relaxation. 'Although we might get back to you with something.'

'Make sure you do.' Joel nodded to Drew, smiled at Sophie and got to his feet.

After Joel left, they were silent for long minutes. Drew was the first to break.

'Josh took compromising pictures, didn't he? Then he leaked them onto the internet, out of spite.'

'Spite and money. All of the gossip about the photographs didn't do him any harm when it came to selling his story. He's got a reality show on the back of it. I suppose he'll have a few things to say about me then.'

Just when she should have been elated, full of the suc-

cess of finally getting things under control and being
able to talk to Joel, she was suddenly beaten again. It
was almost too cruel to bear.

'That's just sick. Can't you get them taken down?'

'Not legally. My lawyer tried, but they're Josh's copy-
right. His story is that I leaked them, for the publicity.
Maybe I did... I don't remember.'

'I haven't seen them, Sophie. I won't be looking for
them either.'

'Thank you.' She hung her head so he couldn't see
her tears.

'If you ever want to talk about it, you know I'm here
for you. But since you obviously don't...'

'I'm so ashamed, Drew.' She blurted out the words.
For once he didn't seem to know what to do. He reached
forward to touch her, and ended up grazing his finger-
tips against her sleeve.

'Don't be.' He was thinking before he spoke, long
gaps of silence between each sentence. 'You have nothing...nothing to be ashamed of. And you don't have to
explain anything to anyone, least of all me. I know you
didn't leak those photographs because I know you.'

They sat in silence. A minute and then two. Five and
then ten. It was as if the photographs could be somehow
wiped away if they didn't talk about them.

'Soph.' He finally spoke.

'Yes, Drew.'

'Do you want to get some ice cream?'

Somehow ice cream was the only thing that made
sense. 'I'll call down to room service.'

'Or I was thinking maybe we could go into town
for it.'

A twenty-mile round trip to get ice cream. That made
sense as well, in a crazy kind of way.

'We'll go on the bike?'

'Yeah. I'd like that.'

'Good. Ice cream, then.'

The bike was always the place where Drew worked out his problems. Perhaps it could work the same magic for Sophie. She had to cling to him, her arms tight around his waist, and he sensed that the enforced proximity was as comforting to her as it was to him. Closeness that held no unwanted implications and none of the awkwardness that a hug might have engendered.

How could he not have known? Her agonised insistence that she had to retrieve the memories of those lost days. The morning he'd found her going through his phone. The idiot at the hospital. It was if he hadn't wanted to know.

Maybe he hadn't. Maybe he'd been afraid of what the photographs might show him. Gina's photographs had shown him much, much more than he'd ever wanted to know.

A slight change in the angle of the bike, reflected by a synchronous moment in their bodies, his and hers. He couldn't imagine the agony that Sophie must be in. Not being able to remember how something like that had happened. The constant questions, none of which had any answers.

Her hand moved, tapping his right side. She wanted him to go right at the next junction. It would take them on a huge detour along miles of country roads, which finally curved back on themselves and meandered into the high street. Drew smiled, turning the bike. Somehow, he and Sophie would get through this.

CHAPTER THIRTEEN

DREW WAS FEELING pretty pleased with himself. He'd succeeded in what he'd gone out to do and that always pleased him. They'd made the trip to London by train the previous evening, leaving his bike packed securely on one of the lorries that travelled with the crew and Jennie in charge of Sophie's luggage. Sophie had gone upstairs to unpack her overnight bag, returned to sit with him for half an hour and had then started to yawn so had gone straight to bed.

This morning she was fresh, rested and already settling in. By the time Drew was finished in the shower, she'd made breakfast, and then she'd sat down with her script, studying her lines for that afternoon. He'd pushed back the chairs in the sitting-room and she'd read them out loud, over-acting for laughs. She was spreading her wings, gaining in confidence and learning to do all the little things she'd once depended on him for. Soon she'd fly away.

Not today, though. The cast was meeting on set at one to take a look around and go through a few scenes. Inhabiting the place, Joel called it. Sophie was eager to get going, and by twelve they were already on the road.

'Stop here, will you? I think we need to take a turn soon.' She was studying the map on her phone intently.

'No, it's not for another few miles.' Drew stopped the car even so, and leaned over to peer at the screen in front of her. 'We're here.'

'Right under the blue dot. Yeah, I got that.' She smirked at him.

'And you need to scroll up a bit to get to where we're going. The Hazlemere Estate.'

'There's somewhere I want to stop off. It won't take long.'

'But rehearsals…'

'They're at three o'clock. I lied.'

'You lied? You need a good memory to be a good liar, don't you?' Sophie was up to something. He just couldn't fathom what.

'I wrote it down.' She picked her notebook up from her lap, flipping it open and displaying a page.

Rehearsals at three.
Tell Drew to leave at twelve.
Belltower Hospital.

'No. Not a chance, Sophie.'

She turned to him, the slow burn of her mismatched eyes boring through his defences. Maybe he'd have to give up trying to fight her on this one and just beg.

'I've heard an awful lot about my needs. What's best for me. And I'm sick of it. What about the things you need?'

'I don't need to go back to the hospital. It's closed. Finished.'

'Did you say goodbye?'

He'd been too busy to say goodbye. Writing references for the people who'd worked for him, arranging transfers of patients, speaking to the doctors at the new hospital to ensure that no one fell through the cracks of the bureaucratic process. He'd simply gone home one night, so tired that he could hardly stand, and had woken up the next morning with nowhere to go.

'Since you're not answering, I have to assume that's a no.'

'I didn't need to. It's done. Over.'

'Humour me.'

If he was humouring her, it wouldn't hurt so badly. If he thought that Sophie needed to go to the hospital for some reason, he'd bundle away his own feelings and go. 'You really think I should go?'

'Yes, I do.'

Wordlessly, he started the engine. There was only one person who could have made him go back and say the goodbyes he'd shrunk from before. And he had the misfortune to be in a car with her and heading towards the hospital entrance.

It was Sophie's face, not his own, that got them past the security guard at the entrance. That was almost the hardest thing to take.

'How did you do that?' He accelerated past the wooden hoardings.

'Jennie found out who to call for me. Then I got on the phone and said I was looking for a location.' She grinned. 'Sometimes having a well-known name works.'

'A location for what?'

'I didn't say. I said it was top secret and that probably nothing would come of it. Park over there.'

Drew swung the car into the ambulance bay in front of A and E. It seemed strange to be able to park here without causing an obstruction, but he imagined that the entrance to the pay-and-display car park would be chained shut. He got out of the car, stretching his legs and back.

'We can go in here, I think.' She handed him the keys that the security guard had given her and Drew sorted through them to find the right one. His hand shaking, he unlocked the door.

Sophie slipped her hand into his and Drew stepped inside. The smell of disinfectant had given way to a slight musty smell, and there was a layer of dust on the long, curved reception desk. Beyond, the cubicles had been denuded of their curtains, and all of the medical supplies and equipment had been removed, probably to be used somewhere else.

'It's so quiet.' Sophie was looking around, seeming to be trying to take in every detail of the place.

'Yeah.' There was nothing here. Nothing that he remembered, only bricks and mortar. 'Would you like to see my department?'

'Yes.'

Neurology was the same. Drew's old office was quiet and dusty, the room completely cleared apart from his desk and a couple of chairs. He flipped open his desk drawer, realising that he'd never thought to empty it before he'd left, and felt a stab of indignation when he found that someone else must have done it for him. Vaguely he wondered where his mug had got to. Broken and put into a rubbish bag, to be carted away, he supposed.

'This must be yours.' Sophie appeared in the doorway, holding his racing green and gold 1936 Grand Prix winner's mug between her thumb and forefinger. 'I tried to wash it but there's no water in the taps.'

'Where did you find it?' Drew took the mug from her, inspecting the mould culture that was growing inside.

'In the cupboard over the sink in the main office. Someone must have stuck a load of them in there without washing them.'

'Hmm. I'll take it home with me.'

Sophie produced a plastic carrier from her handbag and handed it to him, sitting down in the visitor's chair on the other side of his desk. 'This is where it all happened, then?'

Drew dusted off his chair, and sat, facing her. 'Yeah. All of it.'

'When I think of what that hour in Dr Chancellor's office meant to me…' She gave a little shrug. 'All the patients you saw here, each one of them must remember this office, and what you did for them.'

'Sometimes I wasn't able to give them good news…'

'No, I imagine not. But I know you still helped them.'

'I did my best.' It felt as if the most important part of his life had been lived in this place. The work he'd done. The people he'd worked with.

'You wrote your academic papers here? In the dead of night when everyone had gone home?' Her lips twitched into a smile in response to Drew's surprised glance. 'I saw them in the bookcase in your sitting-room.'

'Yeah, I spent a few nights here. Drank quite a bit of coffee.'

'And you feel you've left all that behind?'

Drew looked around the bare office. 'It's not here any more.'

'No, it's not. That's because you already took it with you. All you left behind was bricks and mortar. And your coffee mug.'

Something fell into place. When he'd left here he'd felt numb, not able to comprehend that it was all over. Now he realised that it wasn't.

'I worked so hard to keep this place open. When it closed, I felt that everything I'd done here was a failure, wiped out somehow. But it's not, it never was.'

She smiled. 'No. I used to hate moving from place to place when I was filming, but I learned that you take the good things with you. Which is why you have to do as many good things as you can, so you've got plenty to take when you go on to the next place.'

He smiled. 'That's a very nice thought. So I'll be taking lots of you with me, then. All the good things you've done for me.'

'Have I?' She seemed genuinely surprised. 'I thought I'd just be taking lots of you.'

'Let's not think about that now.' One parting at a time. However much she'd eased the pain of this one.

'No. Best not.'

He reached for her hand, curling his fingers around hers. 'I'm glad we came, but I think it's time to go now.'

'On to the next place?'

'Yeah.' He smiled at her. 'On to the next place.'

He felt somehow lighter when he got back into his car. Sophie returned the keys to the guard with a smile and a thank you, and he opened the gate, letting them out. He would never have come here again without Sophie, and this time he was leaving well. Moving on, instead of crawling away, paralysed by failure and regret.

The Hazlemere Estate was another fifteen minutes drive. A three-lane motorway gave way to leafy country lanes, and when he turned into the gates Drew saw one of the set security guys, waving him through and along a long gravel drive.

He hadn't known this house was even here. Buried in the countryside, behind wrought-iron gates and surrounded by trees at the perimeter of the estate. It was a hidden gem, its architecture spanning a hundred years from Georgian to Victorian as successive generations had added to the country pile that they'd inherited. And now it seemed to have slipped back in time, and sat in the sunshine of an afternoon some time in 1944.

Drew took a long look at the vintage car parked outside and wondered if it was driveable. One of the set mechanics strolled over to look at his own car.

'This is yours?'

Drew nodded. 'I restored her myself.'

'Nice. Shame she's not a little bit older, we could have used her.'

'Betty would like that.' Sophie got out of the car and joined them.

'Betty?' Both men turned to Sophie at the same time, and Drew raised an eyebrow. Not only had Sophie taken the radical step of naming his car, but it seemed that she remembered what she'd called it.

Sophie shrugged. 'She seems like a Betty to me. A bit old-fashioned, but kind of sleek and beautiful.'

The mechanic shot Drew a look that suggested that somehow Sophie didn't understand the lure of engine oil and grease, and asked Drew if he could take a look at the engine. Drew passed his car keys over and they were pocketed carefully.

'So this is the hospital?' He looked up at the impressive façade in front of them.

'Yes. Apparently a lot of country houses were converted into hospitals during the war.' She gave the information with a hint of relish and Drew smiled. Three weeks ago she would have probably kept her mouth shut, feigning disdain, but now she was willing to risk being interested.

'Shall we go in?'

The massive wooden front doors were open, and inside the place was a different world. A huge hallway, which had been converted into a reception area, in nineteen-forties style. Right in front of them stood a carved wooden desk, with a visitors' book, paper and a fountain pen.

Sophie picked the pen up, examining it, and then put it back in place. They followed the signs and found themselves in a large room, complete with fireplaces and chandeliers, that contained rows of beds, placed close enough together to give a modern staff nurse a seizure.

'Amazing.' Drew looked around him. There was nothing which could possibly be traced back to the last seventy years here. It was just as if a snapshot had been taken of the house's chequered history, and re-created perfectly.

'Yes. This is very good.' Sophie was studying the space carefully, and he knew that she was running through her own lines in her head, putting them in the context of their surroundings.

Suddenly, Dr Tara Green surfaced. Sophie even walked slight differently, her own personality subsumed by that of the serious, yet unworldly Dr Green. She moved around the space, looking at everything, testing the height of the beds with her hand, trying random lines from the script under her breath.

Then she was back again. 'How do you do that?' Drew grinned at her.

Sophie shrugged. 'It's about getting yourself into the mindset. People think that learning lines is the only thing an actor has to remember. It's a lot more than that.'

He was beginning to see that. And the more he saw, the more he understood Sophie's achievement. Keeping going, telling no one. 'It must have been very hard for you, Soph.'

She nodded, her face suddenly pinched with stress. 'Yes. It's better now.' She brushed the thought away, smiling again as she looked around the room. 'You need a good memory for make-believe.'

It was just make-believe, all of it. But it was underpinned by serious work and research, not the useless, brittle dreams he'd first thought it was. Drew could respect that.

They explored some more, popping their heads around doors to find rooms that remained untouched and were part of a modern family home, albeit rather grand, next door to rooms that were part of a different time and space.

'Are you going to get some tea? While we rehearse?' The corridors were filling up now, familiar faces greeting them, and Joel's voice sounded, booming from the main hallway.

'I'll watch if that's okay.'

'You can go. I won't fluff my lines.' She seemed unaccountably reluctant to have him on set this afternoon.

'Nah. I'll watch.'

The actors spent some time walking around, discussing with Joel how they wanted to use the space. Drew was becoming used to the process. Reading through the script. Talking about how the words would work in the three-dimensional context of the set. Then a run-through of the scene that Sophie had been learning that morning.

It was different this time. As she and Todd worked together, the lines he'd heard took on emotion and a subtle depth of meaning that he'd missed the first time around. Between them the tension started to build, and even though neither was in costume, the spell they wove was so complete that Drew forgot that what they were saying wasn't real.

Drugs had been stolen from the medicine cabinet. Sophie accused one of Todd's men and he responded with denials. The argument that raged between them mounted in intensity, the atmosphere made all the more compelling by the fact that they kept their voices low, as if afraid someone would hear them. Joel was nodding, letting the scene play through in its entirety, allowing the actors their heads.

Then the climax. Todd pulled Sophie against him, and she struggled. Instinctively, Drew almost propelled himself forward, ready to extract her from his grasp, and then she melted into his arms. The words that Drew had imagined would have been spoken as a curt acceptance of his story fell from her lips in a husky whisper. Then she kissed him.

Drew's hands fisted at his sides. He knew what was in the script. But somehow his mind had skirted around the kiss, imagining only a chaste peck on the cheek. This was nothing like that. She was standing on her toes, her fingers caressing his neck. And his hand was sliding slowly down her back.

'Steady, tiger. They're pretending.' A quiet whisper in his ear jolted him back to reality and he looked round to see Jennie standing beside him.

'Yeah. Powerful scene,' he whispered back, so as not to break the silence, and Jennie nodded, seemingly mollified.

When he looked back at them they were *still* kissing. Dammit, this was a rehearsal wasn't it? Couldn't Todd save those moves until the cameras were rolling? Then Sophie pulled away from him, flattening herself against the wall, and raised her arm. The slap was pulled at the last moment, and her fingers hardly touched Todd's face, but his head rolled as if he'd taken full force of the blow. He caught her wrist in his hand, stopping her from delivering a second.

Oh, for crying out loud! Really? He kissed her again, with savage intensity, and she responded, whimpering with what Drew fondly supposed was a fake reaction. Then Todd turned, storming from the room, leaving Sophie leaning against the wall, her fingers over her lips as if something had just happened and she was wondering quite what it was.

'Great. Do that again tomorrow.' Joel's voice broke the silence.

Sophie and Todd exchanged a nod and a smile, and a buzz of conversation filled the set. Drew silently slipped away. Perhaps it *would* have been better to spend his time in one of the chairs that surrounded the catering truck, reading a book and drinking tea.

CHAPTER FOURTEEN

HALF AN HOUR LATER, she found him doing just that. Or, in truth, pretending to do just that. The tea tasted foul, and he hadn't read a word on the page in front of him. He forced a smile when she asked him if he was ready to go, and, not trusting himself to talk to her, resorted to the pretence that the busy roads required his full attention all the way home.

She followed him through into the kitchen. 'What?'

He'd just been shown his place, that was what. He'd told Sophie that a relationship between them was a bad idea, they'd talked about partings, and she'd taken him at his word. All Drew could think about was the way she'd kissed Todd.

He turned, manufacturing a smile. 'Nothing. I'm just tired.' He reached for the cups in the cupboard, putting the kettle on to give himself something to do. 'Are you hungry?'

'Not really. Upset's a better word for it.' She was eyeing him steadily.

'There's no reason—'

'It's just acting, you know. That's what I am. An actress.'

'You don't have to explain yourself to me, Sophie.'

'Right. Which is why you're sulking, is it? It seems

that I *do* have to explain myself.' She sat herself down at the kitchen table, rubbing her face with her hands.

'You're just tired, Sophie.' The words slipped out before he had a chance to stop them. *Way to go. Blame her condition for your own hang-ups.*

She shot him a look that would have probably sliced the kitchen table in half, had it not been directed straight at him. 'That's your excuse, is it? Poor little Sophie's tired? Grow up… Taylor.'

'Forgotten my name again?' It was a cruel taunt, and he should have known better. Sophie's confidence was fragile…

'Is that all you can say? Yeah, okay, I get angry and I forget things. Big deal.' She jutted her chin confrontationally. 'Now who's being a diva?'

'What exactly are you accusing me of, Sophie?'

'This is supposed to be a friendship, you're not my doctor. It's not all a matter of me spilling my guts and you listening. And you can't pass your own moods off as me being tired.'

He wondered whether she was going to walk away from him, and realised that was just what he wanted right now. Sophie would walk away, shut herself in the spare room for a while and the matter would be closed. That would have suited him just fine.

'Well…?' Sophie jabbed the table with her finger. Clearly she was going nowhere.

'It just…it pushed a few buttons. It's nothing to do with you.'

'Only you made it to do with me, didn't you?'

He supposed he had. Drew sat down at the kitchen table, opposite her. 'It was a long time ago, Soph.'

'And…?' She wasn't letting him off the hook. Somewhere, deep inside, he was glad of it. This new Sophie, the one who was more than a match for him, was much more tricky to deal with, and infinitely more alluring.

'It's a stupid thing…'

'They usually are. Go on.'

Drew sighed, and gave up. 'I had a girlfriend. Years ago. She was beautiful, long dark hair, bright blue eyes…'

'I hate her already. So what did this lustrous-eyed temptress do, then?'

'Gina worked in local government but all she could think about was being a model.'

'Fair enough. Sounds better than local government any day.' Sophie's tone had softened. She knew she'd won, and she was tender in her victory.

'Yeah. I encouraged her, it was what she wanted. She got a few minor jobs, and loved it. Landed a bigger contract and gave up her day job.'

'Okay. Risky, but I can't talk. I took a few risks myself when I was starting out.'

'She didn't show me the pictures. The first I saw of them were a couple of nurses laughing over them in the canteen.'

Sophie gave a pained look, as if she knew just what was coming. 'Were they any good?'

'They were fabulous. She looked like a million dollars. She was posing with this guy, and he was…' Drew tried to put it delicately. 'Let's just say that if he hadn't had his hands strategically placed…'

'Okay. I get it.' Sophie took a deep breath. 'You do know, don't you, that what the camera sees really isn't what's going on. Models, actors, we all work pretty hard to construct something imaginary.'

'The camera always lies?' Drew still wasn't quite convinced of that.

'No, not always. But a professional model's job is not to show the truth. It's to sell a fantasy.'

'I... I don't know about that. I tried to talk to Gina about it, and she wouldn't...'

'Maybe it was something she was trying to get to grips with. We all have to.' Sophie shrugged. 'I'm trying to give her the benefit of the doubt here. Even if I'm not sure I want to.'

'I know. You don't need to be that generous, Soph. I know what happened. She got lost in it all, spent more and more time away from home, and I resented it. There were rumours about what was happening and...in the end she didn't deny them and we split up.'

She nodded, pressing her lips together. 'Personal relationships are tough in this business.'

'In my business too. I went to pieces over it. Henry Chancellor was my professional mentor at the time, and he called me in and hauled me over the coals. Told me that I could let everything slide, or I could work it out of my system.'

'And you worked?'

'Yeah. I've never let a relationship get in the way of my work since.' Drew turned the corners of his mouth down. 'As a number of my ex-girlfriends will tell you.'

'I'll take your word for it. I'd rather not take up references.'

Despite himself, Drew smiled. Sophie had a way of making almost anything seem possible. 'I'm sorry, Soph. It's about my own hang-ups and nothing you've done. You understand that, don't you?'

'Yeah. And tonight's not the time to argue.'

'No. I'm not sure any time is.' Suddenly Drew was trapped, between the enticing thought of what he wanted tonight to be for and the sure knowledge that the idea was impossibly reckless.

'Tonight…' She seemed to be pondering the options. Drew was wondering whether he ought to offer her a cup of tea when she rose, her movements slow and purposeful. Pulled the elastic tie from her hair and shook her head. Drew felt himself falling.

She leaned towards him, palms flat on the tabletop. Then one knee. Slowly, like a beautiful tiger, stalking its prey. He was caught motionless in her gaze. 'Soph…?'

Her lips brushed his. So soft. So sweet. And then he was on his feet, lifting her across the barrier between them, holding her tight against him. He felt her legs, curling around his hips, the high heels of her boots against the backs of his thighs, and he settled her weight against him. They fitted together like the last two pieces of a jigsaw puzzle.

She kissed him again. Annihilating his sense of anything other than her lips, her body.

'That's real. You get the difference?'

'I get it.'

He felt her smile against his lips. 'Come to your senses then, Taylor?'

Not even close. If his senses hadn't been scattered like broken glass on the floor, he wouldn't be doing this. Wouldn't be loving it, far more than he had any right to.

'This is not a good idea, Sophie.' Still he couldn't bring himself to let her go. 'You're going back to the States, I have a job here…'

'I know. Not tonight, though.' She moved against him in a way designed to arouse, and got exactly what she wanted.

'You're not making this easy, Soph…'

'You want me to?'

'No.' He kissed her again, meaning to make it into a regretful parting, and found himself taking every last drop of pleasure from it, then going back for more. 'Are you sure, Sophie?'

He needed more than just the messages her body were giving. He needed her to say it, so there was no mistake. Without that certainty, he would find a way to tear himself away from her.

She looked up at him. Clear-eyed and meltingly beautiful. 'I understand exactly what we're doing. I won't forget.'

She wriggled out of his grip, her feet finding the floor. When she reached for her bag, Drew thought she was going for her notebook, and smiled to himself. Maybe not the most romantic of gestures, but in this context it was everything.

Turning her back on him, she nestled against him. It was sweet agony. She pulled his arm around her, pulling up the sleeve of his shirt. Then he felt the tip of her magic marker against his skin.

'Sophie...' He kissed the top of her head, and then bent to kiss her neck, pushing the bright strands of hair out of the way. Even the touch of the pen on his forearm was making the small hairs stand on end.

'Is that clear enough?'

He looked, and saw the words. *Yes. Everything. Just for tonight.*

'It's clear.' He turned her around, taking the pen from her and pulling her into his arms. She clung to him, laughing with delight as he lifted her, bending forward to lay her down on the tabletop. Her breathing quickened, and he wondered if she thought he was going to take her right here.

Not a chance. If this was just for tonight, it would

happen well, not in a haze of rushed passion. He stretched her arm over her head, tugging at her sleeve, and pulled the cap from the pen with his teeth.

'Now you.'

'What are you going to do?' She wriggled beneath him, and he pinned her down with the weight of his body.

'Stay still. Just a little *aide-memoire...*'

She'd been dozing in the soft warmth of his arms, and it was beginning to get dark when she opened her eyes. Drew greeted her with a lazy smile. 'Hey, there.'

Sophie looked around the room. His bedroom, she supposed, since it wasn't the spare room that she'd spent the night in last night. 'Hey. Who are you again?'

For a moment panic bloomed in his eyes, and then he relaxed into a smile. 'Don't do that to me.'

She kissed him, stretching her body luxuriantly against his. 'I thought you might give me a rerun. Just to freshen up on the details.'

Mischief tugged at the corners of his mouth. 'Where do you want me to start?'

'I remember this.' She held out her arm. He'd kissed her, writing his pledge for the night and drawing little hearts and flowers around it, with shooting stars running around her elbow. 'Does this last until morning?'

'It does. Once it's in writing, it's a done deal. You remember what happened next?'

'You carried me upstairs and took my clothes off. Then yours, and we kissed a bit.' She leaned in close to whisper in his ear. 'That was nice.' She ran her finger over his lips in a broad hint that he might repeat the exercise.

'So we did.' Drew kissed her. Without the hard edge

of uncertain hunger this time. Now he knew what they could do together, knew exactly what response he could tease out of her.

She was more confident, too. She knew how he wanted her to touch him, how a soft stroke made him shiver deliciously, and a harder one made him groan out loud. The circle of cause and effect began to spiral between them again.

'You remember this?' He rolled on his back, pulling her shaking body on top of him, astride his hips. 'I wanted to feel your rhythm…'

He'd been inside her then. This time they mimicked the act, staring into each other's eyes. Stretching each moment to breaking point, luxuriating in the sweet fusion of past and present.

'When you came…' he stretched one arm up to brush his fingers against her lips '…you came so hard, I swear I could feel it.'

The memory of it pulsed through her body, making her shiver. 'You liked that?'

'I loved it. Then you called out my name…'

'Tay—lor…' Sophie bent to kiss him, wondering if he minded. 'You were blowing my brains out, Drew. I couldn't think…'

He grinned. 'If you had called me anything else, I'd have reckoned I needed to try a bit harder.'

'You didn't need to try any harder. If you had I probably would have passed out.'

Her pleasure turned him on. He had seemed to crave it, as if it was the ultimate in sensual gratification. He moved the way he had before, sitting up, holding her astride him on his lap. Face to face. Breath to breath.

'Then you came again.' He held her tight, one arm coiled around her waist, one hand on the back of her head. This was the ultimate in fantasy. She felt his body harden as she clung on to him.

'That one was softer. Longer. All over my body...' She couldn't describe it. A single tear rolled from her eye. She thought that had happened then, and that he'd kissed it away, just as he was doing now.

'I was trying to wait. I wanted to know if you were going for the hat-trick...' He chuckled quietly. 'But I couldn't.'

She'd felt him lose control, his strong body shaking, holding onto her as if she was the only thing in the world.

'How did it feel?' She wanted to share it with him again.

He shuddered, nuzzling at her neck. 'It felt like... being free.'

For a moment they were silent, just letting their hearts beat. Slowly, his hand moved for her breast, cupping it comfortably.

'You up to speed now?' His thumb grazed her nipple and her breath caught, tangled in pleasure. When he ran his tongue across her lips then kissed her again, sweet memories dissolved into anticipation.

'Hold me... Please, Drew.'

'I will.' The promise tore from his lips, and he twisted around, laying her down on the bed. She reached for the condoms on the nightstand, and he caught her hand. 'Not yet. Later.'

'Later?'

'Remember our agreement.'

She ran her finger over the magic marker on his arm. 'I don't need to remember it, I have it in writing.'

He grinned at her. 'Then you'll know we have a whole night. We can take our time.'

* * *

When the alarm went at five the following morning Sophie slept right through it, and Drew kissed her awake. There was no time for anything other than a quick dash to the shower and a grabbed cup of coffee, but that was okay. She'd be coming back home with him tonight, and there was no reason for them not to renew the contract that they'd washed off their arms in the shower this morning.

'I was thinking.' Sophie had decided to put the idea to him in the car so that they could talk about it. 'Why don't you take your bike off the lorry and ride it home while we're filming? Then you could get a taxi back to the hospital.' That would keep him out of the way for a while.

'Or I could do it while you're in Make-up. I'd be back mid-morning.'

'There's no rush. Why don't you have breakfast while I'm in Make-up and then—'

'You can kiss Todd while I'm out of the way?'

Sophie swallowed hard. 'There's that to it as well.'

'You'd feel better if I wasn't there?'

'How do you feel about it?'

There was silence for a couple of miles. It seemed they'd reached an impasse.

'Okay.' He spoke suddenly. 'Let's do this. I'll do what you said, stay until lunchtime and then take the bike home. When I get back, I'll be wanting a little reassurance, though.'

She grinned at him. 'You don't need any reassurance.' Last night had been all the reassurance that either of them could handle.

'I said *wanting*. Not *needing*.'

'Okay. Wanting's fine. In which case I might want a little reassurance back. Just because you do it so well.'

He laughed so hard that he nearly missed their turning. 'Yeah, okay. Flattery will get you everywhere.'

It had been a good day. She hadn't forgotten any of her lines, and the dozens of different disciplines that went into making a filmed sequence work had all fallen into place. She and Todd had clicked together and the gradually building tension, throughout the scene, had been almost palpable. Drew had good-naturedly disappeared after lunch, and she'd heard the roar of the engine as he'd revved the bike past the main entrance of the house.

It had been tiring, and it was almost good to feel this wrung out. She'd given it everything, and everyone had been pleased with the scene. Sophie walked back to her trailer and lay down on the couch, one arm slung over her eyes. She'd get changed out of her dress and take her make-up off in a moment.

Someone tapped on the door, and she answered automatically. Probably one of the wardrobe girls, or Jennie. If it was Jennie, she'd ask whether she'd seen Drew. It was getting late and she could do with going home soon.

'Hey.' His voice, the sound of the door closing, and a sharp click as the lock snapped fast. Sophie sat up.

'You're back.'

'I've been back a while. I took a walk around the grounds. I reckoned you were right in wanting me out of the way.'

'It's the best thing.'

He nodded. Approached her slowly. Suddenly she wasn't tired any more. Suddenly, every nerve was screaming for him. Particularly since she had a pretty good idea of what he was about to do.

* * *

Drew told himself that it was the damn costume. That the green and white print dress, ruched at the top to follow her curves, falling gently over her hips, was turning him into someone else. Someone who couldn't care less that they'd both had a long day. Someone who had conveniently forgotten that last night's promise must have expired by now.

He gathered her in his arms. When he kissed her he knew that the bright smear of lipstick, which made her mouth seem as luscious as ripened fruit, would be on his face too. The thought made him unexpectedly hard for her.

'Careful…' she murmured into his ear.

'Yeah.' He wondered whether she was in costume under that dress as well. He hoped so. He pushed her curled hair back from her neck and found a pin, holding it securely in place. A sudden whiff of Todd's aftershave.

'You smell of another man…' He kissed her neck, tenderly.

'You don't mind?' A little tremor of uncertainty racked her body, and then she relaxed into his arms. She seemed to understand that he couldn't have cared less.

'That wasn't real.' This was all-encompassingly real. It seemed the most genuine thing that had ever happened to him.

His hand skimmed the soft material of her dress and he gathered the fabric carefully in his hand, finding the edge of her stocking tops. Ran his finger around the place where flesh met nylon, feeling the depressions in her skin from the metal clips of her suspenders.

'You do this always? Wear the appropriate underwear?'

'It helps. You move differently…'

'Uh-huh.' He wondered how long it would take to get her out of the dress, undo the row of tiny buttons that ran down the side of it. Then there was the challenge of her underwear, unfamiliar hooks and fastenings and sheer stockings that mustn't be laddered by the clumsiness of his hands. The whole thing seemed impossibly impractical, and headily exciting.

His hands explored a little further, and found silky fabric, clinging to the rounded curve of her hips. He looked for buttons, elastic, something to give some clue about how to get her camiknickers off, and found nothing.

She was having more success. Her fingers loosened the belt of his jeans, and she slid her hand inside. When he felt her touch on his skin he groaned.

'I need some help with this, Sophie.' If he couldn't get inside her clothes soon, he was going to rip them off her.

'Where's the fun in that? Work it out for yourself.' She kissed him on the cheek, and he pulled her in for a proper kiss, his searching fingers dislodging a couple of bobby pins from her hair.

He was going to have to improvise. If his grandparents had managed this complex obstacle course, and his mere presence on this earth told Drew that they must have done at some point, then he ought to have a fighting chance. But he was going to need some help.

He backed her against the cupboard door, kissing her deep and hard, one hand over her breast. Gently, through the layers of fabric, he teased until her breathing started to quicken. He let the tension build, and when she moaned he left her with it, turning his attention to the buttons on her dress.

'Take it off...'

She responded to the low command, pulling the dress

carefully over her head. Underneath, a lace-edged slip, the silken sheen of the material following her curves. He fell to one knee, sliding the fabric up her leg, kissing the inside of her thigh.

'Drew...' She whispered his name and the urgency in her voice almost destroyed him. He tried the camiknickers again, tugging gently downwards but there was still no give.

'How do I...?'

'Hooks and eyes.' Her hands went to her waist, and she unhooked the fastenings. Drew slid her silky knickers down, so she could step out of them.

That was enough. It was all his raging need would allow him to do. Reaching into his pocket, he found the condom he'd picked up earlier, thanking his lucky stars that he hadn't put it back into the box on his nightstand.

'Now... Please.' She pulled him to his feet, tugging at his jeans and dragging them far enough down to free him. He rolled the condom down in one swift movement, and then lifted her body, supporting her weight against the cupboard door. She wrapped her legs around his waist, moving against him.

Slow down. Show her some respect. His heart pounded as he nuzzled against her, opening her first with his fingers and then slipping inside. She cried out in frustration, moving against him, and he lost control.

'Yes...' She arched her back, not seeming to notice when she bumped her head on the cupboard door, and he curled one hand around the back of her skull to protect it. 'Again...'

He pulled out, then pushed inside her again. One hand flew to her mouth, smothering the cry that escaped her lips. He pulled back, knowing this time that this was what she wanted, making her wait as long as he could.

At the next thrust, her body jerked in his arms and he was completely lost. Stripped of everything but the intense need that flashed between them.

'Not yet. Hold onto it, sweetheart.' He whispered the words into her ear. His body was doing everything to hers, driving her to completion, and yet still he wanted her to fight back against him.

'I can't…'

'Yes, you can. Make it last.' He knew that neither of them could hold out for long. But these moments of raw feeling were too good not to try.

In the few minutes before she came, she made him entirely hers. No thought left, hardly anything of him, apart from the need. When he felt her muscles tighten around him, all he could think of was that her pleasure seemed to be washing over him, possessing him. He had no chance to let go, she annihilated him, pulling the orgasm from him in waves of all-encompassing feeling.

For a couple of minutes they didn't move. Letting the shivered aftershocks rack their bodies, hearts beating fast against each other. She let out a little sigh and he kissed her.

'You okay, sweetheart?' He rested his forehead lightly against hers and she smiled.

'Much better than okay. Only I'll have to give you some lessons in vintage underwear. You're not quite as good with it as the modern stuff.'

'I'll practise.'

She laughed, kissing him lightly on the lips. 'Yeah. Practice makes perfect.'

CHAPTER FIFTEEN

IT WAS ALMOST as if he'd been gifted with another sense. One that knew whatever Sophie was feeling and whenever she needed him. On set, the smallest movement of her head made it obvious that she was about to ask for a break, and come to sit with him for a few minutes. In the evenings, the touch of her fingers on the back of his hand was enough to set his body on fire.

Possibly his favourite time of the day was when she got into the car with him at the end of the day. Smelling of soap, the lacquer brushed from her hair, and all his for the night.

'They've missed a bit.' Her hair was still slightly damp, and scraped back from her face, from where the make-up girls had cleaned off the fake blood that had spattered her in this afternoon's scene. A tiny red mark showed at her hairline and Drew leaned over to wipe it away.

She did what he'd been trying to avoid and reached forward, turning the rear-view mirror down to inspect the damage. 'No, that's a scar. From when I hit my head in the accident.'

Drew resigned himself to adjusting the mirror back again, and resolved for the hundredth time to leave a mirror in the glove compartment for her. Only she'd probably forget and still use his rear-view mirror whenever she wanted to check her appearance. The little routine, before he started the car, was more endearing and less annoying than he would have ever credited.

Something nagged at the back of his head as he drove. Something that formed itself into a concrete idea, which suddenly seemed so obvious that he could have kicked himself for not noticing before. He swung the car into a lay-by, and switched off the engine.

'That was where you banged your head?' He was thinking hard, trying not to jump to conclusions too fast.

'Yes, right here. I had bruises down the side of my face.' She reached for the rear-view mirror again, as if to check, and Drew caught her hand before she could get to it.

'And you had bruises on your shoulder?' He remembered that she had a thin red mark on one of her shoulders, the fading remains of a deep bruise, but his mind had been on other things when he'd last seen it.

She undid the top buttons of her shirt, pulling at the collar and squinting down at her shoulder. 'Right here. They were the two worst injuries.' She shivered, watching the traffic move past them on the road.

'Let me see…' He leaned over, running his finger along the tell-tale line, and she giggled.

'Not here…'

'Soph, that looks like a seat-belt injury.' He'd seen hundreds of such marks on crash victims, from where the seat belt had bitten into a shoulder. Right now he was kicking himself that this had never registered before.

'Yeah? I suppose so.' She still didn't see. 'It ran right

across my shoulder.' She traced her finger in the exact line that Drew would have expected.

'And your car was a right-hand drive? Not a foreign import?'

'No, it was...' Suddenly light dawned in her eyes, and her hand flew to her mouth in shock. 'What are you saying?'

'That the location of your injuries suggests you were sitting on the opposite side of the car than you are now. Which is the driver's seat in the UK, but over in America...'

She caught her breath. 'It's the passenger seat. I must have banged my head on the inside of the car door.'

'Unless the impact crushed the cabin...' Drew was trying to ignore the excitement growing in his chest, take in all the possibilities. Right now there was nothing on her right side that she could have bumped her head on, but a crash could do anything to a car's frame.

'No... No, it didn't. I saw the pictures on the police report, I've got them somewhere. The front of the car had been staved in, but I remember thinking how lucky we were that the inside of the car was practically untouched... Drew...' She turned towards him, tears melting her eyes into soft focus.

He dared say the unthinkable. The impossible, and yet yearned-for truth. 'It looks as if you weren't driving...' If Josh had lied about that, then what else had he lied about?

She looked around, as if his own car could provide her with some answers. 'Can we prove it?'

'I don't know. Maybe. If I could get the report from the doctor who saw you at the hospital right after the crash, there might be some notes. He might even have mentioned a seat-belt injury, they're very common.'

Drew bit back his own enthusiasm. 'It may be nothing, Soph. We might never be able to say for sure.'

'But there's a doubt. A possibility.' She snapped open her seat belt and flung her arms around his shoulders. She buried her head in his shoulder. 'Why does this mean so much to me?'

'If Josh lied about this, maybe he lied about other things. You don't have to just believe his version of events, you can make your own decision.'

'Yes... That's it. He...' She seemed to pull herself together a little, relaxing in his arms. 'He had points on his licence. He would have been banned from driving if he was in another accident. Maybe I agreed to switch places with him.'

'Maybe you did. Or maybe he saw that you were disorientated after the accident and took a chance, reckoning you wouldn't disagree with him. That's not what really matters, though, is it?'

'No, it's not. He painted me as a monster, and now one part of his story doesn't hold up. Maybe I'm not so bad...' She started to tremble, as if on the verge of an explosion of tears.

'You're not so bad. Trust me. I don't need to know whether you were driving or not to believe that.'

'Thank you.' She stretched up to kiss him, her lips like the whisper of a summer breeze on his. 'I think I'll have to think about this all over again.'

'You do that.' Drew waited for her to sit back into her seat and buckle her seat belt. 'Is it your turn to cook tonight?'

'Probably.' She reached for her notebook and consulted the pages. 'Yep. I'm doing fajitas.'

'Great.' He reached for the ignition. 'You can think while you're cooking.'

* * *

She knew what she needed to do. When they arrived home Sophie spied her laptop on the coffee table in the sitting-room, and made for it. The pictures still felt like unfinished business. She needed to show them to Drew, before either of them could move on.

'It's time we looked, Drew.' She plumped herself down on the sofa, blinking as the screen in front of her lit up, and wishing that the gazillion-colour picture quality wasn't quite so well engineered.

He seemed to know what she had on her mind. 'Soph, you don't have to…'

'I want to.' This was the test. Whether he had enough confidence in her to look at the pictures, or whether he would just bury his head in the sand, hoping they'd go away.

'Okay.' He sat down next to her, stretching his arm across the cushions behind her. Sophie opened the folder, hidden deep in the warren of files, and typed the password. Five tiny icons appeared in the corner of the screen, which gave no good idea of the photographs they represented.

'Ready?'

'I'm ready. If you are.'

She ignored the implicit question. She was never going to be ready for this, not if she lived to be a hundred. She doubted if Drew really knew what he was saying either, but this was the only way forward.

The first photo wasn't too bad. It would actually have been quite a good one, if taken on its own, Sophie curled up on a bed in a plush hotel room, the sheet that covered her following the contours of her body.

'Okay. That's not so bad…' His fingers found her shoulder, giving it a reassuring squeeze.

'They get worse.'

'Yeah. I'd figured that out.'

In the next, the sheet had been drawn back. She was lying on her right side, but the bruise on her shoulder was just visible, half-obscured by pillows. She felt his body stiffen against hers.

'I...' When she looked round at him, his face had gone suddenly pale. Sophie wondered if he had the same punched-in-the-gut feeling that she'd had when she'd first seen the photos. 'Zoom in a bit...on the bruise...'

If that was the way he wanted to play it. Just look at her shoulder, nothing else. Step back from the rest of it. She magnified the photo, thinking grimly that it must be high resolution, because the quality hardly deteriorated.

'That's... It looks like a seat-belt injury to me. From... what I can see.'

She took a deep breath. 'Next one?'

He didn't reply. Just nodded. In the next photo, she was lying on her back, her hair obscuring the right side of her face, her shoulder out of the view of the camera. Sophie wondered whether he would notice that her nipples were hardened into tight points, as if someone had just been touching them.

A soft curse, under his breath. Yeah. He'd noticed.

'I'm sorry, Drew.'

'Don't... It's not your fault.' His arm finally wound around her shoulder, and she felt herself shudder in response to that small comfort. 'Soph, I'm so sorry this happened to you.'

He was drawing back. Protecting himself from it all. She'd known he must, and all she could do was hope that when he'd thought about it, he'd still be able to touch her. Her fingers were trembling, and she completely missed the next icon and clicked by mistake on the last, and worst, of them.

She heard him catch his breath. She was still lying on her back, her hair still flopped over her right eye, but her face betrayed a languid smile. It was the kind of pose that a model might strike to suggest sex.

But this was obviously not posed. Drew had been humiliated once by photographs, and these *had* to be worse than the ones of his ex-girlfriend.

She turned to look at him. His eyes were dead, staring at the screen, a look of sheer rage on his face.

'I'm sorry. I'm so sorry, Drew.' She slammed the lid of her laptop shut, trying to break the noxious spell, but still it seemed to linger.

'It's…okay, Soph.' She felt his hand, cold on hers.

He pulled her to her feet and her laptop slipped from her lap, sliding onto the carpet. Hugged her tightly. Sophie waited for the warmth, the enveloping feeling that everything was all right, and it didn't come. His hands were planted on her back, still and lifeless. It was as if she were being embraced by a tailor's dummy.

'Drew… Please…' She just wanted to sink into his arms, feel the forgiveness that his words had volunteered. But she couldn't. She'd pushed him too far, and Drew was a man, and a human being. This was too much for him.

'It's okay, Soph. Really. They're a shock, but…'

I still love you. Say it. Say it.

'We'll get over this.'

'Yeah. We will.' Or maybe not. Drew was steeped in his work and his good reputation. This must be sheer torture for him.

'Why don't I go and make dinner?' It was all she

could think of, to bring them both back to normality a little.

'Yeah. Okay.' He agreed a bit too fast. 'I might go for a run, if that's okay with you…?'

He'd never asked before. Just changed into his sweats, bade her a cheery goodbye, and left her to get on with whatever she was doing. Things were different now.

'Be back for dinner. In an hour.'

'Of course.' Finally he smiled. Somehow it was the worst of it all. He was making an effort to be nice, but Sophie knew that he was angry with her. She was never going to be rid of those damn photographs. And now they'd driven Drew away.

Even running, as hard and fast as he could, couldn't get rid of it. The anger that someone could do this to Sophie. When he got to the park, Drew dropped for a punishing round of push-ups, which only served to make his shoulders ache and didn't dispel the rage.

They ate together, talking and laughing. Sophie's laugh seemed somehow brittle tonight, as if she was having to put on an act. Still the anger burned.

When he'd finished stacking the dishwasher, he made coffee for himself and herbal tea for her. She sipped it in silence and then went to bed early, leaving Drew to plot the most horrible revenge he could think of against the man who'd done this to her.

That didn't work either, and when he slid between the sheets she was curled up, fast asleep. He kissed her brow and rolled onto his back, to stare impotently up at the darkness.

They were both groggy and tired the next morning. Drew hadn't slept much, and he wondered whether

Sophie's regular breathing in the bed beside him had been just a pretence of sleep. Perhaps he should have made the effort to rouse her, and to talk to her, but he wasn't sure what he could possibly have said. Just that this hurt, but she knew that already, better than he did.

The weather was forecast as fine for the next week, and Joel had decided to shoot the scenes at the lake that lay in the grounds of Hazlemere House. Drew followed a makeshift sign along a gravelled road and parked next to Sophie's trailer, where Jennie was waiting for them.

In the last month, Jennie's job had suddenly become less fraught. Drew knew that Sophie had apologised to her for her behaviour, without going into any details, and the easier relationship showed in Jennie's smile.

'We're not late, are we?' Sophie seemed on edge this morning.

'No, there's plenty of time. But whenever you're ready for Wardrobe and Make-up...'

'I'm ready now. Thanks, Jennie.'

'I'll catch you later, down by the lake. I'm going to look at this submersible...' He was aware that the smile he gave her felt awkward on his lips.

'Yes. Later.'

Everyone knew him by now, either as a set advisor, the doctor who was useful to have around for minor bumps and sprains, or the guy who always seemed to be somewhere near Sophie. No one seemed to care much which of those hats he was wearing at any given time, and Drew received waves and nods of acknowledgement as he walked down to the lake.

A small jetty reached out into the expanse of shimmering water, a square platform at the end. The timbers looked old, but when he craned to see underneath, he could see fresh wood. The whole thing had been built especially and aged to look as if it had been there for a while.

Next to the jetty a small metal craft bobbed in the water. The submersible. Drew had seen the cramped inside of it built in a warehouse in Devon, and had marvelled at the bravery of going underwater in such a thing. Now the craft looked even tinier and more precariously dangerous.

The early morning chill still hung in the air, and he pulled his jacket around him, settling himself in a seat. Sophie was called straight from Make-up down onto the jetty to go through her scene with Todd. Today she was wearing a red dress with a grey knitted cardigan, her legs bare.

Joel was placing all the actors, marking out their positions on the jetty, supervising the camera angles and checking the direction of the light. So many details that went into just a few minutes of filming. The actors ran through the scene one last time, and then came the moment that was beginning to excite Drew as much as it seemed to thrill everyone else on the set. In response to a call for silence, the bustle quietened and the cameras were ready to roll.

Cups of tea and the inevitable doughnuts. More debate over camera angles, and the sun climbing in the sky began to make Drew feel sleepy. A boom was rigged up on the jetty so that the cameraman could swing out over the water and film the conversation taking place in a small rowing boat, next to the submersible. Sophie joined him to watch for a few minutes and then was called back for one of her scenes.

A shout from the waterside made him jump, dropping his book. Then a scream, which drove him to his feet before he knew what was happening. The boom was

sagging over the water, the three men who had been providing a counterbalance for the long arm grappling to
control it. But all he could see was Sophie.

He ran. There was only one place that he belonged
now, and that was at the end of the jetty, where Sophie
was calling to the cameraman, who was fighting to keep
his balance on the other end of the swaying boom.

'Sophie, get out of the way...'

She either didn't hear him or she was ignoring him.
Drew pushed through the crowd that was milling around
at the waterside and made a spurt of speed along the
jetty.

'Joe... Your safety harness...' Sophie was standing
still, perilously close to the swinging arm of the boom.

If the boom collapsed into the water, taking Joe with
it, he would be trapped. Drew saw Joe respond to Sophie's words, unclipping his harness from the frame.

'Get out of the way...' He grabbed her, pulling her
clear of the boom, and when she struggled he picked
her up bodily. Joe chose that moment to jump into the
water, and now that it no longer supported his weight,
the boom shot upwards, slewing violently.

'He's in the water...'

'I know. I'll get him. Stay there.' He dumped her back
onto her feet, out of the reach of the boom, and Drew
kicked off his shoes.

'Get everyone off the jetty...' Someone had called
for a lifebuoy, but no one seemed to know where they
were. A couple of men were wading into the water from
the shore, but Drew was closer to Joe, who was struggling in the deep water, weighed down by the heavy
safety harness.

'Go, Sophie.'

She hesitated, seemingly confused for a moment and

about to panic. Then she turned, shouting to the people around them to get back, moving with them to safety, as Drew dived into the lake.

He reached Joe before any of the other men in the water, catching his flailing arm and supporting him while he punched the release for the harness and got him out of it. It was easier now to keep him afloat, and together the two men swam for the shore.

'Okay, mate?' Joe was breathing heavily, stumbling out of the water, but there was no blood and he seemed uninjured. Willing hands supported him onto the grass, to sit down and catch his breath.

'Yeah. Thanks…' Joe's head swivelled round in response to a shout, and Drew followed his gaze. Everyone was off the jetty now, apart from a young woman, one of the sound technicians, who was sprinting to the far end of it. And Sophie had left the safety of the water's edge and was running after her.

'Theresa… Leave it…' Sophie's voice floated across to him in the sudden hush.

Dammit! When he'd told Sophie to get everyone off the jetty, he'd taken it for granted that she'd include herself in that instruction. Theresa had reached the end now and was struggling to pull a heavy metal trunk, containing sound equipment, back to safety.

'Duck…' He shouted the word as a sudden gust of wind blew the boom around almost full circle. Sophie hit the deck, but Theresa ignored him, and the boom caught her, propelling both her and the equipment she'd tried to save into the water.

'Soph…' He was running now, as if his own life depended on it. Sophie had got to her hands and knees and was crawling towards the edge of the jetty to see what had become of Theresa. Then she seemed to tip over, letting herself down into the lake.

Sophie. Sophie. Drew saw the bright flash of her hair in the water, and then she bobbed beneath the surface. He dived in after her.

At first he couldn't see them. Then a shadow, moving under the water. Her blonde hair had broken free of the pins that had held it and was streaming behind her. Taking a deep breath, he dived, feeling the water sting his eyes. It was hard to see, but then he found what he was looking for. Sophie's frightened face, streams of bubbles rising from her mouth from the effort of trying to pull Theresa's limp body to the surface.

He grabbed her arm, motioning her out of the way, and she shot upwards, towards the glow of the sunshine above their heads. No longer trapped in the all-encompassing noise of instinctive fear for Sophie, he reached for Theresa.

She seemed to be trapped somehow, and he worked his way down to her legs. One was pinned between the underwater timbers of the jetty and the metal trunk that had fallen into the lake. He tugged at the trunk, the handles tearing into his fingers.

It didn't budge. He braced his legs against the trunk and his shoulder against the jetty and pushed as hard as he could, feeling a sudden sharp pain in his shoulder as his foot slipped and he crashed against the timbers. It was enough, though. Theresa's leg shifted and he saw her body moving upwards in a motion that was almost purposeful. When he looked, he saw that Sophie was there again, her arms around Theresa's shoulders, lifting her up towards the light.

Three heads broke the surface almost at the same time. Two sets of aching lungs gasped for air and the third, Theresa's, couldn't respond. Sophie was struggling to keep her afloat, a dead weight in the water, and Drew took over. Pain shot through his left shoulder and along his arm as he tried to swim and he heard a sickening crunch as the bones relocated into their proper alignment.

Somehow, he and Sophie managed to get Theresa back to the men who were waiting for them, waist deep in the water. Strong arms hoisted her clear, and carried her back to the shore.

'She's dead… She's dead…' he heard a woman sob as he stumbled out of the water, Sophie by his side. Not yet. Not if he had anything to do with it.

'Out of the way.' He heard Sophie's voice, calm and assertive, cutting through the pain.

'Call an ambulance.' Jennie was on hand, as always, and she pulled her phone from her pocket in response to his words. 'Give me some space…'

A small circle formed around Theresa's lifeless body. 'Ian, we need the first-aid kit. Andrew, get a blanket to keep her warm.' Sophie took the words from his mouth, assigning tasks to the people she knew would complete them with the minimum of fuss.

He knelt down next to Theresa, clearing her mouth and tipping her head to one side and then back ready for CPR, using his uninjured left arm as much as possible. Pinching her nose, he delivered two rescue breaths and then cried out in agony as he tried to move on to the compressions.

'I'll do it.' Sophie was kneeling on the other side of Theresa's motionless body, her wet hair pushed back from her face.

'Can you…?' There was no point in asking, really.

Drew didn't have the strength in his arm and couldn't keep up the rhythmic, lifesaving effort that was needed.

'Count for me.' She positioned her body over Theresa's the way he'd seen her do with the dummy, and Drew wrenched his consciousness away from the screaming pain in his shoulder and concentrated on counting, keeping the beat of the compressions for her.

He could use his left hand, as long as he didn't try to raise his arm. After thirty compressions, he delivered two rescue breaths. Repeat. Repeat.

'It's not working...' Sophie ignored the words behind her, and so did Drew. Another repeat. Then Theresa choked, water and vomit bubbling from her mouth.

Sophie wasn't prepared for this. She'd listened well when her father had taught her the basics of first aid, resuscitation, how to stop bleeding. It had all been precious time with him, and she'd practised on her own afterwards, wanting to gain his approval with her willingness to learn.

She knew exactly how to deliver the compressions and rescue breaths. But dummies didn't vomit all over you.

She helped Drew roll Theresa onto her side, and he bent over, clearing her mouth with his finger. Then a tight smile twitched at his lips.

'Theresa. Theresa... It's all right, sweetheart. Just breathe. You're all right.'

She saw Theresa's arms twitch in an involuntary movement. Then a choking sound and another wheezing breath. And another. She heard the sound of someone crying behind her, and realised that her own face was wet with tears.

Drew was talking to Theresa, watching her reactions.

Then his gaze flipped up to Sophie, and he nodded, a smile in his eyes.

'I need you to help me a bit more.' His voice had the same reassuring tone that he'd been using with Theresa.

'Okay, no problem.' She steeled herself, trying to stop shaking. 'What's wrong with your arm?' She couldn't see any blood on him.

'I think I knocked it out slightly. It's okay, I felt it snap back again.'

Sophie rolled her eyes but his gaze was already back on Theresa. As soon as she was safe and on her way to hospital Sophie was going to make him sit down and take notice of her. In the meantime, all she could do was to follow his instructions to the letter.

'Wash your hands.' She looked down at her own hands, realised they were covered with vomit and grabbed at the water bottle lying on the grass nearby. 'Look in the first-aid kit. Get a pair of gloves for yourself, and a pair for me. Find something to wipe Theresa's face with.'

He gave the instructions quietly, one at a time, waiting for her to do each thing before he went on to the next. She could do this. He was there, he wouldn't let her forget anything, or do something wrong.

She rolled up a towel, slipping it under Theresa's head as he told her. Andrew was deputised to watch Theresa, hold her hand and call out immediately if she gave any signs of distress, and Sophie covered her with a blanket, tucking it carefully around her.

'Have we got an ambulance coming?' he called to the group behind them, and Jennie answered.

'Yes. It'll be twenty minutes before they get here, though, they're a way off.'

'All right. Keep me posted.' Drew turned his attention back to Theresa, who had begun to moan, her free hand seeming to reach downwards. 'Steady, sweetheart. Try to lie still.'

Theresa didn't respond, a keening cry escaping her lips. Drew's mouth tightened into a thin line. 'Andrew, keep her still if you can. Sophie, I need you to help me.'

Quietly, he talked her through it, helping with his one good hand wherever he could. Loosening Theresa's clothes to look at her chest and stomach, to check that there were no injuries there. Sophie could already see that Theresa's left leg was swelling under the thin material of her wide-legged trousers.

'You've seen her leg?'

He nodded. 'First things first.'

She remembered that. Breathing. Then bleeding. Stomach and chest injuries first. Sophie took a deep breath and went through the checks, one by one.

'Still with me?' His voice again. Not tender. Not even kind, but there was something else there that made her strong. When she looked up at his face she saw it. A confident half-smile that told her he was in no doubt about whether she could do this or not.

'Like your shadow.' She smiled back.

He reached for the first-aid box, pulling it towards him and taking a pair of scissors out. Carefully, he cut the wide leg of Theresa's trousers, and she helped him to lift it slightly to see underneath, where the centre of the swelling seemed to be.

'What is it?' She'd craned around in an attempt to see what Drew saw, without getting in his way. The whole of Theresa's calf was swollen and a blotchy red colour, with what looked like small blisters forming on the surface of the skin. 'A jellyfish?'

He shook his head. 'Her leg's obviously taken a pretty

hard blow at some point. Could be that there's a break in one of the blood vessels.'

'Internal bleeding.' Sophie whispered the words, almost to herself. They didn't sound good.

'I'll need to make sure there's nothing else.' His gaze flipped to Theresa's face as she moaned and tried to move and Andrew soothed her, stroking her hair. 'I want you to hold her leg still for me while I do it.'

'Okay. Show me where...'

His words guided her hands and she gently supported the leg, clear of the sand beneath it, concentrating on keeping it still. Drew craned round, looking at it carefully.

'The blisters, Drew...' A long blister seemed to have formed before her very eyes, running down the back of Theresa's leg.

'Yeah. I don't want to drain it here, that needs to be done in sterile conditions.' He looked up. 'Ambulance?'

'Ten minutes...' Jennie's voice again.

'Let's hope so.' His whispered words came through gritted teeth and a cold feeling of dread crawled across her skin. What if it was more? What if he was going to need her to cut the leg, to drain it?

If she had to do it, she would. Drew wouldn't let her fail. She moved automatically, responding to Drew's instructions, carefully cleaning the detritus of the lake away as best she could and wrapping a large dressing pad loosely around it. Drew folded a soft quilted jacket that someone had produced, sliding it underneath and covering it with a towel.

'Okay. That's enough. Just lay her leg down carefully.'

Theresa was shifting restlessly, trying to move, and

Drew inched sideways. 'Theresa… Listen, honey, I know your leg is hurting you.'

'Yeah.' Theresa was crying softly. 'Is it broken?'

'No, but you've taken a blow to the back of your leg and it's quite swollen. There's an ambulance on its way and you're going to be just fine.' He waited for Theresa's nod and gave her a melting smile. 'Hang on in there, okay?'

'Yeah. Okay.'

'Can we give her something for the pain? I've got some aspirins in my bag,' Sophie whispered to Drew when he turned his attention back to her. 'Wherever it is…' She didn't have the faintest idea, but she had a good enough excuse for losing it and expected that Jennie would be able to find it.

'No, giving her anything aspirin based is only going to make the bleeding worse. The ambulance paramedics will be far better equipped to deal with that when they get here.' His gaze found hers. Sure and steady, melting away at the edges of her fear. The sound of a distant siren floated in on the breeze.

'Here they are…'

He nodded. 'Yeah. It's time for you to step back now.' He turned, beckoning to Jennie. 'Go with Jennie and let her get you into some dry clothes.'

'But you—'

'I'll be with you as soon as I can. I need to talk to the paramedics when they arrive.'

'You're not going in the ambulance.'

He shook his head. 'I can't help them, and I'll just be in the way.'

She frowned at him. 'That's not what I meant. I meant you need a doctor to have a look at *you*.'

'It's okay. I dislocated my shoulder when I was a kid.

I banged it underwater, and it slipped out very slightly and then back in again. I just need to rest up a bit.' He turned to Jennie. 'Will you get some warm clothes and a blanket for Sophie, please? Make sure she sits down and has a hot drink.'

'Gotcha.' Jennie held out her hand to help Sophie to her feet, and she ignored it.

She didn't want to leave him now. She didn't want to leave Theresa. She couldn't. She was sure that if she went along to the hospital there was something that she could do.

'Stepping back's the hardest thing, Soph. You have to do it now, because if you don't you'll be in the way.' His voice *was* tender now. Full of everything that she felt, and everything that he knew.

'Come on, Sophie.' Jennie bent down, taking her by the shoulders, trying to avoid the bits of her dress that were stained with vomit. Numbly she got to her feet.

'I'll see you soon?' She could see the ambulance crew now, walking towards them.

'I'll be right there.'

She allowed Jennie to lead her away, but suddenly clean clothes weren't uppermost in her mind. She broke away from her, gagging as she ran to the water's edge, and then retching violently into the water.

CHAPTER SIXTEEN

DREW HAD BROUGHT the ambulance paramedics up to date, and they'd carried Theresa to the ambulance, making her comfortable for the ride to the hospital. Andrew climbed in to go with her, and she managed a small smile and a wave in Drew's direction. Then he made himself do what he'd told Sophie to do, and turned away.

His shoulder throbbed mercilessly. He should find a sling, that would make it more comfortable while he rested it up for the next couple of days. Easy enough, this had happened before a couple of times, and he knew exactly what to do.

But first he had to find Sophie. He wanted to make sure that she was all right, and that she was out of her wet clothes. He walked quickly to her trailer, tapping on the door and grunting with pain as he automatically reached for the handle with his left hand.

Inside, Sophie was showered and dressed, sitting down and protesting as Jennie tried to wrap a blanket around her.

'He said blanket. Clean clothes, hot drink and a blanket...' Stress showed in Jennie's face as the conflict between following a star's every command and doing as the doctor said seemed to overwhelm her.

'Nice going, Jennie.' Drew grinned at her and Jennie relaxed a bit.

'Drew. Sit down.' Sophie lost interest in the blanket, and Jennie surreptitiously tucked it over her legs. When he didn't obey straight away her face took on a determined look. 'Sit, will you?'

'Feeling better?' Out of the corner of his eye he'd seen Sophie run to the water's edge and throw up, then allow Jennie to lead her away.

'Yes.' She dismissed his enquiry with an imperious wave of her hand. She obviously *was* feeling better. 'Jennie, can you get some dry clothes for Drew, please? And a triangular bandage from the first-aid kit.'

'Right.' Jennie brightened considerably at the prospect of a task that didn't involve blankets.

'And some paracetamol, if you can find any.' Drew lowered himself slowly into a seat.

'Sure thing. How many?'

'Bring me the packet.' He might well need some more for later. Jennie disappeared, and Sophie fixed him with a glare.

'Well?'

'Well, what?' He was beginning to shiver now, his wet clothes sticking to his skin.

'Are you going to do as *I* tell you now?'

He'd thought about getting her to lie down for a while and waiting until she had recovered enough for him to scold her for running back down that damn jetty and putting herself deliberately in danger. But right now his whole body ached, and the thing he most wanted was for Sophie to hold him.

'Yeah. Okay.'

She helped him out of his clothes, and shepherded him into the tiny shower cubicle at the other end of the trailer.

Rolled her sleeves up and soaped him clean, then dried him and wrapped a large towel securely around his waist, leading him through to the seating area.

'Where's Jennie got to?' She peered through the window.

'Soph…'

'They must have something in your size. What's the point of having a wardrobe department if they can't rustle up some dry clothes?'

'Soph…' He reached for her and she turned, her vexed expression softening suddenly. 'Sophie, come here.'

She walked towards him, and he wound his good arm around her waist, pulling her close. She hugged him awkwardly, trying not to touch his injured shoulder, ending up holding his head to her chest. That was okay. That was right where he wanted to be. He could hear her heart beating, smell the delicate perfume of her body.

'I'm so cross with you…'

'I know. I know, the photographs.'

'What? No!' Was that really what she'd thought? 'Sophie I was angry *for* you. Not *with* you. How could you have thought…?'

She shrugged wordlessly. Of course she'd thought that his anger had been directed at her. Everyone else seemed to blame her for the images.

'Soph. I'm sorry. Why on earth didn't you say something?'

'I was hoping you'd come around. That you might think they weren't so bad after all.'

'They're horrible. I hate them, because they hurt you, and because people think that they're your fault in some way. That's all. You have nothing to apologise for.'

She seemed almost breathless with relief. 'So why are you cross with me, then?'

For a moment Drew couldn't think. 'Oh. Yes, I'm cross with you for running down that jetty. Putting yourself in danger.' He tugged her closer, wincing as pain shot through his shoulder. He didn't care. Only Sophie mattered.

'Oh. Well, I'm not sorry for that.'

'No, I didn't think you would be.' This was *his* Sophie. Spirited and brave, a woman with her own opinions. Not the bullied, frightened person who either lashed out or apologised for everything.

'We did okay, didn't we?'

'A lot better than okay. You helped save a life.'

She nodded. 'That feels good. I'm so proud of you, Drew.'

His heart warmed and he held her close, catching his breath as he pulled her against his injured arm. 'I'm always proud of you. Most especially today.'

She bent, kissing his forehead, a tear rolling down her cheek and splashing onto his. 'Thank you. That means a great deal.'

A tap sounded on the door of the trailer and Sophie backed away from him quickly, rubbing her face with her sleeve. 'Come in…'

Jennie appeared, a bundle of things in her arms. 'Clothes.' She draped a pair of combat trousers and a T-shirt over the back of a chair. 'I found your shoes on the end of the jetty. Triangular bandage.' She fished in her pocket for something. 'And some safety pins.'

'Thanks, Jennie.' When Drew reached for the bandage, Sophie picked it up. 'Did you find any paracetamol?'

'Yeah.' Jennie gave the packet to Sophie, and Drew realised that there wasn't much point in trying to take control here. She squinted at the instructions.

'A thousand milligrams.' He prompted her with the dose.

She broke two tablets out of the foil, letting him see the label on the packet. Sixteen five-hundred-milligram tablets. Put the tablets into his hand and the packet into her handbag. Drew grinned. No one, *no one* else would have got to do that with him. Except Sophie.

He downed the tablets and she handed him a glass of water. Drew took a couple of gulps and handed it back to her. If she wanted to play nurse then she could put the glass back on the table. He wondered vaguely whether she'd consider giving him a massage later.

'We're going to be breaking for the day now?' Sophie turned to Jennie.

'Yes. They'll have the set builders in tonight, repairing the damage, and Joel's sending in the second crew to film the shots of the submersible going up and down tomorrow. There are a couple more things he needs you and Todd for, and he'll do those tomorrow afternoon.'

'So we get a lie-in?' Sophie grinned.

'Yep. Would you like me to get one of the drivers to take you home?'

'Thanks. I think it would be better if Drew didn't drive tonight, at least.'

'I'll find someone.' Jennie disappeared, and as soon as the door of the trailer slammed behind her Drew had Sophie back in his arms again.

'Are you going to help me on with my clothes now?'

She giggled. 'That'll be a first. I suppose it's just the same as helping you off with them, only in reverse.'

'I expect so. And then home.'

She nodded. 'Yeah. Home. That would be just wonderful.'

CHAPTER SEVENTEEN

THE WEEKS THAT had stretched out ahead of them began to trickle away and became days. Ten days before they were due to wrap the film it was announced that they'd made good progress and should be finished in seven. Sophie wanted to personally shake everyone on set who'd worked so hard to deprive her of three precious days.

That evening she told Drew that she was tired and went to bed early. When he padded quietly into the room and slipped under the duvet next to her, she pretended to be asleep. It was another night wasted from their precious, ever-dwindling supply, but she couldn't fake it. If she let him hold her, let him make love to her, she wouldn't be able to stop herself from crying.

When the alarm went the following morning she got out of bed and locked herself in the bathroom, staring into the mirror. Today was their last day in London, and tomorrow they'd travel up to Bath to shoot the final scenes. Then the end-of-shoot party. They still had six days, and she should make the most of them.

When she went downstairs Drew kissed her as if nothing was wrong, and she kissed him back. They talked in the car on the way to the set, and she tried to laugh, even managing it a few times. Today was going to be a good day. She'd make it so.

It was a long day, Joel making sure that they had everything they needed before they had to leave the Hertfordshire set. Drew sat in on the shooting as usual, there to help her through if she needed it. Sophie almost wished that she did need him, but somehow even her unpredictable memory chose today to retain every single word of the script.

They got back to his house at ten in the evening. 'I can't wait to just soak in a hot bath…' Sophie made for the stairs.

'Can we stay here a moment?' He opened the door to the sitting-room. 'There's something I want to talk about.'

The arrangements for travelling to Bath tomorrow maybe. Whatever it was, he didn't look particularly happy about it.

'What is it?' Sophie followed him into the sitting-room and perched on the edge of the sofa. Something was wrong, she could feel it, buzzing in the air between them.

'Carly's going to be coming by in the morning.'

'Yes, I know.' Carly had decided to fly back for the last week of shooting and the end-of-shoot party. In reality, Sophie suspected that decision had been made with Drew, and that it had something to do with making sure that she got back to America in one piece. Right now, she was tempted to tell him that he didn't need to have bothered about that. She wasn't going.

A thought suddenly hit Sophie. 'She's all right isn't she?'

'Carly's fine. She got an earlier plane and landed this morning. I spoke to her today.'

'Why didn't she call me?' Something was going on.

Both Carly and Drew were in on it, and it wasn't good. 'Stop beating around the bush, Drew, and tell me.'

'I'm not coming with you to Bath.'

'What?' She felt sick. She knew the answer to the next question, but there was no way she could prevent herself from asking it. No way that she could roll time back and not have this conversation. 'Why?'

'Because we've come to the end of things. We've already taken as much as we can from this relationship, and there just isn't anything more.'

He might have come to the end of it, but she hadn't. There was still so much more she wanted to do with him.

'You're wrong.'

'Maybe. But I've made my decision. I'm not coming with you to Bath.'

'Then I'll come back here in a week's time. We can decide what to do then.' All Sophie's thoughts were beginning to splinter in her head. Everything was shattering around her. She willed herself to breath, to hold on. She couldn't lose it now.

'It's not just a matter of geography, Sophie. I'm ending this now.'

'Well, you can't. What about me? Don't I have a say in it?'

He shook his head slowly. Of course she didn't. If one partner wanted to end things then the other one just had to put up with it.

'At least tell me why. I deserve that, don't I?'

Something softened in his eyes. For a moment she thought that he was going to relent. He'd examined the reason and found it wanting.

'I'm a doctor, Sophie. I give a lot of time to my work, it's what I am. Who I am.'

'And you can't be seen with me, is that it?' Cold dread

crept over her. This was the one thing that she could never change about herself. Her past. Everything she touched would be tainted by it.

'Your life and mine...they're different. I can't give up my career and follow you, Sophie. I thought that none of it was worth anything any more, and then I met you and you taught me different.'

'Who said you had to give it up?' It was make or break now. Dammit, it wasn't going to be break. 'I'll retire.'

'Don't be ridiculous. You're twenty-eight years old.'

'Yeah, well, they say that you don't get the parts when you get past forty.' She shrugged. Was it really that easy? Allow her whole career to dissolve with a shrug of her shoulders?

'No. I won't let you.'

'You don't have any choice in the matter. You don't get to say what I do with *my* career.'

'Exactly. And you don't get to say what I do with mine either. We can't be together because we have different lives. We're different people.'

'You want me to beg? Is that it?' She would. Five minutes of his time every day, that was all she wanted. Five minutes and the chance to sleep beside him.

'No!' He turned on her, rage showing in his face. 'You should never beg, Sophie. Never.'

Something cold settled around her heart, like frost in July. 'Fine. Then I won't.'

She turned and marched out of the room. Drew didn't think that she was good enough for him. He hadn't said it, but he hadn't denied it either. He got to have his photo in respectable magazines, and hers was plastered up on the internet and in scandal sheets. *That* was what he meant by *different people*.

He didn't even try to stop her. In that moment she knew that he wouldn't stop her from leaving tomorrow either.

He wasn't there the following morning. Or in the other bedroom. When Sophie crept downstairs she saw cushions and a blanket scattered on the sofa, and heard the noise of the shower downstairs in the utility room next to the garage.

She showered and got dressed, applying her make-up carefully. She knew Drew well enough to know that he wouldn't have changed his mind. That he thought this was the right thing to do and would remain steadfast. Maybe he was right. She'd made the decision years ago that she didn't want to live the way her mother did, never knowing when her father was going to come home.

Even so, walking out of here with Carly, leaving him behind, was going to have to be the best performance of her life. She applied a little more blusher and then wiped it off. Against the paleness of her face, and her hollow eyes, it looked like red cheeks painted on a doll.

She heard the doorbell, and Drew answered it. Carly's voice and then footsteps on the stairs. The bedroom door opened.

'You okay?' Carly walked into the room. Tanned and frowning.

'Yes. You?'

'Me? I'm fine. Tired of sitting around doing nothing.' Carly came forward for a hug, and Sophie clung to her.

'So, we're off, then?' Sophie tried to smile and wondered if it was as brittle as her voice sounded.

'Don't you want to say goodbye to him?' Carly's face was suddenly tender.

'I... No. I don't think I can say goodbye to him.' That

would break her. Maybe if there were no goodbyes, she could pretend that she might see him again.

'Okay. Finish getting ready, and I'll throw the rest of your stuff into a case. We can sort it all out when we get to Bath.'

When Sophie took a deep breath and went downstairs, Drew wasn't there. She could see him sitting in the kitchen, the door open, watching for her, but she turned away and he didn't move. She carried her case out to the car and put it into the boot.

Carly had stopped in the doorway with the smaller case, and was looking back into the house. Drew appeared next to her, and they exchanged a couple of words. Then he bent, kissing her on the cheek, and Carly hugged him.

Sophie knew that he was watching as they lifted the second case into the boot and got into the car. When she finally looked behind her, she could see him at the end of the path, hands in his pockets, watching the car disappear along the road.

'I'm not heartless.' Carly must think she was a monster for not even saying goodbye. 'He ended it.'

'I know. He told me that.'

'He did?'

'Yep. He said that you weren't to blame for anything.'

An agonised wail, which didn't seem to belong to her, rose from her throat. Carly stopped the car and hugged her, while Sophie cried on her shoulder.

CHAPTER EIGHTEEN

THE LAST MONTH had been a whirl of activity. Almost since her plane had touched down Sophie had ferociously pursued all the things she'd tried not to think about when she'd been in England. She'd rented a house, spoken to her agent and to the studio. She'd done screen tests, had talked to a guy from one of the major perfume houses with the aim of being the face of a perfume she didn't wear, and had spent a lot of time talking to doctors. None of whom had been Drew.

When Carly had mentioned that she might like to slow down, she'd ignored her. Drew had given her up because of this life. If it wasn't a success, then nothing meant anything any more.

'Ready?' Carly lay on the bed in Sophie's hotel room, watching her apply her make-up and straighten her jacket.

'Think so. How do I look?'

'Businesslike and feminine. Is that what you were going for?'

Sophie laughed. 'Yes, I think so.' She was more nervous than she'd ever been. That she didn't want to show.

'Got your speech?'

'Probably.' Sophie looked in her handbag and found the sheets of paper, clipped together, right at the top. 'Yes.'

'Let's do it, then.'

Everyone had warned her that this wasn't the best idea she'd ever had. Carly first, but when Sophie had shown herself to be determined, she'd capitulated. Then her agent, who had been mollified by the studio's reaction when they'd been told. She'd chosen her charity carefully, speaking to a number of different CEOs and selecting the organisation that she felt suited her best.

Now the crunch. After a brief introduction Sophie stood up in front of two hundred people and the line of cameras ranged behind the seated guests, and went public. A concise description of her injuries and the symptoms. A slightly longer insight into the charity's aims and how it helped people with traumatic brain injury. Sophie's own heartfelt plea for better understanding and help for those who, like her, had been brain injured. And a final personal statement.

'Everyone has their own demons to face, their own difficulties. In the past months I've learned that my memories are important to me, but there's one thing that's more important. With the help and support of people I hold dear, I've learnt to define myself by who I am and not by what I can, and can't, remember. Thank you, ladies and gentlemen.'

Her legs gave way and she sat down with a bump. A moment of silence, and then applause, rippling around the room and growing until it practically deafened her. Carly leaned across, whispering in her ear.

'In other words, watch out, Josh, because we're coming to get you.'

Sophie grinned. 'We don't need to. The charity's arranged for Dr Chancellor to give an interview as a follow-up to today. I've given him permission to talk about the particulars of my case, and he says he'd like to touch on the impact those photographs had on me. I said I'd welcome that.'

'So he puts your side of the case.'

'No, he gives the facts. If they contradict what Josh has said, then so be it. I know what I think, and I believe in myself. That's what matters.'

Carly squeezed her hand. 'You've come a long way, Soph.'

If only Drew had been here to see it. The one desire of her heart that she hadn't expressed today. That would have to remain wished for ever, and silent for ever.

'Look...' Carly nodded over to where one of the reporters had for the moment ignored the news potential of the story and was clapping enthusiastically. 'That's a first. Getting a newshound to drop his pencil.'

The CEO of the charity rose, his avuncular face wreathed in smiles. He thanked Sophie, and announced that she would be available for questions this afternoon, and that after the next speaker refreshments would be available.

He offered her his arm and led her off the stage. Sophie's knees were shaking.

'I can't thank you enough, Miss Warner. We would never have been able to attract this much publicity on our own.'

'It's my pleasure. Do you have the list of papers interested in an interview this afternoon?'

The CEO nodded. 'We'll take it in your time, not theirs.' His portly, middle-aged appearance didn't remind her of Drew in any respect, but his attitude did, and that was one of the reasons she'd chosen his charity. 'Whatever you can do is a bonus. There are no expectations.'

'Thanks.' Sophie scanned the list. 'I'll see them all. Which is the most important to you?'

'This one. We've been trying to place an article with them for a long time.'

'Perhaps he'd like to join me for lunch, then.' Another name on the list had caught her eye. 'And this one. I read that paper when I lived in England.' Actually, she hadn't had much time, or inclination, for newspapers. But it had dropped through Drew's letterbox every morning.

'I'll see him for...' Sophie frowned. At the moment she was too overwhelmed to organise the list in her head.

'A chat over afternoon tea maybe?' The CEO's eyes twinkled.

'Yes, that would be good.' The adrenaline rush was beginning to subside now and she wanted to sit down.

'Leave it with me.'

'You want him to read it?' Carly was watching the CEO's retreating back with the thoughtful look that always seemed to accompany any conversation about Drew.

'I just want him to know.'

'After today, there won't be many people who don't know. But that's what you want, isn't it?'

'Yes.' The feeling of achievement was taking over from the nerves now. Steadying her, allowing her to face a long afternoon of interviews. 'It's what I want.'

Maybe it was jet-lag but Drew had found the choice slightly bewildering. At home, a rental car was just a rental car. In LA, you could rent a dream car. Whatever your dream happened to be. In the end he'd gone for a classic nineteen-fifties model with red paintwork, chrome trims and a roll back roof. If he wasn't sure how this journey was going to end, he may as well complete the last leg of it in style.

He checked out of the hotel early, unable to lie awake, working through the different possible outcomes for today any longer. He left the heavy traffic of LA behind, and the air became crisper and fresher as the road climbed and scissored, winding its way into the Hollywood Hills.

He almost drove straight past the property, which nestled among the trees, clinging tightly to the slope of the hillside. Carly had said it was a small property, and he supposed that in comparison to some of the places he'd driven past it was, but by London standards it was big enough.

Could he live here? It was quiet, beautiful, and yet you could see the morning mist covering the buzz of LA from here. Drew was under no illusions that it would be tough at first, but he could make it work.

He parked the car and walked up the steps leading to the front door. Above his head, floor-to-ceiling windows looked out onto the valley below him like blank, expressionless eyes.

Steeling his determination, he knocked. When no one answered, he wondered whether this wasn't his last opportunity to come to his senses. The trustees of the memory clinic in London had asked him to reconsider his resignation and had given him a week to get back to them.

He wouldn't change his mind. Sophie had left him a message. He knew that what she'd said in that newspaper interview was for him to read, and he wouldn't ignore it.

He got back into the car, picking up the book that lay on the seat beside him. Despite all the uncertainties, he knew he had to wait and play this thing through to the end, however long it took.

* * *

'Nice car.' Drew had deliberately stopped looking along the road, forcing his attention onto the words in front of him. When he heard Sophie's voice, the hairs on the back of his neck suddenly stood to attention.

At least it had given her some time to get her head around it. When he looked up at her, her face was composed, but her eyes were bright and alert. She was wearing trainers and running gear, holding the lead of a mid-sized, indeterminate breed of dog, which looked up at him with a great deal more interest than Sophie was showing at the moment.

'What are you doing?' She couldn't quite meet his gaze and was fiddling abstractedly with the dog's lead.

'I came to see you.'

And in the first moment he'd seen her he'd known. His decision was made. Drew knew what he wanted, and he suddenly felt that he was strong enough to move heaven and earth to get it.

Her face was still impassive. 'You'd better come in, then.'

She felt numb. Maybe that was the effect that extreme joy and extreme terror had, cancelling each other out to leave only numbness. Sophie climbed the steps to her front door and led the way upstairs to the large, open-plan living area of the house. The steeply rising ground meant that the front afforded fantastic views of the city below, and at the back there was a good-sized yard, shaded by tall palm trees.

'This is nice.' Drew glanced around, taking in the magnificent view.

'I like it.' She seized a bottle of water from the fridge and two glasses. 'Water?'

'Yes. Thanks.'

'Shall we sit outside?' She opened the patio doors, and the breeze caressed her face. This was what she'd wanted. It was what she'd planned for, even if Drew had taken matters into his own hands and forced the pace a little. Nothing could stand in their way now.

'I saw your speech. It was well done, Sophie.' His eyes softened. 'And, from what I read, it hasn't done your career any harm.'

'No. It was a calculated risk, but in the end I wanted to do it.' She ventured a question. 'You didn't come all this way to say that, did you?'

'No, I didn't. I wanted to tell you that I'm currently looking for a job.'

'What? What happened?' Her thoughts began to splinter, and she fought it. Struggled to keep it all together.

'Sophie?' He leaned forward, his gaze searching her face. 'Stay with me...'

'Give me a minute.' She closed her eyes, and took a breath. Calming herself, levelling her thoughts.

'Just breathe.'

'Yeah, I'm breathing. I'd have thought that seven years of medical training might have taught you how to recognise that.'

He laughed. 'I love it when you put me in my place, Soph.'

'Someone has to.'

She opened her eyes. 'What's all this about your job? It was such a great opportunity, and you wanted it so much. What have you done, Drew?'

'There's something I want more, Soph. I want to be with you.'

'But you can't work as a doctor here.'

'I know. I'd have to resit some of my exams. From what I hear, it might be a fairly long process, but I can do it. Medicine's my calling Sophie, but you're the woman I love. I'm putting my career on hold.'

'But… My life is not what you want.' Tears blinded her eyes. 'I'm not good enough for you.'

'That's never been true, Sophie. You're the best person I've ever met. I thought that our lives were just too different, and we could never compromise enough to be together. But we're going to have to if you love me as much as I love you.'

'Drew, you idiot. Of course I love you.' Emotion drove her to her feet and Sophie began to pace restlessly. 'I've got a flight booked to go to England in two weeks, and now you turn up here and say you've given up your job.'

He stared at her. 'But you've got a dog.'

It was a new experience to see Drew completely at a loss, saying the first thing that came into his head. 'It's Carly's dog. I'm looking after her for the week while she's on holiday. I turned the offer I had here down, because I wanted to be with you. I wanted to be the person that you could love.'

He seemed to gather his wits, getting to his feet and pulling her into his arms in one fluid movement. 'Sophie. You can't do this.'

'Why not? You did.'

Now was the only moment that mattered. Drew knew she'd need time to think about it, but he'd already made his decision. And it was only fair that she knew that. 'Sophie…'

'Yes?' She looked up at him. So beautiful. Every time

he saw her the words just floated through his mind, an instinctive, unbidden reaction.

He had nothing to give her. No candlelight, no dressing up. There was at least one thing he could do. Drew fell to one knee.

'What are you doing?' He curled her arms around her waist and she struggled a little. 'Think about it, Drew.'

'I have. I'm not planning on giving up medicine, and you're not going to give up your career either.'

She quieted in his arms, perching on his knee so that he could hold her close. 'I would have. I would have come to England and been a doctor's wife...'

'That's a fine thing to be. But it's not *your* thing. We can work this out if we both give a little. There's only one thing that I won't compromise on.'

'Which is?' She wrapped her arms around his neck, her body trembling with his.

'I love you, Sophie. Please, marry me.'

'Yes.'

It was if he'd been clinically dead all these years and suddenly shocked back into life. His heart seemed to stop beating for a moment, then found its rhythm again. 'Do you need some time to think about this?'

'I've thought about it already. And my answer is yes.' She dropped a kiss onto his cheek and it was as if he'd been touched for the first time.

'You want to write that down?'

'I'll do it when I go inside. In the meantime...' she traced her finger along the line of his jaw, and Drew shivered '...we'd better start thinking about how we're going to pay the bills. Since we're both unemployed.'

'Can you go back and say you're taking the offer after all?'

'Maybe. But your job, Drew. You wanted it so much. I want it so much.'

'They said they wanted me to think about it, and go back to them in a week's time, but I said my decision wouldn't be any different.'

'Ring them. Tell them you've changed your mind.' She tried to get to her feet, almost knocking him over in the process.

'It's too early. They'll be asleep.' He held her tight, kissing her. 'Anyway, we've got something far more important to do first.'

They crossed the state line into Nevada two days later on a glittering morning. Drew was in his element. Driving a vintage car, on his way to a wedding. Their wedding. Sophie repeated the words to herself. *'Our wedding.'*

He turned to her and smiled. 'Yes, sweetheart. Our wedding. I'll be Mr Sophie Warner soon.'

'And I'll be Mrs Drew Taylor.' Sophie rehearsed the name a few times in her head.

He laughed. 'Sounds good to me. You can always keep Sophie Warner in reserve for when you want to get things done.'

She grinned at him. 'Sometimes it's useful to be able to do a bit of name-dropping.' The exquisite location, next to a waterfall. The rings, each one engraved on the inside with a promise, and the beautiful white lace dress. Everything had dropped into place, as if the world understood and blessed what they were about to do.

'I love you, Sophie.' He'd said it a hundred times, and the words still thrilled her.

'I love you too. And I trust you with everything. My life, my career.'

'And I trust you with mine.' They'd talked about it,

and agreed to keep their options open but not make any final decisions yet. The one decision that they needed to make was that they wanted to be together, and that they'd both compromise to make it happen. This was no risk, no stepping into the darkness of an uncertain future and hoping things would work out. It was a step into the light.

The car sped along the highway, almost as if it too couldn't wait. Sophie consulted the map. 'We have to turn off the highway soon. We're nearly in Paradise.'

Drew chuckled. 'Nearly?'

'Yes, it's just up ahead. I want to stop at the "Welcome to Fabulous Las Vegas" sign for a photograph.'

'Another one?'

'It's a landmark. And I want a complete photographic record.'

'So you can remember who you married?'

'No.' She pulled a face at him, and he laughed. 'So I can remember how happy I am.'

EPILOGUE

DREW HAD DRIVEN all night to be with her. He parked his car in the hotel car park just as dawn broke over the harbour, and grabbed his weekend bag from the back seat.

The receptionist knew him from his previous weekend visits, and smiled at him. '*Ciao*, Dottore Taylor.'

'*Ciao*, Elena.' He took the key that she proffered and punched the lift button, smiling to himself.

The suite was in darkness, and Sophie was still asleep. Quietly he removed his clothes and slid into the warmth of the bed. She turned over, nestling against him, and Drew was suddenly entirely happy.

The last year would have been difficult to plan in advance but in practice had been the happiest of his life. Drew had negotiated a four-day week at the memory clinic, which had flourished under his guidance and hit the headlines a couple of times on account of Sophie's patronage. Sophie had landed a part in a West End theatre production, which had turned into a hit, had spent three months renovating and decorating their new home, and then two months on location on the Italian Riviera, shooting a new film.

The weekends when Drew had travelled down to see her had made the weeks without her worth it. In three weeks, when filming finished, they were going back to Vegas for their first anniversary.

'Dr Taylor.' She snuggled up against him and the long foreplay of phone calls and an eleven-hour drive suddenly began to heat up. 'I thought you wouldn't be here until this afternoon.'

'Couldn't wait.' He slid his fingers inside the long T-shirt that she was wearing, feeling the smooth warmth of her skin.

'And I had lace, to surprise you with.'

'Lace?' He would enjoy stripping the cotton T-shirt off her every bit as much. 'I'll look forward to that tonight.'

She brushed a kiss onto his lips. 'There was something I was going to tell you.'

'Yeah? What's that.'

'Don't remember.'

He could hardly tell whether she was teasing or not. She very rarely had lapses in memory now, and she didn't let it bother her when she did.

'I dare say it'll come to you.'

'Something to do with...that.'

Yeah. She was definitely teasing. Her hand had wandered down his stomach, and her fingers brushed against the increasingly prominent evidence that he was glad to see her.

'Any more clues?' He waited, every nerve tingling.

'You and me... That discussion we had...'

Something thrilled deep inside him. 'But that was only last month...'

'I suppose you must have got it right first time.'

He rolled her over, suspending his weight above her, making sure that not an ounce of it pressed down onto her body. She giggled, aiming a play punch at his shoulder.

'I'm pregnant, not ill. You're allowed to touch me.'

'Sophie…' He'd thought that he couldn't possibly love her any more, but this moment had proved him wrong.

'Happy?'

'More than I can say, sweetheart. I love you so much.'

'I love you too.' She dropped a kiss onto her finger-tips, reaching up to brush it to his mouth. 'This'll be a new adventure. You and me and a baby. I'll be at home a lot more…'

'Or I'll be at home. I'm going to insist on my right to be a great father. And a supportive husband.'

She seemed to shine with happiness. 'We'll work it out. We've done pretty well with that so far.'

He bent to kiss her. 'Yeah. Write that down, Mrs Taylor. It's a promise.'

* * * * *

5_ST19

  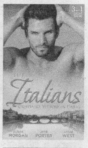

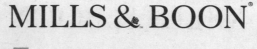

MILLS & BOON®

THE ULTIMATE IN ROMANTIC MEDICAL DRAMA

A sneak peek at next month's titles…

In stores from 2nd October 2015:

Available at WHSmith, Tesco, Asda, Eason, Amazon and Apple

Just can't wait?
Buy our books online a month before they hit the shops!
visit www.millsandboon.co.uk

These books are also available in eBook format!

0915/03